MEDDLERS IN THE CARDINAL'S SONG

Meddlers in the Cardinal's Song

WALLACE ELDRIDGE

A NOVEL

Cover Photography by Pexels, Joáo Silas & Robert Hambley
Used by permission from
www.pixabay.com, www.unsplash.com & www.dreamstime.com

Cover Design and Formatting by anigrafx, LLC
www.anigrafx.com

I dedicate this book to my parents, Wallace and Muriel Eldridge. Thanks for giving me life and the encouragement to live it in full.

The Cardinal's Song

Flash of red in the wind-bent pine;
First to sing in the budding spring,
With voice of cheer and song of hope.

Oh, mortal weary from winter's siege,
Cast off your cares and listen to me,
For joy redounds from the top o' my tree.

Lift up your heart, sing along with me,
For sorrows pass and hope's reborn,
You man below in the melting snow.

Prologue

October, 2006

The street dead-ended at a limestone-pillared gate. Because his passenger said nothing Lucas realized their destination. After a moment's hesitation he drove his grandfather's Cadillac through the open gate. Acres of granite-studded lawns appeared.

Bryson Roberts' sinuous left hand appeared in front of Lucas' face and pointed northwest.

"Head down that lane. Stop by the far pin oak." The voice's harsh rasp conveyed a menace Lucas never had heard from his grandfather. It sent chills down the teen's spine and he felt his pulse surge. He managed to pull over at the oak and turned off the ignition. Lucas started to get out of the car but froze when his grandfather's hand clamped his forearm.

"Stay here, Lucas." Again there was that chilling rasp to the voice, and no "please" to soften the order, or the vice-like grip.

What is with him thought Lucas, but he obeyed and let go of the door handle.

Lucas watched Bryce get out of the car. The tall man with graying dark hair and deeply tanned face hesitated, looked skyward for several heartbeats, then he firmly closed the door.

His late afternoon shadow walked as a giant among the lesser shadows of the gravestones, and stopped at the head of a packed gravel path. The man tugged at the cuffs of his camelhair topcoat and then clasped his hands behind his back. Rays of sunlight, broken by the oak's wind-rustled leaves, played across his still handsome face. He ignored the annoying kaleidoscope of light and, lips compressed into a thin line, retreated into his own thoughts in the timelessness of the place. Then abruptly, chin at the precise angle, the gentleman marched down the pathway.

Lucas could almost hear the beat of snare drums and clash of cymbals as he watched his grandfather's precise cadence. *Ah, so that's it,* thought Lucas. *He's going to visit the grave of one of his Navy buddies.*

The march halted where the man and his shadow towered over an unkempt plot that held a single gravestone. Bryson Chester Roberts turned his back to the wind and unbuttoned his topcoat, revealing a dark blue suit, white shirt and regimental necktie. He wiggled a bit as he unzipped his fly, and then leaned forward so he wouldn't wet his perfectly shined plain-toed shoes.

"Oh, good God!" cried Lucas. Incredulous at what he was witnessing, the teen sat momentarily stunned as the stream of urine splattered over the gravestone. Then he sprang from the car, looked around for other people, and strode rapidly through the rows of gravestones toward the man whose face now glared hatred intense as hammer blows.

Lucas cringed inwardly before the look, but conquered his fear and embarrassment.

"Grandpa! What are you doing? What will people think!"

The pissing ended with a final, forced spurt and the man's angry face began to lose its intensity. A slight upward curl appeared at one corner of his lips.

"Get back in the car, Lucas." The order was conveyed as much with his obsidian-like eyes as with his voice that still held its harshness.

"I will. But, please, come now, Grandpa!"

Bryce Roberts turned away to close his fly. Lucas used the moment to watch the last of the yellow droplets roll down the name chiseled into the desecrated stone. The boy grew puzzled. The inscription told only the month and year Charles Coe died.

Lucas, still anxious to leave, began to walk away as if to lead the man into following him across the grass.

Bryce Roberts ignored his grandson's entreaty. After a final disdainful look at the gravestone, he returned to the path and, topcoat still unbuttoned, strolled back to the car.

Lucas had the Cadillac's engine running. The moment the passenger door closed he pulled out onto the lane and desperately looked for a turnaround. He found an intersection, K-turned, and accelerated toward the gate as fast as the winding lane would allow. He slowed as they passed the gatehouse, but the windowpanes' reflections blocked his attempt to see if anyone inside was watching. Lucas aimed the car between the stone pillars and resisted the urge to speed through the leaf-strewn neighborhood that now seemed so tranquil in the golden late afternoon sunlight.

His grandfather's erect bearing gave way to a relaxed slump against the seatback.

"Now, just maybe, we can forgive that son-of-a-bitch," he said in a deep voice that, thankfully, had returned to normal. "Lucas, take us home."

Lucas drove out of the village and remained silent as the car rolled southward on the narrow road that passed through woods and fields of Bucks County, Pennsylvania. Then the boy's curiosity broke through his reticence.

"Grandpa, who was Charles Cue?"

"He was a man who stole a lot of my heartbeats."

"And that's why you, uh . . . peed on his grave?"

"It finally was time for me to keep a promise."

Lucas waited for his grandfather to explain, and when he didn't, Lucas tried a different tack. "So, why did you say 'now *we* can forgive him'?"

"I said 'Maybe.'"

Bryce remained silent as the tires thumped out the rhythm of the expansion joints in the old concrete road. Finally, he spoke. "Lucas, how many more miles of driving lessons do you need before you reach one thousand?"

The teen glanced to his right and was surprised to see his grandfather apprising him with eyes that had gone wet. Lucas quickly refocused on the road.

"About four hundred fifty. Then I can go for my license." He stole another glance at his grandfather.

The man's voice turned gruff, but his lips curled into a half smile. "Of course, that's in addition to all the unofficial miles your buddies let you drive their cars after your parents docked you for your grades."

Bryce watched his grandson blush to the roots of his blond hair, but the teen couldn't hide the twinkle that appeared in his hazel eyes.

"Damn, you remind me so much of her," said Bryce.

"Who, Grandpa?"

"Lucas, you come by tomorrow afternoon and you can drive again. I'll tell you about her then. And I'll tell you about Charlie Coe."

Chapter 1

February, 1964

Bryce Roberts' contentment was full as he jiggled the mobile toy suspended above the crib and watched for Eddie's reaction. Home, at last, with thirty days leave from the Navy, Bryce was relishing this new taste of fatherhood. He'd held his son for the first time yesterday when Marilyn brought Eddie to the airport to welcome him.

Now, Marilyn was out shopping.

"You guys get to know each other while I'm out," she'd told him. Then she kissed Bryce passionately.

"Lord, woman, you make my spirits dance." He continued to hold her until she kissed him again and then slipped from his embrace.

"Wait till you taste the special dinner I'm going to cook. And dessert . . ." She left with a flirtatious wink

He smiled now, daydreaming about their lovemaking last night. Marilyn and he had been lovers since their senior year in high school. Marriage had not dulled their passion for each other. Lucky you, Roberts, he told himself. No, lucky us. We have something special. And to top it off my wife's my best friend.

His musing was interrupted by the apartment doorbell. It surprised Bryce who heard it for the first time.

"Who's calling this early in the morning?" he asked Eddie, and then headed for the door.

Homer Miller stood on the small stoop, shifting from one foot to the other, his police officer's hat in hand.

"Bryce, may I come in, please?"

Bryce Roberts reached to shake his friend's hand and invited him in. "Homer, what's up? Lord, I haven't seen you in a heck of a long time . . ." Bryce's voice trailed off as the distress in Homer's face grew.

"Bryce, I have bad news. Try to get hold of yourself. Marilyn's been in a car wreck."

Bryce's huge hands gripped Homer's shoulders. "Oh, my god! Is she hurt?"

Homer ignored the tremendous pressure from the grasp. "She's hurt badly and they've taken her to the hospital."

"I've got to get to the hospital! But Marilyn has the car! Homer, can you take me?"

"Yes. The station called your parents' home and Marilyn's parents. They're on the way to the hospital, too."

"It's that bad?"

"I don't know for sure. Get your coat. You'd better come with me right away. Bryce . . . Bryce, did you hear me?"

"I . . . I have to find someone to watch Eddie. Oh, Lord, let me think! . . . Yes! There's a woman who may be home in the next apartment." He grabbed his coat and moved quickly to ring his neighbor's doorbell and introduced himself. He explained what he needed as Homer stood slightly behind him signaling the urgency of the moment with his expression, and mouthing the word "please."

"He's only seventeen weeks old, Mrs. Campbell," said Bryce. "He shouldn't be any trouble."

Mrs. Campbell understood Homer's silent plea and agreed to watch Eddie. The men ran for Homer's patrol car.

Over the siren, Bryce turned to Homer, and, voice tight, demanded, "What happened?"

"That drunk, Charlie Coe, hit her car head on. He came at high speed down the hill west of Minnich's grocery store and just swerved his truck right into her. When I got there that bastard got out of his pickup and walked away from the crash."

"Coe? I'd forgotten about that crazy son-of-a-bitch. He . . . just walked away?"

"He said, 'Say hello to Bryce for me' and then staggered over to a tree and leaned against it."

"Say hello to Bryce for me?" Bryce's mouth hung open as he shook his head back and forth and tried to deal with what he'd heard.

Homer nodded, and swerved around a car that had pulled to the side of the road at the sound of the approaching siren.

"So he knew he'd hit Marilyn," said Bryce. "Damn him! He's always tried to harass Marilyn and me. But, Homer, I never thought he'd go this far. That bastard!" Bryce sat forward as if he could urge the cruiser onward toward the hospital.

"Bryce, sit back and fasten your seat belt! You'll go through the windshield if we hit something!" Bryce settled his large frame against the seatback and buckled up.

Siren wailing, Homer drove straight to the emergency room entrance, skidded to a halt, and the two men ran inside.

The clerk at the desk stopped them.

"I'm Bryce Roberts. Where have they taken my wife?"

"The doctor will be with you shortly, Mr. Roberts. Please sit down in the waiting area."

"I can't sit down! Where's Marilyn?"

"Sir, please." She looked an appeal at Homer and then again said to Bryce, "The doctor will be with you shortly."

Bryce ignored her officiousness, turned toward the doors that lead to the treatment area and charged through them. He froze as the doctor removed his stethoscope from Marilyn's chest and pulled his surgical mask down. The physician shook his head from side to side, and said, "What a shame."

Marilyn's body lay on the gurney with a limpness only the dead maintain.

Bryce bellowed in agony at the sight and the words he'd heard. "Ah, God, no! God, nooooo!"

A wail came from him as he pushed past the doctor and reached for Marilyn's body. He pulled her to his chest and caressed her bruised and pale face with a lover's touch. "Oh Marilyn, no . . . Oh, Sweetheart," he keened again and again between sobs. He continued to cradle and caress her until the ache inside him demanded relief.

Bryce gently laid her down. Staring in agony at the lifeless body of his wife, he raised his fists high above his shoulders.

The E.R. nurse shook as the most primitive scream she'd ever heard tore through her senses.

Then Bryce turned away. The tormented man brought his fists slamming down on an empty gurney, denting the stainless steel. He slumped over the gurney and hung his head in despair.

"God, why her?" he bawled. "Why not me?" He returned to Marilyn and again gently cradled her body in his arms as his sobs and groans resumed.

A nurse who'd left when he'd burst into the room returned with Homer Miller and a doctor who Bryce recognized as Mort Kincaid. Homer and Dr. Kincaid stood quietly in deference to the agonized man.

Finally, Dr. Kincaid put his hand on Bryce's shoulder. The surgeon could feel the vibration of Bryce's low-pitched groaning. The sound reminded him of the day his prize bull had broken his foreleg.

"Bryce," he said, still gently touching his shoulder, "I'm so terribly sorry this has happened." He paused, waiting for a reaction. There was none except a momentary glance in his direction.

"Bryce, I want to take you to a room down the hallway for a few minutes. Will you come with me, please?" Bryce looked up, his face contorted with agony, and he would not let go of Marilyn's body. Silence built in the room, punctuated only with his sobs.

"Please, Bryce, we all can handle this better if your family can join you in a room we have down the hall," said Kincaid. He turned and walked toward an exit.

Bryce still cradled Marilyn. Then, reverently, he laid his wife's body down, covered her as if tucking in a child, and followed Kincaid in a walk that reminded Homer of a feeble old man.

Homer moved forward, and draped Bryce' arm over his shoulder to steady the man who had been his high school teammate.

"Please use our chapel," said Kincaid. He saw a look of panic and desperation form on Bryce's face as a renewed realization of his wife's death struck him. "Officer Miller told me your families are on the way, and I think it would be best if you stay here until they can join you. Officer Miller told me he'll stay with you until they arrive. It's private and you can remain as long as you need to.

"Bryce, I want you to take some medicine a nurse will bring to you. It's a sedative that will help you get back in control."

"I don't want medicine. I just need to cry."

⟨≈⟩

Noah Coleman was trying to be stoic, but failing, and Stella Coleman was weeping uncontrollably as they entered the chapel.

She reminds me so much of Marilyn, Bryce thought. But now her usually coiffured hair was disheveled and her eyes were dulled. Bryce stood and embraced his weeping mother-in-law and held her as her tears spilled on to his shirt, joining with his.

Homer Miller shifted from one foot to the other. "Bryce, I'm going to find your parents."

"It's okay, Homer, someone will bring them back here when they arrive. Could you please stay for a moment?"

Bryce let go of Stella, guided her to a seat beside Noah, and led Homer to a far corner of the chapel.

"What'll they do with Coe?" Bryce's deep voice had turned to a harsh rasp that made the hairs on the back of Homer's neck stand up.

"We'll throw the book at him and hope the judge locks him up for a long time."

"How long? He could get away with it because that son-of-a-bitch is half nuts."

"I can't say for sure what they'll do to him. It'll depend on what the judge decides."

Homer left when Harry and Rosalie arrived. Bryce's mother was tearful but surprisingly calm. Rosalie hugged her son for a long time and then asked him to sit with her and Harry.

"Bryce, this is awful, but somehow we'll get through this as a family," said Harry. "Together we've faced rough times before and we'll overcome this one too. We'll be with you and Eddie as much as you need us."

"Eddie! Oh, Lord! I left him with a neighbor who doesn't even know me. We have to go to the apartment and get Eddie."

Harriet, his younger sister, heard him as she entered the chapel and said she'd met Mrs. Campbell when visiting with Marilyn. She volunteered to take Eddie back to the nursery that Rosalie had prepared in their home on the news of Marilyn's pregnancy.

"You're going to have to stop and buy bottles and formula, Harriet," instructed Rosalie. She handed money to Harriet and said, "That baby is going to miss . . ." and then she stopped as she realized that Bryce had heard and he again began to shake with sobs.

Later, the two families agreed upon a funeral home and departed. Bryce told his parents that he'd meet them outside and he headed for the emergency room.

The treatment room was empty, quiet. Marilyn's body was gone. He stood quietly for moments and then raised his face. "God, what am I going to do without her?"

He stopped himself in the lobby and tried to get control before joining his parents. Then his focus shifted. *God damn that bastard, Coe!* His anger at Coe grew until it consumed him. Nausea rose in his gut and he dashed for the men's room. Shaking with rage, and embarrassed over the need to do it in a public restroom, he knelt over a commode and puked. When the man finally raised his head from the toilet bowl and took in the stained tile floor on which he knelt, and the graffiti etched into the stall walls, his unrelenting hatred of Charles Coe rooted.

He lifted his head, and then forced himself to stand erect. *Somehow, I have to get through this.*

But how?

Think about Coe later. Stay in control for now.

Now I have a funeral to plan.

Chapter 2

I t was snowing when they laid Marilyn to rest. The mourners were shielded from the late February weather by a large tent that Harry had ordered from a summer picnic service.

Bryce withdrew into an emotional fog as the service progressed. He was aware of his family and friends who surrounded him but they weren't enough to relieve his terrible ache.

A gust of wind blew snow under the tent. Snowflakes fell on the coffin, beautiful delicate snowflakes.

Like her, he thought. Why didn't I pay more attention to Coe's threat? I knew he was dangerous. I just forgot about him after the passage of time.

◦❦◦

On a late afternoon in August of 1958 Bryce and his father were sitting next to the pool at the lower terrace of their backyard after swimming laps. Their bathing suits dripped water through their Adirondack chair bottoms. Harry sat with his back to the sun. Bryce faced him.

"Great way to cool off after work," said Harry. He was shorter than his son, but had the same dark hair, squared jaw and full lips. He prided himself in staying in good shape. His waistline had no flab that adorned many of the contemporaries of the forty-seven year-old man.

Bryce knew that something was bothering Harry because his father was rubbing his badly scarred knee, a sure sign of his discontent. Bryce waited, alert and apprehensive.

"By the way, have you heard from Marilyn lately?"

"Yes. She writes every week."

"How does she like Paris?"

"Fine. She's made some friends, as she always does."

"Have you written to her?"

"I did a couple of times, but it's hard to write when I haven't been doing much but work and baseball. There's nothing to write about."

"Write about what you think of things. That makes for an interesting letter and it's a way to share a little of yourself."

"I'll try that."

Harry paused for a long moment, as if thinking how to begin. "I knew her mother when we were young. But I guess you already know that."

"Yes, you told me that a long time ago."

Harry hesitated again and then said, "Bryce, it's time we start talking like men."

Ah, now we're getting to what's really bothering you, thought Bryce.

Harry stopped rubbing his knee and leaned forward in his chair, his forearms resting on his thighs, hands together between his open knees.

Bryce waited for the next words with the nervousness that comes with a new experience and curiosity over what was to follow.

Curiosity won. He assumed a similar pose to face his father.

"Don't you ever talk about this with anyone," said Harry. "Before Marilyn's mother married, Stella was one hot woman. Nobody said much about it back in those days but some of the men in our crowd knew it and would try to get past first base with her. Somehow she had the talent for sniffing out the guys that just wanted to get in her pants; and they never did. But if she liked you . . . I just hope Marilyn doesn't have that reputation."

"She doesn't, Dad." Bryce felt his armpits begin to sweat profusely as he waited for the next question. But his father was too circumspect.

"I haven't heard anything, either," said Harry and he leaned back just a bit. "Oh, don't look at me like that. Parents in this community hear things, too. We just have a little more experience than our children in sizing up people.

"For instance, this Charlie Coe may seem harmless to you, but he's not."

Bryce sat up straight, ready to argue, but his father held up a hand and continued.

"I know he tried to meddle on Prom night, and I think you handled it well. But, Bryce, I'm telling you, that kid is unstable. I play golf with one of the doctors who treat him and Forrest went out on a limb to warn me. He's really concerned that Coe kid is going to snap. That whole family is strange. Keep your distance from the Coes, particularly Charlie. I understand that he's taken to drinking and that he gets even more volatile under the influence."

"I know he drinks. He came to class drunk a couple of times. They sent him home."

"Yes. His father promised he'd keep Charlie under control if the Board would just let him finish his senior year. So we voted to allow that."

Bryce beamed inside because he'd figured that was the situation and it gave him another small notch of confidence in his own ability to analyze a situation. But he was upset with himself for not pegging Coe's menace.

"Okay, he's more volatile than I thought, but I can handle him. I always have."

"Don't be too cock-sure of that."

Harry again began to rub his knee. "There's something else you should know. Charlie Coe told his psychiatrist that he had a gun with him on prom night. I don't know whether that's true, but the psychiatrist thinks it may be. The doc told me it's a way people like Charlie feel power. Coe believes that if he uses the gun, he'll get recognition. That's more important to Charlie than the consequences he'd face."

"Claiming he had a gun probably is just Charlie's braggadocio," said Bryce. "At least he hasn't been around this summer, so I guess he's found someone else to bother."

"Bryce, has it occurred to you that he's not around because Marilyn's in France? It seems he only bothers you when she's with you. You may want to reconsider whether you should continue to date Marilyn if it means Coe will make you a target."

"I'm not going to allow that creep to interfere in my relationships!"

"He already has. And I don't think he's going to stop. Bryce, there will always be people out there who deliberately interfere or meddle in other peoples' lives—"

"He won't have a chance. He can't follow me to Dartmouth and he's not going to get to Marilyn at Penn State."

"The Coes of the world have a way of turning up unexpectedly. Keep that in mind."

Harry was called to the house to answer the telephone. He stood and looked at his son.

"You're beginning the final steps of your journey into manhood, Bryce. We need to talk more often. Man to man. No lectures. It's just that I want you around for the long haul and I want to see you succeed. And I'll be damned if I want to see you shot by some crazy kid."

Chapter 3

A snowflake blew onto Bryce's lips. He brushed at it and refocused on the coffin that was suspended over the neatly edged hole dug in the frozen ground.

Inside, Bryce was racked with guilt. *Marilyn, I'm sorry. I was so joyful over our reunion I just didn't think about anything bad. Now you've paid the ultimate price . . . All because Coe wanted to get at me.*

The graveside ritual ended with The Reverend Jacob Knox sprinkling the customary dust over the coffin. Then he signaled the men from the cemetery company to lower the coffin into the ground.

Bryce's eyes flowed tears but he fought to control the sobs that threatened to erupt. His brothers, Phillip and Stephen stood beside him, their shoulders pressed against his. As the coffin sank below ground level Bryce's spirit sank with it.

God, Marilyn, I don't want to say good-bye like this. It's not what was meant to be.

Stephen handed him a clump of dirt and Bryce tossed it reverently on the coffin. He walked away while other family members took their turn to do the same.

⌒═◎

One person in the cemetery was smiling. Charlie Coe, out on bail, watched the ceremony through a break in the evergreens that partially hid a maintenance shed. He had to adjust the eyepieces of his binoculars to accommodate the thick lenses of his glasses. Once more he brought the grieving face of Bryce Roberts into focus.

Coe shivered, but it wasn't from the cold and snow.

Chapter 4

When the funeral reception at the Roberts' home ended, Jacob Knox found Bryce sitting outside on a second story balcony overlooking the distant snow-covered hills. Bryce's topcoat was open, his hair and shoulders were dusted with snow, and he was drinking a scotch.

"Jacob, I am one lonesome man right now," said Bryce.

"I know."

The pastor hesitated and then began. "Bryce, I'm not going to talk to you about God. You know He's there when you need Him. I think we should talk about grief and how you might handle it. Would you mind if we went inside?"

Bryce fought the urge to tell his pastor to go away. Instead he dumped the contents of his glass over the balcony rail and led Jacob inside to a small, paneled sitting room. He remained standing and faced the cleric. Then Bryce's restraint gave way.

"How dare you say God's there when we need Him! If that's true why did He allow this to happen? Huh? Tell me why, Jacob! Marilyn was so full of life and we had so many years to live ahead of us! Damn it! We didn't deserve this . . . *I* don't deserve this!"

Bryce put the empty glass on a table, removed his topcoat and violently threw it toward a chair.

"Jacob, don't take this personally, but right now I'm madder with God than you could believe!"

Bryce's dark, almost black, eyes blazed with anger and he moved even closer to look down into Jacob's face. "Jacob, I cannot fathom God. I've tried to lead a decent life, to do the right things, study hard, work hard. And how do I get repaid? Tell me! How has God repaid me? Huh?"

Jacob didn't back away. "Bryce, God doesn't *owe* you anything." Jacob paused until his words hit home. Then he continued. "Sometimes there's a brutality about life, and about death, that makes God hard to figure out. But understand this: God hasn't used Marilyn's death to punish you. As time passes you'll believe that."

"That still doesn't answer my question, Jacob." Bryce stepped back and raised his arms, as if beseeching the God he now railed against. "Where's His justice? Where's His love?"

Bryce's eyes continued to blaze across the room. It was all Jacob could do to meet their intensity. "Bryce, at least you're not keeping that anger inside. One of these days, tell God why you're angry with Him. If you do, He won't turn into a wimp, and He will, I guarantee, understand your anger."

"Even if I do that,' said Bryce, "I'll go through life hating one of His creations. That bastard Coe didn't even give me a chance to say good-bye to my wife."

At the mention of Coe, Bryce's voice took on a harsh rasp that sent shivers down Jacob Knox's spine. "Lord!" thought Jacob. "That voice . . . I've never heard such hatred."

Jacob winced and regrouped. "You'll probably hate Coe for a long time. Just don't let it consume you. Like a lot of feelings, it'll be tempered by time. Just let time do its work. Someday you may even find it in yourself to forgive Coe."

Bryce's face turned fierce. Jacob recognized the expression from his days as a Marine Corps Chaplain. It was a warrior's look, one that men get when about to enter battle.

"When Marilyn and I were at a swimming hole with a bunch of friends from our Bucks senior class, I think Coe tried to shoot us when we were running to our car through a thunderstorm. There was a sound that was more like a high powered rifle than thunder. I couldn't prove anything. But two days later Coe pulled into Smitty's Texaco right behind me. He had a crescent-shaped wound over his right eye, the kind that you get when a rifle's recoil kicks the telescopic sight into your face. He smiled that smug, weird way of his and said, 'Say hello to Marilyn for me.' He didn't get any gas, he just swaggered over to his car and drove away.

"Another time, a week after Marilyn was my Winter Carnival date at Dartmouth, I received an anonymous letter with a drawing of a gravestone. The gravestone held Marilyn's name and birth date and had the word 'soon' for her date of death. I knew it was Coe, I just couldn't prove it because it came up negative for fingerprints and the handwriting expert Dad hired was no help.

"So, let me ask you something, Jacob. If a man who, for years, stalked and deliberately tried to torment you, then killed your wife and best friend, who you love with all of your heart, could you forgive him?"

Bryce sat down and continued to look accusingly at Jacob, as if he were God's personal agent. Jacob didn't answer. Instead he waited calmly for the next outburst. Finally, he sat down across from his grieving parishioner.

An antique French clock ticked in the silence. As the moments passed Bryce's face went from anger to anguish. "I apologize, Jacob. That wasn't fair."

Jacob watched him struggle to hold back the tears that sought release. Bryce regained enough composure to continue.

"I feel at loose ends, Jacob. Marilyn's murder has wiped out my plans for our lifetime together. And that's really all I wanted. Just a loving marriage, some kids . . . a challenging job. Jacob, I believed in that dream and I've worked damned hard to earn it!

"I've tried to think things through, find a reason I've not been allowed to have that dream . . . why I didn't deserve it. All I keep coming back to is the fact that I'm now a twenty-four-year-old widower with a baby son who I don't know the first thing about raising and caring for. Christ! There's really no instruction book on that. Things are so out of my control!"

Chapter 5

"You'll learn to handle things," said Jacob. "And Marilyn's parents and your family will step in and help with Eddie while you finish out your Navy obligation. Midge and Harriet told me that Eddie's learned to feed from a bottle when they hold him; and, they're going to do alright with the boy, particularly Midge. She once told me she felt like a second mother to you and your brothers and sisters. Now she's going to help raise a third generation of the Roberts clan."

Jacob saw Bryce's posture relax a shade and his face mellow at the mention of his family.

"Now, let me speak for a few minutes," said Jacob. "You have to accept the fact that Marilyn's gone, Bryce. I think you've started to do that, but there'll be times that you'll find yourself talking to her. Go ahead and do it, but then take a time out and tell yourself that you need to move ahead. You're going to yearn intensely for Marilyn to the point that you'll feel as if your heart has been ripped out. Just don't let it consume you. That will pass. And for a while you're going to stay angry at the world and God for the raw deal you believe life has handed you. That's normal. Just don't let your anger take complete control."

The warrior's face reappeared, full of challenge. "Just how am I supposed to manage that?"

"Understand that God is still with you. You still have a strong faith that will, if you call upon the Almighty, help you through the coming months. And you're strong in other ways. Tom, your roommate, told me how you were nicknamed 'The Machine' by your fraternity brothers because you used to get up at 5:30 in the morning and start your day with swimming and piano practice before most of them were even out of bed. He also said you studied with incredible concentration. I think you learned that at Bucks Academy. Anyway, I know you have the self-discipline and strength to handle grieving. I just want to tell you what to expect so you understand what you're going to experience is normal for a man who's lost his wife. It'll probably take you about two years to get through most of the process—"

"—No it won't," said Bryce, "I don't have that kind of time."

Chapter 6

B ryce used Bucks Academy's swimming pool to work out every morning for the last weeks he was home, but it wasn't enough to regain the fitness he demanded of himself.

When he returned to his Navy Underwater Demolition Team 41, Bryce's commanding officer had him running on the beach with his platoon and doing calisthenics until he thought he was back in "hell week." It helped the grieving man turn his focus away from what he left behind. For that Bryce was grateful to his C.O. and the men in his platoon who volunteered to go through his reconditioning with him. In the evenings he turned in to his bunk too exhausted to linger long on thoughts of Marilyn before sleep overcame him. Eight days later he told his C.O. he was again fit when the team began training with an advanced underwater breathing apparatus that didn't leave a trail of large bubbles in the water.

Before Taps he tried to read a book on naval history, but thoughts of Marilyn at last filled his mind. "Ah, Marilyn, I can't shut you out any longer. Today I thought about our senior prom and the way Coe almost ruined it when he showed up in his father's tux. I never told you, but I learned later that he had a pistol and would have shot you if I hadn't phoned his old man to come get his drunken son. A lot of good that did. That loony finally got to you anyway, all because he wanted to make me hurt. God! You were so innocent, so kind. I always thought we could handle Coe. You'd be alive today if I'd have taken his threat more seriously. Now I feel so damned guilty over what he did. But from whom do I ask forgiveness?"

He put the book down and ground his fist into his palm.

❧

On Saturday evening he declined an invitation to go off base for bar hopping and socializing. Dressed in fatigues, he returned to the beach, sat at the seaward side of the dunes, and, alone in his agony, bawled his heart out into the sounds of the surf and the wind.

When he was spent, he rose from the dune, strode to the water's edge and looked out over the ocean. He raised his finger to point.

Where do I point in this vastness?

He settled on the starlit horizon. "Coe," he screamed, "you little turd! I'll never let you hurt me again! You hear that God? Do You? I'll never let him hurt me again!"

Chapter 7

Evars Dombrowski's father was Polish and his mother was of Lithuanian heritage. He was all American. Boatswain's Mate First Class Dombrowski stood a shade over six feet, but that's not what one noticed about Evars. He had a huge, muscular torso and arms to match. He taught judo and hand-to-hand combat as if they were a religion. And God help any student who didn't follow the credo. If he thought a trainee wasn't working hard enough to learn the moves he'd look at him with contempt mixed with anger from over his high Slavic cheekbones. He didn't need anything more than what became known as "the look" to make a point to his students.

Judo training was new to UDT 41 but they took to it gladly. Many sensed it was connected with the next class of men who would be drawn from UDT units to train as SEALs. Bryce had been offered the opportunity to join the next SEAL class but he declined. He had no desire to make a career of the Navy, and the men who went to the SEAL units were mostly career-oriented. But he willingly embraced judo.

Dombrowski singled him out on the first day of training because Bryce was the biggest man in his platoon. Dombrowski wanted to make the point that in judo, size was not everything. Lt(j.g.) Roberts found himself flying through the air and landing flat on his back with embarrassing regularity with what seemed almost no effort on Dombrowski's part. That was all the motivation Bryce needed. He vowed that he'd work hard and learn to do the same thing to his instructor. He checked out a book on judo from the base library and studied and practiced the balance techniques and moves illustrated in the text. He also began to run and swim longer distances and at greater speed than he'd ever done before. And he built up his upper body strength. The extra conditioning was for him. The quiet practice was for Dombrowski.

Just as he had done at Dartmouth four years ago, Bryce formed a "study group" to work on their judo lessons but also to learn and repeat more advanced moves. They quietly left their barracks in the evening and practiced on the beach before it became too dark to see. Bryce didn't realize it at the time, but he was building leadership skills that would serve him well.

A week later during an afternoon practice one of Bryce's men threw Dombrowski. Somehow Evars understood that Bryce was behind the extra skills the platoon was showing and Dombrowski didn't appreciate being upstaged. There began an almost vicious competition in the teaching sessions that had the men working even harder to practice the skills that Evars Dombrowski worshipped.

Bryce again was a target, but this time the balance he had practiced along with his superior reach had its effect. Evars went down. The boatswain tried "the look" on Bryce but his student just smiled and didn't offer his instructor a hand up. He knew that if he did so, Evars would find a way to take him down.

Dombrowski got up and said, "You guys have learned your lessons well. Now maybe you'll stay alive if you have to defend yourselves." He then reached out to shake Bryce's hand. Bryce accepted the gesture and landed on his butt. Evars, whose grin was more a grimace, grinned and, gravel voice low in his throat, said, "Mr. Roberts, I think you're learning this—almost."

Chapter 8

Bryce had no intention of spending another Saturday evening alone on the beach racked with grief. When the weekend arrived he accepted the invitation from his fellow junior officers to dress in civilian clothes and head downtown for a few beers and the companionship the evening offered. They found themselves a table in The Blue Crab next to men in their unit and bought them a round of beers.

Dombrowski and Bryce had called an unspoken truce. Had they admitted it, a growing respect was budding between the career enlisted man and the junior officer. Evars sensed that there were no pretenses about Bryce. And accepting the company of enlisted men didn't seem strange to Bryce, who'd spent his summers among working class men in sawmills or clearing and replanting logged-over forests.

The Blue Crab featured a piano player who was a retired Navy Chief. He led the patrons in singing many of the old favorites from the 1930s to the present. Customers requested the songs from a selection in tattered books with the words printed in them. When the drunks would begin to get off-beat or off-tune, the chief beat out the rhythm with one hand on the paneled wall next to the old upright and the other hand managed the keyboard.

The third round of beers arrived at the officers' table and the waitress asked if they wanted something to eat. A marine at the next table made a crude remark about eating something. Ignoring the vulgarity, the waitress moved to the other side of the UDT tables to take their orders. None of the navy men paid any attention to the marine and his buddies . . . at least not directly.

By the time they finished their food, the chief began a medley of the four service songs. "Anchors Away" resounded out into the street. When the Marine Battle Hymn began, the Navy men chanted "Cha-Cha-Cha" at the end of each stanza, so that by the time the words "on the land the air and sea" were sung, and they were augmented by another Cha-Cha-Cha, the navy men had the marines' attention.

Bryce began to look for a corner he could put his back to, but the place was packed and there was hardly room to push his chair back. At the end of the song, as if on cue, beer bottles flew and the few women in the place were shoved unceremoniously under the tables. The marines next to the UDT tables leaped up, knocking over their chairs in anticipation of the fray which rapidly escalated into a donnybrook. A marine charged at Bryce swinging wildly with his right arm and Bryce, using the lessons of the past month, put the man down with a hip throw. The marine landed in a pile of chairs and disappeared under the melee.

Another, who had the misfortune of vaguely resembling Charles Coe, came at him. Anger erupted in Bryce at the thought of Coe. Forgetting all about the fine points of judo, Bryce delivered a crushing, hate-fueled punch to the man's jaw and the hapless marine staggered backward and dropped to his knees. Bryce waded into the group of marines as if he were Patton after Rommel. He didn't stop beating the daylights out of all of the Coes masquerading as marines until the shore patrol arrived outside and Dombrowski hauled him out a rear exit into an alley filled with the stench of garbage and vomit.

"Holy shit, Mr. Roberts, you aren't even breathing that hard," said Evars.

Bryce's temper cooled. "Must be all that conditioning I'm doing. You know something, Ski? That almost was fun."

◦◦◦

The men of UDT 41 referred to their commanding officer as "Old Iron Tongue" because when Lt. Commander Standring was annoyed, he had a habit of curling his tongue against his lower front teeth. He was displaying his trademark as Lt.(j.g.) Roberts stood at attention in front of his desk.

"Mr. Roberts, the marines are on the same side as we," he began. "You sent four of those men to the hospital, Mr. Roberts. That's four good men down, Mr. Roberts, and that means their buddies may have to stand their watches and pick up their slack, Mr. Roberts." He paused, tongue curled, and then continued, "Do you have anything to say, Mr. Roberts?"

"Sir, one of those marines looked like the bastard that killed my wife, and after that I just lost control, Sir." Bryce was going to continue to explain and conclude with an apology, but Standring stopped him with a gesture. The C.O. turned, looked out the window behind his desk for a long minute and then faced Bryce again.

"I know about your wife and I'm sorry about that, Mr. Roberts. Hell of a thing to have happen. If I didn't understand that circumstance, you'd be in serious trouble.

"Mr. Roberts, when you do go on shore leave again, stay the hell out of bars frequented by enlisted men. An officer and a gentleman just doesn't behave as you did. Understood?"

"Yes, sir."

"As it is, you're confined to base for three weeks.

"Now, your new assignment has come through. I've been asked to transfer you to the group that's training the incoming class of SEALs. Do you think you're up to that?"

"Yes, Sir. They're going to be the best conditioned men of the bunch, Sir. Oh, uh, by the way, Sir, my parents are bringing my son down to see me this coming weekend. Do you think I might be able to serve my restriction after that?"

The tongue resumed its curl and then, exasperated, the C.O. shook his head back and forth. "Yes, Mr. Roberts. Now get out of here and report to Lieutenant Farnham over at the SEAL barracks. You can move your gear later today."

Chapter 9

When his parents brought Eddie to visit, Bryce was tentative around the baby. He couldn't help thinking of Marilyn when he held Eddie, and the baby seemed so fragile in his hands. But soon he was relishing the opportunity to gently bounce him on his knee. He thought of a letter Marilyn had written to him about a mother's love and he began to understand the father's version of that emotion as he held his son and gave him his bottle.

"Will you look at this boy chow down? We have to do this more often," he said to Rosalie.

"You can take a weekend and come home, too," she replied.

"Bryce, what did you do to your hand?"

"Oh, uh, hand to hand combat practice, Mom. Got a little out of control. It's okay."

Bryce didn't miss the roll of Harry's eyes.

"How are Noah and Stella?" he asked.

"She's been taking turns caring for Eddie, and Noah is beginning to come out of the shell that he went into after the funeral. Eddie seems to do that for him, so we share him with them quite often. This child is going to be terribly spoiled if we keep it up."

Eddie got his first taste of sand and the ocean when they drove to Virginia Beach that late May afternoon. As the baby inched his way across the blanket under the umbrella, Rosalie smiled in that gentle way Bryce had appreciated since childhood. Bryce's eyes began to fill, and abruptly he rose and walked away toward the surf to keep his tears private.

"God," he mentally shouted at the deity, "When Marilyn and I took leave in Cape Cod, I dreamed about us on the beach with our kids. Now that dream is ruined and I want the pain to go away." He looked out over the ocean and continued addressing the Almighty.

"Jacob told me I'd have to get used to reminders and flashbacks, and that eventually they'd soften, but, God, please hurry up with that part." He ran down the beach along the waterline until he could control himself. Then he returned to his son for another round of joy and pain.

"We really have quite a family," he thought as he watched the youngest generation of the Roberts clan crawl toward his grandmother. I'll have to tell him about us the moment he's old enough to listen.

⊙≋◦

In the year 1705, in a letter to William Penn, the Proprietor of Pennsylvania, James Logan referred to the area around what is now the Borough of Quakertown as a "Great Swamp." The Quakers who settled the region drained the swamps and farmed the fertile lands thus exposed. The locale became known as "Richland" for the abundant harvests the land yielded and for its vast stands of heavy forests.

The Quakers also proved to be canny businessmen, and when German settlers moved into the area in the 1730s a thriving trade among the peoples took root. During the Civil War era the Quakers, following their philosophy of the worth and dignity of all people, operated one of the largest stops on the Underground Railroad.

Rosalie was descended from these farmers and craftsmen of northern Bucks County. She met Harry Roberts when he made a sales call upon her grandfather, a cabinet maker who was able to stay in business during the Great Depression by making caskets.

Harry's family harvested and marketed hardwood for generations. While still in his late teens, Harry took to the roads as a salesman to help the business keep going during those tough financial times. Harry was impressed with Rosalie's quiet strength and charmed by her pleasant disposition, and he often found excuses to stop at the shop to talk with her in the small office she maintained in immaculate order. The young woman with the lovely smile and lively dark eyes finally accepted his offer of a soda at the local drugstore and their courtship blossomed.

Harry's Scotch-Irish ancestors had settled in Newtown in the southern section of Bucks County in the early 1700s. They couldn't believe their good fortune in finding the perfect stream to dam for a saw mill. They built their dam and millrace with native stone. The mill pond was created with earthen banks shoveled into place with back-breaking labor. They never complained that the work was hard; they just did it and thanked God for their freedom and the living they earned from the mill and their farm.

Seeking more lands, Harry's ancestors removed to central Bucks County where they continued to farm and build an expanding lumber business with a larger mill. Keeping alive a family tradition that began in the Revolutionary War, they always sent their sons to serve their country in times of war.

When the Japanese struck at Pearl Harbor, Harry Roberts, despite being the father of two children with another on the way, volunteered for the army and fought in North Africa. He was wounded at El Guettar, mustered out at the insistence of his colonel who knew he had three children, and welcomed home to recuperate under a grateful Rosalie's care. When his knee finally healed after another surgery to remove more shrapnel, he managed the family's forest products business and Rosalie helped to supervise the farming operations, all the while praying for the war to end.

Harry and Rosalie, descendants of the colonists, children of the Great Depression, and survivors of World War II, deeply appreciated the blessings that hard work and tenacity began to bring them as they left the war behind. Neither of them, however, could anticipate the changes the approaching decade of the 1960s would bring to their family.

◦≈◦

And what a decade it's been so far, thought Bryce as he came back to the present.

Harry was standing there, looking out over the ocean, as if toward a distant shore. "I wonder if he's thinking about the past or the future?" thought Bryce. "Well, Eddie, you're the future. The one whole egg left in the henhouse after the fox went through. Don't worry, son, I won't let the fox get you, too.

"Do I tell him about Coe someday, or do I just keep that to myself? No, I can't do that.

"But what do I tell him, and how? Coe is never again going to meddle in our family's business . . . and neither is anyone else."

Chapter 10

Saturday, October 7, 2006

Bryce handed the car keys to Lucas. "Let's head for Bucks Prep. You pick the route."

"Why there, Grandfather?"

"I'm going to show you a stump."

"Huh?"

"Drive, Lucas. I'll tell you when we get there."

The prep school's campus was a collection of slate-roofed Georgian brick buildings and native limestone dormitories that conveyed a tone of strength and permanency. Brick pathways wound among them, adding warmth to the landscaped grounds. The mature but carefully maintained trees that gave a lasting grace to the school's appearance had lost most of their leaves to a recent frost.

Bryce led Lucas to the side yard of Macleod Hall and stopped at an aging stump that barely rose above the ground.

"This is where it really started all of those years ago," said Bryce. "It was in the spring of 1958. Back then this stump was a huge oak that only seniors were allowed to gather under. Some friends and I were standing right here . . ."

⊙≋◎

Bryce felt a hard tapping on his shoulder, turned in response, and looked down to see Charlie Coe's intense light brown eyes staring up at him through thick glasses with heavy black nylon frames. "Man alive," thought Bryce, "those eyes still have a crazy gloss to them." Bryce controlled an urge to shudder.

"You gotta break your prom date with Marilyn, or else!" snarled Coe. Dried spittle stretched at the corners of his mouth as he spoke, and his sparsely whiskered chin started to quiver.

Bryce inhaled deeply to calm down and asked himself, "Do I just flatten the little twerp, or do I try to reason with a loony? God! What a choice!"

"Charlie," said Bryce, deliberately keeping his tone level but firm, "I'm not going to break my date with Marilyn. Look, you're no dummy. You know Marilyn and I are going steady."

Then Bryce hit the button he knew would get Charlie's attention. "And something else: your father's going to hear about it if you go near Marilyn again. She was really upset after you tried to get in her car yesterday. Just stay away from her. Find your own date and stop bugging Marilyn and me."

The gloss in Coe's eyes took on greater intensity. "She's the only girl who even says hello to me. If she doesn't go to the Prom with me, I'll make damn sure she's not going with you either!"

Exasperated, Bryce sought to break through Coe's fantasy. "Charlie, don't threaten me. Just go away and leave us alone. You have no right to annoy other people. And, Charlie . . . Marilyn says hello just to be polite."

"That's a lie! She likes me a lot." Coe moved even closer to Bryce, but Peter Chase, who saw Bryce's eyes darken with anger, grabbed Coe from behind by the belt and pulled him away from Bryce. Peter turned him toward a chartered school bus that took local students home.

"You're going to miss your bus, and your old man will whip your butt if you aren't on it," said Peter.

Fear appeared in Coe's eyes. When Peter let go of him he trotted toward the bus. Then he turned and shouted, hand cupped to his mouth, "I mean it, Roberts, you better break your date or I will."

Bryce squelched a response to Coe's melodrama. The three friends watched Coe board the bus, and then Dean Brooks said, "Bryce, how do you keep your cool around him? Man, if I'd have been you I'd have punched his lights out."

"I almost did, but Peter saved me. I'd love to beat the crap out of the twerp for the way he's frightened Marilyn, but he's half my size and I won't let myself get angry with a crazy. Besides, the little creep knows that if I beat him up, I'd get kicked out of school and there'd be hell to pay with my parents."

"Old man Kelly doesn't have your self-control. Our vaunted Assistant Head Master lost it with Coe in the hall yesterday," said Dean. "I saw him slam that jerk's head into the lockers . . . wham, wham, wham. Jeez, Coe's glasses went flying down the hall, but he held onto his books. Kelly was so red-faced I thought he was going to do the twitch. He stopped it when he saw me coming down the hall."

"What did Coe do then?" asked Bryce.

"He just picked up his glasses and gave Kelly the finger."

"Charlie needs to go back to the funny farm," said Bryce. "The only reason they let him out is to give him a chance to graduate so the school won't have to deal with him and his old man next year. But I don't care about that. I just want him to stay away from me and Marilyn. Damn it! People shouldn't have to put up with his kind of meddling!"

⟨⟩

"So, did you take your girlfriend to the prom?" asked Lucas.

"Yes, but it was in a beat-up old Dodge, not a limo like you kids use today."

"Did Coe try to stop you?"

"He showed up at the prom, but I called his old man and told him his son was drunk. Coe's father came and took him home. Marilyn and I were lucky that night. I later learned Coe had a gun with him and he intended to shoot Marilyn."

"Were you scared then?"

"I should have been. It might have saved a lot of grief later. But let's talk about that lesson on the way home."

Chapter 11

May, 1964

Lt. Farnham and Bryce outlined a training schedule for the SEAL class that would drop most ordinary sailors to their knees. Much of it was based on the initial weeks of UDT training, plus more. Reveille at 4:00 a.m. and a run on the beach followed by strengthening exercises and then breakfast. Then on to inflatable boats in the surf and more running on the beach by teams with the boats over their heads.

"See that post that is sticking up about a mile down the beach?" shouted Lt.(j.g.) Roberts to his trainees.

"Yes, Sir!" they shouted in unison.

"We're going to run down there and back." He led them through the soft sand to the post and began the leg back. When they arrived at the start some of the men began to slow down to take a breather.

Bryce shouted, "I didn't say we were only doing one lap, you worthless squids! Turn around! We're going for another lap!" And they ran through the sand again, legs aching and lungs on fire. He heard one of the men mumble, "What's he trying to prove, anyway?"

Bryce ran alongside the panting sailor and shouted, "It's not what I'm trying to prove, Johnson, it's what you're trying to prove to yourself. What are you going to prove, Johnson?"

"I can make it, Sir," came the reply from the panting man, and he picked up his head and continued to run.

"Who can make it, Johnson?" ground Bryce's voice.

"We can make it, Sir," answered Johnson, cursing himself for opening his mouth and now having to pay the price of talking while running.

Bryce wanted all of his men to succeed, but, from experience, he knew that many would not get past "hell week," just as many in his UDT class had not. He watched his men for any sign of a true medical emergency as they worked and hustled through the obstacle course and then when they were required immediately to repeat it. Men began to drop out and Bryce removed their names from his roster. He had less than a quarter of them by the time "hell week" was over.

☞

When his confinement to base expired Bryce bummed a ride to Philadelphia with a chief who was going there to visit his family. Bryce caught a train to Doylestown and called Ralph, their hired man, to come for him.

Eddie had changed, even in that short month. He now was crawling more effectively and getting into everything that was at floor level. Rosalie and Midge had removed to higher locations all of the items from the lowest shelves in the house to preserve them from the havoc Eddie created when he found a new item.

Bryce was watching him now as Eddie spotted a distant toy and began the trail across the oriental carpet in quest of new adventure. The boy turned his head back toward his father as if to ask if it was okay to keep going and Bryce told him to "go for it." Eddie began to baby-laugh and Bryce's heart melted. He silently thanked God for his family and Marilyn's parents who so willingly took on the responsibilities of parenthood for him.

Midge entered the room, sniffed, picked Eddie up, looked at Bryce, and said, "Follow me. You have to learn to do this." Midge showed him how to clean the baby and then had him re-diaper Eddie a second time just to make sure he performed to her standards. His large hands were not well-suited for the job but he persisted until he had it right, being careful not to stick his son with the diaper pins. Eddie yawned and began to nod off and they put him in his crib with the promise of more time with his dad.

As the infant's eyes closed, Bryce saw Marilyn in Eddie's features. Bryce had to walk away.

Then, knowing he must get used to it, he forced himself to return to the crib to again see Marilyn in his son, something he knew would endure for his lifetime. He felt his eyes begin to tear and fought to stop it.

When he had himself under control Bryce went downstairs and played the piano for the first time since Marilyn's death. He practiced the scales and then selected the third movement of Schumann's "Fantasie." To those who heard the serene reverie, played at first with mistakes and sour notes, and then more smoothly as his hands loosened and the memory channels of his brain reopened, it was as though the house had again begun to breathe.

Chapter 12

"**B**rother, you Navy guys aren't that tough," said Phillip. "I'll bet anyone in good shape can keep up with you."

Bryce just smiled and said, "We'll do some 'training' tomorrow morning. If you're standing when it's over you just might be a candidate for the SEALs."

In the morning Bryce started Phillip swimming laps at long distance speed in their pool which still had not warmed in the early summer. The brothers swam beside each other, stroke for stroke, and then, as Phillip began to tire, Bryce told him, "Okay, we do more, faster." He led Phillip on more laps until his brother was flailing ineffectually at the water. Still they weren't finished. Bryce handed Phillip two buckets and made him swim a lap holding one in each hand. Bryce pulled him out and said, "Now, we go for a run."

Phillip looked at him incredulously and then with hands shaking from fatigue, tied the laces of his sneakers and silently prayed for a short run. They ran for over two miles along the trails through the fields and woods behind their home until Phillip could go no farther. He wouldn't go down; he just stood there breathing as if he was suffocating. Bryce admired the fact that he still was standing.

"This is just a taste of what it is like the first weeks of SEAL training. Are you still interested?" asked Bryce.

"Man, I thought I was in decent shape, but you just ran my butt ragged," panted Phillip. "Is that really what I'd have to look forward to?"

"That and much more. At least fifty percent of it is mental toughness. You have that in your genes, but get yourself tougher physically."

"I'm going to do that, because after what you told me of the SEAL's mission, I really want to get in."

As they walked the path back to the house, a buck deer flushed from the undergrowth and the brothers silently watched it gracefully bound across a field. Then Bryce spoke.

"Did you know," he said, smiling broadly, "that the Indians who used to live around here would chase a deer until they ran it to ground?"

"If you think I'm going to run after that deer, you're nuts!"

"Come on," said Bryce, "I'll race you back to the house."

Phillip groaned and doggedly trailed his brother home.

⌀⌀⌀

That evening Bryce again had to turn away as he looked across the dinner table at Stella, his mother-in-law, but he stayed seated because he knew that he always would see Marilyn in her, too; and he had to get used to it.

"I was looking away from you, Stella, because Marilyn resembled you. I just want you to know that I won't do that after a while." He looked her straight in the eyes and said, "I think in the end it'll bring a gentle reminder. I saw her in Eddie's face this morning and I had the same reaction. I made myself look at him because I know I'll see Marilyn in him as long as I live."

"We see the same thing," said Noah, "but we also see a lot of Roberts in him, too. Pretty good combination if you ask me; Marilyn's sense of humor and your courage." Then the man's eyes filled with tears and he excused himself from the table.

"We've had a lot of that at this table lately," said Harriet. "But we can't ignore what we're thinking and Jacob Knox says it's good to get it out. Are you going to church tomorrow morning, Bryce?"

"I might try for the late service before I fly back. Dad, what does your pilot like to do?"

"What I want him to." The diners laughed and Harry finished, "So, let's allow him to sleep in."

Noah returned to the table and sat quietly while the conversation flowed. Bryce felt Noah's eyes on him and he looked at his father-in-law and asked, "What are you thinking, Noah?"

"Harry said you're planning to go back to school for a business degree. Stella and I hope you'll still share Eddie with us while you do. We've really become attached to him."

"I've been accepted by The Wharton School of Business at Penn. I start in September. I plan to live here while I attend, so I'll be looking for your help babysitting while I'm at school. Will you do that?"

"Need you ask?" Noah smiled and reached for Stella's hand.

The conversation moved on to a discussion of the growing conflict in Vietnam and ended with the debate over U.S. involvement unsettled.

The Colemans left and Harry took Bryce aside. "Coe goes on trial next month. Do you want to come home for that?" asked Harry.

"No, Dad. I talked with the D.A. in February and he told me that, if possible, he'd like me here for the sentencing, but he doesn't need me for the trial. I'd just rather not listen to that story all over again. It's been tough enough dealing with memories of the good times."

Chapter 13

December 2006

"Lucas, you're going to learn to drive in city traffic today," said Bryce. "There are plenty of holiday shoppers driving into Philadelphia, so if you can handle that kind of traffic, I may recommend that your parents let you go for your license."

"Grandpa, you've already delayed my getting my license. How come?"

"Lucas, your parents are relying on me to prepare you. I just want to be sure that you're ready. Now, did you study the road and street map for the best route into the city?"

"Yes."

"Show me."

Bryce nodded his approval as Lucas traced the route he would take to Macy's Department Store. "Okay. Let's roll. I'll tell you some more about your grandmother on the way in to town. You know, Lucas, that store used to be known as Wanamaker's. I have some good memories of Christmas back in 1961. It was the time Marilyn and I made up after I fouled up the relationship . . ."

⌖

By Christmas of 1961 the holiday season at Wanamaker's Department Store was an enduring Philadelphia tradition. Bryce, carrying his shopping bags, made his way among the crowds, enjoying the store's decorations and displays. The organist in the alcove above the main floor was playing Christmas carols and Bryce began to hum along with "Deck the Halls" as he maneuvered toward the bronze eagle that was a Philadelphia landmark. It stood on a granite pedestal on the first floor and its location had served as a meeting place for generations of Philadelphians.

He'd met Marilyn earlier in the day in a women's shop where he was looking for a gift for his mother. Marilyn had reluctantly agreed to have coffee with him when she finished her shopping.

Now he watched as she approached. Marilyn was dressed in a tailored red wool topcoat over a grey pleated wool skirt and a white blouse with a rounded collar under a navy cardigan sweater. Hanging from her neck on a gold chain was a clear glass marble that Bryce knew contained a mustard seed. Her blonde hair was swept back in a practical but attractive bun, defying the style of the moment that tended toward mid length perms and bouffants.

Growing up around her made me lose an appreciation of just how beautiful she is, he thought. He watched a young man in a business suit turn his head to stare at her and then bump into another shopper as his distraction became complete.

Marilyn's face broke into a hesitant smile as she spotted Bryce.

First smile of the day, thought Bryce. Good. She's had time to think about things. He pressed through the crowd toward her.

"I've been shopping here," she said, "so I put in our reservations at the restaurant. I practically had to bribe the hostess, but I think we have a table by now if we hurry.

"Bryce, this is just going to be a friendly chat. So don't put any more meaning into it."

"Okay."

She ordered German chocolate cake and stirred three creams into her coffee.

Bryce shunned the fancy desserts and had black coffee.

"I took the train in so I'll eat when I go home," he said.

"Good, I took the train, too. If you're nice to me we can ride home together and you can carry all of my packages," she teased.

He smiled, pleased that she still had her blunt sense of humor.

"Besides," she continued, "you'll be able to explain why you never apologized for treating me so badly. You never wrote anything or tried to see me over summer breaks. And you've otherwise ignored your first love for the past two years."

Ouch, thought Bryce, this isn't going to be as easy as I thought. Well, in such matters, the best defense is a good offense.

"Well, the postman didn't exactly wear out my mailbox with letters from you, either."

"How dare you! You were the one who created the trouble, in case you've forgotten. By the way, how is . . . what was her name . . . Karen?"

"I don't know. I haven't seen her since that summer. Anyway, to get back to your first question, I thought you were so angry that an apology wouldn't do any good. For what it's worth now, I'm truly sorry and I ask your forgiveness."

"Thank you. I'll think about it."

His face remained pleasant, but she saw the disappointment in his eyes despite his attempt to hide it.

"Oh, all right, I accept. You're forgiven, this being the season and all."

"Do you really mean it?"

"Yes, I'm too young to hold a grudge forever . . . Bryce, why didn't we make the effort to reconcile?

"I think we learned that living away from home at college offers a lot more options for our time and we made other choices because we weren't next door to each other. I often thought of you, I just found it difficult to force . . . uh, to discipline myself to write, particularly under the circumstances. And last summer I was up in the north woods of Michigan studying wolves."

"And the summer before?"

"Marilyn, your turn. What did you do last summer?"

"I spent a lot of time taking care of Mom. She had a serious case of pneumonia and really kept us all in suspense for a while. I was her nurse and chauffeur for most of last summer."

"I wish you'd called or written to me about that. I could've at least sent her a card."

"I wasn't sure you would've cared. Anyway, what did you do the summer of your freshman year?"

"I went to a baseball camp in South Carolina and then I came home and worked in Henry Morton's cabinet shop."

"And you didn't call me to beg forgiveness." Her face turned into a teasing pout.

"So, where were you?"

"Ah, Bryce, I've never been able to snow you. I was in the Poconos, working as a senior counselor at a girl's camp. And then our family vacationed in California before I went back to Penn State. In God's name, why were you studying wolves?"

"You're changing the subject which means you don't want me to ask about your social life."

"Darn," she snapped her fingers in a 'bright idea' way. "You notice everything. Okay, I joined a sorority and we date guys who we get to know, but nothing serious has come of it."

"I don't have any attachments, either," said Bryce. "Dating at Dartmouth means taking a road trip to a girls' school and my fraternity brothers and I do that, but it's tough to keep a relationship going long distance."

"No kidding," came the teasing, sarcastic response.

Then their eyes met in their merriment and the unspoken hope each held.

Chapter 14

The train for Doylestown, Bucks County's Seat, was a local. When the train slowed and pulled into the station at Warrington Bryce felt Marilyn's hand slip into his. He was pleasantly surprised. But then she shifted in the seat beside him and stopped talking about her college friends. He looked up at the entering passengers and understood the reason for her actions.

Charlie Coe was coming down the aisle toward them.

Of all the times that jerk has to show up, thought Bryce, this is really the worst.

Coe saw them and deliberately sat in the vacant seat in front of theirs. He turned around, and stretched his arm across his seatback. He stared unflinchingly at them through dirty-lens glasses that magnified the size of his eyes so they dominated his face.

"Well, if it isn't the prom queen and Prince Charming."

His breath was a rotten mixture of poor dental hygiene and cheap booze.

"Bryce, I know it was you who let the air out of my tires on Prom night. Don't think I'll ever forget it, either."

"Charlie, I did that. But you were looking to be a total pain in the butt and I didn't want anything to happen that anyone would later regret.

"So, uh, Charlie, what are you doing with yourself these days?"

Coe scratched his beard stubble, reached inside his stained and dirty canvas coat, and pulled out a paper bag that obviously contained a pint of whiskey. The movement of his coat wafted a strong odor of stale sweat toward them.

"I'm drinking," he said, and took a swallow from the bottle. "And I cut firewood for my regular customers." He belched loudly and several passengers on the train looked at Marilyn and Bryce in sympathy.

"Marilyn, I'm going to call you for another date, now that I know you're home. I betcha that you'd go out with me, too, if Bryce isn't around to tell you what to do."

"Charlie, I won't go out with you if you call. I'm sorry, but you're just not my type."

Coe's face turned ugly with anger so quickly that it took Bryce and Marilyn by surprise. He reached back across the seat with his grubby hand and dirty, broken fingernails extended toward Marilyn. Bryce firmly caught his wrist and powered Coe's arm back over the seatback and held it there.

"Charlie, cool it or I'm going to call the conductor and have you arrested for public drunkenness on a railroad." Bryce had no idea whether there was such a crime, but he wanted Coe to leave them alone. At least the threat might make him back off.

"Won't be the firsht time. Marilyn, can I give you a ride home in my truck?"

"I don't ride with drunks," snapped Marilyn.

Bryce looked at the passenger across the aisle from him who was coolly observing the scene and said to the man, "I can't leave the lady. Would you mind finding the conductor, please?"

"Sure, son. You have your hands full with that guy." He got up and moved forward in the train.

"Gotta call for help, huh? I'm too much for you to handle, huh?" jeered Charlie. He took another swig from the bottle and with a look of drunken cunning tucked it back inside his coat. "All right, I'll be nice for now. I might even be real nice, seeing that it's the Christmas season."

The conductor, a skinny black man in an immaculate uniform, appeared. He was followed by a uniformed policeman who was on his way home.

"You again, Coe." The conductor shook his head back and forth good naturedly and said, "I think you'd better come up to the next car with me and the officer so there's no more trouble." He stepped back and the policeman moved next to Coe's seat and gestured him forward.

Coe began to protest and then thought better of it when he realized that the policeman had a look of anticipation on his face that Hannibal must have had as he approached Rome. He stood, wobbled, and began to move toward the front of the car. Then he turned and gave Bryce the finger. The policeman shoved Coe forward and he shuffled onward and out of the car, with the policeman and conductor behind him.

Bryce felt Marilyn begin to shiver and he put his arm around her shoulders and held her until the train began to slow for their station. When it stopped, the conductor returned and helped them remove their packages from the train and stack the bags on a small luggage wagon.

"I've asked the officer to detain Charlie until just before we go back to Philadelphia," said the conductor. He smiled at them. "You folks will be all right. We have a few minutes before we're scheduled to leave, so you'll have time to make it out of here before I ask the policeman to let that man off the train."

Marilyn thanked him profusely and Bryce offered a tip, but he declined. "You folks just have a nice Christmas," he said, and then returned to his train.

Bryce pulled the wagon tongue and they moved the creaky contraption among homebound commuters to the parking lot and her car.

"Marilyn, I'm going to follow you home. I don't want to take a chance on Coe following you. Is that okay with you?" She nodded and helped him load the packages into the trunks of their cars.

"Bryce, that's beautiful wrapping paper, the one with the brilliant cardinals. Where did you find it?"

"It's special. I'll tell you about it when we get to your house." He seated Marilyn in her car, made sure she locked the doors, and returned the wagon.

Bryce looked through the darkness toward the train. He waved his thanks to the conductor who still was watching from the steps of the train; then he jogged back to his car and drove out of the lot behind Marilyn's car.

Marilyn came back to sit in Bryce's old Dodge when they arrived at her home. She was sobbing. He reached out for her and she willingly came into his arms.

"That creep ruined what was a lovely afternoon," she said. "Can't somebody have Coe committed or do something to have him treated for his drinking?"

"Unless his mental problems can be treated, I doubt if much can be done about his drinking."

"What about a peace bond? Rick Biddle's dad had one put on a fired employee who kept coming back and threatening people at the shop. Maybe we could get one on Coe."

"We can ask our parents to look into that. But for now, let me change the subject. How long will you be home?"

"I have to be back at school by the fourth of January. Why do you want to know?"

"I'd like to spend time with you while we're home," said Bryce.

"Let me think about that," she said. "I may need to be persuaded."

"Why?"

"I really cared for you, Bryce, and you hurt me very badly. Then you just went away and closed out our relationship. Now I'm not sure I want to open that door again."

"You kept hinting at a commitment from me and we were too young for that, and we still are. We had a lot of growing, a lot of things to do before we could even think of settling down."

"You could've told me how you felt. I'd have understood. Instead you just tried to string me along."

He kissed her warmly on the lips; and then tilting her chin up, looked her in the eyes and said, "I still had a perfect afternoon. Seeing you again is all it took for that."

Even in the faint light from her porch, he saw her eyes begin the twinkle he cherished.

"Oh, Bryce, don't sweet talk me. You just want to get in my pants again."

○≈○

Bryce was in the Dartmouth drama club. It took all his newfound acting skills, six telephone calls, a visit to Marilyn's home, a long walk together in her neighborhood, and a promise from him that their time together would be "just casual" before Marilyn finally agreed to see him again.

It was then that she remembered the wrapping paper and asked about it.

"Those cardinals have a special meaning to me and my family," he told her. When I was four years old, my father and I were walking outside on a sunny, late February morning. A bird was singing high in the bare branches of the treetop beside the house.

They tell me I looked up and asked, "Daddy, what kind of bird is that?"

"He's a cardinal" said Harry. "They're the first birds to begin singing in the springtime. Their song is a message of hope for a blessed year."

"I watched as the bird puffed up its chest to sing again. Then, according to family legend, I asked, 'Do you think he knows that?'

"Harry says he looked at me in astonishment over the question. 'I don't know, but God sure had a reason when he gave that cardinal his song,' he told me.

"Ever afterward, when I needed to be cheered up, my family would tell me they had heard a cardinal singing and I'd rush outside to listen. Somehow, the bird's song did just that. As time went by the cardinal's song was adopted by the whole family as a message of cheer and hope. So, when I saw that wrapping paper I knew I was going to wrap at least one of your presents in it."

Marilyn hugged him.

Chapter 15

July, 1962

"**M**r. Roberts, your tour of duty has been extended until thirty-one December this year," Lt. Farnham told him. "The Navy wanted to keep you for another twelve months but I told them you're a hardship case with a young son at home without his mother, so you go home this December rather than next September."

He saw the consternation on the junior officer's face and said, "Bryce, they're doing it to everyone now. They need men for the build-up in Vietnam and you have to stay to help train another class. The men respect you and you get them to give the most they're capable of. We need you until I can find someone else."

"Sir, any number of men can do what I do. Why not have someone coming back from 'Nam assist with the training. I'm supposed to start grad school in the fall."

"I know, you mentioned that, but I can't help it, Bryce. I did the best I could and Lieutenant Commander Standring pitched in for you, too."

Bryce telephoned his parents that evening to deliver the news. He tried to put it in the best light by promising to be home for Christmas.

Several days later he received a letter from Jacob Knox. He read and reread it until he almost committed it to memory.

Dear Bryce,

It was good to see you in church and I was glad to have the opportunity to walk you back to the parsonage to chat for a few minutes. Sorry it wasn't longer, but Sunday is my busy day. When you mentioned that you're working hard to accept reminders of Marilyn, I did a silent cheer because that's a huge step forward in the grief process. I know it's hard to do, but keep it up. It will help you begin to think of her without being overwhelmed by emotions. No doubt you're thinking that if you had gone for the groceries she'd still be alive, and you may feel guilty over not having spent more time with her. But guilt is normal. It's another way of wishing you could have her back. Understand that and the guilt will fade.

Just don't keep your grief inside. If you inhibit your grief, it, and you, will become distorted. I know it may be difficult to let it out with men who have the mindset of your buddies, but call upon some of the more mature of them, particularly one who may recently have lost a loved one, if you feel the need to talk. It won't hurt to do so over a couple of brews.

I don't think you're one of those people who pray to God for impossible things. Instead, ask Him to help you use your own courage and strength to see you through the times ahead. Just as you made it through "hell week" you will make it the rest of the way through your period of grieving.

In the end, your loss will become a part of you . . . who you are, your fiber. And believe me, you shall have a new dimension to your strength. Keep the faith.

Yours in Christ,
Jacob Knox

Bryce felt himself choking up when he finished the letter because he'd been thinking of Marilyn and the days they'd spent together after their reunion during his junior year at Dartmouth. They had been some of the best of times for them. *But I can't allow myself to dwell on them.*

Chapter 16

Chief Willie, the piano player at the Blue Crab, looked popeyed as Bryce entered and sat on the barstool next to his. It was early Saturday afternoon and most of the tables were still empty.

"Easy, Chief. I'm not going to start anything. I'm just looking for a good piano."

"Sir?"

"I play classical music for relaxation and I need to find a good grand piano in this area."

"Why ask me?"

"Instinct. Plus my sources tell me you have a lot more talent than you show here. I figured you might know where I can find a good piano."

"You're serious aren't you?"

Bryce nodded.

"Sir, what I don't understand is why someone who plays classical piano would risk breaking his hands in a bar fight with a bunch of jarheads."

"It's a long story."

"I have time. Do you want a drink?"

Bryce sized up the situation and decided. "I'll have a beer."

Over their drinks he told the chief about what set him off the night of the fight.

Chief Willie listened and at the end asked, "Have you seen this Coe guy since he killed your wife?"

"No, service in the Navy has kept me away from home and when I am home I've deliberately avoided going anywhere near him. Hell, just thinking about him and what he did gets me in a terribly foul mood and then I can't concentrate on what I really need to be doing."

"And what you need now is a piano?"

Bryce nodded.

"Want to play something now? I have some Chopin etudes tucked away in that box next to my piano."

The chief was testing him but Bryce went along. He sat at the battered upright and was surprised at how well-tuned it sounded. The former Navy Band leader listened intently until the last notes faded.

"You're rusty but you're good. Sir, can you stay here for a minute? I want to look up a phone number. I might be able to help you with your mission."

Bryce watched him use the phone book from behind the bar and then dial a number in the booth in the hall near the men's room. The chief turned his back while he spoke and then hung up after several minute's conversation. He jotted a note and handed it to Bryce.

"Captain Craig said it would be okay to call him. His wife died about a year ago and he has a baby grand piano that she played. I used to play cocktail music there when they had parties. He lives in officers' housing on base so you should be able to get there without too much travel from your quarters. And the Captain is in line to make Admiral, so be decent to him. Could pay you dividends some day."

"Thanks for the skinny, Chief, but I'm out in December. But I'll call the man anyway." He did and was invited to the home of Captain Bartholomew Craig on Sunday afternoon at fourteen hundred hours.

⊙〰⊙

Bryce appeared at the home dressed in his summer whites uniform and shook hands with a man in neatly pressed civilian clothes who had the look of a hawk: big piercing dark eyes under heavy, dark eyebrows, a generous, aquiline nose and a full head of close-cropped salt and pepper hair.

"May I offer you an iced tea, Mr. Roberts? There's some in the refrigerator so it won't be a bother to make."

"Yes, Sir. I take mine plain, please."

"Well, follow me to the galley. A cold drink will do us good on a warm day like this."

On the way back to the kitchen, to the left in a room off the hallway Bryce saw a beautiful Steinway, with the top raised, apparently in anticipation of his playing.

"At ease, Mr. Roberts. We're not on duty."

He filled two huge glasses from a covered pitcher. "See that aluminum wrap? My wife, Marjorie, showed me that trick. Keeps the tea fresher. She's gone a little over a year now but sometimes she still is right here with me."

"How long were you married, Captain?"

"It would have been twenty-five years next month," Craig replied. "Cheers and thanks for humoring a lonely man, Mr. Roberts."

"I know the feeling, Sir. My wife died in February of this year. She was hit head-on by a drunk driver."

"To die so young is really tough on a family. Do you have any children, Mr. Roberts?"

"A son; he'll be a year old in November. How about you, Captain? Do you have children?"

"We have two boys. One will graduate from the Naval Academy in June and the other is a sophomore at Duke. That was his mother's school."

They chatted about Captain Craig's career and Bryce's training duties and then the captain showed Bryce the piano. Bryce played a few scales and appreciated the perfect, rich tones of the instrument. He turned to Craig and said, "This is an honor to play. Thanks for the opportunity."

"Go ahead and play whatever you'd like. I'm going to go sit in the parlor."

Bryce paged through the extensive collection of sheet music that was on bookshelves in the room, and then decided to look inside the piano bench where he found only a neat stack of Chopin works. He was about to practice one of them when he realized that they probably had been left there by Marjorie as a handy place to store her favorites. He replaced them because he didn't want to put the captain into a maudlin and sentimental mood with her music. He chose instead "The Moonlight Sonata" and began to practice it with joyful emotions that he had not felt for a long time. For a precious while Bryce lost himself in the music. When he finished he found a collection of Brahms' works. He chose "Intermezzo in E Major" and began to practice the piece. He ended with another Brahms Capriccio as his hands and wrists began to tire from the unaccustomed exercise. He found Captain Craig sitting quietly with a book on his lap but there were tears in the corners of his eyes and Bryce knew he'd reacted to the music. The captain brushed the tears away and stood.

"That was wonderful. You have quite a talent. You mustn't let it get rusty. Why don't you think about stopping by next Sunday if you have the inclination?"

"I'd like that, Sir. When should I call to confirm?"

"Call my office. I'll get the message if I'm not there. Here's the number," and he handed Bryce a business card. "Anytime except Sunday morning. I'm either in chapel or out on the golf course then."

Bryce called, and again, the two lonely men went through the steps of the iced tea and conversation before the young officer played. They discussed their grief and yet, as men, couldn't let themselves completely show the anguish each still felt; but they shared what the other was willing to speak of, and so, with understanding, their acquaintance deepened and layers of their grief were ground away.

When Bryce sat at the piano that afternoon, he found that several of the Chopin pieces had been moved from inside the bench to the music rack above the keyboard.

Chapter 17

L t. Farnham read the letter from the Bucks County District Attorney and then signed Bryce's leave orders. He handed the papers to Bryce, who began to about-face for the door.

"Wait one, Mr. Roberts," he said and then was quiet for a moment after Bryce turned to again face him.

"Let me give you some advice," he counseled. "When you face that man in the courtroom, no matter what he says, unless it's an apology, do not respond. Gauging from what the District Attorney wrote that . . ." he looked at the letter again, ". . . Coe deliberately caused the accident. That kind of man will continue to want to make trouble and so he'll bait or taunt you in front of others. If you lose control, people will remember that, and in the years to come, that'll work against you. If you keep above it, they'll respect you and that's where you want to be."

"Thanks for the advice, sir. How is it that you know—"

"That is all, Mr. Roberts." Farnham picked up another piece of the paperwork he abhorred.

Bryce did an about face and left.

⊙≈◦

Bryce considered cars a necessary nuisance, but he wasn't able to find a practical, low- mileage used car he'd sought. So, as he entered Delaware, and drove northward toward Bucks County, he was behind the wheel of a shiny new red Pontiac sedan that had an infant's car seat in the back. He tuned the radio to a station that played the popular music of the day and tapped the steering wheel to the rhythm of the Beatles and sang along with Roy Orbison's latest hit, "Oh, Pretty Woman."

Barbara Streisand was singing "People" as he pulled into the lane leading to his home and Eddie. He thought about what he would do with his son while he was home, but couldn't get past the hug stage. "To heck with it," he muttered, "let's see which way the boy is inclined."

Eddie was napping. Bryce greeted his mother and Midge who were the only ones home. His brothers and sisters were all away at college, or working, and his father was traveling on business. Harry had promised to be home tomorrow when Bryce was to appear in court. Feeling at loose ends, Bryce opened a beer and walked out to the large multilevel flagstone terrace behind the house. Ralph, the handyman and gardener, and Rosalie kept the terrace in beautiful condition with flowers in the beds that were cleverly integrated into the design of the terrace. There always was something blooming there from early spring crocuses to the late fall chrysanthemums. Now it was Dahlias, and Bryce enjoyed their pastel colors before his gaze turned toward the ripening cornfields and forested hills in the distance.

"Maybe I can take Eddie on a horseback ride tomorrow," he thought. "I'll have to rig some kind of front papoose-like holder, but maybe we can do that." Bryce put his mind to the design but eventually decided to consult Rosalie about child carriers.

He heard a door open at the lower level of the house and heavy, precise footsteps that definitely belonged to a military man approached. He turned, and with surprise and delight, saw Peter Chase walking toward him. They shook hands and then hugged as old friends, Bryce exclaiming, "What brings you here? How did you know I was home?"

"I'm home for Sandra's wedding and my sister is one nervous lady at the moment, so I just needed to get out of the house. I started calling around and your mother told me you were home, so I figured I'd stop by. You look good. How have you been?"

The comfort of long friendship allowed Bryce to be himself. "It's been a roller coaster. Most days I can think about Marilyn without tears coming. Meanwhile I've been busy training volunteers for a special unit called SEALs."

"Them? We had some of those guys come through my Special Forces Unit for training. They're good men, Bryce." He paused and then a look of recognition lit his face. "You know, a couple of those guys were reminiscing about their instructors back at Little Creek and they had some particularly choice words about a big son-of-a-bitch who used to take them for long swims in the cold ocean and then run their butts off on the beach. Anybody we know?"

Bryce tried not to blush. "Might have been me. We sent some men who made it through to Fort Bragg for additional training. So, what are you going to do? Stay in the Army or get back to civilian life?"

"I'm getting out. I got back from Vietnam about two months ago, and now I'm helping to train some of our men before I wind it up. They asked me to stay in, but I want to get into journalism and see what I can do there. There's so much going on in this country right now. Johnson's Great Society, the war, the protesters, the space race, campus radicals. It's endless. Now, let me ask you something. What are you doing home?"

"Charlie Coe gets sentenced tomorrow and they asked if I could be there. They want to hear from the 'victim's' family. I'd like to take Eddie in to show to the judge, but I'm not going to let Coe set eyes on my son. I'm trying to think of what to say without giving Coe the satisfaction of knowing he's hurt me. But that's not possible, nor would it do Marilyn's memory justice."

"Bryce, do you have another of those beers? I can stick around and we can talk about what you could say. Then maybe I could help you write a 'prepared statement' as they say in journalism." Bryce nodded thankfully at his friend, left; and returned with more beer, a pen and a tablet.

The two young men who had been friends for almost twenty years worked together until Peter had to leave to attend a pre-wedding function. Bryce hadn't felt as drained but relieved for a long time. When Peter left, Bryce studied the written statement and made a decision. I'm going to deliver this personally.

Chapter 18

Coe had gained weight on prison food but he still maintained the cocky manner he displayed to cover his self-doubts. He was standing in front of the judge's bench now, dressed in prison clothes, with a large deputy sheriff on either side, as he listened to the judge tell him that he had been found guilty in the non-jury trial and now it was time for his sentencing. The court asked if he had read the pre-sentence investigation report that the Probation Office had prepared and Coe told the judge it was "all a pack of lies."

Judge Cohn turned to the defense attorney and asked, "Mr. Lee, did you review the pre-sentence investigation report with your client, Charles Coe?"

"Yes, Your Honor, several times."

"Without breaching any confidences, are you satisfied that your client understood what he read?"

"Yes, Your Honor."

"Mr. Coe, you have called the report a 'pack of lies,' which means that you've read the report and understand the words that you read, even if you don't agree with its statements and conclusions. Correct?"

"Yes, Judge, but I did not say at the accident that I was sorry. I just told Homer, here, to say hello to Bryce for me, 'cause I knew it was his wife that I hit."

The judge carefully confirmed the statement Coe had just made. "At your trial you testified that you saw Mrs. Roberts' car coming up the hill and you deliberately drove your vehicle into hers?"

"That's what I said, Judge. But I didn't say I was sorry." Coe, gloating, turned and looked at Bryce.

Bryce, seated in the first row of spectators, clenched his fists, but held them low, next to his thighs.

"Before I impose sentence, do you have anything you want to say to the court?" continued the judge. "And, Mr. Coe, as you know, I've found you mentally competent to stand trial, despite a history of some treatment for mental issues, so you may want to be careful about what you say now."

"I don't want to say anything; I did what I did and that's it."

"Mr. Richards, does the District Attorney's Office have anything to state?" asked the judge.

"Yes, Your Honor. We ask that you impose the maximum sentence for second degree murder upon the defendant. He hasn't shown any remorse for his deliberate and cruel act.

"Your honor, Mr. Roberts, the victim's husband is here. He has a statement he would like to deliver to the court."

"Come forward, Mr. Roberts," ordered the judge.

Bryce, clothed in his dress blue navy uniform, rose from the front row of spectators and moved to the lower bench directly in front of the judge. He had memorized the statement he and Peter had prepared.

Coe, a deputy on either side of him was to his left.

Bryce ignored Coe and addressed the court. "Good morning Your Honor."

The judge nodded in acknowledgement and said, "Proceed, Mr. Roberts."

"Your Honor, my wife and I were longtime sweethearts who married with boundless love for each other, strong hope for our future, and dreams of a family full of children and happiness. Our only child was seventeen weeks old when Marilyn was murdered, so our son, Edward, will never have the privilege of knowing the wonderful woman and mother who gave him life. She was a woman of high but gentle spirits; indefatigable humor and wit; a loving wife who comforted me in times of challenge; and, she was my best friend and confidant. Even before we married we had grown so close to each other we truly were one in spirit; and so, our marriage was the natural progression of our lives together.

I have deeply grieved her passing."

Bryce paused and then, his black eyes intense, faced Coe and spoke.

"Charles Coe, in killing my wife, tried to destroy our relationship, and thus me. There is no purpose in that. Coe's crime neither disabled me nor empowered him. It was the act of a coward who believes himself to be weak, and seeks to create within himself a false sense of power—power that he never will achieve on his own—by harming one whom he considers strong."

Coe turned and glared at Bryce when he heard those words.

Bryce met Coe's stare, returned it, and remained in total control, face taut and eyes now boring into Coe's.

"But what he does not understand, and probably never will, is that Marilyn always was, and always will be, mine. Marilyn is gone, but I still have those wonderful memories of her that Charles Coe cannot change and cannot take away. Therefore, it is on behalf of my son, Edward, who will face challenges in this life without his mother, that I respectfully request the maximum sentence be imposed upon Charles Coe."

Bryce turned and faced Judge Cohen who told him, "Thank you, Mr. Roberts. You may be seated. I see other family members in this courtroom. Does anyone else wish to make a statement?"

Charles Coe's father, a little pug of a man, rose, identified himself, and asked to speak. "Judge, Charlie is a bright young man and I don't know what went wrong with him. I beat him good when he needed it, but apparently the lessons didn't sink in. I offer our apologies to Mr. Roberts, his family and to Marilyn's family."

Charlie Coe turned, glared at his father, and shook his head no.

"Thank you, Mr. Coe," said the judge. "Does anyone else with an interest in this matter wish to make a statement?" The courtroom was silent. Then Noah Coleman stood.

"Your Honor, I am Noah Coleman, the father of Marilyn Roberts. If it were up to me, I would see the man hanged. Coe deliberately took an innocent life without any justification. He has shown no remorse. Please impose the maximum sentence."

The courtroom again sank into silence as Coe stood smirking over the attention he was receiving.

The Judge responded. "Mr. Coleman, I understand your position, but this court must follow the law and its conscience."

He turned to the stenographer and said, "Very well. Now take this order: In the matter of Commonwealth of Pennsylvania versus Charles Coe, Number 4822 of 1964, the court having found the defendant, Charles Coe, guilty on the charge of Murder in the Second Degree, hereby sentences the defendant, Charles Coe, to a term of imprisonment in a state correctional institution for a period of not less than seven and one-half years nor more than fifteen years. Defendant shall be given credit for all time served to date. A further condition of this sentence is that the defendant's driver's license shall be suspended for the duration of this sentence." The judge went on to advise Coe of his appellate rights and then the court recessed.

Just before Coe was handcuffed and led out of the courtroom, he turned and gave Bryce the finger. Bryce remained stone-faced, but behind the mask his hatred burned.

Peter Chase drove Bryce and his father home. "How long do you think he will serve before they let him out on parole?" Peter asked.

"The D.A. told me he must serve at least half his sentence before he can be considered for parole," said Bryce.

"Seven and one-half years for murder?" said Peter. "What is this world doing to itself?"

"Actually, we were lucky to get a homicide conviction," said Bryce. "The DA explained to me that because there's a specific law against drunk driving and another that punishes someone for involuntary manslaughter, Coe's attorney argued that he should have been prosecuted for those lesser offenses which don't carry as severe a penalty. But Coe's admission that his act was deliberate, even though he was drunk, was enough to go for a second degree murder charge. So Coe got a tougher sentence than otherwise would have been imposed."

"He could be eligible for parole at the end of his minimum, but I don't think they will let him out that soon," said Harry. "Because he hasn't shown any remorse for what he did my sources tell me that factor will weigh heavily against his chances for an early release."

Harry didn't identify his "sources", but if Bryce knew anything about his father, it was either the judge or someone on the Parole Board.

At that point Bryce silently admitted that he really cared more about building a life for himself and his son than how long Coe served time in jail.

But I still hate the bastard.

Chapter 19

Before returning to Little Creek, Bryce took his son horseback riding. He contrived a rig of suspenders, several belts, and cloth that had Midge shaking her head in dismay.

"Bryce, don't ye dare put the wee bairn in that nightmare getup! He'll fall out and be trampled!"

Bryce smiled to himself. A sure sign of Midge's distress was her reversion to Scottish expressions that she brought with her when she'd arrived over forty years ago.

"Now, Midge, humor me and the boy. Look, he's smiling. Besides, I'm not going to take him over jumps or anything. Just a little ride around the fields. Nice and easy, and I'll hold on to him." Bryce looked down at the baby suspended in front of him and had a few qualms, but headed for the mare he'd saddled minutes before putting Eddie in his "rig" as Bryce referred to it. He allowed the mare to sniff Eddie who reached for her ear, and then Bryce gently mounted from a block and held Eddie while the horse got used to him and her strange little rider. He walked the mare out of the stable yard and into the field beyond.

Eddie started to do his baby giggle and Bryce kept his gentle grip on him. All was right with the world as the father and son began to enjoy their first adventure together on that sunny summer day.

"Look up in that tree, Eddie," said Bryce and he pointed skyward. The child's gaze followed his hand upward.

"That's a cardinal singing."

Chapter 20

December 1964

B ryce was discharged from the Navy and journeyed home, still worried over how he was going to raise Eddie without Marilyn's love and help. He stopped at a bookstore and purchased a copy of every book in stock on how to raise children. Over the next weeks he devoured each of them and, in order, pitched every one of them into the trash. They all advised paying too much attention to the child's wants and sensibilities and mentioned little regarding his self-discipline and learning through the experience of hard knocks and tough love.

Although Bryce enjoyed spending time with Eddie, he was restless for much of the balance while he pondered his future.

For the winter Harry had installed a translucent arched cover over the swimming pool. Bryce rose early and swam in water that barely reached 62 with the help of a heater. He polished his skills at the piano and tried to master a Rachmaninov piece, but his heart wasn't in it. Many of his friends had found employment away from the area and others were too committed to their own new families to spend time with him. He telephoned Dean at his brokerage office. As he waited to be put through, memories of their prep school friendship brought a smile and an eagerness to reconnect.

"Hi, Bryce," said Dean. "Where are you?"

"I'm at home. I just finished my active duty in the Navy. I thought it would be good to get together and catch up on what we've been doing."

"Uh . . . sure. Do you want to meet for a drink somewhere? If you can make it into the city I can leave work a little early and we can chat before I have to catch my train."

"I was thinking more along the lines of a game of tennis at the club's new indoor courts."

"Sounds like fun, Bryce. But I'm really jammed for the next couple of weeks. Can we do it after the New Year?"

"Sure, Dean. I'll call you after the holidays."

⊙≈⊙

As Christmas approached Bryce hurriedly shopped for those who would be home that year, but without Marilyn to buy for he did it mechanically. The little joy he was able to muster was shattered when, carrying his gifts, he returned home and entered the kitchen.

He put the boxes on a chair and Rosalie handed him an envelope with his name and address crudely printed near the bottom.

"This arrived today," she said.

"Hmmff. No return address," said Bryce. "The handwriting looks so childish. I wonder who it could be? Maybe a card from one of Margaret's kids?"

He used a kitchen knife to slit open the envelope and withdrew a folded sheet of paper. Bryce's face turned white with anger as he opened the sheet and saw its message. A gravestone with Marilyn's name and date of death was drawn on the paper. Kneeling before the grave was a grieving man. Inscribed on his back was the name Bryce Roberts and under it the words, *mea culpa.*

"Goddamn that bastard!"

Rosalie looked with shock at her son. "Don't you dare use such language in this house . . ." She stopped when Bryce wordlessly handed her the drawing.

Rosalie looked at the drawing, dropped it on the counter and hugged her oldest son.

"Who would do such an awful thing?" she asked. "And at Christmas?"

"Coe. Even from prison that S.O.B. still is trying to harass me." Bryce moved toward the window that looked out over a grove of white birch trees, and stood there trying to calm himself. Then he turned to Rosalie. "Well, I'm not going to let him get to me. I'm just going to put an extra effort into Eddie's Christmas."

Henry Morton allowed Bryce to use his shop to make a rocking horse for his son. One of the first phrases Eddie learned to say was "giddy up" as his father held him on his new toy on Christmas morning.

The day after Christmas Bryce realized he'd been pacing inside the house like a caged tiger. He turned to hiking and horseback riding to burn off his frustration and disquiet. It was then that he found himself at his father's hunting cabin, *Sunrise*, on a cold grey winter morning at the end of a long ride. Years ago Bryce and his brothers had watched the workmen haul the massive logs and timbers to the site using draft horses to traverse the long fire trail that led to the eastern promontory of the hills. The boys joined in the construction by running errands for the carpenters and they "apprenticed" for stonemasons who used the local rock to build the cabin's massive fireplace, hearth and chimney.

Harry ordered well digging equipment dismantled, hauled to the site, and then reassembled. The well produced especially sweet water. An outbuilding held maintenance gear and a stable for four horses. As the years passed an electric generator was installed. But most of the visitors to Sunrise preferred the lanterns that gave the cabin a special glow that comforted of an evening. The main feature of the cabin was a wall of windows that gave hunters a view of the sun rising over the valley below.

Now, roof shingles were curled or missing; plaster caulk between the logs needed renewal; and the floorboards on the front and side porches were aged beyond repair.

"Dad's been too busy to come up here," he told himself. "Otherwise this place wouldn't look like this." Bryce found pencil and paper and set about measuring the porch with a tape measure from the well-stocked tool bin. He made a list of supplies that were needed, closed up the cabin and started home.

As he rode down the fire trail on the big hill that some Easterners called a mountain, he was surrounded by one of the oldest stands of timber in the eastern United States. Trees over one hundred feet tall with trunk diameters measured in feet rather than inches bordered the trail and grew in the surrounding woods. Other trees had fallen to the forest floor, giving the place a look of chaos. Bryce noted with apprehension the accumulation of underbrush, downed trees and branches that littered the hillsides. It was the stuff that forest fires fed upon and the forest floor hadn't been cleaned up for generations since his grandfather ordered the trees preserved. He thought about the possibility of winter work for a lumberjack crew clearing all but the large downed trees. His last stop was at the trail that led down to a gorge with a waterfall at its western end. The wood steps leading to the pool below were rotted or missing.

Bryce reported all of what he'd seen to Harry who authorized all of the repairs but limited the clearing operation to along the fire trails and around the cabin. Bryce, ignoring the January cold, personally rebuilt the porches. He wanted to keep busy as the first anniversary of Marilyn's death approached.

When April arrived stonemasons rebuilt supports for the steps down to the falls and carpenters replaced the wood steps and railing down the steep grade.

By then Bryce was gone. He traveled south for a tryout with the Founders baseball team after an acrimonious discussion with his parents about the conflicting demands of his parenthood and his own future. Even worse was Harry's anger and disappointment that Bryce had postponed working for Sunrise Lumber Company.

Chapter 21

It began with a telephone call and a fight. Bryce telephoned the Founders organization to inquire about a tryout. He was told that he wouldn't be allowed to try out because he was too old and he hadn't been seen by any of the scouts.

Harry angrily refused to speak with a man who he knew in the team's management. "You have a duty to your son and a duty to this family. By God, stay here and live up to your duties!"

Bryce refused to give in. He asked his former college coach to call the Founders' head scout. The coach told the scout that Bryce had all of the tools: "He can run, field, throw, hit and hit with power; and he's a leader," the coach reported. "I tried to get him to try out for professional ball when he graduated but he joined the Navy instead."

The scout telephoned Bryce and inquired about his availability for a tryout. Bryce asked if there was a tryout session other than with the team at Florida spring training and he learned of one in South Carolina near the town where he had practiced with the Dartmouth team during Spring Break. It was all Bryce needed.

"Kid, you're really blowing a golden opportunity to get ahead," Harry told him. "If you do this, you're going to abandon your fatherly duties, your duties to yourself, and a solid career."

"Don't call me kid!"

"Men take responsibility. Boys run from it."

"I'm not going to be controlled by you!" shouted Bryce. "I will be my own man and decide my own future! I want to prove to myself I can make it without this family's help."

"My, God, boy, what do you think families are for?"

"Well and good. But there are still too many memories of Marilyn here."

Harry kept his voice calm. "Don't you understand that if you run, Coe has won? That he's controlling what you make of your life?"

"No he isn't. And, by God, don't you try to manipulate me with crap like that. I'll decide my future, not you!"

"I'm not 'manipulating' you and I never have."

"That's bullshit! I think you set me up to meet Karen Howe in the hope of getting me away from Marilyn. I'm not going to be manipulated like that ever again."

For once Harry's ability to maintain a poker face failed him. His fleeting expressions of consternation and remorse were all that it took to convince Bryce that his shot in the dark had hit home.

"I'm not running away from problems or challenges!" shouted Bryce. "I just need more time to get over Marilyn's death and make my own way."

"Balls, boy! You're running."

"The hell I am! I'm going to prove to myself I can make it on my own. Then maybe I'll think about coming back and working in the family business. I love Eddie and this family. But I have to find another reason, just for me, personally, to really want to live again."

"I thought you said you were going for an MBA. Are you going to abandon that too?"

"No. I'll figure a way to do that, too."

"*Playing baseball?*"

"Watch me."

☙❧

Bryce headed to South Carolina, found a cheap rooming house, and practiced for a week with his old college coach and members of the team. He worked on his fielding, but concentrated mostly on the timing of his hitting.

The team thought he should stay on as an assistant coach but Bryce left the day of the tryout and headed to the field at a minor league stadium near Spartanburg. There were dozens of young men there with their own gloves and spikes. They were timed running the bases, and carefully observed when they threw the ball from third base to first, and then from the outfield to a cut-off man. The scouts realized Bryce had a "gun" of an arm from the outfield and his speed on the base paths was better than most big men. But what sold them was his hitting. Bryce's week of practice with the college team had helped him get his timing back and his form in swinging the bat was classic.

"He has a swing that reminds me of Yastrzemski," one of the scouts told the other.

"Yeah, but can he hit good pitching?" was the response. They brought in two AA level pitchers to pitch to a small group of the players who were asked to stay after many of the others had been excused.

Batting right handed, Bryce fought to keep his nervousness from showing and he powered some of the decent pitches over the left centerfield fence and several of those left the ballpark entirely. He had trouble with curve balls but he clobbered the left hander when he tried to pitch him inside. What really had the coaches shaking their heads was the surprise perfect bunt he laid down the first base line. Years of practice with his brothers had honed that skill and he had fun showing he could do it. The final workout had him chasing down fly balls in the outfield and his long legs ate up the ground as he charged after some well-hit balls near the wall.

"Where is it you said you played?" asked the scout.

"Bucks Academy and then Dartmouth College."

"Ivy League? Didn't know they had your caliber of player. You look older than a kid fresh out of college."

"I've just finished a tour of duty in the Navy."

"Play any ball in the service?"

"No. I was in a UDT unit and we spent too much time offshore to get in much baseball."

"Bryson, what do they call you? Bryce?"

"Yes, sir, I've just always gone with Bryce."

"Well, Bryce, we want some other people to have a look at you. Can you make it down to Clearwater in the next couple of days?"

"You bet. Who do I see?"

"We have some people there at this time of year and they might want to ask you to stick around for a few days. Come on, I'll give you their names and then call them about you and a couple of the other fellas here."

They liked him well enough to put him under contract to play on one of their class A farm teams in Virginia. He received a generous signing bonus that he immediately sent to his bank for deposit in an interest-bearing account. He promised himself to invest it wisely after he finished the season. "I'll call Dean about that," he figured.

By mid-July he was leading the league in RBI's; had acquired the nickname "Frogman" when one of his teammates learned he'd been in UDT; and, he learned how to sleep on a bus. He roomed with three other teammates in a boarding house run by Mrs. Winton, the widow of a Baptist minister who brooked no nonsense from "her boys." They learned that a night out on the town had to end early, or the latecomers were locked out and had to sleep on the porch furniture. That irritated Shortstop, Mrs. Winton's cat, who tended to bite people whom he found sleeping on the glider he considered his turf.

The saving grace to Bryce's living arrangement was the presence of a decent upright piano in Mrs. Winton's parlor. While the younger players were out trying to get served in one of the local bars, Bryce practiced his scales and other short pieces, and he often found time to humor his landlady by playing a few hymns. He sometimes unlocked the front door for his returning teammates if Mrs. Winton had retired for the evening and Bryce had stayed home to practice the piano.

Then, in the next home game, it happened.

Chapter 22

It started with a razz. On his way to the outfield, he heard a woman in the stands heckling the opponents. His gaze played over the stands until he saw her. The fan's appearance didn't resemble Marilyn in the least, but her voice and mannerisms did. He began to think of Marilyn while he watched his pitcher succeed in getting three ground outs, and then his thoughts shifted to Charles Coe.

That summer Bryce had tried to avoid thinking about Coe's words in the courtroom. Getting angry distanced Bryce from his game, his teammates and coaches, and drove him into a funk. But tonight his rage at Coe began to simmer as he trotted toward the dugout. He was due to bat second that inning and was still steamed at Coe when he got to the plate. He found himself intensely studying the pitcher's movements and imagining that the ball was Coe's head. He relished the chance to smash Coe with the bat. He took an outside pitch, waited for the next pitch, and then hit a fastball so hard it not only cleared the left center field fence but sailed well beyond into the parking lot where it broke the windshield of a fan's car. It was remembered for years afterward as the longest home run anyone ever hit at that ballpark. All Bryce saw was Coe's head, face still wearing his thick glasses, disappearing into the twilight sky over left center field.

He stayed angry for the rest of the game. His teammates sensed it, wondered what had sparked the normally implacable older man into his quiet rage, and they gave him a wide berth on the bench. He hit two more home runs to tie a club record for a single game. He didn't care about the record; all he thought about was how good it felt to smash that bastard Coe's head.

Bryce's anger left him as he showered after the game, but he analyzed what he had done at the plate that worked so well. The trance-like total concentration was all he could credit because he hadn't changed his swing or stance. During the next days he worked hard at practice and ran extra laps to work off the frustrations he felt over not being able to forget about the man who had dealt him such grief. His coaches thought it was just an intense work ethic that drove him and gave him high marks for the effort and the effect it had on the rest of the team who didn't want to be "shown up" by Frogman. During the next two games Bryce's concentration at the plate was so intense that the crowd noise and the dugout chatter became distant in his consciousness. He went three for four in both games with two more home runs to show for his effort.

The performance brought the attention of the Founders' management and the local newspaper, whose sports reporter had pitched for the town's high school team. The interview by the reporter appeared in the next edition.

"Bryce, your batting average over the last three games has climbed to an incredible .422 for the season. How do you do it?"

"Well, I've been working extra hard at batting practice and I'm really concentrating at the plate."

"Every player concentrates. What's your secret that makes the tactic work?" asked the reporter.

If I told you the real story, they'd pack me off to a mental institution. So what should I say to get this man to stop his inane questions and go away?

"I'm seeing the ball better. I watch the pitch from the time it first leaves the pitcher's hand right up to when I decide whether to swing. It just looks bigger now."

"Coach Henley says you discussed going to Reading pretty soon. How do you feel about that?"

Kid, I heard that from the coach this morning, and I'll be one happy man to get away from all of these children and begin to play ball with men.

"I'd be grateful for the opportunity. But I doubt I can keep up my batting average at its present level. Those pitchers in AA ball know a lot more ways to get batters out. If I'm sent up I'll just try to contribute to the team effort any way I can."

Chapter 23

Reading, blessed Reading. It wasn't the brightest city in Pennsylvania, but it was closer to home and he could spend time with Eddie when his parents came to see a game and brought his son along, which Harry insisted that they do to remind Bryce of his fatherly duties.

Bryce's prediction about the league's pitching proved true. Most of the pitchers in A ball concentrated on throwing heat—fast balls. In AA they threw all of the pitches. He struck out the first two times he was up to bat, but hit a bullet off the left field fence for a double his third at bat. The bonus was that it happened with two men on base. To continue his education and to see what he could do, the coach allowed him to play the next game. Again Bryce got a hit with a man on base, but he struck out twice, once swinging wildly at a high fast ball and on the other at bat he got frozen by a nasty curve ball.

"Bryce," the coach told him, "you have a good, level swing, but you have to learn to hit a breaking pitch better. If you don't do that, the word will get around that you can't hit breaking balls and you'll never see a fast ball when you're at bat."

They practiced with the pitchers throwing him curves and sliders until he began to recognize those pitches and to hit them in batting practice. After regular practice was over they used a former minor league pitcher who could still throw a good curve ball to help Bryce get used to that pitch. It was a long week, sitting out every game, a situation that Bryce never had faced. Always before, he'd been one of his team's best players, depended upon for his bat and his leadership. Now he just hoped that his batting coach would recommend that he get some playing time.

The opportunity came in the next game when his team's pitcher was scheduled to come to bat with a man on second base. His team was behind by a run. The coach told Bryce to pinch hit for the pitcher and gave him a pat on the back as he left the dugout.

"Remember, lay off the high stuff," he was told as he rubbed pine tar on his bat handle.

The opposing catcher went to the mound when Bryce was put in the game and came back to the plate smiling.

"He's just going to throw you junk, Frogman, and you're goin' to swing at it anyway," he taunted. The taunts meant nothing to Bryce, as he'd endured much worse during UDT training, and especially during hell week. Instead, he invoked the same concentration as when he'd hit Coe's head out of the park. The first pitch was a high fast ball that he stayed off. Again he drew the catcher's hazing.

"Shoulda' swung at that one baby, it had homer written all over it."

Bryce didn't respond. The high heat was followed by a curve ball outside the strike zone, and by now the noise of the crowd and other players' chatter had begun to fade from his hearing. With two balls and no strikes, Bryce thought he might get a fastball and waited to see the pitch.

He's throwing a change up, thought Bryce as the ball was released from the pitcher's hand. He counted an extra beat before he started his swing and connected hard. The ball careened off the center field fence for a double and Bryce had his teammates slapping his back as he scored on the hit the next batter made. He stayed in the game to play left field and hit a curve ball for a single his next time at bat.

"Now, yer gettin' it," his batting coach told him. "Be out here early tomorrow for practice. We're goin' to work on layin' off or hittin' sliders." Bryce finished the season with a .301 batting average, a generous addition to his bank account, and, high hopes for the following year. But he still had to contend with Wharton.

Chapter 24

On a cold November afternoon on his way from school to the train station, Bryce found himself walking behind a woman with blond hair in the classic bun-in-the-back that Marilyn had favored. The woman was dressed in a red coat of the same shade Marilyn wore the day they reunited at Wanamaker's. Bryce lengthened his stride and, heart racing, caught up to her. She heard his footsteps and looked at him. Her face belonged to a complete stranger.

The woman's expression turned to alarm and Bryce stammered, "I'm . . . I'm sorry. I didn't mean to frighten you. I thought you were someone I used to know." He quickened his pace and moved on. It was the first time in several days that he'd allowed himself to think about Marilyn in more than a passing moment. He realized that his time in the Navy and playing ball hadn't finished off his grief.

That weekend he went alone to visit Marilyn's grave for the first time. It wrenched him emotionally, but he forced himself to go after avoiding it for so long. The grey November sky was low, but the air was crisp. Patches of the grass still held a shade of forest green.

"Her color," he told himself.

The epitaph on her gravestone read: "All we have is the Almighty's. And shall not God have His own when He calls for it?"

"Ah, William Penn, you were a wise man." It was then that Bryce accepted the finality of Marilyn's death and the fact that there was not a damned thing he could do about it. He reached out and touched her gravestone and thought about how poor a substitute the cold granite was for the warmth of her twinkling eyes.

Love left him and hatred boiled over to destroy his reverie. *Goddamn you, Coe! Someday I'll piss on your grave!* He stomped back to his car and tore out of the cemetery.

Chapter 25

E ddie said "no" to everything Bryce told him to do.

"It's the terrible twos," explained Rosalie. "Now you know what I went through raising you kids."

"How did you deal with me?"

"You went to your room until you listened."

"Did it work?"

"Eventually. Now, you're too old for me to send to your room, so please say yes, you will come to church with Midge and me."

Bryce had forsaken church in his agony over Marilyn's death and his inability to reconcile why God had allowed that.

But he had to admire the way Rosalie had used his own maturity to work him into a box. He reluctantly agreed to accompany his first and second mothers that Sunday.

After the service the young father spoke in earnest with other parents about putting Eddie into small groups of children to begin the development of his son's social skills. He received plenty of advice on toilet training and dealing with Eddie's "no's."

He also received an invitation to a church supper the following Thursday evening. He started to decline, and then caught himself.

Come on, man, he thought. *You have to get yourself back into life, even if you don't feel like you want to. You're not going to let Marilyn's death put you down on your knees forever. Remember what you told Marilyn that day at Winter Carnival . . . how you try to savor every heartbeat of life. She told you later that was one of the things about you that made her love you. She'd tell you to get going again, so, do it, man, do it.*

He accepted the church supper invitation and was assigned to the kitchen where he endured a share of good natured ribbing as he cleaned pots and pans. Afterward several of the older women politely asked him if he was feeling well enough to "get back in circulation."

He talked with Jacob Knox and told him that he'd replied that he was not up to anything but enjoying group activities. Jacob promised to quietly spread the word of Bryce's continuing non-availability. Then Jacob began to question him about what he was experiencing over the last year. Bryce told him everything, including his thoughts when he finally visited Marilyn's grave.

"Ah, Bryce, you're in the last stages of the heavy grief that comes when one loses a spouse. And from what you tell me you're beginning to think life still has something to offer. That's good news. Sometimes you're going to feel disillusioned about the path God's chosen for you, but that will pass. I think one of these days you'll begin to date women again, but take it slowly. There sometimes is a tendency to rush into a serious relationship with the first woman you meet when you do rediscover the opposite sex."

Chapter 26

At the beginning of his second semester Bryce sat in the Dean's office, ready to put his dreams on the line.

"So you still want to play professional baseball?" The Dean had Bryce's student record open on his desk and noted his high grades at Dartmouth and over the past semester. Bryce took the lead and spoke at length about his last four years and the need he felt to pursue the new life he had charted for himself.

Dean Harris got to the nub. "The problem, of course, is that your team's season begins before school ends. We can't give you any special treatment. That would set a bad precedent. Do you have any ideas on how to deal with your dilemma? I don't think you would've come to me without something in mind."

"Let me take the full course load but study ahead of where the rest of the class will be. I can talk to my professors about doing that and then, hopefully, they'd be willing to discuss the advance lessons with me after I do them. I could then join the team a few weeks after spring practice starts and come back here just for final exams."

"But Bryce, even supposing your professors would agree, you'd miss lectures and class discussions that really benefit every student in the MBA program. This school prides itself in graduating people who have received the best we have to offer. Have you talked with your team's management about the possibility of reporting late?"

"Not yet," replied Bryce. "I wanted to get your reaction first. I believe I have the potential to make it to Triple A ball this year and maybe play in the majors next year. And I want that opportunity."

"Let me know what your team says. Maybe we can work something out, but don't count on anything. Wharton prides itself in graduating fully qualified people. Bryce, I think you're going to have to choose between Wharton and baseball."

Chapter 27

Bryce called Beanie George, his coach, and explained what he wanted to do.

"Yeah, I have a daughter in college and I know how important a good education is these days, but you'll have to talk to the GM." Beanie gave him the General Manager's number.

The GM's reaction wasn't encouraging. He suggested that they meet at the office at Connie Mack Stadium when he would be in town later that week. He told Bryce which entrance to use and they set a time.

Bryce hung up, determined to find a way to convince the GM that he could start late.

Then Bryce went fishing, not by a stream, but in his living room. He knew Harry Roberts couldn't resist a business discussion that included negotiation strategies. Bryce told him of his discussions with the Dean and GM. Harry assumed a courteous, formal attitude, but Bryce detected the underlying interest he'd predicted. His father maintained his silence for such a long while that Bryce thought he was drifting off. The same tactic had fooled many others in business discussions with Harry. Then Harry took the bait.

"Who's your competition on the Double A team and potential competition on the Triple A team?" he asked.

Gotcha, old man. You're on your way back to respecting me.

Bryce and Harry then went over each outfield player on the Reading team who could hit the ball for power or for average and they covered the AAA team as well. They concluded that if Bryce continued to progress this year, it was likely he'd be called up to the AAA team.

"Your team's management have done the same kind of analysis," Harry told him. "So they probably believe that you have pretty good potential. That gives you a little leverage in your discussions, but not much. Keep in mind they can always make a trade to fill a gap.

They may want to talk about a pay reduction if you can't start every game, but don't give in on that at first because I also think they look at the long term, and if you convince them you're aiming at the same thing, they may listen to what you want. Just make sure they know it's this year and next year that you'll be in school when spring training starts."

◦≋◦

The taxi dropped him at the corner of West Lehigh and North 21st Streets. The cabbie thanked him for the tip and jokingly told him the season hadn't started yet. Bryce entered the main gate in the Beau Arts cupola/tower that was the trademark of the stadium and found his way to the stairs leading to the offices. The GM must have heard him approaching because he was standing in an open office door waiting for Bryce. He shook hands warmly and ushered Bryce into the office decorated with shelves full of baseball memorabilia, photos and trophies.

"Beanie and I have talked about your request," the GM began. "I've had some time to think about it, and I'm not keen on the idea. But I want to hear more from you before we decide what to do."

Bryce told him that he used the Bucks field house batting cage to keep his timing. He described the Wharton MBA program and how, someday, he hoped to work in the forest products industry as his father did. But for the time being, his sole ambition was to play professional baseball.

"Then why go to school at all?" asked the GM. "Couldn't you go when you finish playing ball?"

"I have a two-year-old son. He'll need a lot more of my attention later than he does now. So I chose school now while his grandparents are still young enough to take care of him while I study."

"When does school end?" asked the GM.

"This year and next finals are the last week in May. I can join the team a couple of days later."

The GM thought for a while. Beanie George had told him that Bryce was one of the hottest prospects he'd seen in years. So, how do I keep the man happy and still use him?

"You're going to have to see the team doctor in March. I wouldn't be surprised if he has to put you on the disabled list with a bad case of 'studyosis'. You probably won't be well enough to report for at least two months. Of course your pay is suspended, but only while you're out with your disability."

"That's fair," said Bryce. "There is one thing, though. I want a clause in my contract that says I can't be traded without my consent if I keep my average at .300 or above for the season; or, if I hit fifteen home runs or better during the season if I play in eighty-five percent of the games left after I join the team."

"With that kind of performance, who'd want to trade you?"

"Then you won't mind putting that in my contract, will you?"

"Why those terms?"

"I want to be within traveling distance of my son."

"Okay, but it'll have to be confidential. And if you don't make those numbers, there's no guarantee about whether you're protected from a trade. And if you don't make your own numbers your pay goes down too. By 12 percent."

Prick. "No. It's already docked while I'm out."

"Six percent."

"Three percent."

"Agreed." And they shook hands. The two men knew that most minor league baseball player's contracts weren't negotiable. Thus, Bryce had obtained a substantial concession.

Lord!, thought Bryce as he left the stadium. Now I have to hit a lot better than I did last year or I get traded and I may not be able to see Eddie during the season. And I'm not going to get spring practice to get used to the pitching. That MBA had better be worth it.

Still, Bryce was pleased with the discussions. In the mid-1960s the minimum salary for a major league player was about $7,000. Bryce earned more than that as a minor leaguer because he was considered a good prospect, but he wanted assurance that he really was going to have the deal he negotiated. He spoke with his father about his idea to write a letter to his GM confirming the discussions so at least management would be reminded to think about putting the authorization for the late start in writing.

"Bryce, baseball management are some of the toughest people going," said Harry. "I agree with your idea. That way your GM knows he's dealing with someone who's responsible and serious . . . about baseball."

Bryce didn't respond to that twist of the knife.

He did as he planned and two weeks later a revised contract arrived in the mail for his signature. He signed it, made a copy, and then mailed the original back. A notice to report for a medical exam was included with the contract. He reported to the University of Pennsylvania Hospital, where, surprisingly, he was put through a complete battery of tests and full examinations.

Then he figured it out. "Management wants to be able to tell another team I'm physically sound if they offer me as a trade. Now I have more pressure to perform. Well, I asked for this."

Chapter 28

The examining physician told Bryce that he suffered only from excellent health and youth; and that his exam records would be forwarded to the team doctor in Reading. Two weeks later Bryce received notice that he had been put on the disabled list, but the reason for his status was scribbled illegibly in the space provided on the form. Bryce could have sworn it read "studyosis."

☙❧

A surprise awaited him when he appeared for his regular off-season batting practice at the Bucks fieldhouse. Gino, "The Hammer," Berrio introduced himself. He'd pitched in the minor leagues for years and now coached at a small college in the area. He mentioned that the GM had given him a call about throwing curves and sliders to a young hitter at Bucks and he'd been so intrigued he stopped over to see what it was all about.

So, maybe that GM's really not such a prick.

From then on, early Tuesday and Friday evenings found the two men talking pitching and situational hitting after Gino threw curveballs and sliders to Bryce with a surprising "pop" for a man his age. He taught Bryce the fine points on how to read a pitcher's motion and then threw him change-ups that caught Bryce thinking fastball. The sessions taught Bryce to begin his swing later, and he developed better bat speed as the workouts progressed. Gino set the pitching machine to throw low strikes at the outside and inside corners of the plate and taught Bryce how to foul them off rather than being counted out on such pitches; and, he preached patience, patience, patience at the plate. Most of all, Bryce learned how and when not to swing at pitches that umpires would call balls rather than strikes.

Their sessions continued until the week before final exams. Bryce thanked Gino and wished him Godspeed.

"Just remember," Gino told him, "believe in yourself."

"I do, in spades."

"What makes you say that? You don't impress me as an egotist."

"Thank you. I'm not. I just have confidence in my ability to deal with what life throws at me . . . I suppose part of that's my upbringing in a family that preaches self-reliance. But there's more to it, I think."

"Oh? In what way?"

"When a new challenge comes up I find myself relishing it rather than fearing it."

"You must fear something, even if it's just an inside fastball."

"I sometimes fear for my son, for his safety and his future. He's all I have left and he's everything to me."

Chapter 29

Bryce often read to Eddie and tried to spend more time outdoors with him as the weather warmed. The boy loved to run and cheerfully chased after Bryce in their games of hide and seek among the trees around their home. Eddie's laughter and development were constant joys to Bryce as he entered the push to complete his study team projects and prepare for final exams.

"But how do I get back in Harry's good graces?" Bryce asked himself. Bryce and his study group worked hard on a Management problem they had been assigned; and, his Finance and Marketing classes had been joys to him. But Bryce needed something more immediate.

Then fortune smiled. His marketing group had selected, at his suggestion, a real problem from his father's business and so the students had an opportunity to work in an actual situation rather than in a hypothetical one. They decided to recommend that a composite wood sheet that was a replacement for plywood be marketed for interior use only, and so labeled, because the weathering test results were still incomplete. Harry's engineers and marketing people protested, but the students held firm and Harry nixed an extra production line that would have been installed had the composite been marketed for sub-roofing purposes. The group then developed a marketing plan that was adopted by the company for its first phase, or market entry campaign.

Another step back into Harry's good graces, thought Bryce. He won't admit it, but I know he's proud of our team's effort.

He didn't wait to receive his final exam grades. By then he'd hugged Eddie and the rest of his family good-bye, and driven to

Reading. He found a rooming house near the stadium, signed a lease for a month and headed for the team physician's office.

"Man, I hope this layoff hasn't screwed me for the season," he told himself.

Chapter 30

The doctor finished his cursory exam and told Bryce, "They can use you, young man. From what I saw last year, you have a potent bat and they aren't scoring many runs per game thus far." He handed Bryce a form that he'd signed and told him to put his shirt back on.

"Practice probably has started, so get on over there. And, good luck to you."

Bryce was assigned the most inconveniently located locker, but he didn't complain. He knew that the good spots had been reserved by the players who'd appeared for spring practice weeks ago and who had earned them by their performance. He donned his practice shirt and pants and walked in his cleats toward the exit leading to the field.

The trainer came out of the toilets, looked at Bryce, and said, "What the hell is 'studyosis'?"

"It's a condition that affects the brain, but I'm okay now," replied Bryce with a straight face.

They walked to the field and Bryce greeted Beanie who put him through fielding practice most of the morning. Bryce had to charge a fast sinking fly ball, field it on the first hop, maintain his forward inertia, and accurately throw the ball to second or third base. The skill was in detecting the arc distance of the fly ball and maintaining his forward movement to get the best speed on his throw after he caught or fielded the ball.

Bryce worked hard at the drill and pushed himself to make the extra effort necessary to catch the ball on the fly rather than the first bounce. They finished up by running laps and then had a scouting report on the teams they would play that week and the pitchers who they probably would face. As he was getting dressed after showering, three of his teammates from last year greeted him and told him they were glad to see him back.

"We're going for lunch down the street, want to join us?"

"Sure," said Bryce. "But I've sworn off beer for a while. Just so you guys know it's not the company that keeps me from having a brew."

Calvin Lyle, the shortstop, laughed and responded, "This place doesn't have a liquor license. If we want to drink there we have to bring our own. So we'll stop for a six-pack on the way."

The neon sign over the door they entered was not lit. A large hall with an elevated platform down the center of the room around which barstools and tables were located was the first to catch Bryce's eye. Then he understood.

Strip joint. Ah, well, too late to leave now, but this is the last time I'm going to get dragged in here. They paid their "club dues" and ordered sandwiches. The food arrived, served by a waitress who was topless and feigning interest in the men at the table. Bryce watched as Calvin and Brady tried to tease her and she just held out her hand for payment of the tab. The prices, as expected, were outrageous and the food was just awful. Bryce figured the cook hadn't changed the french-fry oil for about two weeks.

A scratchy record started to play over a set of speakers at one end of the platform and a woman dressed in a worn, tight sequined dress strutted on to the stage and began to move to the music. She was the "headliner" for the week and drew cat-calls and whistles from the lunchtime crowd. Bryce watched as she unzipped and removed her gown after only fifteen seconds of gyrations. The woman was overweight and flabby, but Brady, Calvin and Harper, the catcher, hooted and cheered as she did the bump and grind around the cheap stage. Bryce had more fun watching the guys' reaction to the stripper than he did in observing her. But he joined in clapping her off the stage when the music ended.

"Do you guys come here often?" he asked.

"No, we save that for later," said Harper. The three of them laughed and Bryce managed a weak smile at the gutter humor. "Actually, we hardly ever come here. We just wanted to celebrate you joining the team. What the hell was wrong with you anyway?"

"I had a condition that was affecting my brain," said Bryce. "Seems it was getting full of all kinds of strange stuff that the doctors couldn't figure out. Then it cleared up about a week ago and they released me to play."

"Man, that's weird shit," said Calvin. "You ain't goin' to go whacko on us are you?"

"Nah. I'm okay now," said Bryce, grinning despite himself.

⟨◦≋◦⟩

The next morning they boarded a bus for Trenton and Bryce had the opportunity to talk with Bob Keller, one of the better pitchers on the team. They talked pitching for a while and the conversation then turned to women. "I hear a couple of the guys took you to The Arcade," said Bob. "God, what a hole that place is. Did you actually eat there?"

"I had a couple of bites and then I picked up a deli sandwich later."

"What did you think of the women?"

"Matched the food."

They continued their conversation and agreed to be road roommates. Bryce told him about Marilyn's death and Eddie.

"Sorry to hear about your wife. Were you married long?"

Easy, Bryce, he told himself. Get used to people asking you that question. They're just trying to be decent.

"Just over a year. It was rough for a while after she died, but I'm getting back into life again. I still think about her, but now I can at least talk about it, when before I couldn't."

They made it to Trenton early in the afternoon in time to check in to their hotel and then have an early meal before the pre-game practice started. Bryce's season began with him going two for four at the plate and cleanly playing everything that was hit to left field. He couldn't do anything about the two homers that went out of the park over his head. His team lost, 4-2, and returned to the hotel in a lower mood than when they had left.

Chapter 31

In the 1960s, attendance at minor league games had shrunk to eleven million per year, down from a high of over forty million in the late 1940s and 1950s. The number of teams shrank. Youngsters who'd grown up in those decades worshipping the likes of Joe DiMaggio and Robin Roberts still found a home in minor league baseball, but the competition was fiercer and only the brightest prospects were kept for eventual placement on major league rosters. It was into that world Bryce thrust himself, knowing that he had to be among the best if he was to reach his goal.

The lessons with Gino Berrio had their effect as he wore out pitchers by fouling off strikes that weren't hittable and taking pitches that were out of the strike zone. He maintained awesome concentration at the plate and walked so many times he developed an unflappable self-confidence, to the point he believed he'd always reach base one way or another. Of course I don't, thought Bryce, but I know I can do it a lot of the time. And knowing that about myself is as important as anything I can have in this game.

IIe batted fifth for the first month he returned to the team, and then was shifted to clean-up when Bo Richards, the first baseman who filled that batting slot, went into a slump. Bryce hit his first grand slam home run the day after he was moved to the clean-up spot and he stayed there even after Bo Richards got his swing back. He felt sorry for Bo, but not enough to let it bother him. After all, baseball success belongs to those who can play well and take advantage of opportunities.

In late July he noticed a couple of Founders scouts attending the games and he wondered why they were at the field in Reading rather than out looking over high school prospects. The answer came later that week when he was called into Beanie's office and told by him and the GM that management wanted to give him a try at the AAA level.

"You can't learn much more down here, and they want to see if you can handle that level of pitching. If you can, you'll stay there. If you can't we can use you back here to finish out the season and you might get to Triple A next year."

Bryce showed he could hit AAA pitching. By the end of the season, he knew he'd be invited to spring practice in Clearwater the following season. He had his chance for the majors. Now, all he had to do was figure out a way to finish school and not irritate the Founders management by reporting late for spring practice and the season.

Chapter 32

B ryce settled into his second year study routine and times with Eddie as a welcome change from the travel and hotel living he endured to play the game he loved.

But all was not well on the local trains he rode to and from school. Hoodlums now menaced the passengers. Bryce traveled the trains frequently but, due to his size, he wasn't bothered. Often he'd sit in the cars near elderly people to discourage anyone from victimizing them. Things changed one evening when he arrived late at the station for the trip back to Doylestown. As he stood on the platform he saw in the next section that an elderly man was being taunted by three punks.

Do I mind my own business or not? If nobody does anything, the old guy will get mugged. I can't let that old man get mugged. So even though there are three hoods I have to do something. Maybe if I just go over there the hoods will leave.

Bryce walked toward the elderly man. As he got closer he noticed the yarmulke that covered the crown of his head. One of the teens shadow boxed around the man, imitating a prize fighter in the ring. The shadow boxer was tall but thin. He was dressed in a cheap imitation leather jacket and bell bottomed, pin striped trousers. His pointed toe shoes were worn and scuffed. He had a thin moustache under a broad nose. The moustache did nothing to distract from a bad case of acne.

The older man stood there unflinching, but his face was beginning to express the fear he felt over his situation. The man brought his hands up in a defensive gesture and Bryce saw his wedding ring. *That man has family at home waiting for him. I've got to help.*

He quickened his pace.

"Come on ole Jew boy, we know you have a wallet somewhere under that coat," mocked one of the hoods. "You jus' going share a little wit us so's we kin get lit up tonight."

The three of them laughed because they believed that, out of fear, no one would pay much attention in the almost deserted station. They didn't sense Bryce's approach.

Bryce continued toward the old man and called loudly, "Israel, my old friend, how are you? It's been quite a while since we had a chance to say hello."

The hoods turned to Bryce and the shadow boxer said, "You know this honkey? We jus need a few mo minutes wif yo frien'. Then you kin have him back."

Then his two accomplices made a mistake. Rather than spreading out, they moved between Bryce and their intended victim and stood next to each other, arms folded across their chests in attitudes adopted straight out of the "tough guy" TV shows of that year.

Bryce sized them up. They were dressed in dirty warm-up jackets that covered old sweat shirts. Their jeans were bell bottomed with the oversize cuffs enveloping dirty and worn sneakers. There was a hint of uncertainty in their faces as the man with the broad shoulders came purposefully toward them. They looked at each other for encouragement.

"Boys, get out of here," said Bryce.

The hoods laughed derisively.

Evars, here I go. Please, God, help me do it right.

Bryce dropped his briefcase at the hoods' feet and kicked it between them. When they both dodged and looked down they gave Bryce the opportunity he needed. He quickly moved slightly between the off-balance hoods, grabbed each one's neck in his big hands, and violently smashed their heads together. Once . . . Twice . . . The adrenaline was flowing now . . . The third time he banged the hoods' heads together he gave it all he had and heard the grunts of pain he listened for. He shoved the dazed thugs toward the shadow boxer and they sprawled on the platform surface. Bryce then stood between them and the older man.

"Gents, this man is my friend, so just leave him alone and everything will be cool."

The two hoods with the now booming headaches dizzily began to move toward the exit gates and stairway, but the shadow boxer didn't follow. He put his hand into his coat pocket and Bryce told him, "Don't. Just keep your hands where I can see them and get out of here."

The thug pulled a switchblade knife from his pocket and the noise of it flicking open made a loud snick that echoed off the tiled walls in the night quiet of the station. Bryce kept his eyes on the man's waist and feet as he advanced. The hood gave away the coming slash by a change in the rhythm of his heavy breathing and the way he planted his right foot. When the slash came toward him, Bryce reacted as he'd practiced the many times under Evars' tutelage.

The hood felt a powerful vise close on his wrist and begin to twist as if he had the arm of a child. The hand pulled him past and out of reach of his intended victim. Pain like an electric shock began to spread as his wrist was twisted. He felt his grip on the knife loosening, and then his elbow suddenly began to move at an odd angle as Bryce's other hand pushed it forward from behind the joint. The knife clattered to the concrete floor. The shadow boxer tried to turn toward his antagonist but he felt a powerful kick to the back of his knee that dropped him toward the cold, dirty floor of the platform. The hand continued to push at his elbow and the hood heard a sickening squish and felt a shooting, excruciating pain consume him as his elbow was dislocated. He screamed in agony and the other two hoods took off toward the gates, jumped them, and disappeared into the exit stairs.

The train arrived at the platform, bringing a transit authority policeman who ran toward them when he sensed that something was wrong. The cop took one look at the now groaning man on his knees and said, "Well, if it's not Leroy, finally paying the price up front. What happened here?"

"Officer, my name is Abraham Rabinowicz and I saw everything. This gentleman, thank God, protected me from an attack and from being robbed, and it looks like he broke, ah, Leroy's arm in the process."

"We know Leroy pretty well. We've just been waiting for him to do something stupid so we can nail him," said the policeman. "Last couple of times the judge just gave him probation. This time I'm going to insist the DA put him in jail. That switchblade ought to land him there. Were there two other punks with this hood?" asked the policeman.

Bryce told the officer about the two others and stayed to give a brief statement. He agreed to make himself available as a witness, but asked that he not have any publicity. The policeman said he'd try to honor Bryce's request.

Abraham Rabinowicz was a chubby man with a neatly trimmed grey beard. Bryce saw the extra wrinkles around his right eye from years of using a jeweler's loupe. He introduced himself and began to chat with Bryce as additional police arrived to take Leroy away for booking and medical treatment. Bryce and his new friend boarded the train and learned that each was headed for Doylestown. Rabinowicz was in Philadelphia to visit relatives and to purchase at wholesale jewelry for his shop in Doylestown. When Abraham learned that Bryce was a baseball player, their friendship blossomed as Abe confessed he had been a lifelong Founders fan.

"Why did you help me, Bryce? Most people wouldn't, you know."

"I just figured a family man like you could use some help."

Abraham gave Bryce a questioning look and Bryce said, "I saw your wedding ring."

Abraham heard the barest hint of melancholy in the words and made a decision.

"You must come to my home for a family dinner Bryce," he said. "I want to thank you for what you did. Will you do me and my family that honor?"

Bryce accepted and they agreed that he'd visit the following week. It was then that Martin Luther King was murdered, and unrest in the city made it particularly dangerous to travel in certain sections. Bryce continued to take the trains, but he avoided cars that were almost empty.

Chapter 33

When, for the first time, a state prison door slams closed behind a man there is a universal reaction. Leroy Carter was no different. As the heavy, clanging boom of the cell block door echoed down the concrete-walled passageway, he felt a deep chill run down his spine and his legs turned rubbery. The guard who escorted him toward his cell watched closely because he had a bet with the other guards on his block that Leroy would shit his pants on the way to his cell. The guard lost his bet, but only because Leroy bee-lined it to the metal commode in his cell before he said anything to his new cell mate. The guard laughed and slammed the cell's door closed.

His cellmate faced out toward the passageway as Leroy finished his business. The commode flushed, the cellmate waited a decent interval, and then turned toward the new arrival.

"A lot of new guys do that. What's your name, anyway?"

"Leroy Carter. How 'bout you?"

"Charlie Coe."

Chapter 34

They assigned Bryce to play with the AAA team because he'd missed spring practice and there was no room on the Founders' roster for him. During the off-season he'd stayed with his usual exercise program and so he didn't have to get in shape as some of the other players did each spring. The only thing he lacked was a book on the opposing pitchers, so he began to compile one, and he spoke with his coaches and teammates about their knowledge of the opposing pitchers. He practiced hard, asking the batting practice pitchers to place the ball low and away or low and inside, just within the strike zone. They got it there more times than not and Bryce practiced either fouling off those pitches or hitting them down the lines over the heads of the third and first basemen. The coach moved him from sixth in the batting order to fifth.

Maintaining a batting average above .300 in AAA ball is almost as difficult to do as in the major leagues. But Bryce did it as he developed the ability to hit a less than perfect pitch for a base hit. In mid-June when a regular outfielder for the Founders went down with an injury, Bryce was called up to join the team. He flew to Cincinnati. The coach chose to watch Bryce in practice and played another outfielder instead. The first day after they returned to Connie Mack Stadium, Bryce took his turn at batting practice and hit one over the scoreboard in right center field. That almost never was done and he got the attention of the coaches and players who saw it.

"Roberts, you do that in a game, maybe I'll buy you a steak dinner," said the coach. Bryce didn't do it in a game, at least not that season. But he did manage to keep his batting average above

.300, a factor that helped the team toward a respectable won-loss record at the All-Star break. He went home for the break to spend time with Eddie, who now was four years old.

⊙≈◎

The sunshine lured Bryce and Eddie out of the house to the side yard where they enjoyed a game of Frisbee. Eddie chased the dish into a shrub border and, moments later, began screaming in pain. Bryce rushed to his son and found him under attack from yellow jackets whose nest the boy had disturbed. Bryce brushed and swatted frantically at the stinging insects, picked up his son, and ran as fast as he could to the house. He pulled the boy's clothing off, killed several more of the yellow jackets that they had brought into the house and shoved Eddie under a cold shower. His parents ran a cold tub and brought ice to chill Eddie's stings. They used tweezers to pull out the stingers that were visible, but it didn't seem to help much and the child's breathing became labored.

"Dad, call an ambulance, we need to get him to a hospital!"

Harry went for the telephone and called the emergency number at the ambulance company. The ambulance was out at a traffic accident and unavailable. The standby vehicle was in the southern section of the county. Harry stood there and thought as coolly as if he were analyzing a business problem and then dialed again, this time to his daughter.

"Margaret, I don't have time to explain," said Harry. "Is that helicopter that was crop spraying still working the fields? . . . Good. How do I contact him?" He listened for a moment and then said, "Well, then you get him on your radio and tell him to land in the front yard of this house. Tell him it's an emergency and there's not much wind so he can come down away from the trees. Do it now while I hold on." He listened while Margaret contacted the pilot and repeated his instructions.

"Okay, Dad," said Margaret, "he's on the way. What's going on?"

"Eddie's been stung by a swarm of yellow jackets and he's going into anaphylactic shock. We have to get him to a hospital."

"Oh, no!" she cried. She was quiet for a moment and then said, "Have Ivan fly him to Children's Hospital in Philadelphia. He can land at the stadium nearby."

The helicopter, with its spray pipes furled, landed outside. Bryce wrapped his son in one of his own terry cloth bathrobes to hold as many of the ice packs as would fit. The pilot helped Bryce strap himself into the seat and then looked at Eddie as he was handed up to Bryce.

"Hold onto him, Mister, this is going to get bumpy."

Bryce felt as if he was riding a bucking bull as the chopper gained altitude and headed south. He held onto Eddie and prayed. The bumpiness evened out as they rose above 2000 feet altitude and the pilot handed Bryce a chart.

"See if you can locate the hospital and the field."

Bryce held the chart awkwardly while he still tried to cradle the whimpering Eddie. He found the curve of the Schuylkill River, and searched to the west of the curve. There! He folded the chart to manageable size and handed it back to the pilot and pointed. Ivan acknowledged the position and adjusted the throttle and rotor to get maximum speed out of the aircraft. Then the pilot got busy on the radio. Bryce held onto Eddie and watched the boy's breathing. He was semi-conscious and still weakly crying from the pain, but his breathing became labored as his airways constricted. *Oh, hurry, hurry,* cried Bryce to himself. *I can't lose him too.*

Harry had called ahead to the hospital and there was an ambulance and crew waiting for them as they landed at the field. The nurse had been advised of the problem and immediately injected Eddie with epinephrine as they loaded him into the gurney. Bryce prayed silently as they sped toward the emergency room. Fresh ice packs were applied when they arrived, and Eddie was hooked to equipment that monitored his heartbeat and respiration. Bryce watched as the electronic blips moved across the screen and held steady . . . steady . . . steady.

Oh, God, please don't take him from me, pleaded Bryce. *You know he's all I have; and I don't have the strength of your Abraham.*

Eddie's labored breathing began to ease and they gave him medication for the pain that would increase upon his reaching full consciousness. The doctor told Bryce they wanted to keep Eddie overnight and would transfer him to a regular floor unit. Bryce thanked the ER staff and followed his son to the ward where the boy would spend the night. The pain medication made Eddie drowsy and he fell into a restless semi-consciousness. Bryce left him to telephone his family with the news.

When he returned to the ward the worried father paced up and down the hallway, past the nurses' station, looking in on Eddie every few passes. The Charge Nurse suggested that he might want to sit in the room with Eddie. Bryce stopped his pacing and asked if they'd monitor his son while he went for a sandwich. The Charge Nurse on an adult ward would have been insulted by the comment, but years of working with distraught parents gave her understanding.

"Sure. There's a cafeteria downstairs. You can bring the food up here if you'd like." She turned to speak with another parent standing behind Bryce.

"Mrs. Davis, I was just telling Mr. Roberts that there's a cafeteria downstairs. If you're hungry you can get a sandwich there and bring it back here."

Bryce turned to see who the Charge Nurse was addressing and looked into the deepest blue eyes he'd ever seen. The elevator chimed and Bryce said, "I'm going to bring back a sandwich. May I get something for you, Mrs. Davis?"

"Oh, that's not necessary. I'll just ride along to see the selections they have. I can use the break anyway."

Bryce moved toward the elevator and held the door open for her. When the door closed they stood in silence as strangers do on elevators. Finally Bryce introduced himself as the doors opened and they followed signs to the cafeteria.

"Bryce," she repeated. "That's an unusual name."

"It's a family name."

"I'm Candace Davis."

"Do people call you Candy?"

"My older brother did when he wanted to tease me."

"What did you do about that?"

"An hour before he was to play in the league championship game, I hid his favorite baseball glove. I made him promise not to call me Candy ever again if he wanted his glove back."

"Did he keep his word?"

"Yes, but he found other ways to torment me."

They were quiet for a time as they found the cafeteria, selected their food and paid.

As they returned to the ward she told him, "My daughter is here for treatment of an inner ear infection. She got dizzy and fell and I thought I'd better bring her in and they found the infection. The doctor wants to keep her overnight to make sure she didn't suffer a concussion in the fall."

"My son, Eddie, was stung by a swarm of yellow jackets. He went into shock so I brought him here."

"Looks like some yellow jackets got you too."

"Yes."

They ate beside the beds of their children. They didn't see each other in the hospital again.

Bryce slept in a parents' section. The following morning he took Eddie home in the car his family sent. He couldn't help but remember the woman with the strikingly beautiful eyes. He wondered about her and then his thoughts turned elsewhere as they arrived home.

Chapter 35

When Candace Davis was eight years old she ran in tears to her mother, Alice. "Oh, mothuuurrr," she wailed, "Jimmy said I have purple eyes and he said it in front of all the other boys at the playground."

"Don't pay any attention to your brother teasing you, dear. Boys say things that they think are funny, but they don't mean to hurt your feelings when they say them."

"Mom, do you think I have purple eyes?"

"No, honey. Your eyes are a beautiful shade of deep blue. You're very fortunate to have such pretty eyes and I think they're just fine. Now go on outside and tell your brother to come in for a minute. I want to talk to him about his chores."

Mollified, the tallest girl in the third grade ran from the house to find her brother.

❧

By the time she was twelve Candace was taller than many of the boys in her class and had a reputation as a tomboy who could throw and hit a baseball as far as her brother and his Little League teammates. But, at that age, she was more interested in horses.

Her father, David Hawkins, a public defender attorney, could not afford to buy her a horse. But he and Alice sacrificed for riding lessons, and later, to part ownership of a hunter that his daughter rode in the Montgomery and Chester County areas of Pennsylvania. One of her proudest moments was when she won her first jumping competition.

Candace's best friend, Florence "Flo" Davis, was boy crazy and often tried to get Candace to double date.

"Flo, boys don't want to date me. They get embarrassed because I'm too tall for them."

"Candace, you're gorgeous, and besides, Tommy Mason will go out with me if I fix you up with his buddy, Danny Riker. He's only a little shorter than you."

Candace wore low heeled shoes and sometimes slouched in an effort to appear shorter. In the end, she accepted her stature, dated boys who weren't as tall as she was, played clarinet in the school band, and prepared for college by achieving excellent grades in math and physics.

What Candace did not accept was that she was becoming a beautiful young woman. Her deep blue eyes were perfectly at home in a face with high cheekbones, chiseled thin nose, and full lips set off by pale skin, all surrounded by curly black tresses. Others noticed and she was asked to model in local fashion shows. Candace finally agreed to participate after Flo practically dragged her to the first one.

"Flo, what if the dresses don't fit me? I can't do this!"

"Oh, Candace, be a sport and do it just this one time. Most of the women there won't even know you and some of the clothes are bound to fit."

Candace watched the more experienced models move and walk and became adept at mimicking their movements and the poses. The modeling gave her self-confidence and she continued to work fashion shows in department stores and at charity events after she entered college at The Massachusetts Institute of Technology on a Merit Scholarship.

At MIT she became hooked on the intricacies of physics and often spent time reading theoretical works in the library. She excelled in advanced seminars, much to the admiration of her professors. One of those academicians invited Candace to dinner and she accepted in the expectation of meeting other people through him. Hope turned to disillusionment when he tried to take her back to his apartment.

"I thought we were going to Professor Blaine's reception."

"Oh, Hugo's such a boor. All he wants to talk about is the new tectonic plate theory."

When her date tried to kiss and grope her she punched him with all her might and took a taxi back to her dormitory. The professor spent the next week lying to his colleagues about the origin of his black eye. Candace's professors winked conspiratorially at her when they passed in the hallways.

Near the end of her sophomore year Flo's cousin, Jake Davis, called to introduce himself. "Flo found out I'm at MIT and she said that I should call you."

They agreed to meet for coffee and by the end of that day he was hopelessly in love with her. It took Candace three more dates to likewise succumb to cupid's arrow.

He was six feet two inches tall with dark auburn hair, flashing brown eyes and a totally charming smile. Candace called Flo.

"Thank you, thank you. He's wonderful, and I love the fact that I can wear low heels when we go dancing."

"Their song" was Henry Mancini's "Moon River" and they held each other particularly close when they danced to it.

Jake could laugh at himself and he treated her with respect, two qualities that endeared him to Candace. He lived in an apartment off campus his senior year and Candace spent her evenings studying with Jake in the tiny third floor walk-up. It could have been half way to Mars for all it mattered to the happy couple who often finished study time with what Jake and she called "reaction research."

To meet his Air Force ROTC obligation Jake entered flight school after graduation. Candace went home to plan their wedding. "Yes, Dear, I'll keep it small. Just Flo for a maid of honor. We owe her that much." They married between his basic flight school and jet training. On weekends they danced at the Officer's Club when Jake could remove himself from the bookwork and training that intensified when he began to fly the F-4 Phantom.

"I'm preggers," she told him when he entered training in close air support and air-to-air fighter tactics. "You'd better become the best pilot in the Air Force because we," and she pointed at her belly, "want you back."

Six months later he was flying out of Saigon, Vietnam in support of the Army Special Forces, and on tactical bombing runs over North Vietnam.

Candace moved in with her parents and began working for her Master's Degree at Penn while she waited for her baby to be born and Jake to come home. She delivered their daughter on a rainy April morning at the Hospital of the University of

Pennsylvania when she unexpectedly went into labor two weeks earlier than her due date.

Jake's parents, Jennifer and Stanley, flew in from Boston when they received the news and helped Candace send word of his daughter's birth to the new father. It was rumored that he did aerobatics on the return from a mission after he heard the news, but nobody was able to confirm that, and his wingman wasn't talking.

Anne Leslie Davis was named after two of her great grandmothers. Her grandparents, David and Alice, had a nursery waiting when Candace came home from the hospital. And they all began praying for Jake's safe return. Candace listened to the popular tunes and often thought of Jake as Mel Carter belted out "Hold Me, Thrill me, Kiss Me."

"Ah, Jake Honey, I know you'll make it home safely," she often told herself.

Their prayers were answered when three months later Jake's squadron received orders to transfer stateside to MacDill Air Force Base in Florida. Candace traveled there and moved heaven and earth to find housing on base for their family. The bureaucratic wheels (and some of the enlisted men whom she charmed) moved forward and they were assigned a small house in married officer's country. By the time her husband arrived, she had the place looking like home with flowers planted in the tiny front yard and a small room done up for Anne. His return was joyous, celebrated with champagne and a bed that was well used in the days that followed.

"You've changed, Jake. You have an assured confidence about you that's replaced some of the cockiness you had before you went to Vietnam."

"Thanks, I think. Experience does that to a man. Now let's talk about my leave."

They spent three days visiting with each set of parents before heading to Niagara Falls and fishing in the Thousand Islands area. There were moments when they would be quietly fishing and in the next spontaneously embracing. They returned via Philadelphia to pick up Anne from her grandparents and then settled into the routine of life on an Air Force base. They made friends with their neighbors and often socialized with the pilots and wives in Jake's squadron.

They both looked forward to the day Jake would leave the Air Force for a civilian pilot's job.

Chapter 36

"**W**hat are you in for?" Leroy asked.

"Murder." Coe said it matter-of-factly, but he watched Leroy's eyes. In prison the inmates who had committed violent felonies were looked up to by the others. Leroy's eyes widened ever so slightly and Coe knew he had the initial advantage. He deliberately avoided asking Leroy the reason he was in prison, but Leroy's nervousness made him eager to talk.

"They rapped me with agg assault," said Leroy. "I went to knife this big honkey and he got lucky and kicked me when I wadn' lookin'."

"Yeah? Where'd it happen?"

"Philly. In a train station. Damn pigs came along at the wrong time."

"Funny, I don't remember reading anything about it in the newspaper."

"They didn't want nothin' in the papers. The honkey plays for the Founders and he said no newspapers."

"Oh? Who was that?"

"Dude said his name was Roberts."

"I know the guy."

"Yo' shittin' me."

"No way. I'm the one who killed his wife."

"What? Were yo' bangin' her?"

"No, but I wish I had been. I killed her because he pissed me off and I wanted to put a hurt on him."

"Yeah? What'd he do to you?"

"Tried to make me feel small, didn't show me respect."

"Yo shittin' me."

"No. Here, I'll show you the newspaper articles. Right here."

"Ah cain't read too good."

"That's okay. I'll read them to you."

Chapter 37

A week after Eddie was discharged from the hospital Bryce returned to personally thank the physician who had treated his son. He found Dr. Wilson reviewing charts at the nurses' station and waited patiently until he finished. The doctor remembered Bryce and inquired about Eddie. He suggested that they see their family physician to obtain medicine they could administer quickly if Eddie were to have another reaction.

"He probably won't," explained the doctor, "because this episode may help him build immunity toward the insect venom. And, likely, he won't get stung as many times if he does get it again."

They continued to chat and Dr. Wilson asked Bryce what he did for a living. Bryce told him.

"Come on. I want to take you on some rounds with me."

Bryce followed and entered rooms where very sick children were being treated and others where they were recovering from surgery. At every room Doctor Wilson introduced Bryce as the "newest Founder" and invited them to shake hands with Bryce. Some of the children were fans and others just enjoyed the extra attention.

Bryce discovered a new joy in their reaction to him.

"These are some of the milder cases," the doctor told him. "Wait until you meet kids on the other wards."

"I can't today. I have to get to practice. But I'll stop by again as I have time."

Bryce kept his word and as the weeks went by he'd stop in and read to some of the children, or play checkers with the ones who could work the board. He always lost. One afternoon when he was on the floor, the hospital's public relations director asked him to pose for photographs. Bryce politely declined, explaining that he didn't make his visits for publicity purposes, but because he enjoyed cheering up the kids. He threatened not to return if he received any publicity. Dr. Wilson heard of the exchange and stored it away for future use.

In August Dr. Wilson handed Bryce an invitation to the hospital's annual charity ball. Bryce checked his schedule and found he had a home day game that Saturday, so he accepted. He figured that he was bound to run into people he knew.

◦≋◦

Off-the-rack tuxedos weren't sized for men with Bryce's broad shoulders, deep chest, and narrow waist. His tailor had to use two different suits, one for his jacket size and one for the trousers. Bryce was satisfied with the results as he dressed for the evening. He reached for his patent leather, ankle-high lace-up boots that he last wore at his wedding. They still fit and he pulled them on and tied the laces with precision.

Marilyn, you should be here.

Stop it, Bryce! She's not. Relax and think about other things.

He stayed in his room at the Warwick Hotel reading a biography of Ty Cobb until he was sure that he wouldn't be one of the first arrivals at the charity ball. Then, with a light application of cologne, he was ready for the evening. He rode the elevator to the ballroom level and walked into the large room that was occupied by men in tuxedos that fairly matched those of each other and women in formal dresses who tried very hard not to dress alike. Bryce smiled at the thought and surveyed the room for people he knew. He spotted a group that included his longtime friend and broker, Dean Brooks, and men he remembered from a recent Bucks' reunion.

As he walked toward them Dean saw him and mentioned his approach to the group. Several of them turned toward Bryce, including a tall, blue-eyed woman, wearing an empire style royal blue dress. The woman's black hair was swept back with a cascade of long, loose curls, intermingled with a thin blue ribbon dropping from the crown of her head. Her neck was accented with a double-stringed pearl choker.

She watched him approach and thought to herself, *that man walks with the fluid grace of a panther.* Then Candace recognized Bryce as the man she had met at the hospital. She smiled in remembrance.

Bryce returned her smile. His composure was so shaken by the beautiful woman that it was all he could do to keep control and remember the names of the men in the group to greet them and their wives. He managed that without revealing his distraction and then turned to Candace to reintroduce himself.

"Good evening, Mrs. Davis. This certainly is a happier occasion than when we last met."

"Yes, it is, Mr. Roberts. How's your son?" *The man's dark eyes are so intense and alive.*

"Please, call me Bryce. And Eddie's fine. He recovered without further problems. And your daughter, Mrs. Davis?" *A man could drown in those blue eyes and those full lips are meant to be kissed. Man, get control of yourself. Her husband will show up any minute.*

"Anne is fine, too. And please call me Candace." *He's not the taciturn man I thought he was that day in the hospital.* She concluded that he probably hadn't been much for conversation due to the self-control he was exercising in order to endure the painful stings. *And I wonder why he isn't wearing a wedding ring.*

Dean recognized Bryce's interest in Candace and thought about what he could say to smooth the introduction. "Candace, you're standing in the presence of the newest Founders star. If you mention baseball, you'll make a friend for life."

Candace accepted the lead and said, "What position do you play, Bryce?"

"Left field, but only in baseball."

She laughed and Bryce thought, *Good, she has a quick wit. But cut and run while you can. She's married. That's a ring on her left hand.*

He turned to Dean and said, "Your glass is empty. Show me the bar and let's get you a refill and me started. Candace, you don't have a glass, may I bring you a drink?"

"Yes, please. Some white wine."

"Chablis? Chardonnay? Fume Blanc?" he asked with the appropriate French pronunciation and accent.

"Chablis, *s'il vous plait*," she responded, and then she turned to face the group. But her eyes followed the two men as they walked across the room.

Bryce tapped Dean on the bicep as they waited in line and said, "With those eyes and that smile Candace Davis could ask a man to walk across hot coals and he'd smile while he did it."

"Down, boy. She was widowed a couple of years ago and really took it hard. She only goes out in groups once in a while, which is why she's here tonight. So don't start anything. She probably won't respond. She told my wife that she intends to stay away from another relationship and devote her time to raising her daughter." Then Dean changed the subject.

"How have you been?"

Bryce knew Dean really was asking about his recovery from grief and he told his friend the truth.

"I still miss Marilyn, but I've built a new life and am doing okay. I'll play ball for a few more seasons and then settle down in business. Right now I just want to be able to set aside time to spend with my son. And I can do that when we have home games and in the off-season. When he starts school I'll have some decisions to make. So for now, things are as good as I can make them and the salary is not too shabby. And, by the way, thanks for all of your investment advice. Those assets are growing nicely."

"You're welcome. Are you dating anyone?"

"No one steady. I haven't made the time to start a relationship. Once in a while I'll take a woman to a concert or a movie, but that's about it. I've not trusted myself to get involved."

"Bryce, it's been over four years since Marilyn passed away. You two had something special, but do yourself a favor and get back in circulation. Look at what Candace's doing. She goes out in a group. Why don't you give that a try?"

Their drinks came and they returned to their friends. Bill Wagner earned Bryce's gratitude when he asked him to fill the last chair at their table.

"Thank you, I'd be delighted," replied Bryce.

Bill pointed out the table that they had reserved and then left with his wife for the dance floor as the band began to play.

Candace looked at the other couples and said, "Don't hang around just to keep me company. Go dance and enjoy yourselves." She made a shooing motion with her free hand.

Then she looked at Bryce and said, "I went to a Founders game in June when they were playing the Pirates. Were you playing then?" The rest of the group faded onto the dance floor and at that point Bryce was about to answer when he noticed that Candace was tapping her toe to the beat of the music. Her feet were encased in royal blue high heels with an open toe and straps that clung to her ankles.

Now those are sexy ankles, he thought.

"I'll talk baseball, but," and he bowed slightly in teasing formality, "may I have this dance first?"

She gave a small curtsey in return, put her hand on his outstretched arm, and said, "Only if you lead."

His chesty laughter rumbled to the surface and he led her to the floor, depositing their drinks on their table on the way. They danced, she adjusting to his style, and then Candace looked up at him and said, "You're a good dancer, Bryce. This is fun. My husband and I used to go dancing and it's one of the things I miss the most about his passing." *There, I said it, and he knows I still miss Jake.*

Then he surprised her. "My wife was killed in an automobile accident four years ago, and I still miss her, too. So I think I understand what you're going through."

"Oh, I didn't know that. My sympathies. How old was Eddie when it happened?"

"Four months."

She heard the gravel in his voice when he answered and put her arm more closely around his shoulder for the rest of the waltz.

He accepted her understanding of his pain. In their closeness he realized that she wasn't wearing any perfume and he surmised that it was something she would do when her grief abated.

The waltz ended and they returned to the table to reclaim their wine.

"So, Bryce, when did you come up from the minor leagues? Were you in the Pirates game that I saw that evening?"

"Yes, I got my first major league hit in that game. The coach put me in to pinch hit and I got lucky and hit one off the fence."

"Seventh inning, right?"

"Yes."

"I am honored, sir. I saw you get your first major league hit."
She raised her glass and toasted, "Here's to many more hits off that
wall."

"Thank you. I'll take as many as the opposing pitchers give
me." *My God, woman! That smile ought to be illegal. And there's
spunk plus intelligence behind those blue eyes.*

"You're being too modest. I think you want to crush that ball
every time you're up to bat." *That half smile is a killer.*

"We haven't talked about you. Do you work?" asked Bryce.
"It seems that more and more women do these days."

"I teach physics at Penn." Then she challenged him with a
look that said, come on, get it over with. Make your wise-guy
remark.

Bryce looked into her blue eyes in a flirtatious manner, but he
said, "Way to go. That's a tough subject to teach."

She was pleasantly disarmed. "Thanks. I do it because I love
my subject and I love to teach. It's just freshman physics, but it
suits me fine. It fits nicely with my laser research."

"Laser research? I'm in the presence of genius."

Bryce sensed that she was uncomfortable over the last remark
and he tried to steer the conversation into safer territory. "Besides
physics, what do you do for fun, Candace?"

She looked at him and concluded that there was no innuendo
in his question. "I've taken up riding again. I used to have a hunter
when I was in high school but the other half-owner bought my
share when I went to college. Now I just enjoy getting out with
friends and riding the countryside on a rented horse."

He didn't tell her that he rode. Instead he asked if she ever
took her daughter riding with her. Candace smiled at the thought.
"Yes, I put her in the saddle in front of me and she's learned to
hang on to the mane and I hold on to her. I put a belt around her
waist and fasten it to me as a safety measure."

They danced another waltz and this time she put her head
lightly against his shoulder. *This man could really get to me if I
allow that. Oh, Jake, I don't know if I'm ready for another man
yet.*

I could get used to this, thought Bryce.

*Slow down, man. Don't let yourself get infatuated with the
first beautiful woman you meet.* Then Bryce stopped himself.
Don't kid yourself. Candace with the blue eyes, I think I'm going

to help you over the final steps of grief that I understand so well. I just can't frighten you away with my efforts. But there will be more dancing after dinner and she fits so well in my arms.

The orchestra took a break and the master of ceremonies welcomed the guests and "friends of the hospital" as dinner was being served. Awards for volunteer service were presented and Bryce looked around for Dr. Wilson. He saw him several tables away, caught his eye, and shook his head in the negative. He saw Dr. Wilson move toward the podium and take the microphone.

"There are some here in this room tonight who give of their time and talents as volunteers who would prefer anonymity," he announced. "I will honor that wish, but I want to tell those people that their selfless giving is much appreciated. They come in, read to the children, play games with them and talk anything from dolls to sports to help the kids forget for a while that they are hurting. I hope someday to be able to identify these people because they certainly should be thanked in a more personal way. In the meantime let's hear it for those volunteers."

Candace noticed that Bryce was applauding but he was not one of the many people looking around to guess who had been recognized. *It's you he's talking about, I'll bet. Should I tell him my guess, or would that embarrass him? Some other time, then, when I know him better. Ah-hah! You've just admitted that you want to see him again.*

They talked and danced for much of the rest of the evening. Bryce persuaded her to give him her address and telephone number which he wrote on the back of a business card. She told him that she still would prefer to go out in a group.

"I understand," he said. "I've been there too. My 'work' usually is scheduled when other people are playing, and vice-versa, so arranging for group activities during the season is a challenge. But perhaps we can think of something. Or perhaps someone in your groups can call to include me." He handed her a business card with his home address and telephone numbers on it and then escorted her back to Dean's group. He took her hand, lightly kissed the back of it, smiled and said goodnight to her and his friends.

Candace watched him walk out of the room which now was largely empty, and her own emptiness returned. For the first time she hated the feeling, rather than accepting it.

Chapter 38

C oe sat in the prison library reading the society pages of a three-day-old Philadelphia newspaper. He liked to imagine himself attending events and rubbing shoulders with the people featured.

"Whoa, what's this?" Coe pushed his thick-lens glasses up his nose and focused on a photograph of four people at a hospital charity ball. "Yes! It's him. And check out the woman with Brycey Baby. Quite a looker. Now isn't that interesting.

"I'm going to get to know her someday."

Coe surreptitiously tore the photo out of the paper. He couldn't wait to show it to Leroy.

Chapter 39

Bryce ended his first major league season with seven home runs and his batting average at a respectable .274. The team did not make post-season play and so he packed his gear and left the clubhouse vowing to do better next year.

He and Harry took Eddie fishing for late season trout and they snapped picture after picture of the boy as he "fished." The excitement peaked when Eddie actually caught a ten- inch rainbow trout in the well-stocked stream. Harry showed Eddie how to unhook the trout and handed it to the boy who promptly released the wriggling fish back to the stream.

"Let's catch more rainbows, Pop-pop" was all that the boy said for the next five minutes. Bryce and Harry tried to convince him to stand still or move slowly near the water's edge, but Eddie was too excited to pay attention.

"This kid is really going to have fun in Maine next year," said Bryce. "Getting all of the family together and going to Maine and fishing are some of the things I've missed the most as a result of playing baseball. And . . . that's it! A group activity."

"Huh?" said Harry. "I think you've lost me on that one."

While Eddie continued to fish, Bryce explained. "Dad, remember the time Eddie got stung and we rushed him to Children's Hospital? Well, I met a woman there whose daughter was ill. Her name's Candace Davis. She has a very pleasant way about her. We chatted briefly when we went to the cafeteria for sandwiches, but I never followed up because I thought she was married. Then I met her again at that charity ball for the hospital and Dean told me she'd been widowed about two years ago. She took her husband's death as hard as I took Marilyn's and she's just now getting back into a social life. We talked quite a bit and I asked her to go out to dinner with me and she declined. She just wants to go slowly and socialize in groups for a while. I couldn't think of anything to do during the baseball season. I've been trying to think of a group activity for her to attend with some of our mutual friends. A day spent deep sea fishing is the perfect answer and sea bass will be running soon," he finished.

Harry just looked at his son for long moments. "You're really interested in this woman, aren't you?"

Bryce nodded.

"What is it about her that attracts you?"

"She's witty and intelligent and I found I can talk easily with her. We share the fact that we lost our spouses and I think that leads to a special understanding. Besides, she loves to dance and likes sports. And she has the most incredible blue eyes I've ever seen."

"If she wants to go fishing, I can give you the name of a good captain my friends and I use. He has his boat in Great Egg Harbor Bay and that baby moves like the hammers of hell out to the fishing areas. How many people do you want to invite?"

"Maybe four other couples."

"He can do ten. I'll give you his name and number when we get back to the house. Call him for open dates first. He's in demand."

☙❦❧

Alice Hawkins knocked on her daughter's bedroom door jam and informed her, "Candace, there's a man with a very deep voice on the phone asking for you. He says his name is Bryce Roberts. Do you want to talk with him?"

Candace looked up from correcting a pop quiz and gazed heavenward from her desk chair. She was out of her room and moving down the hallway by the time she said, "Yes, mother, I'd like to talk with him." She reached the phone stand and subconsciously combed her hair with her fingers. She took a deep breath and picked up the receiver.

"Hello, Bryce, how have you been?"

"I'm fine, Candace, and you?" *It's so good to hear that mellow, liquid voice of yours.*

"I'm well, thanks. How did your season go?" *I read the Daily News' sports pages every day to follow what you were up to, and I even have some of your stats memorized, but I'm not going to tell that to anyone.*

"It went well for my first year up. I just want to improve my ability to hit major league pitching. Now, let me change the subject. Candace, are you still interested in going out in a group?"

"Yes, Bryce. What do you have in mind?" *Oh, please say dancing. I want to talk with you more, get to know you better.*

"Deep sea fishing off the Jersey coast. Have you ever done that?" *Please don't tell me you get seasick.*

"No, but that sounds like fun. When would we go?" *Hey, it's a group date, with him there, so don't be picky.*

"Saturday two weekends from now. The boat is available then and Dean and his wife are already signed up. I'm going to ask another couple. Can you get some people lined up?"

"Sure, Bryce. What's this going to cost? We always go Dutch Treat on these get togethers."

"Probably in the neighborhood of forty dollars each. Is that okay? Everything is included. Boat, captain, assistant, rods, bait, a good lunch and a little wine thrown in for good measure." *And I'll pay the extra cost that you'll never know about.*

"That's reasonable. I still have your card. Let me call you back to let you know if it's a go." *I shall kill Flo if she and her husband say no, which will leave only one more couple for me to get.*

"Candace, I'm looking forward to this. It ought to be fun. I'll wait for your call. Goodnight."

"Goodnight, Bryce."

Candace walked down the hall to her mother's sewing room. "Mom, have you ever been deep sea fishing?"

"No, dear, but I believe your father went years ago. Why don't you talk to him? Who is that Roberts man, anyway?"

"He plays left field for the Founders."

"You're going deep sea fishing with a professional athlete?"

"I am if you'll baby sit Anne two Saturdays from now."

"Of course we will, Dear."

⌒≋⌒

"Deep sea fishing?" echoed Flo over the phone. "Isn't that when you get up before the crack of dawn and then go out in a boat, get seasick and sunburned, and don't catch any fish? I don't know. How did you get 'hooked' into that?"

Candace smiled and then spoke in the tone of voice that Flo recognized would never take no for an answer. "Mrs. White, remember that man, Bryce Roberts, who I mentioned? He's asked me to join a group that's going, and to bring along some friends."

"Honey, you did more than 'mention' him. Okay, we'll go. Bill likes deep sea fishing, so he won't be any problem to convince. Who else is going?"

"Bryce said Dean Brooks and his wife are in, but I don't know the other couple he's asked. And I have to find one more couple. People who are good sports. I'll have to think about that."

"Candace?"

"Yes?"

"I'm glad you're interested in someone."

Candace began to protest, but Flo just laughed, told her to call with the details, and hung up.

◦≋◦

"Bryce, I thought sailing the deep blue was your bag," said Peter Chase. "What's going on?"

Bryce shifted uneasily in his chair and said, "I'm getting a group together to go out Saturday next and I thought you and Marie might enjoy some time away from the golf course."

"Bullshit. You've met a woman who likes deep sea fishing, haven't you?"

"How'd you figure that out?"

"Oh, come on, Bryce. Women usually don't go deep sea fishing in a group and you've just invited my wife. You must really be interested in this lady. Tell me more about her."

"I don't know if she likes deep sea fishing or not . . ." and he explained much to his long- time friend who now worked as a reporter for a Philadelphia newspaper.

Peter agreed to talk Marie into the trip and offered to drive his station wagon. "Get Dean to drive his new Buick station wagon, too," he suggested. "He keeps bragging about how smooth the ride is."

Chapter 40

They met at Dean's home when the moon was still bright in the western sky. Flo and her husband, John, rode with Peter and Marie, and Bryce and Candace rode with Dean. Candace invited Young Kim and his wife, Sue, to join the group. Sue possessed a quick wit that Candace loved and Young taught math at Penn. He and Bryce found common ground when Young mentioned that he'd served in Vietnam with the Army Rangers.

The two men began to compare their training experiences, each topping the other's tales.

Sue and Candace listened in fascination to the men open up about things they normally didn't discuss in the presence of women. Dean's wife slept in the front seat.

This man has more to him than baseball, Candace thought. If half of what he says is true, he's mentally tough as well as charming. And I didn't know that Young Kim served in the military.

When Kim got onto the subject of survival school and how they learned to eat bugs, Sue had enough.

"If I hear that story one more time, particularly before we stop for breakfast, I'm going to throw up in your lap, Mr. Kim."

"The big tropical beetles were the tastiest," responded her husband. Everyone was still smiling as Dean pulled into a diner along the Black Horse Pike.

⟨✺⟩

The thunder of the big sport-fisherman's Caterpillar Diesels' exhaust made the group stop trying to shout above the noise. They relaxed and enjoyed the motion of the sleek boat as it cut through the water at high throttle. The morning had turned glorious with the sunrise.

"Light winds and an Indian summer day," predicted Captain Watts. He was a black man in his early fifties who had built his business with hard work and superb customer service. Claude, his son, who was a sophomore at Rutgers, and home for the weekend, served as the deckhand. The boat was immaculate and the gear well maintained. Watts invited each of the couples, one at a time, to the bridge where he explained how he'd maneuver the boat once they got their lines over the side, and how, when someone next to you hooked a fish, to give that person some room.

"Most of all, don't get your lines tangled. Take turns so we only have two or three lines over the side at a time. Someone can help Claude and me spot for fish. You'll see the water begin to roil as the small fish are pushed to the surface by the big ones feeding underneath. I can put one of you in the chair if you hook something big."

"What's big?" asked Candace.

"A big sea bass, or maybe a tuna. Sea bass out here weigh five to fifteen pounds, but they can get a lot bigger. Tuna are deeper down. If you hook one of them you'll think your line is caught on a rock. Then we definitely put you in the chair."

Flo was the first to catch a fish, a nice sized sea bass. "Do I keep this?" she asked Claude.

"You bet, that's a good eating fish. I have a couple of recipes you can choose from. Simple broiling all the way up to some terrific sauces." He took the fish and put it in one of the huge ice-filled coolers. "I put a green tag through the dorsal fin. That's your color, ma'am."

In the afternoon Candace, whose line Claude had baited for tuna, hooked one. Bryce held the rod, tip up, line running out even with the drag set, until Candace was strapped into the fighting chair and then he helped her place the rod into the holder. Face intense with concentration, Candace began to fight the fish as Claude coached her. The others pulled in their lines.

"Could be a while before we land that one," said Claude. "Mrs. Davis, if you get tired, let us know, and I'll put Bryce in the chair."

"No way," replied Candace. "This is my fish." The rest of them opened beers and watched as Candace worked the rod and

Captain Watts skillfully maneuvered the boat to keep its stern toward the fish.

Twenty minutes later Candace, exhausted but proud, saw the tuna pulled on board by Claude. He 'bonked' it and it went into a huge cooler with bluefish they had caught.

"Ma'am. Put your hands on your hips and try to make big circles with your elbows," Claude told her. "It'll help your muscles stop aching."

Candace did as he suggested and then sat down on a cooler with her back against the cabin bulkhead, arms and shoulders feeling as if they were dead but on fire. Bryce spoke with Claude as the others put their lines out again, and Claude disappeared into the cabin. He emerged with a tube of liniment and handed it to Bryce.

Bryce looked at Candace and said with a smile, "Hold your arms out one at a time." She held an arm out and he began to massage some of the ointment into her forearms, wrists, and hands.

My arms look like toothpicks in his hands, yet he's surprisingly gentle, she thought.

Bryce finished the second arm and hand and congratulated her on the fight she had given her fish.

"You're stronger than you look," he finished.

"I've been working out with some of the exercise equipment Dad has in the basement when I can't get outside. He told me about how sore he got after fishing like that, so I spent some extra time exercising my arms and shoulders. But I had no idea a fish could put up that kind of a fight."

"Wait till you have to clean it," Bryce teased.

"Oh, no. I'm having that beautiful creature stuffed."

"Do you mean mounted by a taxidermist?"

"Yes. I'm going to hang it on my office wall as an example of how a thin thread, properly leveraged, can work wonders."

"Drat! Here I was already tasting grilled tuna steak."

"You may have your wish," said Sue, "it looks like Young has just hooked one and I'm not going to allow a big stuffed fish on our walls."

When Young landed his tuna, Captain Watts suggested they head in. He and Claude cleaned and scaled the catch except for Candace's tuna. Bryce and Sue helped them while Dean steered the course Watts had given him. As they got closer to shore gulls began to follow the boat to feed off the waste they disposed of in the sea. Flo actually picked up fish guts to toss up in the air to the circling birds.

Watts took the helm as they neared the inlet and, later, backed the sleek boat into its slip with practiced skill. He promised to deliver Candace's tuna to a good taxidermist and pointed them to a ramshackle restaurant where all of the locals ate.

Bryce and Candace rode back with Marie, a teetotaler, driving Peter's car. Bryce sat behind Marie's pulled-up seat, grateful for the extra leg room. They talked for a while but the long day began to affect Peter, who had wine with dinner, and Candace, whose excitement finally caught up with her. Marie watched in the rear view mirror as Candace's head sank onto Bryce's shoulder and saw him smile contentedly as Candace drifted off to sleep.

Chapter 41

C andace's shoulders ached when she awakened. Bryce obligingly massaged them while she groaned in pleasure and pain. Peter was awakened by the noise and jokingly inquired if it was okay to look into the back seat. Bryce kept massaging and Candace kept her eyes closed as she felt her muscles begin to relax. *His hands feel so good. It's been so long since I've felt a man's hands on me like that. Oh, but I'm not ready for this.*

"Bryce, I'm okay, now," she said. "That really felt good. Thanks."

"My pleasure, ma'am." *I've got to stop thinking about embracing her. I'm going to do something stupid and I'll ruin the whole day.*

Bryce's trip home passed quickly because he mentally was proposing and then rejecting more group outings. Candace once again had refused his invitation to dinner.

"What do you mean, you turned him down on a dinner invitation?" asked Flo as she looked incredulously over the seat back at Candace. "That man is the most gorgeous hunk I've seen in years!" She turned to John and said, "Sorry, Honey."

"I'm scared, Flo. He's a delightful man, but I just don't know if I want to go out with him yet. I'm finally starting to get over Jake's death but I'm still hesitant."

"One dinner won't hurt," chimed in John. "He seems like a decent man who wouldn't take advantage of a vulnerable woman."

"John's right, Candace. You should call Bryce and tell him you've changed your mind. It's the adult thing to do."

⊙≋◎

Several weeks passed and the telephone in Candace's home did not ring for her. And then late one afternoon it did. But it wasn't Bryce. The taxidermist called to say her fish was ready and he told her the cost. Candace was surprised at the price and the craftsman explained that it was a big item and Watts had put a rush on the order. She inquired about the size of the piece and was told the length and width of the mounting board and the thickness of the total work. She thanked the man after obtaining directions to his shop and his hours. She used a tape measure to check the dimensions of the trunk of her compact car and had her doubts whether the mounting board would fit.

"I should borrow a pickup truck with a cap top just to be on the safe side," she thought. "Now who do I know with a pickup?" She went through a mental check list of friends and acquaintances and it was of no help. She telephoned Flo.

"Call Bryce."

"Flo, he drives a red sedan. I saw it at Dean's house."

"He told me his father operates a sawmill when we got to talking about family. I bet he could get a pickup and you could kill two birds with one stone by having him drive you down there to pick up the fish. After all, dahling," she said in a theatrical tone, "you'll need help lugging that fish and you have no experience driving a pickup, do you?"

"I'll think about it."

❦

Bryce returned home with Eddie after a visit with Marilyn's parents. "Stella's fine but Noah's back is still bothering him. He says he is going to cut back on his weightlifting. They send their love . . . Mom, what are you smiling about?"

"There was a call for you while you were out. A woman named Candace Davis wanted to speak with you. She has a nice voice, I think." She handed him a slip of paper with a number in a Philadelphia exchange.

He telephoned and heard her voice answer very businesslike. "Candace Davis speaking."

"Bryce Roberts speaking. My secretary said you called."

"Your mother is not going to like that, you fraud."

"Actually, that's been a part of her job for a long time. Wait until your daughter is old enough to have friends calling. We used to have a chalkboard in the kitchen for messages. Now, what can I do for you?"

"Remember that tuna I had mounted? Well, the taxidermist called and said it was ready. But from the size he described, I think I should go collect it in a pickup truck. Flo thought you might know where to borrow a pickup. It should have a camper top, I suppose."

"Sure, I can borrow my sister's pickup. She and her husband are away on vacation. So the truck's available. And I'll be happy to drive you. Shall I meet you at your office or at home?"

"Bryce, thank you. Can we go tomorrow morning? My only class ends at 10:00."

"My day is yours. Let me get a pencil and paper and I'll take down the directions."

She gave him the directions in a precise manner and they agreed on a spot on campus where she would be waiting for him.

"It's a blue truck with Eagle Rock Farms written on the doors," he told her.

"Okay, see you tomorrow and, again, thanks." *What a nice man. He probably has other things to do and I've interfered with his schedule. But it'll be good to see him again.*

◦◦◦

"Mom," asked Bryce, "will you please drive me over to Margaret's house? I need to borrow their pickup." On the way he told Rosalie about Candace and her need.

Rosalie said, "Your father mentioned that you were interested in a blue-eyed widow. Is this the same one?"

"Yes."

"Is she someone special?"

"I think so, but I want to get to know her a lot better."

When he returned with the truck he spent the next hour cleaning the interior and washing the dusty vehicle. It still looked like a working man's truck.

"Kind of gives it character," he said. Then the old Dodge in which he and Marilyn traveled over the county came to mind, and with it, memories of the two of them. He squeezed hard on the sponge.

There will be days when I think about her and I'll just enjoy the thoughts rather than getting all maudlin about it. It's the only way I can live again.

Chapter 42

"What I really need to make my collection complete," Coe told Leroy, "is a photo of Marilyn Roberts' gravestone. Since you get out before I do, could you visit her grave and take a picture of it? I'd be willing to pay you good for it."

"Man, I doan' even know where the grave is at. How in hell would I take a pitcher?"

"I can give you directions and I'd really make it worth your while."

"How you goin' to do that, sccin' as how you is locked up?"

"I can. Just trust me on this Leroy. Just trust me."

Chapter 43

B ryce eased the pickup to the curb and watched the tall
woman in a tan car coat, sky blue sweater and grey bell
bottom slacks walk tentatively toward the vehicle until she
recognized him. He leaned across the seat and opened the door
for her and she climbed in, cheeks red from the brisk autumn day.
"You're right on time. I was standing there only a few minutes."

"Being prompt is one of the few things I insist upon. I savor
every heartbeat of life and when someone keeps me waiting I think
of it as a waste of my heartbeats. So I don't do that to other
people."

"Wow! Aren't we getting heavy this morning?" They pulled
away from the curb and he drove toward the Schuylkill
Expressway. "But I suppose it's good to live your life like that. It
keeps you focused on where you're headed, doesn't it?"

"Yes. Now where's this taxidermist's shop?"

"It's in Longport, just north of Ocean City. I have directions
once we cross the bridge into town."

"There's a map in the glove box. See if you can figure the
best way to get there, please."

She studied the map for a few minutes and then told him the
route he should travel.

"Okay, help me keep an eye out for the turns. Do you like to
travel?"

"Sure, I love to see new places. Last year during summer
break I went down the Grand Canyon in a raft. Everybody had a
ball and it's absolutely wild with no modern conveniences. By the
time we came out of it everyone experienced culture shock when
we got to our first town."

"Did you go with a group from around here?"

"No, I just signed up for a raft of under thirty year-olds and made friends."

"I bet you didn't have any trouble doing that," said Bryce.

"It was okay until one of the guys made advances and I had to explain that I wasn't available. When he heard the reason, he was decent about it."

"After Marilyn's death, when I first started to go out socially, I did the same thing you're doing. Just groups. I finally told our pastor to quietly spread the word to a couple of matrons who kept trying to fix me up with the young ladies. It worked for a while. Then they started with the dinner party invitations and there was always some unattached woman at the party. I just wasn't interested so I started to decline the invitations."

"Do you go now?"

"Sometimes. But I prefer dinner parties with an eclectic group of guests who can get some fun conversation going."

"Bryce, you're not at all like what I imagined a professional baseball player to be . . . You have a turn coming up ahead. You want to get in the right lane." He did, and she continued. "You don't chew tobacco and you prefer wine over beer and you're . . . well . . ."

". . . Suave, debonair, erudite, and I don't have a pot belly."

"Yes, them too," she smiled. "But there's more. Look at me . . ." He turned and saw pure devilment in her face. "You look terrific in a tux."

Bryce's deep-chested chuckle rumbled to life.

"Well, turn-about is fair play. You're not at all what I imagined a woman college physics professor—"

"Instructor."

"—instructor to look like. I'd figure at least two hundred pounds with a slide rule hanging from her belt and thick glasses . . . and . . ."

"A hairy upper lip."

He laughed again and asked, "Where did you get your undergraduate degree?"

"At MIT. That's where I met Jake, my husband."

"So he was brainy too." Then he deliberately changed the subject. "How did he die, Candace?"

"Do you really want me to talk about that?"

"I want to hear it all if you'll share it with me. We have time."
This man will understand. He's been there.

"It happened on a windy November morning. Two of my neighbors and I were unpacking groceries we'd bought at the PX, when an official car stopped in front of my home. Jake's squadron commander, Tommy Wells, his wife, and the base Protestant Chaplain got out of the car. The three of us wives froze in fear because when the chaplain is there you know something awful has happened. I stood there, hardly breathing, waiting to see who Tommy would approach. He looked at me the whole time he was walking toward us. I remember my hand going to my throat and thinking, 'Oh, God, please, no, please no. Let it be someone else.' But it wasn't. He led me inside the house and put both of his hands on my shoulders. Then he said, 'Candace, I don't know how to say this, but Jake has had an accident. He wasn't able to bail out . . . he didn't make it . . . he's gone.'

"I don't remember fainting, but they tell me I did."

She turned toward Bryce and asked, "Do you really want to hear the rest of this?"

"Yes. If you want to talk about it."

"I remember coming to on the couch . . ."

⊙≋◯

"He was here this morning," she argued angrily. "I saw him right there at that table when he ate breakfast." Then, pounding on the couch arm in time with her words, and shaking her head back and forth, she cried, "Don't tell me he's gone!"

Tommy was silent.

Candace's expression changed to desperation. "Tommy," she pleaded, "he's one of the best pilots in the squadron. You know that. He can't be gone."

Tommy Wells looked her in the eyes and sadly but firmly shook his head denying her plea.

The chaplain told her, "He was in a mid-air collision with a civilian small plane that was just above a cloud that Jake was going up through. Neither pilot made it, Candace . . ."

She kept thinking, this is all a bad dream and I'll wake up and everything will be all right.

LuAnn Wells looked at the other people in the small living room and asked, "Could the rest of you step outside for a while? Leave us alone for a few minutes and then I'll come get you." The others went outside where more of the neighbors had gathered as the news spread.

"Candace, pinch yourself," said LuAnn.

Candace tentatively did as she was told.

"Harder," ordered LuAnn. Candace gave her own thigh a mighty pinch and felt the pain. Her face bore a terrible anguish as she began to cry. LuAnn held her for a long time as the sobs wracked her.

Eight days later in Wellesley, Massachusetts the tall widow felt as if she'd physically shrunk as she sat by the graveside in a fog of despair. The muzzle blast of the honor guard's rifles performing the three-volley salute made her jump at the first volley and then she sat tensely as the remaining two volleys followed. The bugler played taps, bringing tears to her eyes for what seemed the thousandth time. The flag that draped the casket was folded by the military pallbearers and presented to her. More solemn words were said, the casket was lowered into the grave, and the mourners then slowly retreated out of the wind to their cars.

Flo rode with Candace and her parents to the Davis' home where friends and relatives came to pay their respects. Candace sat quietly through it, not showing the impatience that she felt. After the last of the guests left she asked Flo for a favor.

"Flo, will you drive me into Cambridge? I want to get out and walk some of the campus and then we can come back here. I just want to talk to Jake and I'd like to do it at MIT, where we met."

Flo said, "All right. If it's going to help you say good-bye, I'll do it. Wear something warm, Candace. It's getting colder."

They found a parking spot along Ames Street and Candace got out and walked through the campus. Flo followed at a discreet distance and finally saw her sit on a bench that faced the Charles River. Flo walked away along Memorial Drive and left her friend to her thoughts.

As Candace spoke into the late afternoon cold, the condensate from her warm breath left her mouth in little puffs.

"Jake, I don't understand why God did this to us, but He did. And we can't do anything about it now. I don't yet know how I'm going to go through life without you. I'm so confused and my life is in chaos. But, I'll find a way for Anne and me to live and someday we can be happy again. God, I hope so, because right now this pain is almost unbearable and I just want it to stop. Jake, help me get through this. You always were so confident about everything. Now I have to reach in and pull up some of that for myself, when all I really want to do is curl up in a little ball and cry.

"Why did you have to go fly your silly planes, anyway? You knew you could die doing it. Damn! Sometimes I even get mad at you for what happened! I'm going to live with my parents for a while, and Jenny and Stan are going to come down to visit with Anne every chance they get. When Anne gets older she can come and visit them in Wellesley in the summer. She will never know you, but at least she'll know her grandparents. Oh, Jake, I miss you so."

The little puffs of condensate stopped because she was spent, empty. Flo saw her sitting quietly without making the gestures she had earlier observed, and she returned to her friend.

Candace heard her approaching and looked up as if Flo was a long distance away.

"You can take me back now," she said.

As they pulled away from the curb The Righteous Brothers were singing "You've Lost That Lovin' Feeling" over the car radio. Candace snapped the radio switch off and the drive back finished in silence.

Chapter 44

Bryce loosened his seat belt, reached into his back pocket and handed Candace a clean handkerchief to wipe away her tears.

"I'm sorry to carry on like I have," she said. "I shouldn't burden a new friend with this."

"Don't worry about it. I understand. I've been through the same thing."

He was silent for several miles.

Then he said, "I didn't have any warning either. A crazy drunk driver named Coe deliberately hit Marilyn's car head-on. The S.O.B. walked away from the crash."

"Deliberately? Why?"

"He's a mental case. He did it to wound me and make himself feel like a big shot."

Man, do you realize how your voice has turned so ugly? "That's awful. How did it make you feel?"

"I'm still angry with the guy. If I begin to think of him, which isn't that often nowadays, I pretend a baseball pitched to me is his head. I've hit a lot of line drives that way."

"How fitting. That's perfect," she said, and she meant it. "I just figured Jake and the other guy both went to heaven but not before Jake beat the daylights out of him on the way there. But I like your idea better." She was quiet for a long moment as she again studied the map.

Then Candace asked, "How did you and Marilyn meet?"

"We were high school sweethearts. We drifted apart when I went to Dartmouth. I didn't realize how much I still loved her until we saw each other over Christmas break in our junior year. We were inseparable after that."

"Dartmouth? Did you have Marilyn for your Winter Carnival date?"

"Yes. She had a ball. And so did I."

"What do you do now when you think of her?" she asked, in a quiet voice.

"I still miss her but it's not the same god-awful aching feeling. Now, when I think of her I just kind of smile to myself in pleasant remembrance. What do you do when you think of Jake?"

"Like I told you, I used to talk to him. But not much anymore. Now I just figure he knows what I'm up to and he's there."

Bryce saw a diner up ahead and pulled in so they could stretch and get a cup of coffee. When they returned to the pickup she looked at Bryce with misty eyes and said, "Thanks for drawing me out. It's better to talk than keep it inside. You're a good man Bryce Roberts."

"Likewise, Candace Davis." He wanted to lean over and kiss her then but she obviously was thinking of Jake, so he started the motor and they continued on their journey of discovery.

"Do you visit Marilyn's grave?"

"I didn't go for a long time after she died, but now I visit several times a year. It's still depressing."

"When the school year ended after Jake's death, I took Anne back to Wellesley to visit Jenny and Stan, Jake's parents. Jenny borrowed a stroller and the three of us took Anne on walks in a nearby park. Finally, Stan asked if I wanted to visit Jake's grave. He took me because I was unsure of the way and I didn't want to drive home afterward.

"I still remember straightening the flag holder beside Jake's marker. Stan and Anne waited for me on a nearby bench as I whispered to Jake. I told him what we'd been doing and how Anne had grown and how I missed him.

"Bryce, that 'conversation' was awful. I found myself telling a dead man to cheer up because I wasn't crying all the time; and that I'd even found myself laughing at a comedy on television. When I think now about the incongruity of it . . .

"Anyway, we visited for another day and then flew home. Anne slept in the seat beside me and I spent most of the time looking out of the window of the airliner. When the plane began its descent toward Philadelphia and banked over the Delaware River for the runway, I finally understood the fascination and love that Jake held for flying and I wasn't angry with him anymore."

Bryce slowed for a stop light and turned to her. "Good. Getting rid of the anger is part of the healing. So, tell me about your teaching. What made you decide upon that?"

"I didn't want to work in private industry after I earned my Master's Degree so I spoke with the department head and was hired to teach freshman physics, provided I'd pursue my doctorate.

"I was a little unsure of how it would go on the first day of class. I'd prepared so hard. There were eighteen men and two women. The second day of class ten more men signed up. I decided right then that I'd be tough and demanding so those guys would get serious or drop out."

"I'll bet most of them stayed." Bryce's half smile appeared and she felt herself return it.

⊙≪⊙

She was a serious lecturer but enjoyed the demonstrations she and the students performed to study the science's fundamental principles. The male students redoubled their efforts when they realized that she really expected them to learn the subject. She taught both semesters that year and came to love the expressions that appeared on students' faces when they understood the theories she presented. She began to think about her doctoral dissertation and was undecided until the department head suggested she obtain clearance from the Department of Defense to work on a laser project being conducted on the closed-off top floor of the building.

As the year 1968 arrived, Candace decided to begin socializing with groups of people she knew from school and from her own circle of friends in her community. It was difficult at first but she made the effort and found herself beginning to enjoy the activities. She joined a group that went out dancing once a month and learned some of the classic ballroom dances that the group favored, as well as "the fish" and "the frug." She didn't care that most of her partners were not as tall as Jake.

She and her teaching colleagues were outraged and saddened when Martin Luther King was shot in cold blood that April. They attended a memorial service for him at a church near their physics lab as the nation grieved and cities again exploded in riots.

The faculty group went to a Founders game in June. Before the game began the fans observed a moment of silence over the assassination of Bobby Kennedy. Again, the nation gnashed its teeth in frustration over the violence that seemed to be settling upon it as it endured the Vietnam War and the angry protests that seemed never to end.

Nevertheless, there was something about the excitement of the Founders fans that infected Candace. Amid the smell of peanuts and beer and the glare of the nightlights she welcomed the diversion from her grief and found herself cheering with the rest of the fans when the Founders tied the game in the bottom of the seventh inning.

"Shades of my brother in Little League," she said, and whistled loudly through her teeth in a most unladylike fashion. She was oblivious to the fact that her behavior made a charming foil to the feminine grace that was her usual style.

There was a runner on second with the pitcher due up next when the public address announcer told the crowd, "Now batting as a pinch hitter, Number 51, Bryce Roberts."

"He's a new guy," explained the thermodynamics specialist. "He just got called up from the minor leagues."

Along with the rest of the crowd she whistled and cheered the batter.

◦═◦

"All I remember, Bryce, was this rookie hit a long fly ball off the right field fence and wound up at second base. The runner on second scored easily and the Founders went on to win the game."

Candace reached across the pickup's seat and touched Bryce's arm.

"Later that summer at Children's Hospital I didn't associate the man I met with the pinch hitter in that game. What I remember most about you at the hospital was how stoic you were over your own stings when you were so concerned about Eddie.

"I looked for you the next day but you were gone. Who would've dreamed then we'd now be on our way to pick up a stuffed tuna?"

Chapter 45

The taxidermist proudly showed Candace his handiwork and her tuna. "Captain Watts said this guy weighed sixty-four pounds. Not big for a tuna, but he makes a nice trophy," he said.

"He felt like he weighed a ton when I finally landed him," said Candace. "He's going to hang in my office at school and be my conversation starter for years to come." She wrote a check in payment and parted with it wistfully.

Bryce saw the expression and made a mental note to probe that at the right time. He felt the finish of the wood mounting and admired the smoothness. He turned the display to check the top for hook eyes and found two large ones. Then he helped carry the mounting out to the truck and loaded it. He carefully protected the fins and then wrapped the whole mounting in blankets he brought along for the purpose. Then he tied it down.

"Bryce, thanks so much for your help. I wouldn't have been able to wrestle that thing into my car and secure it to keep from bouncing around."

"I never did get any tuna steak out of the deal," he teased. Then he asked the taxidermist if Cutty's was open and the man told him the restaurant stayed open year round. They thanked him again and drove across the narrow island toward the ocean.

"Bryce, how do you know about this place?" asked Candace as they pulled into the parking lot.

"I telephoned Captain Watts and asked him where he took your fish and where a decent restaurant is in the town."

"Do you think ahead like that all the time?" *What a thoughtful thing to do.*

"Only when it comes to food."

Then something clicked in Candace's quick-witted mind. "You knew all of the time where we were going. Why'd you ask me to read the map?"

"I didn't know exactly how to get here." *Besides, I'll never get serious about a woman who can't read a road map.*

"Baloney. You just wanted to see if I can read a road map."

Okay, when you get caught, admit it. "You're quick. But then, what should I expect from a brilliant physicist?"

"Don't try the charm routine. Why don't you just ask about my abilities?" she challenged, eyes beginning to show a hint of fire.

"I like to explore for them as we go along." he answered.

"So you like to test people rather than just ask?"

"Sometimes it's better to see what people do rather than hear what they say. And it's more fun to learn about someone that way," he said with a half smile.

"What other tests do you have planned for today?"

"None. I promise. Let's just be ourselves."

"You have a deal," she said and shook his hand.

They found a table by the windows looking out over the beach and ocean. Their talk turned to their families. She learned of his brothers and sisters and he learned of her brother who practiced law in Philadelphia. He told her of his summer jobs clearing logged over forests and she told him more about her riding hobby. Bryce refused her offer to "go Dutch" when the check came.

When they returned to the truck he reached behind the passenger seat and pulled out a small knapsack. In it were two pairs of sneakers and socks, one set obviously larger than the other.

"Take off your shoes," he said, smiling. "You're about my sister's size so I brought along some new sneakers that look like they'll fit you. Let's go for a walk on the beach to help work off that lunch."

Candace just stood there smiling. *Oh, man, you really know how to get to a woman. Candace, you'd better be careful.* Then she took off her shoes and put on the heavy socks and sneakers. They fit.

The ebbing tide provided a wide, hard beach surface near the water. They rolled up their pant legs. He held out his arm and she took it as they walked, first into the wind, so it would be at their backs when they returned.

The tang of salt marsh was strong at low tide and the waves churned softly into the beach with their final run-up coming with a pleasant swishing, hissing sound. The water crested to a foamy line, only feet away from where they walked.

"I've loved the smell of the shore ever since I was a kid," she told him. "It reminds me of the taste of clam chowder, and the rough feel of sandcastles, and lifeguard whistles in the wind, and, oh, so many memories."

"So you came here with your family in the summer?"

"Yes. We used to rent a place in Ocean City. I'd stay on the beach 'till the sun went down."

Candace couldn't resist collecting a few shells and Bryce relished the fact that she was having fun. He watched the tall woman with the unassuming, graceful walk allow the child within her to come alive as she examined the simple treasures offered in the sand. The wind heightened her color, giving her cheeks a special glow.

The wonderful thing about her is that with all that beauty, she's not the least bit vain, thought Bryce. No constant fussing with her hair or fiddling with her make-up.

"Here," she said, handing him a perfectly formed, small scallop shell, "keep this as a memento of your day as a tuna chauffer."

Her smile brightened when he pocketed the shell and Bryce's heart responded. *Easy, man, stay in control of yourself.*

"The day isn't over," he said. "We still have to deliver and hang that beautiful fish."

"We have to go back, huh?"

"I'm having a good time too, Candace."

"Let's walk a little farther."

They did and then reluctantly turned, only to be surprised at how far they'd gone. They raised their collars against the wind at their backs, and began the return. As they walked, she put her hand in his.

◦≋◦

On the return trip he talked about life as a professional baseball player. "It's not just the games. It's practice and weird hours and travel. I'm away from home for weeks at a time. We live out of suitcases and eat in hotels. I much prefer it when we play at home."

"How does Eddie handle your leaving?"

"He knows I'm coming back, so he's okay about it. But this past year when I couldn't see him as much, he missed me. My parents told me he would ask about me more frequently than he used to. But he has both sets of grandparents to stay with so that's a big help. And we have Midge and Teensy to give a hand. Midge is our cook and maid. She's been with my mother since before she married. She's more like family, a second mother to me. She's aged rapidly in the last couple of years, so Mom hired Teensy as her assistant. Boy, was that a real adjustment for Midge, but she got over it.

"Anyway," he continued, "baseball players aren't just tobacco chewing, beer drinking jocks. Many of my teammates are married with families and they worry about the same things that concern every parent. Others are young hell raisers off the field, but that keeps a good mixture going. They're a great bunch to be around. I just hope my being away doesn't have a lasting bad effect on Eddie."

Chapter 46

C andace dozed until they returned to campus. Amid stares from students and passers-by, Bryce carried her prize to her office. He had packed a small tool box in the truck and Candace brought it along.

When she unlocked the door to her office his gaze swept the room and stopped on a framed photograph on her credenza. It was of a man in an Air Force uniform. He stepped into the room and looked more closely at the photo.

"Jake," he said.

"Yes, that was taken right after he made Captain."

My competition is a dead man, he thought. He put the mounting down, fished in his tool box, and handed Candace a small level to use in marking the wall where the trophy would be hung. Candace showed him a cleared wall space opposite her desk. He held the mounting up to give her an idea of the height at which to hang the fish.

"No, up a little . . . now to the left . . . no, down a little. No, I like it better up some."

He turned to see her quietly laughing through an expression of devilment that had again appeared. "Oh, Bryce, you looked so serious, I just had to do that."

He lowered the fish to the floor and stalked her. She squealed in laughter and fled around the desk, but he was too quick for her and he caught her and hugged her to him. Bryce looked into her eyes and saw their acceptance. He kissed her long and gently, soft lips to soft lips, and then felt her arms go around his neck. They finally stopped and just held each other as their breathing returned to normal.

She leaned back in his arms, smiled, and said, "Ummm, that was nice." Then her eyes settled on Jake's photo. She stiffened and pulled away, her face gaining a panicked look.

Man, get her away from her panic and let her think about things later. Quick, say something.

"It was, indeed, ma'am. What a great way to thank me for being a tuna chauffer. But it's not getting your fish hung on the wall. Now, let's pick a spot and get it done."

The distressed look faded from Candace's face and was replaced with an all-business expression.

This time they finished the job. As they were leaving, he paused in the doorway and looked back into the office. "Somehow, it looks a lot better in here with that fish on the wall," he said. *And every time you look at it, you'll think of our times together.*

He walked her to the commuter train station. He didn't even try to kiss her good-bye. She stepped up into the car's entry, turned, smiled, and waggled her fingers to him. Then she stepped out of sight.

Chapter 47

"**I** saw Judge Cohn at lunch today," said Harry. "He asked me to say hello to you and to tell you that he's written to the parole board stating that Coe shouldn't be released at the half-way mark of his sentence which comes up next February. He cited Coe's lack of contrition and the fact that he believes Coe is a danger to the community."

"Funny. I had a conversation about Coe the other week when Candace and I were on the way to collect her tuna. That was the first time I'd thought of him in a while. Now he pops up again. I doubt if he'll ever change and there's nothing we can do about that."

"If that man ever is paroled, I'll request that as a condition of his release that he be ordered to stay away from our family," said Harry.

"But now I'm going to change the subject. When do you expect to put your MBA to work and how are you going to do it? I know you've been looking over our lumber broker's shoulder for the last two months. But, you need to get more active. The assistant manager of the saw mill is out on an extended medical leave. I'd like you to fill in for him until you have to go to Clearwater. What do you say?"

"Does the General Manager really need me hanging around? If he's been grooming someone else to come along, I don't want to step on anyone's toes."

"I asked Dave Hayes about that and he says he really can use your help. He remembers you from years ago and told me you worked your butt off then. Now he wants to discuss ideas on improvements to the production lines."

"Okay, I'd like to do that. When I was working there I saw some things that could use some attention. Have they done any modernization lately?"

"Some, but I'd like you to share any ideas that you have with Hayes."

"I'll be there tomorrow morning."

Harry struggled to keep his eyes from turning misty. "Bryce, it's good to have you back in the fold."

"It's good to be here. I told you I'd come back. I just had to do it in my own time."

◔◕◔

Bryce breathed deeply when he entered the mill. The scent of freshly sawed wood mixed with the odor of bark stripped from the logs by powerful water jets mingled with lubricants used to keep the machinery running smoothly. The screaming of the headsaw as it cut logs into lumber was loud enough to require earplugs. It was countered by the higher pitched sounds of the resaws and side edgers that gave the rough boards their final dimensions. He walked the line that morning with David Hayes as a series of poplar logs went through. The resulting lumber would then be cured and later run through a planing mill to produce boards with a finished surface. When dried properly, poplar served as a sturdy base over which furniture makers applied veneers.

At the end of the tour they retreated to the relative quiet of the General Manager's office.

"David," asked Bryce, "if you had a wish list for this place, what would be on it?"

David opened a desk drawer and produced a folder that contained detailed information on a modern sawdust collection system.

"Bryce our dust levels are too high," he said. "I know we use masks near the equipment, but the ambient air is too full of particulate. We need to get it cleaned up to reduce the risk of explosion and for the employees' health. It's a win-win situation because we can sell the collected dust to a composite board maker, or to a paper mill, and thus reduce the cost of the collection system with the proceeds."

They finished their talk about retrofitting the older mill and then Bryce explored the entire facility with an eye out for problems in need of a solution. By the end of the day Bryce had a list of projects. He began to feel alive in the new environment and his thoughts and imagination mushroomed as he considered potential new markets for the mill's products. He took a stack of industry trade journals with him when he left for home.

Chapter 48

C andace was out shopping with Flo in the days before Christmas. The physics instructor had gone over her reaction to Bryce's kiss until she almost made herself sick with remorse.

When Flo couldn't take any more of Candace's blues, she steered them toward a coffee shop to allow her friend to talk it out of her system.

"I never should have teased him like that," lamented Candace, "But what should I expect when I run around the desk laughing? An invitation to a chase means you want to get caught. And I did want to get caught. I just didn't think I was going to get held like that and kissed warmly like that and respond like that. Now he probably thinks I'm a tease as well as a social zero. I thought at least he might invite me to dinner again but he hasn't called, not even once."

"Have you sent him a Christmas card?" asked Flo.

"No. I feel that rather than just signing it, I'd have to write something and I don't know what to say."

"How about 'that kiss felt like more' or something along that line?"

"Oh, be serious for a moment. The card is a good idea but I need to write something somewhere between standoffish and come hither."

"Merry Christmas, Respectfully submitted . . ." then Flo relented as Candace's expression changed to irritation. "Don't put so much emphasis in this, Candace. Maybe the guy is just busy and he'll call after the holidays."

"He hardly said anything to me on the way to the train, even though we spent the entire day, I mean the entire day, talking about everything. He just kept his face neutral but he probably was thinking he couldn't wait to put me on that train and get out of there."

"Don't try to figure out what a man's thinking," offered Flo. "It's useless, unless you're standing naked next to a bed and he turns off the television when he looks at you."

Candace smiled at her friend's humor and said, "Flo, I really do want to see Bryce again. I've done a lot of soul searching this last month and I realized that I've been feeding my own grief rather than letting it fade. I've thought about Jake and have concluded that I owe him respect but not devotion. If I could hear him now I know he'd tell me to get on with my life."

"I've wanted to tell you that for months. Candace, it's your life now, so do what you believe is right, not what you think someone else might expect from you."

"Let's go pick out a card. I can think of what to write later."

◦⧲◦

Their cards crossed in the mail. His showed a cardinal in a pine tree. There was no printed message inside, but he had written: "This is a season that celebrates Hope. May all of your hopes be fulfilled. Bryce."

Her card featured a wonderful classic rendition of Santa Claus. Inside she had written under the printed greeting: "Merry Christmas, Bryce. I still think fondly of our trip to Longport. Candace"

Her card joined a small scallop shell on his bedroom dresser. The card sat there until after the New Year when he finally telephoned and asked her to have dinner with him that weekend. She accepted. Bryce made Saturday reservations at a country inn that was noted for its ambiance as well as its cuisine. The host agreed to reserve a table in a corner away from the kitchen.

◦⧲◦

Because he now was involved with the family business, Bryce had a new telephone installed in his room at home with a new number and a connection to an answering service when he was not available. It sounded more businesslike and it saved his family from answering his calls.

He left a message at Candace's office to let her know his new number and the time he would stop at her home to take her to dinner. Then he returned to the challenge of saw blade maintenance. He left work that evening determined to talk with mill engineers about the problem.

Chapter 49

"So, how do I handle tonight?" Bryce asked himself. "Don't rush things, but man would I like to tell that woman we could have a future. Well, she'll like the inn's menu. It's the plans for the preliminaries that are the question."

"Daddy, what are you talking about?" asked Eddie.

Bryce hadn't realized his son was in earshot. "Oh, nothing, really. I was just thinking about going out tonight."

"Who are you going out with?"

"A lady I met when I took you to the hospital. Now, come on, let's get you zipped up. If we're going to try out your new skis we'd better get going."

He'd given Eddie a pair of short cross country skis for Christmas. Today he and his son planned to take advantage of a new snowfall. They headed for the fields to the west of the house.

As a child, Eddie had a low center of gravity, so when he fell, he was right back up. He was too small to master the big sweeping steps his father took but the boy found a way to "skate" on his skis by the end of the day. "When you learn a little more, we'll take you on some hills, Eddie," his father told him.

"Like the hills back there?" he asked and pointed off in the distance toward the forested slopes north of their home.

"Sure, someday we can go to Sunrise Hills," promised Bryce. "We'll just stick to the fire trails."

"Does the lady you're taking to dinner know how to ski?"

"I don't know. I'll ask her."

They returned to the house and Eddie ran to tell Teensy all about his new-found abilities. Bryce checked his answering service and there were no messages. He showered, shaved and carefully dressed in his favorite blazer and slacks and put on a new conservatively striped tie he had received for Christmas. Then he threw two oversized parkas worn by skiers on chair lifts into the back seat of his car. On the way to Candace's home he thought of things to talk about with her and smiled at himself over the effort.

"Just let it flow, man. It'll be fine. But no kissing her tonight. She's still attached to her ghost."

Chapter 50

D avid Hawkins had a long, pleasant face and graying hair. His handshake was firm when he answered the door and ushered Bryce in to a large living room that was decorated tastefully in the traditional style. Bryce sat in a wingback chair that Candace's father indicated and they chatted amiably about the Founders and the hope for a better season. David's conversation was measured, a habit he had acquired from years of giving legal counsel to his clients. They were interrupted by a girl who had Candace's eyes. Her grandfather introduced them. Anne looked up at the man who had politely stood for the introduction and asked, "How tall are you?"

Bryce smiled and said, "If I pick you up and hold you about where my head is you can guess how tall I am." And he bent and lifted her level with his eyes. She looked around the room, seeing it from that height for the first time and then she looked at Bryce. "Mommy says you are six feet four inches. Is that true?"

"Yes. But when I was young I was only as tall as you are." *I never told your mother my height.*

Bryce put her down and Anne skipped across the carpet and sat at the piano, a Baldwin baby grand with a beautiful finish. She opened the keyboard cover and began to use two fingers to play "Pop Goes the Weasel" and Bryce was hooked. He walked over to the lovely instrument and leaned over to play harmony to the tune Anne was tapping out. David Hawkins watched in appreciation as the tall man stood next to the little girl and kept his notes in perfect time to her notes. He realized that Bryce was watching her hands rather than looking at the keyboard under his hand. Anne stopped her playing and said, "Do you know "Mary Had A Little Lamb?"

"I think we can manage that," said Bryce. "May I sit beside you on this bench to help you play?"

Anne got down from the bench, Bryce adjusted it for his size, and sat down. Then Anne sat on a corner of the bench and leaned forward as they played the tune together, with Bryce giving it quite an ad-lib flourish at the end. Anne's eyes widened and she said, "Play something else, please."

"Okay, what would you like me to play?"

"Just anything you like."

"Well do you know that song, "'Lullaby and Good Night?"

She nodded and said, "Yes, but it's not my bedtime yet."

"Don't worry," he smiled, "you don't have to go to bed yet. I just wanted to tell you that the man who wrote that song also wrote the tune I'll play for you." He began to play a quiet melody from one of Brahms' Intermezzos. The little girl watched in fascination as his hands and fingers moved on the keys.

She listened for a minute and then told him, "My kitty died yesterday."

Bryce seamlessly transitioned into Chopin's Funeral March, and with a straight face asked, "What was your kitty's name?" Out of the corner of his eye, he could see David Hawkins disguising his laughter with a phony coughing fit. The Funeral March continued.

"Lucy. She was hit by a car."

"Ah, that's sad. Let's play something to cheer you up."

Bryce had been practicing a dramatic Chopin etude and launched into it. The music echoed through the house and Mrs. Hawkins entered the living room, drawn by the wonderful playing. Bryce stopped and rose to introduce himself. *Oh, hallelujah! She's beautiful!* Bryce still remembered Harry's admonition that a man should look at a woman's mother to see what he'd have in later years.

Alice Hawkins was tall for a woman of her generation. She had silver grey hair that framed a lovely round face with a forehead that contained few wrinkles. Her cheeks were only slightly rouged and her lipstick was understated. She had given Candace her blue eyes but the intense hue was missing from Alice's eyes. She shook his hand and then said, "I thought Candace said you're a professional baseball player."

"I am, Mrs. Hawkins, but I enjoy playing the piano as a hobby."

"Well, keep playing. I've had that piano for years, but never have I been able to make it sound like that. What's more, I think it needs to be tuned."

"I'll play something else, but first, I'm going to ask Anne if she'll take a note to her mother for me. Will you, Anne?" The girl nodded, and he pulled a small appointment book out and wrote on a blank page: "You would look good in burlap. Just put on your first choice. I'm getting hungry."

Anne asked, "What does it say?"

Bryce tore the sheet out and said, "Ask your mother to read it to you."

Her grandparents smiled as Anne, clutching the missive, ran for the stairs and her mother. He was on his third etude of the evening when Candace appeared in the living room doorway behind him and quietly watched while he played for her daughter. The piece ended and she walked into the room. He stood at the sound of her footsteps.

Their eyes met and she said, "You play beautifully."

She was dressed in a knee length black dress with a slightly flared skirt and cut out arm holes. Above the low, square-cut bodice a string of pearls and matching pearl earrings finished the look. She carried a beaded black sweater.

His irritation at her tardiness vanished. "Thank you. You look terrific," was all the man could muster.

As he stood close behind Candace to help her on with her coat, he received a message that delighted him. She was wearing perfume and the ring was gone from her left hand.

"Uh, Candace, you'll want to wear boots. The snow may still be on the parking lot at the restaurant."

Candace went to the hall closet and withdrew a pair of ankle high boots with faux fur around the tops. She sat in a chair, looked at Bryce and asked, "Would you mind helping me on with these?"

He knelt on one knee in front of her and again noticed her perfume as she placed her feet in the boots he held. *Lord! This woman's legs are so fine. Probably from riding horseback.*

⊙═◑

They bid goodnight to Anne and her parents and walked rapidly to his car. The moon had risen and the air was still.

Okay, we go for it, he thought. He held the door for Candace, then got in behind the wheel, and reached for the ignition switch.

"Bryce, I want to say something now."

He started the engine and turned to her. "Okay, I'm listening."

"Remember when you kissed me at my office?"

"A sterling occasion."

"Thank you. But I think I may have hurt your feelings when I reacted the way I did. I just want to say that I didn't expect you to kiss me like that and it surprised me." She paused. "But I did like it."

He looked into blue eyes that went from teasing to anxiety and back. Bryce placed his left hand over his heart, smiled, and said, "I'm genuinely touched by the confession and apology, but none's needed." Then, eyes narrowing, and still smiling, he asked, "Want another?"

In answer she smiled and leaned toward him. He kissed her sweetly.

"This is an auspicious beginning," he teased. "Now let's see if they're still holding our reservation."

Bryce drove toward the northwest and soon found the country road he sought. Towns gave way to farmlands and traffic thinned to only occasional vehicles.

"I love the way the moonlight glistens on the snowy fields," said Candace. "Someday this probably will be houses or shopping malls, but right now I like it the way it is. Bryce, where are we going?"

"It's just ahead."

Bryce swung the car into a farm's lane and stopped beside a barn. Then he watched Candace's expression. She turned to look at him in the light of the moon shining through the windshield, and voice tinged with suspicion, said, "All right. What's going on? Are you testing me again?"

The big barn door opened and light from the doorway filled the area where he had parked. A horse-drawn sleigh emerged from the barn.

"We're going to use alternate transportation the rest of the way," he said.

Candace's expression changed from suspicion to consternation. "Oh, Bryce, that's so sweet, but we'll freeze to death in that thing."

"Nope. I have warm, full-length parkas for us in the back seat and there's a wool scarf for you, and a buffalo robe as well. Come on, we're going dashing through the snow."

"Oh, Bryce . . . really, this is too much."

"There's a narrow grate where our feet rest. Under the grate is a small charcoal fire in a metal warming box. Come on, where's your sense of adventure?"

Bryce got out of the car, stopped at the rear door, and withdrew the parkas. Then he opened the door for Candace. Overcoat and all, she reluctantly stepped into the parka that he held open for her.

"Amos," said Bryce, "is everything ready?"

"She's all yours, Mr. Roberts." He went to the back of the sleigh and turned on a bright red light that would warn approaching cars. Bryce used a squared iron loop on the side of the sleigh to climb to the seat then reached down to assist Candace. She didn't take her gloved hand from Bryce's when she made it aboard. Nonplussed, Bryce handed her the scarf. She wrapped it over her hair and then pulled the parka's hood over her head.

"You really want to do this?" she asked.

"It's too late to chicken out now. Have a seat." Bryce adjusted his parka, sat down, spread the buffalo robe over their laps, and whistled to the horse.

"Giddy up, Bess."

Candace felt the bumps the sleigh rode over, but by then she was laughing.

"I can't believe that I'm going sleigh riding in a cocktail dress. But you know what? That charcoal fire is working. You'll have to let me take the reins at some point, just so I can say I've done this."

He turned the horse out of the lane and onto the berm of the still snow-covered country road. Bess settled into a steady gait and Bryce handed Candace the reins.

"This moonlight makes it as bright as day," she said. "How far are we going?"

"Not far enough to freeze to death, but far enough to have some fun. The inn is about three miles ahead."

"Do they have a fireplace?"

"We'll have a drink beside it."

"Are we going home this way?"

"No. Amos is going to drive my car to the inn in a few minutes and take Bess home to her barn. Somehow, looking at a horse's butt after a good dinner just isn't what I had in mind."

"Bryce Roberts, you're nuts. How'd you think of this?"

"I was looking through Christmas cards sent to my parents and among them was a Currier & Ives print of a sleigh ride. The rest just followed."

"Here, you take the reins. Even with these gloves on, my fingers are getting cold."

Bryce lightly guided the horse and sleigh through the quiet of the rural winter evening, broken only by the sound of Bess' breathing and the muffled clopping of her hooves.

Candace soon became lost in the moment—until Jake intruded. The puffs of condensate from her breath reminded her of the day of Jake's funeral and the "talk" she had with him by the Charles River. She struggled for a moment to banish the thought and then gave in. *Oh, Jake, please understand. He's a good man and I think you'd like him.* Then she turned toward Bryce.

He smiled and asked, "Warm enough?"

"I'll make it to the inn." *Jake, I'm saying good-bye for the rest of the evening. I'll talk to you later.* By the time they arrived at the inn she found herself enjoying the sensation of being bundled up next to the man who could make the past recede. Bryce guided Bess to the far edge of the inn's parking lot and brought the horse and sleigh to a halt. He tied the reins, helped Candace down from the seat to applause from several patrons who were leaving, and put their parkas in the sleigh.

"Will Bess be okay?"

"Yes. That was my car coming up the road when we came in." They entered the inn's blessed warmth. "Now, let me help you swap your boots for your shoes and then we'll find that fireplace in the bar."

⊙═◎

Candace emptied her second glass of wine while they talked about their children and how they handled their questions about their missing parent. Now she wanted to pry behind the charm that Bryce used to keep the conversation moving.

"What do you miss most about Marilyn?"

"She had a joy of life about her that made the troubles of the world seem insignificant. What do you remember most about Jake? You were talking to him out there on that sleigh ride weren't you?"

Bryce's eyes looked into hers. She was surprised to read compassion in his face.

"You figured that out?"

He nodded.

"You don't seem upset."

"Not over that. He was a wonderful part of your life. But let's talk about the present. I want to spend the rest of this evening finding out more about you. I don't know your birthday or how old you are or Anne's age or anything like that."

"I'm a year younger than you, and my birthday is October 25th. Anne was born on April 9, 1965."

"How do you know how old I am? And, come to think of it, how tall I am?"

"Bryce, don't you realize that you're a celebrity? Lots of things get published about you in the sports pages."

"You read the sports pages?"

"*The Daily News* has much better coverage than the *Inquirer.*"

"I hardly ever talk to reporters. Invariably they're looking for something that will make a 'story.' I play baseball because I love the game and I just don't want to get involved in controversy, most of which is manufactured."

◦❧◦

They realized they were the only people left in the restaurant by the time they had described their lives in the 1950s. Bryce apologized to the waiter for keeping him beyond the usual closing time and left an overly generous tip.

The streets were almost deserted as they drove to her home with the radio tuned to an oldies station that played tunes from the fifties by Paul Anka, Dion, and others. Candace sang along with the words and Bryce added his deep voice to the Do-wops. And, like teens in the fifties, she sat close to him and they kissed at every stop sign and stop light. In between songs and kisses they were laughing themselves silly over the nonsense.

"Oh, by the way. Do you ski?" he asked as they pulled into her driveway.

"I've tried it, but I never really pursued it. Why do you ask?"

"Just curious. This winter weather has me thinking about it."

He walked her to her door and formally shook her hand. "Good night, ma'am."

Her laughter followed him to the car.

◑ ◍ ◐

He sent her flowers on Monday. The accompanying note read: "See what happens when you finally decide to wear perfume? Bryce"

He doesn't miss much, thought Candace.

Chapter 51

He called on Wednesday evening and invited her to go dancing on Friday night at one of the newer discothèques and she enthusiastically agreed. Again, she kept him waiting almost a half hour before she was ready. He swallowed his annoyance but made a mental note.

They had a quiet dinner first, because the noise of the band at the club would be overwhelming. Later at the club a man popped a flash camera at them while they were having a blast dancing. Bryce thought it was just the 'house photographer' who takes photos and then develops them for sale to the patrons. However, no one tried to sell them their photograph and he promptly forgot about it.

The picture appeared in the *Daily News* gossip section with the caption:

Alone In Left Field No More.
Bryce Roberts, the hunk who plays left field for the Founders apparently has found a partner. The mystery woman has not been identified, but with legs like hers it should not take long. The couple was seen together at one of the City's most popular clubs last evening. Wow! Can they dance!

The photo showed them dancing, with Candace in a twirl that had caused her skirt to rise. Bryce telephoned her later that morning and said, "You really do have gorgeous gams. But if you want me to do so, I'll track down the photographer and put his camera somewhere that will hurt."

"Oh, no, that's okay. It's just that I deliberately wear modest clothing when I teach my classes, and this morning I found a copy of the picture on the bulletin board in my classroom. So someone here recognized me."

"We can't do much about the paparazzi if we use normal means. I'm going to have a talk with some gentlemen I know. Maybe we can put a quick stop to this."

"Oh, Bryce, don't bother. It'll blow over by tomorrow."

◦◉◦

The newspaper was read by the inmates at Graterford State Prison, and one of them meticulously folded the page around the article and photo of the dancing couple. Then Coe carefully tore it out and placed it in his collection of newspaper articles. Soon Leroy would have served his minimum and be released on parole. Coe had savored the thought of adding a photo of Marilyn's gravestone to his thick folder of materials.

"And now, I think there's another target," he told himself.

Chapter 52

Three weeks later Bryce and Candace arranged to meet at a downtown restaurant before attending a performance by the Philadelphia Orchestra. He arrived at the restaurant minutes ahead of time so that Candace wouldn't have to sit alone waiting for him. The *maitre d* seated him and he ordered a glass of wine. Bryce reminisced about the fun they'd had over the past month but he was nagged by Candace's constant tardiness. This evening she again was late and the orchestra's performance would begin on time. Exasperated, he finally ordered a sandwich, and began planning what to say to the woman when she arrived. She still wasn't there by the time he finished eating so he paid his check and tipped the waiter generously for taking up a table with such a small order in the crowded restaurant. He left in time to walk to The Academy of Music.

Bryce paused in the lobby to check the orchestra's future performance schedule. He was still fuming when he was greeted by friends of his parents. He swallowed his irritation when they invited him to join them in their box for the performance. One of the selections that evening was Greig's Piano Concerto and Bryce absorbed it with all of his being.

He caught a late train to Doylestown and by the time he arrived home his telephone was ringing.

I may as well talk to her now, he thought, and picked up the phone.

"Yes, Candace?"

"Bryce, I'm so sorry. I really am. I apologize and it won't ever happen again."

"Candace, you know I can't stand it when people are late. And you've been late . . . no, very late, for every one of our dates. It's just plain rude and I'm not going to stand for it any more. Tonight was the last straw."

"Please don't say that. I'm really sorry and I want to make it up to you."

"People are creatures of habit, Candace, and you won't change. We've had some fun and I've loved your company. But I just don't think it'll work with me getting irritated with you all the time over your tardiness. So now it's over. I need to get some sleep so I'm going to say good-bye and I wish you the best." He hung up before she could say anything more. Then he switched to the answering service with instructions not to disturb him.

"I'm nuts about that woman," he told himself. "But if I keep seeing her I won't have the strength to back away and I really should. People don't change habits like that and I'll be damned if I'm going through life waiting for her. That would drive me crazy. So this is the last of it.

"Damn it!"

Chapter 53

B ryce arrived at spring training in excellent shape and worked hard to improve his timing at the plate by picking up pitches as early as he could after the ball left the pitcher's hand. At every game he took careful notes on the opposing pitchers' tendencies and styles, particularly what they liked to throw deep in the count.

They opened the regular season on a long road trip playing the mid-western teams. Bryce did well, hitting .320 for the trip. He knew keeping a high batting average would be tougher as the weather warmed and the league's pitchers got in better shape.

They finished in St. Louis and flew to Philadelphia and their first home stand. The team plane landed near midnight. The usual group of wives was there to meet their husbands, along with a corps of die-hard fans who always appeared to greet the team when it returned from out of town.

Bryce collected his bag and suit holder, descended the ramp steps, and heard the metallic tinking of the plane's hot engines cooling. In the distance other jets roared as they taxied toward the runway. He started toward the terminal, the smell of jet exhaust pungent in his nostrils.

All of his senses went into overdrive as Candace emerged from the shadows and walked toward him in her sensuous model's stride. She wore a belted light grey trench coat that hinted nicely at her figure. Grey pumps emphasized her lovely legs that showed below the hem of her coat. Her dark, curly hair glistened from the tiny dew drops that had accumulated while she waited in the open for him. Her full lips were perfectly painted a deep red and her eye shadow, lightly applied, emphasized her deep blue eyes over her high cheek bones.

Oh, dammit, Bryce lamented. *Lord, she's a beautiful woman. I had no idea it was going to be this tough to stay away from her. But I must. She won't change and I can't abide tardiness. We'd only wind up fighting about that—over and over.*

He nodded, said, "Good evening, Candace," and kept walking as if to pass her by.

She moved in front of him. "Bryce, please stop."

He felt the tiniest chink develop in his resolve because he heard no plea in her tone, only determination. He stopped, stood woodenly, luggage still in hand, and she put her arms around his neck, kissed him fervently and then looked him straight in the eyes.

"I'm so sorry. I promise I'll never be late again."

He continued to hold his luggage. "Thanks for the apology, but people don't change and, Candace, I don't think that you'll be able to keep your promise." *God, I wish it were otherwise because even Marilyn couldn't kiss like that.*

"Bryce, please, may we just talk? I know it's late but I need only a few minutes."

If you keep standing here, she's going to get to you again. Leave while you still can.

"Candace, I'm tired and I want to get a good night's sleep. We have a day game tomorrow."

He saw the resolve in her face wilt momentarily and then she regained her composure.

Lord, this woman has courage. Maybe I could just listen to what she has to say. Maybe there's a way . . . "Tell you what. I'm renting a house in town and I'll be there tomorrow after the game. If you'd like to talk then, I'll listen." He gave her the address and walked toward the terminal entrance.

"You arrogant son-of-a-bitch," she called after him.

He stopped and turned to face her. "Good night, Candace," he said. "See you tomorrow." Then he walked on. She couldn't see the pain in his eyes, for already he was planning how he would tell Candace why he wouldn't continue, even though he wanted very much to be with her again.

Candace mentally kicked herself. "First you kiss him. Then you curse him? Careful, Candace, you don't want to lose control.

And he's so damned much in control. I wonder what really gets that man perturbed? Besides tardiness, that is. Now, it's still on his terms or nothing. Well, he did offer to listen, and I have a point to make."

She started for the terminal. It was going to be a long drive home.

Chapter 54

On the way home she thought about how Rosalie had helped to try to save her relationship with Bryce. Two weeks after Bryce left for spring training Candace, in desperation, dialed the old telephone number on the card that Bryce gave her at the hospital ball. A modulated and polite black woman's voice answered and Candace thought she'd dialed the wrong number. But, she asked for Mrs. Roberts anyway, and was surprised to hear, "May I say who's calling please?"

"My name is Candace Davis. I'm a friend of Bryce and I'd like to speak for a moment with his mother."

"One moment please, I'll see if Mrs. Roberts is available."

There was a long pause and then another woman's voice said, "Mrs. Davis, this is Rosalie Roberts. Is Bryce all right?"

"Oh, I'm sorry to worry you like that, Mrs. Roberts. Bryce is fine according to the sports pages. It's me that's not." *Oh, God, she'll think I'm pregnant. Way to go, dummy.*

"Mrs. Roberts, I've made a terrible mistake and I think I've badly hurt Bryce's feelings. He's meant a lot to me and I don't want to lose his friendship. I need to talk with someone who knows him well. So I'm calling you to ask if you'd be willing to talk with me about Bryce."

There was a long pause and Candace knew Rosalie was gathering her thoughts.

"Mrs. Davis, don't you think that just you and Bryce should talk? He probably will listen. He's not an unkind person."

"Mrs. Roberts, he's not returning my calls. I've left several messages for him and there's just silence."

"Mrs. Davis, I don't want to sound rude or unkind, but if Bryce hasn't returned your calls, obviously he doesn't want to speak with you."

"I just need your advice on what to say to him in person. I'm going to make that effort."

Candace heard a sigh on the other end of the line and then Rosalie said, "I'm going to be in the city on Thursday. Can you meet for lunch at The Masters' restaurant? Say about 12:30?"

"Oh, thank you, Mrs. Roberts. I am a tall woman with dark—"

"Never mind, Mrs. Davis," Rosalie said in a pleasant tone, "I saw the photo in the newspaper." *Besides, now my curiosity has gotten the best of me.*

Candace arrived first at the elegantly decorated restaurant. When she saw the décor she was doubly glad she'd dressed up for the day in a high-necked dark blue silk blouse with a ruffled front complimented by a full, dark grey wool pleated skirt that extended well below her knees. Her hair was done in a curly perm that copied the Elizabeth Taylor look. After she was seated she surreptitiously checked her cash supply and then again made sure her credit card was in her wallet. No way was Rosalie Roberts going to pay for this lunch.

Rosalie arrived punctually at 12:30 and was ushered to the table. Candace stood to introduce herself to the woman who could only be described as handsome. Bryce had inherited Rosalie's dark eyes and patrician nose. Her face was narrower than his, giving her a delicate appearance. Her make-up was subdued and her graying hair was perfectly in place. Her deep maroon two-piece wool suit was of excellent cut and quality. She was wearing mid-height heels that matched her purse and suit. She extended a maroon-gloved hand in greeting and the smile she delivered to Candace was genuine and her manner at ease. Some of Candace's nervousness subsided as they sat down.

Rosalie asked, "Must you teach this afternoon?" as she removed her gloves.

"No, I have the afternoon off. Thank you for agreeing to talk with me, Mrs. Roberts. I'm so grateful that you're taking the time to do so."

"You're welcome. Since you aren't teaching, will you join me in a glass of wine, Mrs. Davis?"

"Yes, I'd like Chablis," she told the waiter who was standing attentively at the table. "And Mrs. Roberts, please call me Candace."

Rosalie ordered the same and then said, "Candace, some time ago Bryce told his father and me that he'd met you. I know that you teach physics at Penn and that you have a young daughter and that your husband perished in a plane crash several years ago. I'm afraid I don't know much else about you except that Bryce was attracted to you."

Rosalie said "was attracted" in a tone that bespoke history and Candace's heart sank.

"Seeing you in person, that's understandable. The picture in the paper doesn't do you justice."

"Thank you, Mrs. Roberts. I know a lot about Bryce's biography, so to speak, but I need to know much more about how he is inside. If I know more about how he thinks and reacts to situations I can figure out a way to approach him in person to let him know I want to reestablish our friendship."

"What happened to get you two off track?" asked Rosalie.

"We had a date to attend a concert given by the Philadelphia Orchestra and we were to meet for dinner first. I arrived at the restaurant an hour late and Bryce was gone. The *maitre d'* told me Bryce had been there but left. I went to The Academy and couldn't find him. After that I called him to apologize and he said that he didn't want to see me anymore. I've tried to contact him since but he hasn't responded to my messages. I want so much to apologize and tell him that I won't be late if we go out again."

"I gather that was not the first time you were late?" said Rosalie.

"That's right. I've never been a tardy person before, but I was really late being ready to go out with him the last four or five times. He just quietly told me he likes punctuality. He even spoke about how he savors every heartbeat of life and that he sees people who show up late as robbing him of those heartbeats by making him wait around when he could be doing something."

"That's my son to a T. Ever since he's been a teenager he's risen early and goes the whole day and evening in action. He has this inner fire to excel. I don't think he really understands people who don't have those same capacities and drive. He's tried to understand, though. Bryce has read quite a number of books on behavior because he wants to know what makes people tick. He's a bright and perceptive man. But he has more self-discipline than is good for him."

They ordered, and then spent the next hour talking over a delicious lunch. Candace found herself being questioned in a gracious way about her life and family. After Mrs. Roberts finished her second glass of wine she asked that she be called Rosalie and then began to regale Candace with tales of Bryce and his siblings as they grew up. She had Candace giggling from that point on.

"Candace," said Rosalie, "Bryce is exercising his self-discipline by not calling you. He probably has decided that your being tardy is just unacceptable and he doesn't want to tolerate it anymore. The only way he knows to deal with that is to cut off the relationship."

"Rosalie, I think I love him," said Candace and the wine.

"I know, Candace," Rosalie said, eyes full of understanding. "I could hear that in your voice when you called. That's why I agreed to meet you. My son needs someone who loves him despite his disciplined lifestyle. But if you want Bryce you're going to have to run next to him. If he thinks that you'll slow him down he won't invite you to join him. If I were you, I'd see a psychiatrist who can help you understand why you're being late. I'll give you the name of a gentleman I know who's very down-to-earth and you can call him if you'd like to."

Rosalie finished with some final advice. "I think Bryce will give you a chance to talk. If he does, be very candid about things because he can detect insincerity from a mile away."

Candace paid for the lunch and then returned to her office where she telephoned the office of Dr. Samuel Friedman, with whom she made an appointment early in the following week.

Chapter 55

While grading papers in her office Candace listened to the Founders first home game on the radio. When it ended with a home team victory she entered the grades on a report sheet and freshened her minimal make up.

As she exited the building a group of male students watched appreciatively. She was wearing navy blue pleated dress slacks and a simple but elegantly tailored white silk blouse under a lamb's wool cardigan sweater that matched her slacks. Matching navy blue pumps finished the look. Lapis earrings were the only jewelry she wore. A three-quarter length, lightweight woolen cape in matching navy blue kept the spring air from chilling her.

Candace and the taxi driver talked about the team. He was surprised she knew so much about their performance so far that season.

The taxi delivered her to an attractive brick row house with freshly pointed and cleaned bricks. The shutters bore a fresh coat of dark green paint. The dark green front door was at the top of three white marble steps and a marble stoop that recently had been cleaned. The door displayed a highly polished large brass knocker at eye level and above it, beveled glass windows made a row across the top of the door. Candace used the knocker and there was no answer. She checked for a key under the milk-box and found none. She tried the door anyway and was surprised that it opened. Candace smiled when she realized Bryce had left the door unlocked so that she wouldn't have to wait outside. She hadn't expected such forethought from him in a city where most people locked their doors.

Bryce, you're a very self-confident man to believe I'd come here. She was stepping inside when she heard a light honk on a car horn and saw his red sedan pull to the curb several doors down the street. He got out and she watched him stride in his lithe gait toward her. He wore light gray slacks and a blue hopsack blazer over a white polo shirt. His black penny loafers were polished to a high gloss. *The power in that man shows even when he walks. Oh, woman, maybe coming here wasn't such a good idea. But it's too late to back out now.*

He climbed the white steps, and, his face unrevealing, said, "Hello, Candace. Please come in." He said nothing more to put her at ease. When they entered the house he helped her out of her cape and hung it in a small closet along with his blazer. Still silent, he led her to the kitchen through the living room that was furnished only with a couch, coffee table, area rug and an over-sized dark red leather chair. A brass floor lamp provided the only lighting to supplement what came through the front windows.

Rosalie had volunteered to shop for the household items and left all of the receipts on the kitchen counter after a cleaning service did the place. Bryce arrived there so late the previous evening he had time only to take a quick tour in the morning. The receipts still were on the counter. Teensy thoughtfully had supplied wine so he poured Candace a glass of Chablis and he opened a bottle of Cabernet.

"You wanted to talk?"

"Here's to winning the first home game. I hope it's a good omen." *Damn, I sound like a nervous teen-ager on her first date.*

He said, "Thank you," and moved to the living room where he sat in the leather chair. He studied her with his dark eyes as she entered and stood in the half-empty room, one hand holding her wine glass chin high, the other arm folded across her waist.

"I'm listening," he said, with the faintest touch of warmth in his deep voice. He sat back in the chair, left ankle crossed over his right knee. *All right, give her a chance. Anyone with the guts to come here has plenty of spirit and you can't help but respect that.* He gestured politely for her to sit on the couch.

Candace ignored the invitation, took a swallow of her wine, and began to pace. His eyes followed her.

"I never used to be late like I was on our dates," she began. "I know it's terribly rude and I apologize again."

Bryce nodded slightly in acknowledgement of the apology.

Then she continued. "I asked myself to look at the differences. Why was I being late for our dates when I wasn't like that before? What had changed?" She looked at Bryce for encouragement to continue. His gaze was inscrutable.

I will tell him. "Bryce, despite the fun we've had, underneath I was scared. I'm still scared. I talked to a psychiatrist about that and he explained it. Some people who were very much in love with their deceased husband or wife get frightened when faced with the potential of a new relationship. Frightened that it won't be as strong, or that it'll be much different than before and they won't be able to adjust. Frightened that it will end with more hurt that they don't want to take a chance on feeling all over again. Frightened that they may appear to be disloyal to their deceased spouse."

She paused and then continued, holding his gaze with hers. "I'm scared that what we may have going is too good to be true and that I just may be in a rebound relationship. I don't want one of them for me and certainly not for you. So, subconsciously I was acting out all that fear by being late." She looked at him for any sign of understanding, but he just continued to contemplate her.

Finally he broke the silence. "That makes sense," he said gently.

Then he challenged her in a stronger voice. "What are you going to do about your fears?"

I'm going to bare my soul because I trust you. "I'm asking you to be patient with me. I think we might build something very special together; otherwise, you wouldn't have invited me here and I wouldn't have come."

Touché, lady. But, first, I want to hear what else you have to say.

"But I want to be sure. I'm telling you this because it's the only way to be with a . . . with a . . . disciplined man like you."

"Oh?"

"Yes. Underneath that smooth and charming exterior you're mentally tougher than nails. I've seen signs of it and people who know you have told me you are."

"Your understanding me isn't going to resolve your fears. What are you going to do about them?"

"Grow out of them. I can do it now that I know myself better." She took a deep breath. "I'm just going to have to risk jumping back into life with both feet and stop giving in to my fears."

Thank God! That's what I've been waiting to hear from you. "I think you'll make it," he said, confidence strong in his tone.

"You do?"

He heard the rising note of hope in her voice and he gave in completely.

"Yes," he said with the half smile that always pleased her. "Anyone with your combination of brains and spirit who can kiss like you do is bound to be a huge success in a new relationship."

She stopped her pacing and Bryce said, "Candace, put down your wine glass and come sit in my lap."

He held her for a long time after she stopped crying.

⊙≈◎

Afterward Candace used the bathroom "to freshen my face" for what seemed to him an eternity. She joined him at the tall kitchen table that had high-backed bar stools for chairs.

"You really spoke with my mother?"

"Yes, she's a very nice lady." Candace reached for a container of Chinese food that a restaurant had delivered and used chopsticks to serve herself. "This is good. How did you find out about the restaurant?"

"I'm renting this house from one of our pitchers who was traded to the Cubs. There was a menu left in one of the kitchen drawers, so I figured O'Rourke was recommending the place. Now, don't try to change the subject; what did you and my mother discuss?"

"Are you upset with me because I talked to Rosalie?"

"No. I'm irritated with my mother. I don't like the fact that she took it upon herself to talk with you. If anything was to be done about restoring our relationship I think we should've handled it. We're adults and we don't need our parents interfering."

"I asked Rosalie for help. And she did help. And I'm very glad she did because you and I weren't getting anywhere on our own. And you're too proud to admit it."

Bryce smiled but refused to admit her point. "So, what did you and my mother talk about?"

"I'm not going to tell you. It was women's talk."

Candace held a food carton toward him and her mischievous look returned. "More chicken and veggies?" she asked sweetly.

Bryce had to smile. He knew he could never pry it loose from his mother and now Candace had sealed her own lips.

"No, thank you."

He raised his wineglass in salute. "Here's to the sisterhood of women. They've always been accused of spreading gossip and not being able to keep a secret, but I've stopped buying into that. It's men who can't keep most secrets. A secret is knowledge, and knowledge is power. So a man with knowledge has power. But the other guy doesn't know that. So in order to show that he has power, a man has to tell what he knows. Women don't think of power in the same way so they keep secrets better."

"Except when we're being catty. And on that note, put me in a taxi. I must get to the station and home. I have a daughter to hug, some quizzes to grade and a lesson plan to review."

Chapter 56

B ryce telephoned Candace and explained he had a rare off-day at home on Thursday.

"What do you have in mind?" she asked.

"I know you're quite the equestrienne and we have horses at our home. Bring Anne along. We can put our kids on ponies and go out with them for a while and then hand them off to someone while we go back out. Dinner's included."

"That sounds delightful. What time? I'll see if I can juggle my schedule."

"Can you drive to Doylestown by 10:00 in the morning? Even though you can read a roadmap," she could hear his grin through the line, "I can meet you in town and then drive you to our home. You may get lost otherwise."

She couldn't help but smile in return and they arranged an easy place to meet.

"Oh, one more thing," he said. "If you show up in formal riding gear you'll be laughed off the property. Just wear something comfortable. We're casual at dinner, too."

She promised not to wear her riding outfit and said good-bye. Then she returned to her preparations for participation in a panel discussion on trouble in public schools. To an academician like her, the findings of the panel were horrifying.

⊙≋⊙

The four of them reined in their mounts and stopped at the crest of a hill to overlook fields to the right planted with sweet corn, lettuce varieties and other vegetable crops.

Eddie, who had seen it all before, ignored the huge field of tomatoes off to their left. He broke the silence. "Mrs. Davis, are you going to marry my dad?"

Candace put her hand over her mouth to help quiet a laugh.

Bryce told Eddie, "That's not a question children ask adults. That's something only adults talk about."

Candace lowered her hand and looked Eddie in the eyes. "Your father and I are just friends now, Eddie. We're still getting to know each other, and people don't marry until they've spent lots of time together to find out if they're a good match. So 'I don't know' is the answer to your question."

Bryce cleared his throat, gave thumbs up to Candace and gently heeled Thunder into a walk. The riders followed along the trails bordering the fields. As they passed under a stand of tall oaks that divided two fields of sunflowers, a bird began to sing.

"Listen to the cardinal sing," said Eddie. "He brings hope to everyone with his song."

Candace looked up into the treetops and finally spotted the bright red male. "Why do you say that, Eddie?" she asked.

"That's what my dad tells me."

Bryce explained the family tradition that a cardinal's song meant hope and that good times were on the way. Then Candace remembered his Christmas card, and another page was written in her book on Bryce Roberts.

The tolling of what Candace thought was a distant church bell drifted out on the breeze.

"That's our signal for lunch. We can return to the house that way," Bryce said, pointing toward a stand of tall pine trees to the south.

Candace found herself listening for a cardinal's song when they rode the trail that passed through the stately evergreens. The pines gave off their aroma, and the clops of their mounts' hooves were muffled on the layers of needles covering the ground below their branches, but she didn't hear the vibrant birdsong for which she listened.

Chapter 57

After lunch with Rosalie, Bryce and Candace left the children with Midge and Teensy and headed for the stables to re-saddle their horses.

Thunder, Bryce's stallion, sensed that this time he could run. He strained at the reins as they got outside the stable yard and Bryce let him get it out of his system on trails to the east.

On first seeing Ghost, Candace appreciated the depth through the gelding's girth and knew his bloodlines also came from horses meant to run. She gave Ghost his head and pursued Bryce, delighted in her mount's speed. They slowed as they entered a trail that led along a tree-lined stream and allowed the horses to drink before moving on. The trail was wide enough for side-by-side riders and Bryce brought Thunder next to Ghost. Candace's smile was radiant.

"Oh, Bryce, thank you for this day. I've so enjoyed riding again, and doing it here in this beautiful countryside with you makes it even more special." She reached toward his hand across the narrow space between them and they reined in their horses, leaned across them, and kissed. "I have wanted to do that since you showed me to my room back at the house," she said, and her face took on the expression Bryce knew meant teasing or mischief was on her mind.

"We won't wait next time," he said.

"Oh, but we need the suspense of when we'll have that first kiss of the day. Without anticipation we'd miss half of the fun of the first kiss."

"For someone with a streak of tomboy in her, you're quite the romantic. So, we'll wait for at least an hour every day."

She smiled and leaned over for another kiss. Then she pulled away, dug her heels into the surprised Ghost, and shouted over her shoulder, "I'll race you to the clearing down there."

Thunder sensed the challenge but he was several lengths behind when he hit full gallop. Bryce urged him on. As the trail widened near the clearing Thunder and he were gaining until Candace leaned forward over Ghost, assuming a jockey's racing crouch and got just enough speed out of Ghost to keep the lead for a precious few more strides into the clearing.

They slowed the horses gradually and then brought them to a walk.

Bryce looked admiringly at her and teased, "You really know how to ride . . . for a woman."

"You chauvinist pig. I'm going to use the language of some of my students if you keep that up."

"While I'm being sexist, I have a question. How do you keep those beautiful breasts of yours from bouncing all over the place when you ride like that?"

She blushed and Bryce thought he'd gone too far, but the look of devilment appeared on her face. She removed her gloves and slowly unbuttoned her shirt. Then she pulled it open.

"See? I wear an athlete's bra, just like some of the women sprinters wear at track meets." Then she quickly closed her shirt and slowly buttoned it, never taking her eyes off Bryce's.

"Bryce, the expression on your face is priceless," she said as she put her gloves back on. "I'll remember it for years to come."

He knew he'd been had and just laughed at himself with her. "Candace, you're definitely a woman of the sixties."

"Aren't you glad? Bryce, where are we going from here?"

Ignoring the real thrust of her question, he responded, "Toward the river. You must see it from the cliffs." He led them eastwardly, Thunder slightly ahead of Ghost.

He looks like a Greek god mounted on that beautiful horse, she thought.

"Thunder is magnificent," said Candace.

"Quiet. He'll hear you and he already thinks he's king around here."

"Where was he bred?"

"One of the friends I made at Bucks Academy is from a wealthy Arab family. I used to invite him here to go riding. His family owns a horse farm in Kentucky. They have Arabians and Quarter Horses as well as thoroughbreds. One of the Arabian stallions jumped a fence and found romance with a quarter horse mare. Thunder's the result. Taleh offered him to me a couple of years ago when I stopped by to visit him when he came back to this country. I couldn't say no, it would have been an insult."

She grew pensive and Bryce waited for her to open up.

"You never mentioned that you're from a wealthy family," she said.

Bryce heard the tone of semi-reproach. "We don't think of ourselves in that way. We just find ways to keep on striving toward success, and that's had its rewards. I think it's in the genes."

Her blue eyes took on a special intensity that said, don't try to snow me. "What's the real reason that you play major league baseball?"

"I love the game. It pays a good living to those who do well. So, baseball's been a haven for me while I regrouped for my next steps in life and earned my MBA."

She tilted her head to the side with a look that said, There's more, isn't there? Then she held her hand up and gestured, like a traffic cop, for him to keep coming.

"And?"

Tell her the truth, he thought. She needs to know if we get serious.

"I had to do something while I regrouped after Marilyn's death and I didn't want to settle into a business mode right away. I needed to spend time away from this community for a while—all of the memories it held—even if it meant being separated from Eddie, for which I shall feel eternally guilty."

She nodded in understanding, face still serious. "But you were here in the off-seasons."

"Eddie needed me. And I needed him. Satisfied?"

"What are your plans for your future?" *I'm not going to marry a playboy.*

"I'm going to work in the family forestry products business. I have some ideas about how to make our mills more efficient." He paused and his smile began. "I may even want to borrow your laser expertise for the business of measuring and cutting."

Not so fast, Buster. Wanting to change the subject, she reigned in and silently looked out at the distant fields and woods. Still facing the view, she said, "This is Heaven."

"I agree. This is where I've grown up. With the exception of college and the Navy, I've lived here all of my life. I love this place."

Candace thought about their arrival earlier that day . . .

They'd turned into a gateway defined by weathered limestone pillars topped with slate and drove slowly down a long lane lined with alternating evergreen and maple trees. Beyond the trees on the right grew fields of early sweet corn and row upon row of lettuce varieties.

"The lettuce will be harvested in a couple of days and trucked to wholesalers in New York and Philadelphia," he explained. "On the other side are pepper and tomato plants just getting beyond the seedling stage. Those crops go to the wholesale markets also. We have a food processing plant a couple of miles from here where a lot of the vegetables from our farms and others are canned or frozen. My sister, Margaret, is in charge of the operation. We may run into her when we go out riding. She sometimes is out in the fields on horseback."

"When you said that you lived on a farm, this isn't what I imagined, Bryce. This is a commercial venture far beyond a house with a couple of horses in the barn out back."

Eddie spoke from the back seat. "We have peach trees behind our house. The barn is at the side."

Bryce tapped the side of Candace's knee and she turned to look ahead as they crested a small rise. Before them stood a three-story stone colonial house set near the top of a sloping green lawn highlighted with flowering shrubs. Later stucco and clapboard additions branched from the original central structure. Shade trees softened the house into the setting.

Bryce turned into the cul-de-sac to the right, parked and held the door open for Candace. Then they released the children from their car seats.

One half of the double front door opened and Midge stepped out onto the slate block stoop to greet them. She was in her early seventies but still stood erect. Bryce hugged her and introduced Candace and Anne to Midge. His second mother paused for a moment and frankly appraised Candace. Then she smiled, said,

"Nice to meet you," and took the children to the kitchen for a drink.

◦◦◦◦◦

Candace returned to the present. "Do you think I passed Midge's inspection? Boy, did she give me the once-over when we got here."

"Yes, she approved. She asked what took me so long to invite you here."

"What did you tell her?"

"I don't think she wanted an answer. That was just her way of approval. Now, let me change the subject back to your question.

"There's another reason I've played professional baseball. I'd appreciate your keeping this to yourself."

She nodded and he continued.

"I've saved a lot of the money I've earned from my bonuses, salary and the endorsements I do for advertising. I want to put enough aside to be financially well off at an early age so I'm never dependent on anyone in my family for support.

"We're a close family, so I don't plan on telling any of them to go to hell, but I want to be able to if the situation ever arises. I've had some very good financial advice and I'm well on my way toward a target sum I have in mind. If I can play baseball for a little longer I'll have a good nest egg. Then I'll keep it invested and let it build. I'll live on the earnings I make from whatever jobs I have." *Now she knows. I'm not going to live on the family money. Let's see what the lady says.*

Candace pondered over his revelation and then made her own confession.

"I have the same kind of thoughts about my income. I've been almost miserly, saving and investing most of my earnings and the survivor's stipend I get from the government for Anne and myself. My parents gift some to Anne and me each year and Stan and Jennie have a trust set up for Anne, so her education will be taken care of. I want to teach long enough to qualify for a pension." *Now you know I'm not a gold digger.*

Bryce remembered her expression of pain on the day she had reluctantly parted with the check in payment for the mounted tuna and he understood. Then he asked, "Have you ever thought of going into business for yourself? With your savvy about lasers, you have a huge opportunity."

"Maybe someday. Right now I just want to get my Doctorate. My salaries will be increased and I'll have more choices open up in my career."

They reined in at the heights above the wide Delaware River, dismounted, and walked the horses in silence along the tree line at the edge of the fields. Bryce pointed to a woodchuck grazing in the shadows of a clump of trees. When she said she couldn't see it, he stood behind her and pointed over her shoulder. It was an easy step from there and he took her in his arms and kissed her lovingly.

"I know where I'm headed," he said. "I just want to make sure you do."

She tried to keep her expression businesslike but her half-hooded eyes betrayed the emotions she felt. "I think I know where I'm going too," she told him, "but I need more time."

He didn't respond. Instead he handed Thunder's reins to Candace and walked to a patch of wildflowers and picked several. He returned and slipped them in her hair under her riding helmet.

"I can be a patient man," he said. Then he pulled her to him and kissed her with lips parted and tongue gently teasing her mouth.

Chapter 58

"Leroy," said Coe, "when you get out later this year, you have to go to Bryce Roberts and tell him what I've told you. I want that bastard to sweat. When I get out, I'm going to go after him and his family. But I'll be real slow and casual about it so he's always worried about what I'm going to do next."

"I doan' want nuthin' to do wit dat honkey," said Leroy. "Besides, how am I goin' to get near him? He won't give me the time a' day.

"Oh, he will, Leroy. He will. When you talk to him you'll just use the words I'm going to teach you."

Chapter 59

Bryce and Candace were greeted at the barn by Ralph. After introductions Ralph offered to curry Ghost. Candace politely insisted on doing it herself when she saw Bryce begin to brush Thunder. *I'm coming back here,* she thought, *and I want this horse to get used to me.*

When the saddles were put up and the horses groomed, they began the walk back to the Homestead, both stinking of horses. Bryce stopped her before they arrived at the rear terrace and turned his head toward the east. Then she heard it too. An ancient motorcycle ridden by a man who looked very much like Bryce appeared around the barn and headed for the garage. Bryce gave a loud whistle through his teeth and the rider looked in their direction and headed toward them. The rider braked to a halt and turned off the motor of the machine.

"Candace, I want you to meet Phillip, my brother. Phillip, meet Candace Davis."

Phillip dropped the kickstand to rest on a flagstone and dismounted. He removed his helmet to reveal hair still styled in a "buzz cut" favored by the SEALs. But the style couldn't disguise a striking resemblance between the brothers. Bryce was slightly taller but Phillip walked with the same self-assurance. His eyes were lighter, but his smile, thought Candace, was just as charming. She offered her hand and Phillip took it.

"Candace, my brother is a lucky man to have found you first. Welcome to our home."

Okay, he's a bigger flirt than Bryce, but I must get along with him. Talk to him about his bike and let him know I'm committed to Bryce. But how do I do that since I haven't even told Bryce yet?

"Thank you. Phillip, that's a beautiful motorcycle. Have you had it restored?"

"Actually, Dad had this old Indian restored last year after it took two decades of abuse from Bryce and me. I've been hogging it since my return home, but you and Bryce should take it for a spin. We have a lot of fond memories and a bunch of skinned knees and elbows to show for it."

Bryce sat on the bike and looked at Candace. "Interested?" he asked. "It's a lot different from Ghost."

"Bryce, it has only one seat."

"So, hold on tight from the back of the seat."

"Some other time," she laughed. "I'll stick with horses for now."

Bryce and Phillip reminisced for Candace's benefit over their motorcycle riding adventures and then Phillip took the machine to the garage. Bryce's eyes followed and his expression became wistful.

"Someday, I'm going to have a motorcycle, but not before I find a good piano."

⊙≋◎

Candace showered, dried her hair, and put on an informal ivory-shaded shift dress that complimented her tanned face and neck. She finished her outfit with golden topaz earrings and headed downstairs. Bryce had told Candace enough about Harry's strict fatherhood to have her half-terrified of meeting the man. *I have to get over my nervousness about his father, she thought. He can't be that tough or Rosalie wouldn't have married him.*

She stopped for a moment near the front door.

A wide plank floor surfaced the broad foyer and hallway. The lower walls were covered with beautifully finished Black Walnut wainscoting. The wainscoting continued up the staircase she'd just descended. Wallpaper that showed a muted formal pattern of blues covered the rest of the walls that were topped with ornate crown molding stained to match the wainscoting. A pure white ceiling kept the dark woods from making the space gloomy. Portraits of men and women who she guessed were family ancestors were hung along the left side of the hallway that led toward the rear of the house. A thick, wide, oriental carpet runner dominated with shades of navy blue padded the oak steps that were stained to match the wainscoting. A chandelier enclosed in beautifully etched and beveled glass, suspended from the high ceiling over the stairway, was lit, banishing the shadows. An antique grandfather clock that displayed an ornate face through its upper glass door ticked through the silence. The right side wall was fronted with an antique Queen Anne hunt table over which hung a painting of a beautiful woodland scene that Candace recognized as an original work by a member of the Hudson River School of artists.

"Well, what do you think about when you look at that painting?" asked a male voice from behind her. The voice was not as deep as Bryce's but it had the same timbre. Candace turned to see an older gentleman with an erect bearing standing in the doorway to a sitting room off the hall. He was dressed in light gray pleated wool slacks and a freshly pressed lime green linen sport shirt that had long collar points. His penny loafers were black.

"Oh, you must be Bryce's father. I'm Candace Davis, Mr. Roberts. And the painting makes me think of the scenery I saw on today's ride."

"Call me Harry. Now, may I offer you some Chablis?

He ushered Candace through the sitting room into a study next to the dining room where he poured a glass from an open bottle sitting in a bucket of ice.

Bryce has told him what I like, she thought. *I wonder what else he's told you. You have that same inscrutable expression Bryce sometimes shows.*

"Thank you, Mr. Roberts. Ummm, this wine is delicious."

"Rosalie and I found it in France when we were there last year and we brought two cases home. Bryce said that you enjoy Chablis, so I opened a bottle. Here's to horses," he said and raised his glass. "I hope that you enjoyed today's ride."

"It was delightful. I know now why Bryce speaks so fondly of home. The forested hills and rolling fields make quite a sight. And the river is beautiful. I understand you have always lived here?"

"Yes, I have. I wouldn't live elsewhere given another choice." He looked over her shoulder and said, "Phillip, come meet Candace Davis, Bryce's friend."

"Dad, we had a chance to meet outside a while ago, and the pleasure was all mine."

We have to find a woman for this man, thought Candace, *and she again deftly changed the subject.* "Bryce mentioned that you've just returned from a tour of duty in Vietnam. You must be thankful to be home, now, Phillip."

"Yes, but I'm still readjusting to our civilization," said Phillip. "The unit I served with spent a lot of time in the bush. We had none of the comforts of home and I feel almost overwhelmed around such luxury as plentiful hot running water."

Bryce entered the room. "Serves you right for joining that gung-ho outfit," he said, and then poured himself a drink. "My crazy brother joined the Navy SEALs," he told Candace. She looked blank so Bryce explained, "They're like commandos, only better."

"Much better," said Phillip.

Harry raised his glass again and they toasted Phillip's safe return.

Bryce said, "Little brother, tomorrow we need to catch up on lots of things. Want to get up and go for an early morning run?"

"You're on as long as you don't want to chase after deer." He then told Harry and Candace of the day Bryce had introduced him to SEAL training.

"Did you really do that to your brother?" she asked Bryce with a note of mock sympathy directed at Phillip.

"Yes, he damned near ran my, ah, butt off that day," said Phillip. "Tomorrow I'll have my revenge."

"Where are our children?" inquired Candace.

Harry told her that Rosalie and Midge had taken them fishing but that they ought to return shortly. A few minutes later they arrived with several sunfish to show for the effort and they all congratulated the kids on their catch. Candace took Anne to their room to get her cleaned up and Eddie got the same treatment from Midge. Phillip looked at Bryce and said, "Brother, don't take this the wrong way, but if you ever get tired of that lovely woman, let me know."

"That will never happen," said Bryce.

⌒⬤⌒

After grace, Harry began the dinner conversation over a salad of home-grown greens. "Candace, Bryce tells me that you teach at Penn. What made you decide to take up that profession?"

"At first I did it because it was a good way to occupy a very sad and lonely time in my life," she replied. "It was shortly after my husband died. But then I found that I loved the experience of challenging students and watching their progress as the courses develop. Now, I find myself looking forward to the time when classes begin each semester."

"Ah, the country needs more teachers with that attitude," said Rosalie. "From what I've been reading lately, our inner city schools are really in trouble."

"That's true, Rosalie," replied Candace. "I've been participating on a panel that's studying the problems, but it's not all the teachers' fault. It's a lot more complex than that."

"How so?" asked Phillip.

"There's been a whole change in social attitudes," replied Candace. "Up until 1964 discipline in the schools was strict, so there were few problems. There was a disincentive for students to act up because they knew they'd be suspended or expelled. And that was an embarrassment they didn't want to suffer in front of their classmates or families."

"Ah, yes, 1964," said Harry in mock enlightenment. "Wasn't that the year President Johnson really got his arms around Congress?"

"It's more than just new legislation," said Candace. "Two years ago in 1967 the Supreme Court decided the *Gault* case. Now, the schools have to hold a hearing before a student can be expelled. The court in one swipe took away much of the discretion from the local school principals and teachers and added what has turned out to be a whole new dimension to public education."

"Do you think it's needed?" asked Phillip.

"Not for the education process," replied Candace. "But it does serve the social purpose of giving a minority student the sense that he or she is being treated the same way everyone else is disciplined."

"That doesn't work," said Teensy who was standing in the doorway to the kitchen. "They still think they're being railroaded. The only thing the hearing does is satisfy the guilty conscience of some liberal white man."

The black woman who spoke entered the room, and Rosalie said, "Candace, meet Teensy, our resident philosopher. Teensy, this Candace Davis, Bryce's friend."

The two women smiled at each other and something pleasant, but intangible, clicked as Candace offered to shake hands.

"Nice to meet you Mrs. Davis." Then Teensy started to chuckle.

"That picture in the newspaper doesn't do you justice, Mrs. Davis."

"Please, call me Candace. I'd forgotten all about that. The good thing is that not many people recognized me in the photo because I'm not a socialite. And the name 'Teensy' doesn't suit you very well. You're not the small person who I expected to meet. You're taller than I am, and I'm six feet. Who gave you that nickname?"

"My father has a twisted sense of humor. My real name is Sara Washington. I don't mind the nickname. It used to get me a lot of blind dates I otherwise never would've enjoyed. Now, does anyone care for more salad?"

They declined and Teensy retreated to her kitchen. Harry steered the conversation back to the schools. "So, why does it take a hearing to throw a kid out of school for punching a teacher? There is no question that behavior is wrong and shouldn't be tolerated."

"Dad," said Bryce, "ask the Supreme Court, not Candace. I'm more interested in why they're promoting students who don't really merit that."

"Sometimes it's the parents who blame the schools for not teaching their children," said Candace. "When a student flunks, it tells parents they've been failures by not insisting that their children study hard. Parents don't like to hear that and a lot of school administrators don't have the courage to address that point with parents who themselves don't have a fundamental education. But it's more than just that. The whole situation is a product of a changed attitude that puts social issues ahead of practical concerns."

"It's the damned liberals in Washington," said Harry. "I'm on the Board at Bucks Academy and those government jerks tried to tell us how to run our school until we told them it is a private, religion-based institution. Why, they even wrote us a letter telling the school that federal funding would be withheld if we didn't institute a non-discrimination policy. Hell, we had one of those long before the government got on that horse. We told them to pound sand."

"Harry, you know I don't like vulgarity at the dinner table," said Rosalie.

"Sorry, Dear," said Harry, who then finished, "Of course Bucks never has accepted a dime of government money, anyway. That way they can't tell us what to do."

Teensy chimed in again. "A lot of poor people don't think about the long term benefits of a good education. Students from those families think ahead only about this week, or maybe even less; so, you can't sell a long term program to them. You have to figure out how to sell a bunch of short term benefits that add up to a long term one.

"Now, how do you want your steaks?"

The conversation drifted toward the Vietnam War while Teensy prepared and served filet mignons. Candace's suspicion that Bryce had suggested the menu was confirmed when peach ice cream was one of the dessert options.

Bryce had to travel with the team on a road trip so they made it an early night. On the way back to her car, he asked her to make sure she marked the All Star break as a vacation and she promised to do so.

"There's a place I want to show you that we didn't see today," was all that he would tell her. "Of course I want to see you before then."

They put a sleepy Anne in her car seat and Candace left with a wave of her hand and a fresh kiss on her lips.

Bryce held a gift she had given him right before she drove away. He unwrapped it to reveal a tastefully designed brass table clock. Her note read: Thanks for understanding.

Chapter 60

"We can swim instead, if you'd like," said Bryce. "Makes a little more sense in this rain."

"Let's swim and then run," said Phillip. He took off his sneakers and dived into the pool. It was 5:30 a.m. Bryce followed and the younger brother set a fast pace. Bryce reached down inside himself as he had during his UDT training and kept up. But Phillip got the best of him in the last 300 yards of their run in the rain toward home. "At least you kept up most of the way, old man. For someone who doesn't work out as hard as you used to, you're in damned good shape."

"I never want to lose it," said Bryce. "There's too much to do in life not to stay in shape. Let's clean up and eat. Then I have to leave."

They talked about Phillip's Vietnam service over breakfast, but the younger brother was not ready to speak about details and the hardships that he'd endured. Bryce mentally plotted to get his brother drunk to begin the purge of some of the bad stuff.

⊙⊜⊙

Phillip drove Bryce to the airport so that he could use Bryce's car during the Founders' road trip. Then he set out on a quest for a used Jeep by following up on personal ads in the newspaper. He found one in good condition in Warminster. After a test drive and an inspection up on a garage lift, he and the owner discussed price and shook hands on the agreement.

They went inside Glen Foster's offices and Phillip couldn't figure out what business the man was in. Then he saw some photos on the wall of Foster and buddies in fatigues taken in a jungle setting. "Vietnam?" asked Phillip.

"Yes. Army Rangers. I've been out now for about eighteen months." He looked at Phillip and said, "What outfit were you in?" Phillip looked surprised for a moment and then ran his hand over his close-cropped hair, a dead giveaway in the age of long hair styles.

"I'm going to have to let this grow in. I've just been released from active duty with the Navy SEALs."

"Did you guys really spend half of your time crawling along muddy river banks as I've heard?"

"We did some of that but a lot of it was sneak and peek stuff. And we worked with prisoners to obtain intel on local VC leaders. Then we went after those guys."

Foster explained that he and two other veterans had started an investigation business that focused on difficult cases that involved long hours of surveillance and information gathering, but also required the ability to get physical, if necessary.

"We use a lot of very sophisticated electronic surveillance equipment and we always work in teams," he explained. "We've been able to obtain some very decent night vision equipment that really helps. When we interview people, it usually is under a ruse and false ID, and most folks don't realize there is an investigation going on. We don't advertise. Our business is generated when we see an opportunity or by word of mouth. We're looking for one more man and one woman to fill out our group. Would you be interested?"

"Thanks, but I'm going to med school."

◦≋◦

Bryce was having a good season at the plate. His average hovered around .300 and he was hitting well in the clutch. Opposing pitchers and catchers read the scouting reports on him and he became the target of occasional "brush back" pitches, particularly when he came up to bat with a man on base. Bryce took no offense, because "high hard ones" had been pitchers' weapons for decades and they were understood as just part of the game.

But Johnny Grass was a different kind of pitcher. The man had a reputation around the league as just plain mean-spirited. He threw at a batter's head more often than any other pitcher, particularly if the game was close. Bryce knew that, and had watched his wind up and delivery in several of the games that year. Grass finished his delivery somewhat off balance with his landing on the first base side of the mound. There was a brief moment when he lost sight of the ball due to his finish and Bryce saw that as a vulnerability to use if Grass made him a target.

In the fourth inning of a Saturday day game Grass was on the mound when Bryce came to the plate with a runner on second. Bryce was ready and he jumped backward as the second pitch came for his head. The ball hit the catcher's mitt right behind where his head had been a moment before. Bryce changed his grip on the bat so that he could hit a line drive more easily than a fly ball. When he got back in the batter's box he looked for a low fast ball, which he knew often followed Grass' "brush backs." The next pitch was true to habit and Bryce hit a vicious low line drive at the spot he had picked at the right side of the mound. People in the stands heard the ball hit Grass' knee and he went down, writhing in pain. The ball ricocheted toward the right field dugout, the runner scored, and Bryce wound up at second base. Grass had to leave the game.

In the locker room after the game a sportswriter came up to him and started to talk about the play in which Grass went down. "That was really a vicious hit, Bryce. How did that feel coming right after the beanball Grass threw at you?"

"Every once in a while a pitcher takes one, and it happened today. But that's part of baseball. I was just trying to hit it to the right side to move the runner along and he threw me a pitch I could really lay into."

"But didn't it feel like things evened out for you after the brushback?" persisted the reporter.

"I don't keep that kind of score, Bert."

Chapter 61

The All-Star break arrived and, competitive as he was, Bryce was glad there were too many outfielders with bigger reputations than his, and he was not selected. Before the break he'd directed preparations, including having Sunrise cleaned until it practically shone. Because the cabin's refrigerator was powered by propane, he could leave it on for a day or two before his planned arrival. It was filled with gourmet fare. Ralph, the handyman flushed the plumbing free of any rust and made sure the well was working. The batteries for the electric generator starter were charged, and the stable was stocked with hay and feed for the horses. Candace would arrive at the family homestead the next morning, following a detailed map that Bryce had labored over. Anne was in Wellesley with Jake's parents.

Bryce spent the after dinner hours with Phillip enjoying the sunset from the terrace. He poured several shots of good scotch into Phillip's glass in the hope of loosening his tongue about Vietnam. But Phillip talked about the job he had been offered by Foster.

Bryce asked for details, listened, and then asked, "What qualifies you to do that kind of work?"

"We did a lot of snooping around when we were assigned to IV Corp, especially at night and early in the morning before the sun rose. Bryce, I had VC walk within three feet of me and never even notice."

"What if they'd noticed you?"

"They would have been eliminated. Hell, it was them or us."

"You aren't going to be asked to do that around here. What else qualifies you for the job?"

"I know how to handle myself in a ruckus. Foster said there may be some of that once in a while."

"That's not what you need, either. Man, you need to unwind more and get into life back here."

"I've been thinking about medical school. Our corpsmen really had my respect. I figure it's a long haul but it'll be worth it if I can help save lives."

"Better idea. Somehow I see you helping people after what you've been through."

"The med board exams are next week."

"Are you going to take them?"

"Yes. I really wasn't serious about Foster's job anyway. I just wanted to jerk your chain."

Chapter 62

Candace arrived the next morning with her bag packed for five days even though her stay was scheduled for three days. This time Bryce kissed her in her guest room when he put down her bag.

"We're not going to wait this time, and you can anticipate the next one sometime before midnight," he said.

"Mr. Roberts, control yourself."

"Meet me on the terrace after you freshen up, and we can sit and talk for a few minutes about what we can do this weekend."

"What?" she said in mock shock, "You don't have the whole time planned?"

"Well, I have some ideas but we can talk when you come down to the terrace. There's some iced tea ready. Or do you prefer something else?"

Candace smiled flirtatiously and looked at his lips. "Tea is fine . . . for now."

They sat in the late morning sunlight, glad of each other's company. Candace studied the distant scenery.

"Those hills really make the view. Do you ever go there?"

Oh, Hallelujah! "Yes, there's a stream that flows behind that first ridge. It's fed by a pond in the saddle of the hills and it's absolutely beautiful in those woods. My brothers and I spent much of our boyhood hiking all over them. Years ago Dad built a cabin up there. It's called Sunrise for obvious reasons."

So that's what you've been planning. "When I was here last time you said there was a place that you wanted to show me. Is that it?"

"Yes."

If I go there with this man, I'm going to be hard-pressed to say no to what I think we both want. So do I go there or not? Candace, you told him that you want to jump back into life with both feet. Did you mean it?

Candace felt her throat go dry and she knew it was the old fears returning. She sipped her tea and said, "It's probably cooler up there than it is here. How long does it take to get there?"

"Sunrise is a long ride by horseback. If we go, we should plan on staying overnight."

She looked at him with a questioning expression.

"Don't worry, I'll sleep in the guestroom," he said.

"What will your parents think, Bryce? I don't want them to believe that I'm some kind of floozie."

"They know you aren't. My mother really likes you. As a matter of fact, I bet that if we ask, she'll help you pack your backpack for the trip. Mom's often been there and knows what a woman should take with her. If we're going to go we should have lunch and leave so we won't be rushed," he said.

Candace's gaze returned to the hills. *Decision time, woman. What's it going to be?*

"Well, we certainly don't want to be rushed on a hot day like this, do we?" The mischief expression lit her face.

Rosalie didn't help her pack, but she did sit with Candace when she chose items to take along. When she saw the large pile, Rosalie gently persuaded Candace to halve it. Then she took a bottle of cologne that Candace had removed from her suitcase and put it in a pocket of the now stuffed backpack. The last thing that went in on top was a bathing suit because Rosalie had talked about swimming in the stream.

Her son's behavior and that of his girlfriend were not what Rosalie would have approved, had they been younger; but Bryce and Candace were adults who could make their own choices in life. She sighed and hoped that they would find happiness in these now-turbulent times. She watched from beneath a table umbrella on the terrace as they left the paddock. Her son wore a baseball hat and Candace wore a straw cowboy hat. They were talking animatedly as they rode side by side into the heat of the day.

Chapter 63

The sun was scorching on the humid afternoon and they both were glad to dismount and walk the horses through the gate at the base of the fire trail leading into Sunrise Hills. The gate had a prominently displayed sign that read: No Trespassing. Private Property. Fire Restricted Zone. Bryce closed the gate after them and gave Candace a leg up.

It was immediately cooler under the canopy of trees. Many towered over 90 feet into the sky and formed a canopy over the clusters of late blooming mountain laurel that grew in the few sunny patches on the forest floor. Ferns grew in green swaths up one hillside and creeping wintergreen bloomed along the trail bordered by thickets of rhododendron. Huge fungus growths, some with bright colors, protruded from decaying trunks of downed trees. New growth had taken root in the chaos of the forest floor, and everywhere there was moss. The light was dimmer and had a green cast that made them each look pale-skinned.

The horses' hooves made only muffled sounds on the trail that was covered in thick layers of pine needles and macerated brush from the clearing operations. The forest seemed to encourage silence or lowered voices.

"These woods are incredible," she said in hushed tones, "How long have they been here?"

"They're more than two hundred years old. My great grandfather wouldn't allow them to be logged over and, except for the fire trails, they've remained untouched ever since. There's a stream up ahead where otters sometimes play. If we're quiet we may be able to sneak up on them and watch them if they're around. Want to give it a try?"

Candace nodded and they dismounted at the edge of the trail, tied their horses' reins to waist-high tree branches and left their packs on the fire trail. Cat quiet, he led the way down a game trail, helping her over deadfalls, through twisted roots, and new growth that had sprung up along the tiny trail. Candace watched where he stepped and did likewise. They emerged from the green shade onto a rocky ledge above the stream and sat in the shadow of a hemlock. In a slow motion he pointed across the narrow stream to the head of a swimming animal that moments later disappeared under the water. They waited patiently in the shade.

Almost silently a pair of otters broke the surface and climbed out onto rocks at the edge of the opposite bank. They shook the water from their fur, a small patch of sunlight creating tiny rainbows in the sprays of droplets. Two more otters shot out of the water and the first pair ran up the bank, followed by the new arrivals. Bryce pointed to a well-worn mudslide to the left of where the animals had disappeared into the undergrowth and moments later an otter slid headfirst down the bank and into the water. The others followed and they did it all over again. Bryce and Candace watched the playful animals until they stopped their antics. The couple returned to the horses, stopped to allow their mounts to drink from a spring, and then continued.

The fire trail wound upward through the woods for another quarter mile before they came to the steps leading to the waterfall and the pool below.

"You should see the falls," said Bryce.

They dismounted, unshouldered their backpacks, and hitched the reins to posts that had been placed at the trail's edge for that purpose. He led her half way down the steps and paused on a small landing that gave a perfect view of the surroundings. The falls were not a big, thundering cascade but, rather, a fine, shimmering veil of water that his grandmother had named Whispering Falls. It suited the spot perfectly because the muted sound matched the quiet of the forest.

"If you look carefully," he said, "you may be able to see some of the big trout in that pool at the base of the falls." She looked for the trout and then, without waiting for him to start, descended the remaining steep steps and walked to the sandy edge of the pool.

Candace looked up at the falls and then at Bryce. She blew him a kiss. He caught it and began the climb down. She picked up stones flattened by the action of the water and skipped them across the surface of the pool.

"Those trout will never come up now," he teased.

She washed sand off her hands and said, "It's not as cold as I thought it would be. Let's go swimming. It's such a lovely place for a dip and I'm still warm from our ride."

"Ah . . . Candace . . . I forgot to pack swim trunks."

"You, the totally organized man, forgot to pack a bathing suit? What a shame," she teased and tisked her tongue. "Mine's in my backpack. But, you know what? I'm not going to climb all the way back up there." The mischievous look appeared on her face and she said, "If you'll turn your back I'm just going to undress and go in. Then I'll turn my back for you." *God, I don't believe I said that!*

"What makes you think I won't peek? Besides we have to dry off when we get out."

She ignored his teasing and logic. "We'll think of something. Turn around."

He did so, and listened to the rustle of her clothes being removed. Moments later he heard her sharp intake of breath as she waded into the deeper water that was cooler. Bryce turned in time to see a beautiful bottom slip quietly under the surface. Her head came up from underwater and she was facing him.

"Now it's your turn," she called.

He stripped to his skivvies.

She swam a few strokes closer to shore. Breasts floating just under the surface, she stood on the bottom in the deep water and looked at him. He signaled her to turn around and she shook her head no.

What the hell, if this weekend goes as planned it's not going to matter. He put his back to her and dropped his skivvies. Then he turned and walked very deliberately into the water.

"Man, you are beautiful! Not that much hair on your chest, but incredible pecs. Is that from all of your swimming?"

"Fibber," he called back, dived forward, and swam under water to her. She watched, almost apprehensively, as if the big white shadow swiftly moving toward her was a shark. Then she felt powerful hands clasp both sides of her waist. Bryce surfaced, stood on the bottom and raised her part way out of the water, breasts at his eye level.

"No hair on your chest, but gorgeous breasts, and nipples stiff from the cool water." He held her above him, studying her face in appreciation. Water droplets in her eyelashes and hair glinted in the sun. He grinned, looked up at her face and exclaimed, "Woman, you're beautiful."

She looked down at him with teasing eyes and said, "You swim like those otters we watched." She wriggled out of his grasp and splashed water on him.

Bryce swam away toward the falls and got out on the rocks beneath them. He let the falls cascade down on him. Candace joined him there and sat on a submerged boulder. The falling water formed a shawl over her shoulders.

She looked at the rocky cliff sides, verdant with trees and rhododendrons. "This is wonderful after that hot ride. And this place is beautiful. I had no idea this pool would be as large. I was imagining just a little stream."

He looked frankly at her and said, "You look like a nymph that just belongs here." He reached for her hand and they jumped back into the pool together. He swam from side to side to stay warmed up and she did the same before resting in chest high water nearer the water's edge.

He swam over to her, stood on the sandy bottom, embraced her, and kissed Candace with a passion he'd reserved until this day.

She thrilled with the feel of her breasts against his chest, wrapped her arms around his neck, and returned his kiss with equal fervor. Under the water she pulled her legs up around his waist, locked them behind him and kissed him again as he held a strong hand firmly under her bottom. His other hand on her back kept her pressed against him.

He felt himself getting hard despite the cool water. He looked at Candace, and between kisses said, deep voice husky with emotion, "Do you want to wait until we get to the cabin or is here the place?"

"Oh, Bryce, let's not wait. I may be too scared later." She lowered her hips and guided him deep into her, then embraced him again with arms and legs. They remained there, thrilled by the sheer pleasure in each other's faces and the sensations of their bodies' joining, neither wanting to speak first and break the magic of the moment. Then, arms enfolding her, he began to move very slightly within her.

"My God, woman, you're like hot silk down there. I've wanted you for so long. Now I want to pleasure you endlessly."

She grinned wantonly, and said, "Show me." She tightened her arms around him and pushed her womanhood hard against him. Then she lightly put her tongue in his ear and whispered, "I feel so good floating here in your arms like this."

The blue in her eyes began to deepen as he moved within her, and then, she, too, began the rhythm of the most ancient man-woman dance. They kissed deeply, passionately, relishing and loving the pleasures they felt and gave, wanting only to give and receive more. As she neared her crescendo he moved toward shallower water and took her breast in his mouth. She held it at his lips and he eagerly kissed and tongued the nipple as they reached the peaks together.

Heart pounding, she held on tightly, savoring their rapture. Then slowly she relaxed her embrace and dreamily enjoyed the feel of his arms around her and his heat in her and against her. She moaned quietly in pleasure, half floating in the crystal water. When her breath in his ear slowed, she leaned back slightly, looked into his half-closed eyes, and whispered, "You're very dear to me Bryce Roberts."

He nodded slowly in acknowledgment and then pulled her to him again.

Candace returned the embrace. Then she leaned a bit farther away and said, face getting the mischievous look, "What do you suppose the trout think of us?"

"'Biggest fucking otters we ever saw.'"

Her melodious laughter echoed off the water and cliff sides in that serene place. It was the first time since their sleigh ride that he'd witnessed such hearty laughter from her and he found himself glad to hear her laugh so, and glad she shared his humor. He continued to hold her close, still firm within her, not wanting to let go of the woman he'd desired for so long. But he could feel her beginning to shiver.

"Hold on to me," he said; then he put one arm under her bottom and the other around her back and carried her out of the water to a large flat rock that formed a dry platform warmed by

Chapter 64

J ust for the atmosphere they lit a small fire in the mammoth stone fireplace. Candace meandered around the great room, admiring the way the magnificent logs in the walls had been fitted together. Her gaze drifted upward. Rough-hewn beams supported the upper floor and the roof rafters lay exposed under wide roof boards.

The cabin was furnished in rustic early American furniture. The accessories were eclectic items that had found a last home. A balcony extended across the second level allowing a view of the great room from upstairs. A large bank of tall windows in the eastern wall overlooked the valley.

He opened wine for each of them and turned on a radio that ran on batteries. The Carpenter's new hit, 'We've Only Just Begun' floated into the kitchen where they prepared hors d'oeuvres. "Did you order the disk jockey to play that tune now?" she asked.

"I'd like to take credit but it's just a coincidence," he said and then he hugged her to him. She held her cheek to his shoulder and enjoyed the sound of his heartbeat.

The radio gave off bursts of static and the wind began to blow in gusts over the chimney as a thunderstorm approached. He checked the horses and closed the upper doors of the stalls and turned on an emergency lantern to comfort the horses for the coming weather.

When he returned, Candace was standing at the breakfast area window looking southwest at the approaching storm. He stood behind her and put his arms around her. Between kisses to her neck and caressing her he told her about the time the lumberjacks installed lighting rods in the trees near the cabin.

The storm rolled over the valley toward them and she leaned her backside into him and pulled his arms around her tightly as the winds hit the hillside. The tops of the closely growing trees banged into each other and branches split and fell as the wind increased. They watched as lightning shot from cloud to cloud and then a bolt hit one of the grounded trees outside with a terrific crashing boom. Bryce walked to the other side of the cabin and looked out the window to check for any damage but he could see none. More lightning bolts, followed by torrential rain, continued for the next quarter hour. They watched it all from the safety of the cabin, arms around each other.

"This is what stone age men must have felt when they stood at the mouth of their cave and watched," she said. "Only they didn't understand the basic scientific principles governing the storm."

"I wonder what they thought about lightning?" he asked. "Their explanation probably was a lot more interesting than our science. But even with understanding, it's still awesome, isn't it?"

"Yes, it is . . . Bryce?"

"Hmmm?"

"I'm very glad I'm here with you tonight."

"Me too. Are you hungry?"

"Ravenous."

He fixed thick veal chops in a wine sauce with mushrooms and wild rice and Candace made a salad dressing that was superb with a combination of Radicchio and Boston Bibb.

He moved the kitchen table so that they had a view of the valley as the lights came on in the farm houses in the distance below. The convection of the warm air gave the lights a twinkling effect to match the candles she lit for the table.

"I noticed that your mother had candles lit at the table when I was at your home and it made such a nice effect, even when there still was light outside. Does your family use candles often?"

"Most of the year. It's what I've grown up with. Let's make it a habit anytime we eat dinner together."

"That's something I'll look forward to. Honey, this veal is delicious. Where did you learn to cook like this?"

"On rainy days Midge used to get us children in the kitchen and give us cooking lessons. She's expert at it, although she now lets Teensy do most of it for the family and guests. I like to cook for up to four people, but above that, I don't do that well."

"I took some lessons from a Cordon Bleu chef at an Air Force base where we were stationed. If we stay here tomorrow night, I'm going to prepare those steaks I saw in the 'fridge with a very special dipping sauce. I checked and all of the ingredients are here. Bryce, this place is stocked with enough food for a week. What were you thinking?"

"I just wanted us to have a selection."

"So you planned this all along. That's why you had us take in the view from your terrace. You wanted the subject to come up." *Another page in my Bryce book.*

"I admit it." Then, reaching for her hand, he said, "Here in these woods it's just the two of us and nature. I didn't want us to be interrupted. I wanted our first time together to be special and so I thought of this place. I've felt very close to you since we left the homestead and began our ride here."

"I've wanted you, too, Bryce, and I can't think of any place I'd rather be with you," she told him. "I've thought long and hard about whether to give of myself with you."

"What made you decide?"

"Trust. I really do want to jump back into life with both feet and I want to do it with you. I chose you because I trust you. And," she said softly, "you're a very special man."

After dinner they sat on the front porch swing listening to a screech owl and Katydids add their music to the night air. He had his arm around her shoulders and she leaned her head against him.

"Bryce, tell me this is really happening."

He reached up, gently squeezed her earlobe and caressed behind it. "More?"

She turned toward him and the fire built as their lips met, softly at first and then with more urgency. She felt him move his hand under her blouse, unhook her bra and cup her breast, gently teasing the nipple.

"Inside, lover boy," she said. "I'm not exposing my naked body to these night insects."

⚬▬⚬

They found blankets and a soft comforter in a chest in the great room and almost bashfully spread them and pillows over the rug in front of the fireplace. He put another small log on the coals and the flames pushed the deep shadows away from the hearth. They watched each other undress and then lay together, savoring the feel of their embrace, kissing passionately, hungrily. The new lovers caressed gently, then deeply, as they explored for the sensual places each knew they would find.

The radio was still playing quietly when a new tune began.

"Candace, will you dance the tango with me?"

In answer she got up and held her hands out to him, inviting the dance. Bryce stared up at her as the golden firelight played across her body.

"You look like a beautiful, primitive enchantress," he said.

She didn't answer. Instead the tall woman lasciviously curled her tongue across her teeth, and bare feet moving in perfect time, began to dance alluringly toward a clear space away from the blankets, all the while keeping eye contact. He rose and they danced together, bodies touching, faces telling each other of their yearnings. By the end of the tango they both were tremendously aroused and she welcomed him into her the moment they again lay on the comforter. Their arms went around each other and they lost themselves in their passion.

Heartbeat going wild she told him, "Yes, oh yes . . . oh, God, yes . . . like that . . . Now, keep him deep . . . yes, like that . . . yes, oh, Bryce . . . yes!"

This time he was patient beyond her first climax. When she sensed that, she wrapped her long legs around him and renewed her own movements with abandon. She cried out when they together arrived at the moments of ecstasy. Then, almost breathless, she asked, "Oh. Lover! How do you do that?"

"The way you respond makes it easy," he told her.

They lay together on their sides for a long time afterward, he moving gently in her, she with her womanhood gripped tightly around him, each pleasured by their still excited and sensuous state. They lightly caressed each other, kissing wetly and lovingly, delighting in the closeness after enduring years of longing and loneliness.

As their arousal receded Candace's eyes began to tear and a feeling of helplessness came over Bryce as he watched tears slide down her cheeks.

"Honey, what's wrong?"

"Nothing, you wonderful man. Don't you recognize tears of happiness when you see them?"

"Well, then, your tears are okay." He smiled and gently caressed her face to wipe the tears away.

"Bryce, you've been gentle, yet you hold me so . . . and this is going to sound old-fashioned, but I mean it . . . you hold me so ardently, so warmly. I'll always treasure the way you've held me tonight. I've been so . . . lonesome. Yet, I was afraid to be with just any man for the sake of . . . of . . ."

"Temporary satisfaction?"

"Yes. And now I'm so happy we've shared ourselves with each other."

"I'm glad, too, Candace. I've wanted you since that first evening at the hospital ball, but I knew you had to heal first. I thank God you have."

"Bryce?"

"Yes?"

"Will you just hold me while I cry?"

"Go ahead, cry all you want to. I'm here." He guided her cheek against his neck and wrapped his left arm around the woman he wanted to hold forevermore. With his other hand he caressed her neck, her face, her hair as her tears fell warm and wet against him. Deep, aching sobs erupted from Candace, purging the loneliness, the fears, the pain that she'd held inside for so long.

Finally her convulsions ebbed. Still, Bryce held her and caressed her until her sniffing stopped.

She lifted her face to his to thank him.

"Oh, damn, I've made you cry, too."

"Nah, those are just your tears on my cheeks."

"You make a terrible liar." She kissed him then, slowly and completely, as if it were the last one she had to give.

Later, sitting with their backs to the fire, they talked about their childhood dreams and fears, and discovered more to love about each other. He'd been afraid of heights until he learned to fly a glider and she was afraid of a big neighborhood dog until he had come into their backyard and played fetch with her.

When the fire began to die he said, "I wonder if my parents ever had a night like this up here?"

"I think they did," she said, remembering Rosalie's placing the perfume in her knapsack.

"Why do you say that?"

"Just a hunch. Your mother really lets her hair down with a little wine in her and I bet old Harry learned that early on."

The couple stepped out onto the porch to watch the distant lightning from another storm silhouette the forest heights. She again stood with her backside against him and he wrapped his arms around her. Their contentment lasted until a mosquito bit him and he slapped at it. She went inside to the hearth and he put on his shoes and went to check the horses.

When he returned to the cabin he did his evening ablutions and then led the drowsy Candace upstairs to the master bedroom. She walked sleepily toward the bath and a few minutes later returned to their bed and found his arms. They smiled often in sleep that granted each of them a serenity that was complete for the first time in years

Chapter 65

He arose before dawn, put on shorts, started coffee percolating and checked and fed the horses. When the coffee was ready he placed two steaming mugs on a tray with cream and sugar servers and carried them to the bedroom where Candace still slept. He doffed his shorts, kissed her awake, and turned a lantern's flame up so she could barely see him.

"What's wrong?"

"Sunrise in about ten minutes. Get up and have some coffee with me."

"Just this once I shall humor you," she said, yawning. She stretched, got out of bed and headed for the bathroom. When she returned she put a little sugar in her coffee and then told Bryce, "Sit on the bed with your back against the headboard. Put a pillow between you and the headboard." He did so and she climbed into bed.

"Okay, Mister, spread your legs." He did and she sat between his legs, with her back against his chest, and had a sip of coffee. "You're going to be my lounge chair—"

"—Ah shucks, ma'am, I thought we were going to do something kinky."

"Maybe later. When does the sunrise start? I feel like a kid waiting for the fireworks on the fourth of July."

"Give it a minute. We're going to have a good one because there are some clouds in the eastern sky." He nuzzled her neck, and caressed her breast with his free hand.

"Do you want hot coffee all over the place?"

He didn't take his hand away. Instead he continued to tease her by gently caressing the nipple and tip of her breast with a feather-light touch until he heard her begin to breathe in shorter rhythm. Then he stopped.

"Devil." She pinched his thigh and he had to hold still or risk a coffee spill.

The bellies of the clouds began to glow with pinks and oranges. The colors strengthened as the sun neared daybreak. As the orb's top edge arrived just below the horizon the colors of the sky and clouds intensified into a spectacular crescendo of deep crimson, red, gold and a multitude of lumescent oranges, pinks and purples. The couple sat there in the golden light that filled their bedroom, spellbound by what they were witnessing together.

"I think this is God's morning symphony," she said. "Are you a spiritual man, Bryce? You sometimes talk as if you are."

"Yes and no. I think spirituality begins at the border between knowledge and mystery. The more understanding a man has, the more deeply recessed are the edges of his spiritual beliefs, but they're always there in some form, because we're all spiritual beings.

"When Marilyn died I tried to forsake my faith. I reasoned that God couldn't be a loving deity because He took her from me. That was me relying upon human rationale. But, eventually, as I've thought much more about the complexities of this universe, and the order of it, an element of spirituality crept back into my life."

"What was it Thoreau said? 'With all your science, can you tell me how it is that light comes into the soul?'"

"Exactly."

Slowly the sunrise palette faded as the star that warms the earth rose above the horizon and behind the clouds. Candace took a sip of her coffee in silence and then put the cup back on the nightstand's tray.

"Thank you for the sunrise, Darling," she said. "You really know how to treat a woman." Then she rolled next to him, pulled the covers under her chin, and went back to sleep. For the first time in many years Bryce did likewise.

When they reawakened she felt his hardness against her, nuzzled his neck, and whispered, "We can't waste that beauty. But let's scrub our teeth first."

Later, as they were lying there in that languid state that follows, she began, "You know something, Jake . . ." and then she was mortified at the slip.

"Yes, Marilyn?" he responded.

He hugged her to him and said, "We'll do that from time to time and that's okay. Our former spouses can't just be erased. So when they come up like that, let's just understand and remember them fondly."

"That's a deal . . . Bryce . . . do you want to tell me about Marilyn now?"

"You probably are wondering whether I ever was here with Marilyn. She was here once, before we married, on a family day trip, and that was it. I just wanted you to know."

"It doesn't matter now, but thanks for telling me."

They lay facing each other, heads propped up on hands, and he talked with utter frankness and affection about the woman who was his first love. He spoke about their growing up together, her zest for life, their separation during the early college years and, later, during his Naval service. He told her about Coe and all that he had said and done; the terrible shock and grief he experienced; and the recovery he undertook. He told her how Marilyn's parents and his parents were so wonderful with Eddie, and he ended with a gentle reminder that Candace was now first in his thoughts.

She stretched and then curled back close to him. She thought about the best way to begin and then spoke.

"You remember Flo, my friend?"

He nodded.

"Jake was her cousin and he was very much like her in some ways . . . because he was my best friend." Her story of their time together at MIT and in the Air Force unfolded as the morning sunlight filled the room and she spoke from her heart . . . "Memories and Anne are all he left to me, and for a long time that's what I lived on. But now things are different. Now, I remember his quiet seriousness that made his sense of humor all the funnier when he showed it; but, mostly, I remember his self-confidence and intelligence and how those strengths helped him deal with life and me. You have them too, and I think that's part of what attracts me to you. That and one of the most beautiful bodies I've ever seen," she teased.

She leaned across and kissed him. Then she caressed his cheek and said, "Hey cave man, are you going to shave before we cook breakfast?"

After breakfast they hiked on another fire trail that led over the crest of the hill and ended in a high valley. He guided her to a clearing and watched her face as she enjoyed the double image on the surface of a pond that reflected the blues of the sky, brilliant white clouds and surrounding treetops that appeared almost as a dark lace upon the still water.

"This pond is the source of the stream we swam in yesterday," he said as he uncovered a canoe stored on a rack.

They paddled around the pond, enjoying the quiet stillness, broken only by the sound of bird calls and a soft breeze that faintly whispered through the tops of the big trees. He showed her where ospreys used to nest and spoke about how he and his brothers were working with wildlife experts to fledge them at an old nest site on the Delaware River.

As they stowed and covered the canoe she asked, "Why not restore the ospreys to this pond?"

"A couple of years ago Dad had the deadfalls cleared from along the edge of the banks so we could use the pond for recreation. Right after that he discovered large trout are in this pond and he doesn't want the ospreys competing for them. When we come back here again, we can bring the fishing rods from the cabin."

He tied the last knot in the canoe cover and she looked at him with a narrow-eyed appraisal that told him she'd finally detected his ruse.

"Bryce, I just realized that those shorts of yours look suspiciously like swimming trunks. I thought you told me you'd 'forgotten' your swimsuit."

"Oh, I don't swim in these," he said, dark eyes full of laughter and half- grin starting. "I just wear them when I go canoeing."

"Bryce Roberts, you're a conniving rascal." She began to playfully beat on his chest in mock vengeance for being snookered. "How dare you take advantage of such a naive woman?" she asked, her face the picture of perfect innocence.

"Might I remind you that you were the first to remove your clothes?"

"Yeah," she admitted, eyes dancing, "that was fun, wasn't it?" Then she hugged him tightly. "I should've known that you're too organized and disciplined to 'forget' your bathing suit."

After lunch they took books from the cabin's well-stocked shelves, carried them and blankets to the eastern platform and loafed away reading and napping in the afternoon sun. He chose a book of sonnets to read aloud to her when she put her book down to face the sun for its tanning rays. He was just about to put the poetry book down when he noticed a faint inscription inside the cover: 'To Harry with all my love, Rosalie.' He showed it to Candace and said, "Your hunch was right, look what I found."

That evening she prepared the steaks as promised and they talked into the night about people they had known and how they had influenced their lives. He described Evars Dombrowski, his UDT judo instructor's "look," and how he used it to cow his students into paying attention.

"Let me see you do the look, Bryce," she pleaded. He turned away for a moment and then faced her with the best imitation he could muster.

"Good grief! That's scary," she said. "You ought to use that on an umpire when he makes a bad call on you."

"Nah," said Bryce, "They get used to things like that and if you ride them too hard, they can really make life miserable for you."

"Well, then, maybe on our kids when they get out of line," she suggested.

Bryce recognized the opening she had offered but he ducked. "It probably would scare the daylights out of them," he told her and then he was quiet.

"You chicken," she said. Then she studied him in silent contemplation.

"I'm sorry," she said. "It's just that I'm so happy right now, I'm getting ahead of things."

"I think we'd better wait a while . . . before we talk about that," he said. "But I want you to know that being together with you gives me the same hope and happiness I feel when I hear a cardinal's song."

Their lovemaking that evening was defined by their feelings of togetherness and the joy that overflowed with their new beginnings. For the rest of his life Bryce remembered how Candace looked in the lantern light as he lay on his back with her astride him. He marveled over her sensual beauty—arched back, breasts outthrust, face in ecstasy, as she shuddered through her climax only after she alone had timed her pleasure to arrive there.

⌒≋⌒

The last thing they did before they left Sunrise was muck out the stable. They shoveled the manure into an old, iron-wheeled wheelbarrow and Bryce spread it near wild blueberry bushes on the hillside. "Today, I don't even mind doing this," he said.

"Me neither," she added, "but I shall always remember how our first visit to Sunrise ended."

"First visit, Ms. Davis?" said Bryce with raised eyebrows. "Are you suggesting there will be more?"

"I'd love to come back here in the fall with you, when the foliage turns and fish for trout in the pond, just as you suggested."

"Consider it done. We'll return in early October."

Chapter 66

W e're going to have a future together. But what do we do next? thought Bryce as Candace's car disappeared down the lane. Bryce felt emptiness in his gut, almost as if he was grieving. Man, you're hooked, he told himself. Well, don't stand here. Let's get in gear.

He found his father and asked if Harry had time to talk.

"Dad, I'm ready to take a more active role in the family business. When can I start?

Harry thought for a moment and then said, "Candace really has gotten to you, hasn't she? I'll wager that you have plans for a future with her and that's fine."

Bryce could see Harry contemplating his next statement.

"Just don't let her talk you out of staying in baseball if that is what she's attempting to do. You have to decide on your own career timing."

Bryce did a double take. "Why the change in attitude? Always before you've said my baseball is a waste of time."

"Bryce, I've lived for years with the dream of your joining and then running the business. In the process I just never considered your personal goals and situation. I was selfish to approach it that way and it's caused a lot of conflict. It's not too late for me to accept the fact that you have to carve your own path. I know why you've stayed away and it hurt to think that you needed that much space away from your family. Now, I'm telling you not to come back until you're ready. Don't let me, or Candace, make that decision for you."

"Are you going to let me make my own decisions about running the business?"

"As you gain experience, yes. But keep in mind you didn't make it to the major leagues overnight and you have the same kind of learning curve in our business. The big difference is your business decisions could be disastrous for our family and the employees, so you and I are going to confer about most things until I think you're ready."

"What if we disagree?"

"We do it my way," said Harry.

Bryce held his tongue. Then he burst out laughing.

"Dad, I'll go along with that now. Just don't baby me."

"That's a deal. Now, has Candace tried to talk you out of baseball?"

"No. We've talked only once about my career path. She knows I want to work in the family business when I leave baseball. But she's never even hinted about my leaving the game. And you're right, she and I have something very special. Candace is one of the factors that I have to consider when I think about my future. Eddie, of course, is another. He starts school this fall and I think it's best if I'm here more. I want to spend time doing things in the summer with him. I missed too many of Eddie's early years when I was playing baseball and I don't want to do that with my next children, if Candace and I marry."

"You sound as if you've made a decision," said Harry.

"I'm going to leave baseball either this year or next, depending upon what you have available. If you can use me starting in October of this year, I'll bow out of baseball at the end of this season, whether or not Candace will agree to marry me."

"How much do you know about her family?" asked Harry. "That tells you more than you otherwise could ever learn from being with someone in a courtship situation."

"Her mother practiced as a registered nurse for years and she seems like a very down-to-earth lady. Her father is an attorney. He worked as a public defender for years and then got into private practice. I think he's fairly successful. He seems like a decent man. She has an older brother who's also attorney but he doesn't practice with his father's firm. Her parents have been kind to me from the beginning, even when they thought I might be nothing but a dumb jock. The main thing is they've raised Candace to be a very decent person, with plenty of backbone, so I think they're just fine."

"What's his law specialty? Once you know a lawyer's clients you can tell a lot about him, too."

"He practices business law, but I don't have any idea about the identity of his clients. Do I sniff a job for your buddies in Boston?"

"It never hurts. I can find out about her father's practice without doing that. But for the rest of it, we should check and be sure. I'll show you what I learn only if there's something negative that you should know before deciding upon Candace. And, by the way, I think she's a peach. So do your mother, Midge and Teensy. She was absolutely vibrant at dinner last night. What did you do to her up at Sunrise?"

"The same thing you did to Mom up there."

Harry started to sputter, but Bryce, grinning from ear to ear, said, "I found that book of sonnets, Dad. I read some of them to Candace, by the way."

Harry shook his head, "The sixties. We never talked to our parents that way when I was growing up. And we didn't take our girlfriends to a cabin in the woods before we got married, either." Then he smiled at Bryce. "Of course, from the way you're behaving around her, she must have done something to you, too."

"Yes, she did. She's given me reason to feel totally alive for the first time since Marilyn died. Now, when may I start work?"

"This October. You're going to start with a trip to Michigan; only this time, no wolves, just timber and lumber and wood pulp."

Chapter 67

The pitch was low and outside.

"Strike three!" the umpire bellowed.

Bryce showed just enough irritation with being called out on such a bad pitch to let the umpire know he was unhappy, but nothing too blatant, because it was only the second inning. That didn't stop the Founders fans from booing lustily over the call and the chatter from the dugout took on comments regarding the umpire's ancestry, along with medical advice about an appointment with an optometrist. In the 1960s, the umpires could do little about remarks from the bench and so they developed very thick skins. Bryce walked back to the dugout and slammed his bat back into the rack. He wasn't the only victim. Two of Cubs players also had been rung up on questionable calls. Bryce figured the ump was trying to make up for his earlier mistakes by balancing out the bad-call strike outs, something that most umpires avoided doing, preferring, instead, to live with one mistake rather than a bunch of them.

In the fifth inning the Cubs pitcher threw another low and away ball and Bryce laid off of it.

"Strike two!" was the umpire's call.

This time Bryce stepped out of the batter's box and walked in a small circle, muttering comments under his breath, before again resuming his stance at the plate. He fouled off the next pitch and the one that followed and the count remained at three balls and two strikes. He took another low and away pitch and turned to look for the bat boy to hand his bat to before taking his walk when he heard, "Strike Three!"

"Ump, you just hit my limit switch."

Bryce thought about Evars Dombrowski's "Look" and he stood there, bat on his shoulder, and gave "The Look" to the ump. It blazed out from his dark eyes, conveying utter contempt. Their message said that the umpire's abilities were somewhere between pond scum and whale shit. Bryce rarely argued with an umpire and had never been thrown out of a game for doing so. The sports writers and photographers knew that. Telephoto lenses zoomed in on him and the typewriters in the press box began to clack away as he stood there, not moving, just filled with disgust for the man who was doing such an awful job calling the game. The umpire tried to meet "The Look" but couldn't. He dropped his eyes and then ejected Bryce from the game. The stands erupted in boos and Bryce's coach came running out of the dugout to argue the toss and vent the frustration he and the team felt.

Bryce could still hear the foul language his coach was using as he left the dugout for the showers. He showered but waited for his teammates and coaches to come back to the locker room when the game was over. Several reporters attempted to interview him but he only gave them pabulum he knew they wouldn't print.

◦◦

The next morning on the train into the city the newly promoted Associate Professor Davis opened her *Daily News* to the sports section, and gasped at the photo on the lead page.

"Oh, Bryce, you did it. My strong, decent man gave an ump 'The Look.' Honey, the photo doesn't do you or it justice. I've seen that look in person and it's worse than what's shown here, baby." She read on to learn that Bryce had been ejected from the game but had little comment over the incident. When she arrived at her office, Candace tried to telephone him at the townhouse but there was no answer and her class was due to start shortly. She wanted to ask Bryce why he changed his mind and gave "The Look." If it was what Candace thought it might be, she was both overjoyed and a little saddened. Her mind began to race over possibilities as she walked to her classroom. It was not a lab day that required less concentration on her part and so Professor Davis had to devote her full attention to her lecture. It was one of the most spirited she'd yet given.

When Candace finally got through to him, all Bryce wanted to talk about was celebrating her promotion. They agreed on a visit to the Museum of Art and to have a late lunch there on his next off day. In the meantime he invited her for more Chinese food at the townhouse following tomorrow's day game.

"And dessert?" she teased.

She heard laughter in his voice when he responded, "Fresh oranges go particularly well after Chinese food. Would you like to stop for some?"

She appeared early the next evening wearing a light summer raincoat even though the weather was clear. He kissed her in greeting and helped her remove her coat. When he closed the closet door after hanging up the coat she was standing there with much larger than usual breast mounds under her blouse.

"My, aren't we top-heavy this evening. What in the world have you done to yourself?"

"It's dessert." The mischief look began and he reached for her and hugged her again. Then his hands began to explore 'dessert' while she giggled her way through the examination and the puzzled looks on his face. Finally he unbuttoned her blouse and discovered four tangerines stuffed in the cups of her bra along with what usually filled them.

"I had to buy a bigger bra and use the last hook to get them to fit in, but you now have 'dessert,' she said.

"Don't ever change, Candace."

"I already have, you know." She walked to a side table he'd added to the living room and checked the time on the clock she'd given him. "I was on time this evening wasn't I?"

The food was delivered, and over dinner he asked, "Honey, have you ever been sailing?"

"Yes, what do you have in mind?"

"I don't know, I was just thinking about a small boat my brothers and I used to sail when we vacationed in Maine, and before I start boring you with talk about those experiences, I thought I'd ask."

"It won't work, Bryce," she replied, with a knowing look on her face. "You're up to something. What're you planning?"

"You're right; I did that poorly. There's an opportunity to get a good sized sloop for a long weekend on the Chesapeake at the end of the baseball season. I know it's during the school year, but perhaps you can get a Friday and Monday off."

"The biggest thing I've sailed is a nineteen foot Lighting," she said.

"That's okay. Do you still remember the difference between a sheet and a halyard?"

She nodded. "Just what will we do and where will we go? After all, a woman needs to shop for clothes for such an occasion."

"Well, you may need foul weather gear, but you probably have everything else you need. This isn't something that requires you to look as if you have stepped out of the pages of Vogue. The Chesapeake in late September can be chilly so think warm for the evenings and shorts or jeans for the day. If you'd like I can give you a list of things to pack."

"Where do we sleep?"

"On board. There's a galley and head and all the conveniences of home. We even have an auxiliary diesel engine if we're becalmed."

"Galley? Who's going to cook?"

"My dear, this is not a cruise on the Cunard Lines. We can take a lot of pre-cooked items like spaghetti sauce and a bunch of casual things for breakfast and sandwich ingredients for lunch. We keep them in an ice chest cooler that's built in. There's a stove and a small charcoal grill that attaches to the stern railing to do steaks and things in the evenings at anchor."

"Count me in. All I have to do is find someone to take my Monday class. Whose boat is it anyway?"

"It's my Uncle Joseph's sailboat. He said I could use it for having a good season. It's my last season, Candace. I've told the General Manager and it'll be announced after the last game."

She got off her stool and walked around the table to him and put her arms around his neck. "Bryce, I know how you love baseball," she said, looking at him with affection. "And I know we've talked about us. But I want you to know I'd never ask you to quit. If you want to play more years, I can handle that."

"Thanks, Honey, but I want out. I'm tired of the schedule and tired of missing summers with Eddie and my family. I haven't been to our family's Maine vacation home in years. My father is going to need help running his businesses. Dad's still full of life but he's worked hard and I want to help him enjoy his later years. I'm going to start out as low man and try to work my way up. I'll be traveling a lot at first, but you and I will get together over weekends and we'll have time during the summer."

Candace found her substitute instructor. "After all, what are grad students for?" she asked.

Chapter 68

B ryce stopped his car in the driveway of the Sunrise Lumber Company headquarters and looked at the building he'd known since boyhood. Even in his second week, he still was getting used to the idea that he worked there. It was of colonial design with dormers along the third story that broke up the mass of the brick edifice. The grounds held huge evergreen and hardwood trees melding it with the hillside the building dominated.

Late that morning he was reviewing his travel itinerary when his telephone rang.

"Bryce, this is Sarah. I'm at the receptionist's desk. There is a man here who wants to see you. He says his name is Leroy Carter. He says he doesn't have an appointment."

"Can you talk without him overhearing?"

"Yes, I asked him to be seated in the waiting area of the lobby."

"Describe him, please."

"He's a tall, slender black man. His skin has a grayish cast. Pock-marked face, thin moustache. I asked him the purpose of his visit and he just said he wants to talk with you. Bryce, he's kind of creepy."

"Is the conference room clear?"

"Yes."

"Thank you, Sarah. I'll be down there in a couple of minutes."

"Trouble. No rest from it and it just keeps coming," thought Bryce. "What in the world does he want? Revenge for my dislocating his elbow? No, that would just get him into more trouble and he's probably on parole. Do I call the police? No. That won't answer why he's here. And I want to know that. Do I need a weapon? Probably not. But just in case, what do I have?"

His eyes landed on a stout letter opener. He picked it up, turned it in his hands and decided to carry it. It didn't compare to the knife he'd carried in UDT but it would have to do. He took it to the men's room his office shared with his father's, tucked the dagger end into his sock and lightly fastened the handle to his leg with two large band aids from the first aid kit. Then he headed for the service elevator that would allow entrance to the reception area from a side hallway.

◦◡◦

Leroy was dressed in lime green bell bottomed trousers with a matching, loose fitting, long sleeved shirt with puffy sleeves. His shoes were thick-soled patent leather clunkers with thick, high heels—his best outfit. But he still felt terribly out of place and nervous. He sat in the deep leather couch and tried not to look too curious as his eyes glanced around the reception area. He'd never seen such rich furnishings—beautifully crafted wood furniture, thick area rugs over intricately patterned and highly polished wood floors, and tastefully designed and finished desks. Dramatic, poster-sized photos of lumbering operations decorated the walls. He played his hands over the smooth leather of the couch and looked out the large picture window into nearby trees from which were suspended bird feeders. He leaned forward to get a better view of a brilliant red bird and its mate which was of more subdued coloring.

"They're cardinals," said a deep voice from behind him.

Leroy felt his heart skip a beat and his pulse race. He turned to see the man who had confronted and bested him in the train station standing there with those damned black eyes boring into him.

Sheeit! The honkey walked across the floor without me hearing him and he looks like he still could whup my ass. I'm goin' to git down on this act.

"Leroy, follow me, please."

The "honkey" turned his back and started to walk toward a door off the reception area. Leroy arose from the couch and followed. The man paused and allowed him to catch up. Then he gestured politely toward the conference room doorway. Leroy felt his heel catch on the rug edge and he struggled momentarily with his balance. A hand like a vise gripped his bicep to steady him.

Bryce Roberts' expression didn't change. He waited until Leroy recovered his balance, then allowed him to enter the room first. Bryce gave a hand signal to Sarah, followed Leroy through the door, and stood at the head of a long, beautifully crafted wood table. He gestured Leroy into a seat at the side away from the door.

"I gotta' ax, man, what kinda' wood is this table made with?"

"It's walnut burl veneer," said Bryce as he sat down. "Leroy, how did you get here?"

"Borrowed ma cousin's car. I promised to fill up the gas when I take it back."

"How long have you been out?"

"Since twelve days ago."

"Do you have a job?"

"Yeah. I'm workin' at a car wash."

"How many hours a week?"

"'Bout twenty. But the boss, he say I can do more, startin' nex' week."

Sarah appeared in the doorway carrying a tray with Cokes, glasses and an ice bucket. She entered and placed the tray on the table to Bryce's left. Then he passed the tray to Leroy who popped a can open and took a swig from it. Bryce used the silver tongs to put ice cubes in his glass and poured himself a Coke. He passed a coaster to Leroy and took one for himself.

"Leroy, why did you come here and what do you want?"

"I wanted to see what you'd say if I was to mention the name of Karen."

"Go on."

Damn! The honkey's face didn't change and he's still lookin' at me like he wants to bust me up. "Seems like you wouldn't want yo' woman knowin' 'bout her."

"How do you know about Karen?"

"Frien' a mine."

"Who?"

"No need to be talkin' abou' dat. Les jus say ah knows what ah know."

"Why do you think I care about whether 'my woman' knows about Karen?"

"Ma frien' tole me. He said you'd pay to keep it quiet, 'cause you a careful man."

"Who told you that I'm a careful man?"

"I watched you in the courtroom when you tol' the judge how things went down."

"Leroy, you're bullshitting me. You weren't watching me. Hell, you wouldn't even look at me then."

Leroy's eyes dropped to the table and he had another swig of his Coke to hide his chagrin at being called on his bull.

Bryce said, "There's only one other man I know of in prison who also knows me: Charlie Coe. Is he your friend?" The rasp in the deep voice was profound. It made Leroy shiver inside.

"So what if he is?"

Bryce swiveled in his chair, picked up the telephone from the credenza behind him, and placed it on the conference table. Leroy's eyes widened.

"You ain't callin' the fuzz are you?"

"No, Leroy, it's lunchtime and I'm going to order sandwiches. What kind do you want?"

"Uh, do they have burgers?"

"Yes. How do you like yours?"

"You really can pick up the phone and jus order eats?"

"Yes. How do you want your hamburger?"

"Uh, with ketchup."

Bryce spoke their orders and then hung up.

"Did Coe put you up to this visit?"

This ain't goin' the way Coe said it would, thought Leroy. *This honkey ain't scared at all and he looks like he still could get really pissed. And that voice . . .*

"He mighta' tole me a few things."

"Like what?"

"He said he killed your wife. Hell, he bragged about it."

Bryce's anger flashed. He thought for a moment about how he watched Coe's head disappear over the stadium fence when he smashed it with a bat, and all of the rage that went into the swing came surging back. He wanted to smash something now but he resisted pounding Leroy.

Man, Bryce, get hold of yourself! Don't let that son-of-a-bitch get to you from his prison cell. That's really why he sent Leroy here.

Bryce stood up and fear flooded Leroy's face. The honkey's black eyes damned near glowed with anger. The deep breath Leroy had taken slowly escaped as he watched Bryce pace toward a window and then stand there, fists on hips, looking out into the trees. The man returned to his seat at the table, face again impassive.

"Leroy, how's your elbow doing these days?"

"Ah cain't straighten mah arm all the way, but I make out okay."

"Leroy, how about we talk about Charlie Coe for a few minutes till our sandwiches get here?"

"That's cool with me, Boss."

"What else did he say to you?"

"He said he wanted me to take a pitcher of your wife's gravestone and send it to him."

Bryce emptied the last of his Coke into his glass and then, one-handed, squeezed the steel can into a very small scrap.

"But ah doan think I'm gonna do that. Hell, I ain't got no camera and I doan know where the cemetery is."

Bryce gave Leroy the Dombrowski Look. "Leroy," his voice rasped, "if you do that I'll break your other arm."

"Like I said, Boss, I ain't got no camera."

"What else did Coe say about me or my wife?"

"He got a thing about you. Says he goin' to keep after you when he gits out."

"What else?"

"Jus' mostly stuff like that. I think the man is sick in the head."

Their sandwiches arrived and Sarah set placemats and silverware for Bryce and Leroy, served them, and left. Leroy began to eat, and his face showed the pleasure he derived from the good quality of the meat.

"How come you bein' so nice givin' me 'bergers and all?"

"What else did Coe tell you about Karen?"

Leroy interrupted his chewing and said around a mouthful of food, "He said to ax you how come Karen left town so soon after she arrived."

Bryce's thoughts raced. *Coe, you must have been following me that summer without my realizing it. Lesson learned.*

"I don't know, Leroy. Women do things that just don't make much sense."

"Dat's true. You goin' to eat dat other burger?"

"No, it's yours if you want it . . . Tell me something, Leroy. Can you read and write?"

"Not too good." Leroy spread a large gob of ketchup on the second hamburger.

"Want to learn?"

"Why?" He took a huge bite this time and thought, *no sense lettin' this go to waste. 'Sides this honkey may kick my ass outa here real soon.*

"It might keep you out of prison. If you can read and write you can land a job that pays better than the car wash. Once you start a good job you won't want to go back to the pen."

Leroy gulped another bite. "Why you care 'bout dat?"

"It costs us taxpayers money to pay for jail. The fewer the inmates, the lower the cost and the lower the taxes. Now, give me the name of your parole officer and his phone number."

"What you wan' wit dat?"

"He's going to see to it that you sign up for an adult literacy class I know about. That's where guys like you learn to read and write."

"What if I doan want nuthin' ta do wit dat sheeit?"

"Then I find out who your parole officer is and tell him about how you tried to blackmail me, to shake me down for some scratch. Then you go back to the slammer."

"Boss, you one hard man."

"Name and phone number, Leroy."

Leroy reluctantly pulled a slim wallet out of his hip pocket, opened the wallet and withdrew a business card. Bryce took a pen and tablet from the credenza and copied the information from the card while Leroy wolfed the rest of his burger.

"I'm going to call this man today about the class. Then I'm going to call next week and every week from now on just to see how you're doing in class. Keep that in mind, Leroy."

"Yo shittin' me."

"Try me, Leroy." Bryce's eyes affirmed the message.

Chapter 69

A fter the election of Richard Nixon to the presidency the new left weakened. It was not due so much to the change in administrations as it was to the fact the nation had grown tired of the shrill dissent espoused on college campuses, and because the core of the movement graduated from college and moved on to a life where they began to have a stake in the future. The remnants of the 1960s counter-culture concentrated their social agenda on the universities they attended.

The altruism and love many in the movement first espoused was replaced by violence and hatred from splinter groups such as the Weathermen. They, and less radical groups, campaigned to have ROTC units removed from universities and they worked particularly hard to drive research sponsored by the military and big business off campuses.

Their efforts included the secret research being conducted by Candace's group. Because the laser research was a scholarly endeavor in cutting edge technology, the university rightfully refused to close the project, despite threats of violence if the demands of radical groups weren't met.

Following her return to academia, Candace witnessed first-hand the earnestness of the students who advocated against the war in Vietnam and for social justice for minorities and the poor. Few of those students were in her class, because, as she surmised, many weren't interested in doing the hard work studies in the sciences required. Still, she accepted flowers from the hippies in the school's neighborhood and allowed space on her classroom bulletin board for the few handwritten announcements of campus meetings and activities of the left that were posted there.

By the time Candace began to date Bryce, the students knew her only as an excellent teacher who hadn't shown antipathy toward those who led the campus demonstrations. They were unaware of her second job in the research center on the closed-off fourth floor of the physics building, but they were aware that the research was government sponsored.

Candace had grown so accustomed to her work in the laser lab, she no longer thought much about the secrecy that surrounded it. One afternoon she didn't get off the elevator at the third floor, but instead waited for two students to exit. As the door closed, she inserted her key into the switch next to the button for the fourth floor. Her action did not go unnoticed by Nellie Kidd, a student in one of her seminar courses, whose face wore a look of puzzlement and then surprise as the doors slid closed.

Candace found a copy of the local chapter of the Weathermen's underground newspaper on her chair when she entered her classroom two days later. An article headlining the bombing of a physics lab at the University of Wisconsin in which an innocent man had been killed took up the front page. The article crowed about the "victory over the military-industrial establishment." Candace put the newspaper aside, and, without comment, commenced her class. At the end of the lecture Nellie Kidd stayed back and asked if she could speak with Candace.

"I put that newspaper on your chair, Professor Davis," she said. "I just want you to know what some people on this campus think about and talk about."

Candace scanned the article. "Nellie, you're not part of this group?"

"No, but I date a guy who I think is, and I hear things from him that are just plain scary. Professor Davis, you be careful around this building."

Candace thanked Nellie and when the student left, she telephoned Dr. Frankel, the head of the project, and expressed her concerns. He promised to contact the security firm that was responsible for the building. Candace forgot about the matter until she arrived at Bryce's townhouse where they met for dinner. She showed him the newspaper and he read it through.

"That's what you get when amateurs handle explosives," he said. "I read about that Wisconsin incident in the newspaper and those idiots bombed the wrong building. They used stolen dynamite and blasting caps that nobody knew were missing. The awful thing is these nuts are so radical they're not the least bit sorry for what they did. I think they probably will try it again if they get an opportunity."

"Bryce, you once told me that you worked with explosives when you were in the Navy. Are they that easy to get?"

"Not the stuff used by the military. But civilian life is different. Construction contractors usually keep their blasting caps and dynamite locked up, but that's really just to keep snoops and kids out. If somebody's serious about stealing the stuff from a construction site, it can be done." Bryce paused and then changed the subject.

"Candace, I haven't been to your offices since we hung that tuna, and from what I recall people can just walk right into that building. Do you really have any security in that place?"

"Students have access to the first three floors but the fourth floor is sealed at the stairwells with doors that only can be opened from someone descending from the fourth floor. The elevator has a security key that allows access to the fourth floor only by people with clearance and a key."

"If fire or emergency crews have to get access to the fourth floor, how do they do it?" he asked.

"I guess they just break through the security doors. The doors have that wired glass in the top half. Maybe they have a place to get the elevator keys, too, but I don't know about that."

"What about windows on the fourth floor? Are they securely locked?"

"Most of them have alarms and the rest are sealed."

"Candace, that fourth floor sounds like a fire trap. Has your group ever had any fire drills?"

"No, I know we haven't. No one thought about it because only twelve of us work there on a regular basis."

"Honey, is there any way you can get me in there? I want to take a look at what the fire safety and security situation is. People don't think about things like that until it's too late, and I want to help you get an action list together if something's needed."

"Do you really think that's necessary? I can ask my boss, but I'm really hesitant to do that. He's a good person and he doesn't think the secrecy is that important. The only reason he goes along with it is that the government is paying much of the research costs.

But, I don't think he's going to let someone in there without the proper security clearance."

"Tell him I had top secret clearance in the Navy."

"Darling, it's nice to feel so protected, but you have to keep your cool," said Candace. "I'll be all right."

"Candace, humor me. I don't like to insist, but I'm really serious about this. I'll rest a lot easier if I can satisfy myself that you're not working in a firetrap and that the security is adequate for your protection." *And Coe will get out of jail someday.*

Chapter 70

H ow *do I tell her about Coe's intentions and still get her to say yes?*

Bryce and Candace were spending their first evening on the sailboat anchored in a creek off the Severn River. Hills rose steeply from the banks into woods. Houses were set farther up into the hillsides. Lights winked on in some of the houses. The water's surface was barely rippled by the evening breeze. Occasional ring ripples appeared from fish feeding at the surface.

They were sitting on cushions in the cockpit with Candace leaning against Bryce's shoulder. They'd put on sweat suits to stay warm and Candace wore heavy socks. The dinner of steaks, grilled asparagus, and potato salad was a memory. They were under the dodger, a canvas that arched to cover the gangway and forward portion of the cockpit, lending the space intimacy and privacy. It kept the night breeze off them as they sat under its shelter and talked.

"Why do they call this place a creek?" she asked. "It's wider than some of our rivers at home."

"I don't know, but it's that way all over the bay. It probably was a creek to the early settlers who came in off the big rivers. But I'm more interested in your achievements.

"So, again, Dr. Davis, congratulations on your sterling Ph.D. achievement. Are you now an expert on lasers?"

"That's what my colleagues tell me, but I still want to explore more possibilities with different frequencies and mediums. There are surgery techniques that may use lasers. And I want to look at using them to carry sound."

"Do you get to teach more advanced classes, now that you've been named an Associate Professor?"

"Yes, next semester I'm going to lead a seminar course for laser applications. It'll be fun and I get to work with students who have shown real promise."

They could see each other in the dim red cabin light that shown from below and he raised his wineglass to hers in a toast.

"I knew you could do it. You have spunk as well as brains. That's really a lethal combination, you know. May I read your dissertation?"

"Thanks for the compliment. You may read most of it. There's a part I'm not supposed to talk about according to an entity that's funding some of my research."

"You are working for spooks?"

"Not exactly. But you're close." She smiled and said, "Let's talk about something else like the Rules of the Road for boats."

"You must be kidding. Now?"

"Don't all power boats just have to get out of our way?" she asked.

"If we're under sail, yes; except for great big ships that are limited to channels. But when the commercial boats are out here fishing or tending crab pots we should stay out of their way. Those guys are trying to make a living and we're just out here playing around."

"What about all those buoys I saw? I just sailed around in lakes and there weren't any of them."

"That's a nautical exercise for tomorrow on the way out of the river into the bay. For now just remember: Red, Right, Returning. Keep the red buoys on your right when you're entering port. Right now, however, I'm thinking about another port of entry."

He began to demonstrate what he meant.

"There's more room in the V-berth," she said in a voice that told of her eagerness. "You might even show me what you meant by a nautical exercise."

He did. Repeatedly.

☺≣☺

They arose early in the morning and enjoyed coffee while sitting in the cockpit waiting for the mist to clear.

"This is so peaceful," she said. "Did you ever have times like this in the Navy?"

"Nothing like this view, but there were times when we got to enjoy a beautiful sunrise over a cup of coffee. No women, though. Just a bunch of men scratching themselves. I really miss those guys. We depended upon each other and that fosters a camaraderie and closeness among men that lasts a lifetime. There's going to be a reunion next year and I'm planning to attend."

They were quiet in their own thoughts for a while and then he went below to refill their mugs. When he returned he placed the mugs next to the compass on a small table that unfolded from the wheel pedestal. Then he pulled her to him on the seat and looked at her lovingly.

"You've brought joy back into my life, Candace. When Marilyn died a part of me went too. But you've shown me there's a second chance in life and I just want you to know that I love you very much."

She swallowed hard and her wonderful blue eyes began to mist. "I love you too, Bryce," she said, voice mellow but hushed. She put her arms around his neck, her cheek resting on his chest, listening to his heartbeat. They stayed that way, holding each other in the tranquility of the early morning.

Overhead an osprey began its chirping whistle call as it circled, looking for a fish. They watched it and then Bryce broke the silence. He gently tilted her face toward his.

"Candace . . ."

"Hmmm?"

"Will you marry me? I want you completely; not just as a wonderful friend and lover, but as the mother of our children and my life's companion."

She sat up, and tears did come this time. "How many children do you want?"

"Is that a 'yes'?"

"You know it is, you wonderful man. How could any woman refuse on such a beautiful morning when asked so romantically? Yes, I'll marry you. You've been so patient and understanding with me as I worked my way through my grief. I love you for that and so much more."

"Are you sure? I don't want to rush you with a romantic moment that you, uh, may have misgivings about later," he said.

"I think I've known that I wanted to marry you since the evening at your townhouse when you listened to me explain why I was being late for our dates. You were being a son-of-a-bitch, but then I realized that you were just testing me again and that you really wanted to keep the fires burning. It just took me a while to move in confidence to where we are now."

"Then I think three or four more children would be fine. But you're going to have the final say on that. And I want to adopt Anne."

"And I want to adopt Eddie. That boy proposed to me long before you did, and I shall always remember that."

"I have something for you." He reached into his pocket and handed her a small velvet covered box that could be only one thing. She opened it and, through more tears of joy, he slipped the diamond ring on her finger.

"The stones on either side are blue diamonds. They match your eyes," he said. "My grandfather gave this ring to my grandmother on their twenty fifth wedding anniversary and my mother gave it to me when she learned we had this trip planned. She told me 'just in case she says yes.' The weird thing about it is I didn't tell her that I was going to propose to you."

"Rosalie is a very perceptive woman, and the ring is beautiful. But Bryce, are you sure that you want to give me a family heirloom?"

"Give it back if you change your mind. Otherwise, you'll be family."

"That's what I want more than anything."

Several long kisses later he again went below and this time he returned with a camera. They set the timer, rested the camera on the compass pedestal and then posed together for several pictures, one of which featured Candace holding her left hand toward the camera.

More long kisses. Then he said, "Well, let's square away the boat, get a quick shower, and head for St. Michaels. We have a westerly breeze so it's a perfect day to sail over there. We'll find a restaurant tonight so we don't have to cook dinner."

"Bryce?"

"Yes?"

"Will you scrub my back?"

"With pleasure, ma'am."

Before they weighed anchor, he showed her how to set a course using the compass rose on the chart and parallel rulers. On the way out of the river he taught her about the different shapes of the buoys and how to find them on a chart. The sail across the bay was glorious. The breeze was strong enough to push them along at hull speed, top speed for a sailboat. She learned how to steer the larger sailboat in a following wind and to pay careful attention to the fathometer as they entered the shallower waters of Eastern Bay.

"You bring good luck, woman," he told her. "This is one of the best sailing days I could imagine. The wind has stayed steady the whole time, which is a rarity for this bay. And the weather forecast for tomorrow is for more of the same. I'm going to loan you to Uncle Joe when he comes down here."

"When I meet that man I am going to give him such a hug for loaning you this boat," said Candace as he snapped a photo of her at the wheel.

They found an empty slip at the museum in St. Michaels, paid their docking fee, and ordered crab cakes for dinner in a restaurant a few blocks away. The waitress noticed that Candace had become very left handed and guessed they were newly engaged. She confirmed her suspicions and told the other diners who were mostly sailboaters. They took up a collection and bought the couple a bottle of champagne. There followed many toasts and jokes, some risqué but all in good humor. The happy and somewhat tipsy couple was escorted back to their boat by several of the other juiced sailor couples who also had tied up at the museum. They serenaded Bryce and Candace with a terribly off-key rendition of "Indian Love Call" before the couple closed the hatch boards for the evening.

"Are all sailors like that?" asked Candace as they turned in at the forward berth.

"Most of the ones I know are. Some can sing better though." Then a hint of a smile played across his face as he withdrew a coin from his pocket and said, "I'll flip you to see who gets on top tonight."

"It had better be me," she replied. "You'll bang your noggin on the overhead again. Oh, Good Lord, listen to me. I'm already talking like a wife."

☙❧

After a morning tour of St. Michaels and its museum he topped off the fresh water tank and they headed out for a sail north to the Wye River. When they were well inside its waters Bryce bagged the jib sail and furled the mainsail. In the late afternoon they motored into a dead-end creek that was surrounded on three sides by a forest radiant in fall colors.

Candace proudly maneuvered the boat. She backed down the engine as Bryce set the anchor and then gave her a signal from the bow to cut the throttle. As the low rumble of the diesel faded, silence of the kind they experienced in the Sunrise Hills enveloped them. Then, slowly, the forest regained its life in the calls of its birds and the rustle of a deer that grunted at them from the bank before disappearing into the woods. They opened snacks and a bottle of wine and sat in the cockpit enjoying the approaching dusk.

"I was going to propose to you in here but I couldn't wait," said Bryce.

"I'm shocked," said Candace as she helped herself to more Brie and crackers, "that a man of your notable self-control couldn't wait. I'm also greatly flattered that my meager charms apparently overwhelmed you."

"It's for the best. Look at the fun we had last night. And your charms are anything but meager."

"Darling, when we save up some money, let's buy a sailboat."

"I'll make a deal with you, Candace. For every dollar we spend on a boat, we first put the same amount aside for our kids' college education. Of course we won't have any money for groceries, but what the heck, we can live on beans and cornbread."

"We'll find a way," she said and then fed him grapes from a small cluster. She ate the last one herself and announced, "I'm going below to put on my sweat suit."

When they finished dinner, Bryce pulled a special container out of the cooler. It had been filled with dry ice. He opened it and produced peach ice cream.

"You were going to get this whether or not you said 'yes' to my proposal," he said.

"You're the sweetest man. I love being spoiled."

"I love doing it to you." He grinned at the double entendre.

"Later. Let's dig into that ice cream."

They took the last of their wine topside and sat on the cockpit cushions, looking up at a very clear sky painted by a brush full of stars. She surprised him by naming many of the constellations and they determined that their children would learn them too. The moon rose and a school of thousands of small fish played near the surface, attracted by the orb's brightness. The couple watched in fascination as the school brightened as it rose to the surface and faded as it went deep. They lay back on the cushions, mellow from the wine and the day and once again looked up at the stars.

Suddenly a blood-curdling shriek pulsed out of the woods and the hair on Candace's neck stood up.

"Bryce! My God! What's that? It sounds as if someone's being tortured!"

He remained reclined on the long cushion that ran the length of the cockpit, hands folded over his stomach.

"That, my dear, is a barred owl. Settlers called them 'Hooty Owls', but I've always believed that's a misnomer."

A few minutes later the owl shrieked again. Candace took the lead in suggesting they go below where they delighted in each other in ways that they tried for the first time.

Chapter 71

In the morning the wind had backed to the southeast, giving them good conditions for their return sail to Annapolis. They set the sails for the long reach across the bay.

The "Candace Luck" held and the wind was steady for the trip.

"Honey," Bryce said, "there's something I want you to know about me because I don't want us to keep any secrets from each other."

She saw the serious look in his face and swallowed the quip she was about to make.

"Remember my telling you about Charles Coe, the S.O.B. that killed Marilyn?"

"Yes." *Boy, am I glad I held my tongue.*

"He's still in prison, but someday they'll release him. When they do I expect that he'll try to make trouble for us. He's dangerous because he's not all there mentally. Our personal safety and that of our children could be at risk from him. Now, that may sound scary to you, but I want you to understand the risk you take by marrying me. If you want to reconsider your acceptance of my proposal, I'll understand." Bryce mentally held his breath.

There was silence, broken only by the low whistle of wind in the rigging and the hull splashing through the water. Candace removed her sunglasses and looked at him for a long minute. He saw the intensity grow in her eyes.

"With you there to protect us, I'm not going to worry about that."

"Honey, there'll be times I won't be with you."

Again there was a pause. Candace intertwined her fingers and made a steeple of the index fingers. She pressed the steeple to her lips. Then she surprised him.

"Bryce, you own a shotgun, don't you?"

"Several."

"Teach me to use one."

"Okay. That way you'll be able to protect me."

Then Candace did laugh. "Good. I wasn't going to let you out of your proposal that easily."

"Candace, I'm serious. Coe is a danger who I believe we'll probably have to face."

"I understand, Bryce. But we'll have the advantage this time because we know what to expect. Besides, won't the police deal with him?"

"We won't be able to count on that."

"Then we'll count on ourselves and each other. Isn't that what marriage is all about?"

"Thank you. I had to tell you about Coe. It's awful to think about, but you needed to know."

They passed the Thomas Point lighthouse that sat on stilts in the shoal water near the entrance to the Severn River. They were tired by the time they finished cleaning the boat, but more time to talk about their marriage kept them awake for the drive to Candace's home. They decided a marriage in late spring would suit them just fine and Candace began planning their wedding around her teaching schedule.

Then Bryce broached the subject he dreaded. "Candace, there's one more thing we have to talk about."

"What?"

"A prenuptial agreement."

"You romance me, you wine and dine me, and get me all starry-eyed and then you bring up a subject like that on top of telling me about Coe?" He could hear irritation as well as humor and love in her tone.

"When's a good time to talk about it?" he asked.

"Let's get it over with, now that you've mentioned it. If it's any help, I don't want your money. That's the last thing that comes to mind when I think of you." She reached across the seat and caressed his cheek.

"It's not my money that's concerned, it's my family's. Our businesses are owned through corporations and trusts that give us the most effective way to manage those assets. We need the flexibility of making decisions about their management without the interests of spouses having to be considered. Jason, my sister's husband, signed off on those assets and you'll be asked to do the same. As far as my personal wealth is concerned, it'll be there to answer our needs."

"So I can clean you out if I divorce you?" The look of devilment was beginning to play in Candace's eyes.

"You may take everything but my piano."

Chapter 72

"Take Bryce in later in the evening when everyone else is out of the lab," said Candace's boss. "Just let me know what he finds and what he recommends. I don't want anyone's safety jeopardized, either."

"Bryce, that's what he told me, so here we are," she said. Candace watched as Bryce stood on a ladder that rested under an opening in the ceiling of the elevator. He finished his methodical inspection of the elevator shaft that lead to the fourth floor and returned the ladder to the janitor's closet. Then they checked the security doors that sealed off the fourth floor and the windows on that floor.

The security doors had an alarm switch located at the top of the inner jamb and a latch handle that easily could be pushed from the upstairs side. The skylights in some of the offices didn't appear to be sealed or alarmed. He found nothing else of interest, but he did look outside to check the windowsills and the view toward the other buildings and streets below.

Candace watched all of his actions and finally asked, "Where did you learn all of this?"

"When we built an office in Michigan the architect showed me a lot of stuff for our accounting and records room. I also called a man named Foster who deals with security systems and he told me what to look for."

They returned to the elevator and descended to the second floor where Candace led him back to her office.

"Okay. What did you find here?"

"The security probably is good enough to keep snoops out, but if someone really wants to get in there they can," said Bryce. "Fire safety is okay, so long as you can use the stairwells."

She checked her message slips and then walked to the window where she closed the Venetian blinds. "I owe you one in here," she said.

He was looking at the tuna he'd helped to hang and the memorabilia on her credenza that included a picture of them on horseback.

Absently he said, "What, Dear?"

"Come here a minute." She smiled as he walked toward her and she repeated, "I said I owe you one in here." She held her arms open to him and he realized then that she was teasing about the only other time they'd been in her office. He put his arms around her and hugged her firmly to him and then they made up for her moment of panic those many months ago. When he finally stopped kissing Candace, Bryce said, still hugging her, "I still liked the first one. I'll always remember it."

Her eyes had a dreamy look to them that said she was thinking about more than a kiss so he moved to her office door and locked it, turned out the lights and opened the blinds. A view of the campus opened before them. Bryce held her to him and then began to work the hem of her skirt upward . . .

The rest was not what either of them had expected the visit to yield, but later, as he walked her to her train they agreed that spontaneity definitely has its charms.

Chapter 73

Bryce led his fiancé to an attractive jeweler's shop in Doylestown when it was time to choose their wedding rings. Abraham Rabinowicz greeted Bryce like his namesake greeted Joseph. When he learned the purpose of their visit, he made a huge fuss over Candace. He examined her engagement ring, and then led the couple to a display case with a large selection of wedding rings that would complement Candace's ring. As Candace pondered her selection, Abraham began to tell of the time Bryce had "rescued" him from the thugs. Bryce kept trying to say it was nothing and pleaded with Abraham to stop, but the old man continued, and, for good measure, added two more bad guys to the story. Candace looked at Bryce and began to laugh at his discomfit.

"My hero," she teased. "Why do I always have to learn of your adventures from other people?"

"It wasn't five hoods, it was only three. And I didn't throw Leroy across the station floor. Abe, if you keep this up, we're leaving."

"Candace," said Abraham, "you have a wonderful man. Now I'm going to take him in the back while you decide on rings." He led Bryce to a small room toward the rear of the store and pulled a bottle of Kosher wine from a selection he had there.

"This is for your wedding night," he said. "I want you to know I gave a bottle of this to Manny Gerson last month and he told me his bride became very romantic on their wedding night after she had a glass of this wine."

Bryce was touched by the gesture and promised to take the bottle on their honeymoon if Abraham would stop telling the story of how they met. "Now, there's one other thing, Abraham. I want you to charge the regular price for our rings. I didn't come here looking for a discount."

"I'll be fair. Trust me."

Candace decided on a silver ring that matched her engagement ring and Bryce chose a gold band that had a simple design along its edges. Bryce wouldn't show her what was in the bag he carried from the store. Candace asked for just one hint. He told her to wait for their honeymoon.

Chapter 74

The May wedding was attended by family and close friends who rejoiced that Candace and Bryce again had found love and hope for the future. Candace wore an off-white, custom tailored, fine patterned silk dress that had a mid-calf length full skirt. The dress was complemented with a finely detailed silk brocade jacket that was fitted at the waist. The reception got off on the right foot when Candace took off her jacket and opened a foot-long zipper hidden in a seam at the side of her skirt.

The couple's first dance was a tango. "It had to be a tango," she told him.

He looked deeply into her eyes. Then he laughed in exuberance. "Yes, we'll always have the tango."

Their honeymoon trip to Bermuda was delayed until the weather there warmed enough for them to enjoy snorkeling in the shallows bordering the island. When they tired of the ocean, they lazed on the sunny beaches. Candace especially delighted that each of them developed an interest in golf after they took lessons one morning.

"We're going to take more lessons when we get home," she told him.

They returned to Bucks County happy and eager to settle into a life together.

Most of their mail still had to be forwarded from their old addresses. Each delivery included an assortment of junk aimed at newlyweds, advertising the availability of loans, cookware, and the like. It also contained plastic laminations of their wedding announcement that had been published in the Inquirer. The senders asked for a donation to this cause or the other in return.

Candace pitched the junk but did keep a few of the announcements for a scrapbook.

⁘

She was not the only person to save the announcement. Prisoners at Graterford Penitentiary had plenty of time on their hands to read the newspaper and one of them used his child's scissors to neatly cut out the announcement and add it to a folder that now was thick with clippings. But he was still waiting for what would be the crown jewel of his collection. Leroy had yet to send him a photo of Marilyn's grave stone. Coe was growing impatient.

Chapter 75

"Your car is here," said Mabel from his office doorway.
"Thanks," said Bryce. I won't be back this afternoon.
Did you find that folder on the McKean County property?"

"It's in your briefcase along with the certificate frame you ordered."

"Okay, I'm set."

Bryce left the building and entered the limousine where he retrieved the folder and began to review its contents as the car headed for north Philadelphia. Buying forest land was always a risk, but this property had good potential. He studied the numbers as the limo journeyed into the city. Bryce normally would have taken his own car but he wanted to use the drive time more productively—and he had another reason for the limo that he intended to reveal to the chauffer only later that day.

Between Leroy Carter's parole officer's discipline and Bryce's "encouragement," Leroy had completed his adult literacy class and today was the graduation ceremony for his class. Bryce intended to treat both the parole officer and Leroy to an early dinner at a top restaurant. A trip there in a limo would be part of their reward.

When the limo pulled to a stop in front of the building that housed the classrooms on the second floor, the driver, with a worried expression on his face, turned and looked at Bryce.

"Do you want me to wait here for you?"

"It's still daylight, Bill. You'll be okay."

Bryce got out of the limo and was greeted with the stares of neighborhood people who seldom saw a limousine on their streets. He smiled and entered the building where he followed signs up the battered stairwell to a landing that had several doors leading off it. He chose the open door and entered a room with folding chairs arranged to view the lectern that served as a podium for the ceremony. The room was filled with people who had come to receive their diplomas and their friends and relatives who would join in the celebration.

Bryce spotted Leroy in the second row and slid into a seat behind him. He tapped Leroy on the shoulder and asked, "Who is the gentleman next to you." The man turned at the question and smiled because he recognized the voice that he had heard many times over the telephone.

"You know who he is. Jackson, this here is Bryce Roberts."

Bryce reached over the seat back and shook hands with the parole officer.

"It's really good of you to come today," said Jackson. "Not too many people like you do, you know."

"Thanks, I just wanted to see this. I figured Leroy could do it if he just had the opportunity."

"Opportunity, mah ass. Yo' didn't give me much choice," said Leroy.

"Nevertheless, you did it."

The room quieted as the ceremony began. The students went forward to receive their certificates. A newspaper photographer, who Bryce knew, was there to take pictures of the students as they shook hands with their instructors. At the end of the ceremony Bryce stood for a photo of him shaking hands with Leroy who held his newly framed certificate.

The following morning Candace saw the photograph and article in the newspaper and shook her head over the man who had just shown another side of himself.

"He never even told me he was doing this."

Bryce didn't particularly care about who saw the paper but he smiled as he thought about how Leroy Carter, child of the 'hood, had proudly read aloud the entire menu at the restaurant where the limo had taken the overwhelmed con and the two men who had prodded him along to that day.

But Bryce did care deeply about something else. He had the photo and article, which mentioned the trip to the restaurant in the limo, cut out and sent to an inmate at Graterford State Prison. There was no return address on the envelope and no enclosure letter. But the message was loud and clear as a flashing neon sign on the Las Vegas strip.

Chapter 76

C andace's return to teaching was marred by student protesters who became more active with the arrival of warmer weather. Each day as she walked into her building, pickets patrolled outside with the usual signs advocating peace or defaming the military and industry.

On a rainy Tuesday morning Candace entered her office and raised the blinds. She looked outside as she adjusted the blinds' height and saw a group of about fifteen people approaching the building from the other side of the street. None carried protest signs or textbooks but several of them carried backpacks that had begun to be popular.

The telephone rang and she answered a call from her mother who wanted to talk about how lonesome it was with her and Anne gone. Candace had a few minutes before she was to go upstairs to work and so she and Alice chatted about the fun that Candace and Bryce had on their honeymoon. They hung up with promises of a shopping expedition and Candace paused to look around the office before she left for the fourth floor. Her eyes took in a photo of her and Bryce and she shivered deliciously when she remembered how they'd last used her office.

She locked her door before walking toward the elevator. As Candace proceeded down the hall she kept her keys in her hand and they remained there when she got on the elevator. She didn't recognize the two students who were waiting for the elevator when she boarded and she wondered whether they were part of the protest group that may have come inside from the rain. As the door opened for the third floor neither of the men got off the elevator and instead waited for the door to close. The bigger one of the two who was wearing a bandana around his head and surplus army fatigues, turned to her and said, "Okay, beautiful, we're going to the fourth floor with you." He pulled a bulky object from the backpack on his companion and Candace realized it was sticks of dynamite taped together. A fuse dangled from the pack. Candace felt her knees getting weak but resisted the wave of fear that swept over her. She put her key in the switch lock, turned it, and the elevator rose.

She looked at the two men and said, "There's nothing on the fourth floor worth bombing." She felt stupid after saying it. The man with the dynamite reached out for her keys and took them from her. She didn't resist. *I've got to stay calm,* she told herself. *Wait and see what they do. Maybe they'll let me go.*

When the door opened the bigger of the two men put the sticks back into his companion's backpack and said, "Lady, we're in charge here now. Do as I say and maybe you'll come out of this alive."

Candace nodded as they stepped behind her and nudged her out into the hallway. There were four other people at work but they were not immediately in sight. The two men took Candace into an office and told her not to leave it. The smaller of them ripped the telephone cord out of the wall and then stayed outside in the hallway on watch and to keep her confined. Within ten minutes all of the other employees had been "persuaded" to join her. The office door was then pulled shut and a rope tied around the knob on the outside. A metal bar from one of the labs was stretched across the doorframe. They could see through a side window in the doorframe that the other end of the rope had been fastened to the bar, thus locking them in. The two men left the backpack outside the room where their prisoners were confined and moved toward the elevator. They pushed the call button, impatiently moved from one foot to the other, and then disappeared behind the elevator's closing doors.

Dr. Frankel, the lab boss, stood with his head bowed, slowly shaking it back and forth. "We can't stay here," he said. "Those idiots are likely to try to blow up this place. Any ideas, anyone?"

"Look, the hinge pins are on the inside of this door," said Luke Clay. "If we can figure out how to remove them, we might be able to get out of here if there's any slack in that rope."

"Can anyone check the phone line?" asked Candace. "Maybe we can repair it and use the phone to dial for help."

"We're in luck," said Amos Shepherd. "I keep some tools in the bottom drawer of my desk and we can get the hinge pins open." He reached into the drawer and pulled a hammer and screwdriver out. Then he retrieved another screwdriver to unscrew the telephone line wall box cover. He worked at the cover and then examined the connections.

"The wires pulled some screws out, but there may still be a way we can just splice the box wires to the phone. Luke, can you use this pocketknife to peel the wires on the phone's line?"

"I'm going to keep watch in case someone returns," said Dr. Frankel. "If I give the word, stop what you're doing."

Chapter 77

Jerald Fried was born in 1939 to parents who worked in the garment industry of New York City. The couple worked long hours in poor conditions and were paid stingy wages for their piecework. As the country entered the Great Depression in the 1930s, the parents turned to communism, searching for the answer to their plight. They lived in a tenement house with running water only if the landlord paid the water bills, and heat in the winter was mostly a dream. When World War II broke out his father got a job in a factory that made military uniforms. He died in a fire that swept through the building, trapping many inside who could not get out through the exits that were locked and blocked.

Jerry's mother took a job in the Brooklyn Naval Shipyard as a welder and earned enough to keep her family going when her deceased husband's worker's compensation stipend was added to the pot. Jerry's two older sisters worked in the garment trade doing piecework. When the boy was older he refused to work in "the rag business." The most they could get him to do was run errands for the grocery store owner who paid him pennies.

After the war ended his mother still often talked about the communist worker's paradise. Her son read Carl Marx's Manifesto and borrowed other books on the Soviet Union from the public library. At age fifteen he found a job as a clerk in a Woolworth Five and Dime store and was fired for encouraging his fellow clerks to strike for higher wages. He was so angered by what he perceived as an injustice he set fire to the store shortly after it closed for the evening. He was questioned by the police but they couldn't pin it on him.

When he graduated from high school, Jerry applied to City College where he completed two years and then had to drop out for lack of funds and his failure to qualify for a scholarship due to his poor grades in the required courses. He'd spent almost all of his time studying every book that he could find on class warfare, a subject that was not then taught at the school.

Jerry drifted until he found a job writing revolutionary articles for a radical newspaper published in the Village. He also read everything he could get his hands on about Ernesto "Che" Guevara, the Cuban revolutionary. He attempted to travel to Cuba to meet the leftist folk hero, but was unable to find passage on a freighter that would sail there. He nicknamed himself "Che" as the next best thing to do.

Fried moved to Philadelphia where his uncle helped him to get a job at a city newspaper where Jerry immediately became involved in the labor union that worked the presses. When the union members spurned him and his revolutionary rhetoric he found a home with the few radical left wing students at Penn.

Chapter 78

Jerry "Che" Fried, the man who imprisoned the fourth floor scientists, called a press conference at 11:00 o'clock that morning. In front of television cameras and radio microphones he announced that his group had staged a "take over" of the physics building and demanded that the university agree to abandon the use of its facilities for all government-sponsored research. Fried announced that they had "penetrated the capitalist security system on the fourth floor," and now it, and the government lackeys were under control of his "freedom fighters." He gave the university 36 hours to meet the demands or his group would blow up the building. He figured the time limit was long enough to milk the most publicity out of the event but short enough to keep his own people psyched up and interested. Fried said he didn't care if he was now known, because part of any negotiated deal would be amnesty for him and his followers. Then he went inside the physics building to telephone the university administration office. He didn't tell his followers that when the time came he had his own escape plan in place.

Chapter 79

"**B**ryce, you'd better come look at this," said Mabel, who was standing in his office doorway. Her tone made him get up and follow her to the employee lounge where a tape of the "press conference" was being repeated on the noontime television news.

Bryce dashed to his office and dialed Candace's office. No answer. He dialed her mother and asked her if she had seen or listened to the news. When she said no, he asked if Alice had spoken with Candace that morning.

"Yes, she called right before she reported to work at the lab. We had such a nice chat, Bryce. Can you spare her for a day this weekend? We may have some shopping to do."

"Yes, Alice I think we can swing that." *If my wife's not blown to smithereens by then.* He begged off and hung up, thought for a minute, and then dialed Phillip. His brother answered his page and Bryce told him of the situation.

Phillip cut to the core of the matter. "How can I help?"

"Phillip, we have to get into that building and get Candace out of there. I think it'll have to be tonight if they don't release her and the others by then. That Fried is a fanatic and we just can't wait to see what happens later."

"Bryce, why don't you meet me at my place? Bring stuff you think you'll need, including about two hundred feet of rope, pitons, hammers, and grappling hooks that we can use for climbing the outside of the building if necessary," said Phillip.

"Okay, Phillip. I'm going to make a few more calls and then I'll be on my way."

He called Mabel into his office and explained what he and Phillip were thinking of doing. He told her she may have to stay late into the evening to handle the switchboard and relay messages. Mabel eagerly volunteered. Then Bryce called Stella and arranged to have her meet the children after school and kindergarten. He told her about Candace's suspected predicament and said he was going downtown to talk with the university administration and then would stay near the physics building until Candace was freed. Stella told him she'd pray for everything to work out and he hung up after agreeing to call when he had news.

Then he called his sister. "Margaret, do you still use that helicopter service to spray our crops?" he asked.

"Well, hello to you, too, brother dear, and I am fine, thank you very much," she replied.

"I'm sorry Margaret, but I don't have time to explain a whole lot. I need a helicopter tonight and I have to talk to that outfit that flew Eddie and me into Children's Hospital that time he got stung."

Margaret heard the urgency in his voice and said, "It's here in my rolodex . . . let's see . . . ah, yes . . ." and she gave him the number and the name of the pilot.

He told her to tune in the news.

❦

Candace was holding the telephone receiver when the dial tone came on after Luke spliced the last wire. She immediately dialed Bryce's office and the call was taken by Mabel. Candace was dismayed when she learned her husband had left the office, but heartened when Mabel told her of his plans. Then she told Mabel about the knapsack with the dynamite. She asked Mabel to telephone the city police and relate what she had said in case she was unable to complete her call to the police. Then she dialed the police and advised the detective to whom she was connected of her identity and what she knew about their situation. The detective asked for her number, promised to call back, and hung up. Candace handed the telephone to Dr. Frankel. She decided not to tell anyone about Bryce's plans.

Chapter 80

"**B**ryce, how in hell are we going to get in there without tripping the alarms on the windows or the stairs?" asked Phillip. "Besides, there are police posted at the building."

"We get in from the roof. If Ivan, the helicopter guy, calls me back with a go, we jump onto the roof tonight and climb down inside the elevator shaft or go down through a skylight. If Ivan can't swing it we'll climb the east wall. The police are concentrated at the front of the building. There are ornamental brick at the corners, so we'll be able to use that for footholds and handholds. We can heave grappling hooks up on the flat roof and use the lines to hold onto when we climb. There are drain pipes down the wall on the side of the building. I checked them when I scouted it this afternoon. Nobody is keeping watch back there. When we get to the roof we go down the elevator shaft. Then we open the elevator door on the fourth floor and get in there quickly. If any of those assholes gets in the way we flatten them."

"What if the roof entry to the elevator shaft is locked from the inside? It'll take too long and you'll make too much noise trying to break in."

Phillip's telephone rang. Mabel asked for Bryce and filled him in on Candace's call. His felt a chill go down his back when Mabel told him of the knapsack full of dynamite. Bryce told Mabel of their plans to enter from the roof but he didn't tell Mabel about the helicopter.

When he hung up, Phillip said, "You went pale for a minute, Bro. What's up?"

"They aren't bluffing. Candace says they really do have dynamite with them. We'll have to use more finesse or stealth when we enter. If somebody panics before we get control, there won't be time to do anything but pray." He and Phillip brainstormed several options and then he called the number Candace had given Mabel.

The phone was answered before the first ring had stopped. A whispered voice said "hello" and Bryce asked for Candace.

"Candace," he said, voice tight with worry, "Phillip and I are going to get into the building around ten this evening. Ask your boss to request that the university send someone to you all with food and water about seven or earlier. Try to get the delivery guy to the fourth floor."

"Oh, Bryce, be careful. There are two men on guard outside the office where we're being held. The office is located to the right when you get off the elevator. The knapsack full of dynamite is across the hall from us."

Bryce said, "About ten o'clock tonight pound on your door and make them give you and the others a bathroom break."

"We already need that. The two guards who are here now are smoking a joint so if they keep it up they probably will be mellow enough to convince."

"How many people are there supporting the building takeover?" he asked.

"I don't know but earlier this morning I saw more than a dozen people outside who I believe are part of this. Probably there are more."

"Is there a skylight over the room where you're being held?" he asked.

"No, the nearest one is in the hall near the elevator," she told him.

"Can someone on the roof see the elevator through that skylight?"

"I believe so. The skylight's big enough. Bryce, what are you thinking?"

"We may try to enter from the roof. No matter what, just know that I love you and you're going to be okay. Now, please let me speak with Dr. Frankel."

"Bryce, I love you too," whispered Candace and then she passed the telephone to Dr. Frankel who listened for a long time.

His face bore worry when he hung up. Then he dialed the administration office and asked for the Provost.

Chapter 81

" **A** helicopter will make too much noise, Bryce. Everyone in the neighborhood will hear it and the people holding that building will be alerted as well," said Philip,

"Oh, they'll hear it alright, but when they see it they won't be suspicious. They'll welcome it. Ivan is going to hover briefly over the roof and then fly off. I'll shin down a line or drop out of the chopper when he hovers over the roof. The noise will cover my crossing over the roof to the skylight.

"How are you going to pick out that building at night?" asked Phillip.

"It's the only one on that block with a flat roof and it's near the tennis courts."

"Somebody's bound to see you get off the chopper," said Phillip. "Then what?"

"I don't think people will see me. The building is tall enough and wide enough so the bottom of the chopper will be blocked from view when it's right over the roof. I'll get Ivan to drop me closer to the east side."

"Can you see the elevator doors from any of the skylights?" asked Phillip.

"Candace said there is a skylight near the elevator," said Bryce. "It should be good enough to see down inside. I hope."

"What do you mean the people holding the building will welcome the chopper?"

"I talked to Ivan about that and he suggested something that makes sense . . ."

Phillip's smile grew as he listened to the plan unfold.

◦⥈◦

When Dr. Frankel finished speaking with the Provost, he and his group began banging on the door of their office demanding a bathroom break. The pot-mellowed guards allowed them to leave one at a time and they didn't retie the rope to the metal bar when the last of the captives was escorted back to the room. They resumed their seats in the hall near the elevator and turned up the music on a portable radio they'd brought with them.

At seven-thirty the elevator door opened and a man dressed in the college cafeteria uniform got a good look at the area as he handed them sandwiches and soft drinks and left food and water for the captive scientists. When the man left the building, he telephoned a number he'd been given and assured the person who answered that the elevator door could be seen through the skylight.

⚬⚭⚬

At nine forty-five that evening a doctor wearing a white medical jacket and a hospital name tag appeared at the building entrance and said that he'd been sent by the Provost to attend to Dr. Frankel, who was a diabetic and who would go into shock if he was deprived of insulin.

"Che" was called to the door and allowed the doctor to enter. While he searched the medical bag the doctor carried, Che didn't notice that the physician was wearing combat boots under his trousers. Fried led the doctor to the elevator and keyed in the fourth floor button.

Upstairs, the captives again banged on the door, then opened it themselves to request another bathroom break. They had to shout over the music to be heard by the zonked revolutionaries.

Several miles away and fifteen hundred feet up Bryce tapped Ivan's arm and pointed down toward the target. The helicopter with the news channel logo painted all over it began to descend and moved toward the building they'd earlier identified. The chopper leveled off several blocks away and then slowed for the pass at an incredibly low altitude over the people outside the physics building. They last thing they noticed was a crazy camera man leaning part way out the door trying to get pictures of the captive building with the aid of a powerful spotlight that ruined the night vision of many of those outside who looked up. The chopper disappeared over the rooftop and didn't return to view until it was a block away and gaining altitude. Its spotlight was turned off.

The elevator door opened and Jerry Fried smelled the odor of marijuana. He pushed on Phillip's back and the two stepped into the hall. Che screamed at one of the two guards, "You asshole, where's Stokely?"

"He's walking a prisoner to the head. Don't worry, man, he'll be along in a minute."

"Why's the door to that office open?" demanded Che. "Those people aren't supposed to be walking around."

"Easy, man, they aren't going anywhere; they'll set off the alarm if they try and we just bring them back. Besides, that one dude doesn't look so good."

He pointed to Phillip and asked, "Is that why he's here?"

Phillip said, "Yes, where's Dr. Frankel?"

The guard pointed at an office across the hallway and down two doors. Phillip, followed by Che, headed in that direction. As they did, a skylight over the hallway behind them silently opened on newly oiled hinges and a man dressed in combat boots and military fatigues slid noiselessly down a rope that was lowered through the opening. He quietly overpowered the disbelieving man who had remained behind by the radio, quickly gagged him, and dragged the frightened revolutionary into a darkened office where he bound him with duct tape. Bryce checked the hall, and on catquiet feet moved toward the doorway occupied by Che. The man's back was toward him while he observed the doctor taking Dr. Frankel's blood pressure.

Che felt a terrible pain at the base of his neck and yoke of his shoulders as the full force of Bryce's doubled fists crashed down on him, clubbing him to his knees. The dazed man sensed himself being picked up and then a fist slammed like a cannonball into his gut, knocking the wind out of him.

Phillip bolted from the room and ran down the hallway toward a third man he saw approaching. The guard's face got a knowing look and he turned to run toward the knapsack, but Phillip caught him, jerked him off balance, and with a hard downward kick drove the heel of his boot into the man's ankle on the only leg that gave him support. The guard went down, groaning in pain. Phillip, knee in the man's sacrum, tied his hands behind his back with medical tape he retrieved from his pocket. He tied the ankles next, ignoring the cries of pain from the man.

Che tried to get up and Bryce delivered a vicious kick to the man's ribs and would have followed up with more, when he heard Candace's voice coming from the room's doorway.

"Bryce, don't! You'll kill him!" The sound of her voice stopped him. He looked at her and the rage in his face faded.

"Are you okay, Honey?" he asked.

She nodded and leaned against the door jamb. Bryce reached for his duct tape and bound the hands and feet of Jerry Fried, revolutionary. He grabbed the dazed man's hair and growled, "Where's the rest of the dynamite you brought into the building?"

"In that knapsack by the elevator," Fried mumbled.

"Where's the rest of it?" again demanded Bryce.

"That's it. That's all we have," he said and then he gave a twisted grin. "Be careful of that stuff," he said sarcastically, "it's really dangerous."

"If you've hurt my wife, I'll kill you," whispered Bryce. Then he moved to Candace and held her tightly. She put her arms around his waist and returned the hug for all she was worth.

"I'm okay, Honey," she whispered.

They would have stayed that way much longer but Phillip returned. "We should get out of here before someone starts to wonder what's going on," he said.

"Get my keys from that man," said Candace.

Bryce patted down Jerry Fried, found the keys and handed them to Candace. Then he asked, "Where's the telephone that you were using?"

She pointed to the office from which three men began to exit. "It's okay to come out now, gentlemen," she told them. "We're going to leave here in a minute."

Candace gave Bryce the number of the detective with whom she'd spoken. Bryce called and filled the man in on the situation. "I recommend that you use the east stairs to get to the fourth floor," he told the man. "There's a knapsack full of dynamite up here, so bring along your bomb squad." Then he hung up.

He turned to the group and they made their way down the back stairwell, spliced a wire into the door alarm to keep the circuit closed, left the door ajar with a small wedge, and emerged out into the night.

The police had little trouble with those remaining in the building because their leader wasn't there to encourage them. The bomb squad discovered the dynamite was phony like its owner—it was cardboard rolls painted to look like explosives. Che Fried later was convicted of multiple federal crimes and, like most other radicals of his time, faded to oblivion.

Chapter 82

1971

A liberal assumed the Pennsylvania Governor's office in January, much to Harry's dismay. Almost unnoticed in the flurry of proposed social legislation that Harry and his allies opposed were the nominations the governor made to fill vacancies on the state Board of Probation and Parole. By statute, members of the Board are prohibited from participating in any political activities, even to the point of requiring them not to go near an open polling place except to quickly vote and depart. But that prohibition doesn't affect the selection process that takes place before the nominations are sent to the state senate for confirmation. The composition of the Board therefore changed with the addition of women and men whose social philosophies mirrored the Governor's.

One of the new appointees sat on the two-person panel that considered Charles Coe's application for parole upon completion of his minimum sentence. Coe had listened to his jail house lawyer friends and knew enough to express "sincere" remorse for his crime and to profess his rehabilitation through courses (which he considered laughable) that he had been required to take on the impact of violent crime upon its victims and their families.

To the panel Coe spoke glowingly of his high school education, which most inmates didn't have, and he pleaded that his crime was alcohol related. Of course, he would be forbidden to consume alcoholic beverages while on parole. The older member of the panel had read the detailed record of the commission of the crime and of Coe's unrepentant attitude at his sentencing. She reviewed Judge Cohn's letters recommending denial of parole and voted accordingly. The newer appointee voted in favor of granting

Coe's parole request. The tie vote had to be reviewed by a three-person panel, two of whom also were appointees of the new governor.

The Board is required to notify the sentencing judge and District Attorney within ten days of its decision to parole a prisoner. The notice of the grant of parole stunned Judge Cohn, particularly in view of the strong opposition he'd expressed in his letter to the Board when notified of Coe's pending application for parole. The District Attorney was newly elected, but he reviewed the old file and also was shocked at the Board's release of Coe into society. He immediately telephoned the Parole Board district office to speak with the parole officer to whom the Coe case was assigned. Judge Cohn also made a telephone call, but it was more discrete and contained counsel born of long experience on the bench.

Word spreads fast in the law enforcement community and by late that afternoon Detective Sergeant Richard "Homer" Miller received a telephone call from the County's Chief of Detectives.

"Aw, shit," said Homer when he heard the news. "Those assholes have just saddled us with another huge headache we don't need."

"Amen," replied the Chief Detective.

Bryce flew into Philadelphia Airport that evening and called Candace to plan for dinner

"We don't have to worry about that," she informed him, "we're invited to dine with your parents. Stella and Noah are going to be there too."

"Hhhmmff. What's the occasion?"

"I don't know. Rosalie just called a few hours ago to invite us and she absolutely insisted we be there."

"Okay, I'll have the car that is going to meet me drive me home. I don't want you to drive much in your condition. Do you have a baby sitter?"

"Darling," she replied, "pregnant women do just fine driving until we get to about the eighth month, so don't worry about me driving. And no, I can't get a sitter so we'll take the kids with us. What time is your plane due at the airport?"

⊙≋⊙

Margaret and her husband, Jason, were there for dinner that evening along with Phillip. The family said grace and then the meal was served. As always, the conversation was lively as they caught up on each others' news and fussed over Candace's expecting and Margaret's more advanced pregnancy.

Phillip finally turned the conversation to the thought uppermost in everyone's mind.

"What's so important that you yank me out of my clinics and neurology class for a weekday family pow-wow?" he asked his father.

"I received some disturbing news today," said Harry. "Charles Coe has been paroled." He paused to let the news sink in, and then said, "He's going to return here to Bucks County where, I am informed, he'll be on fairly tight supervision as far as parolees go. The police in the area have agreed to keep an eye on him and increase their patrols around our homes just to be sure he doesn't bother anyone. We don't think he'll be doing that, but I wanted each of you to know he again will be around."

"Where will he live?" asked Margaret. "His father died of a heart attack two years ago and I heard that his mother went to Colorado to live with her sister, so he doesn't have anyone here."

"His mother still owns that tract of woodland near town and there's a shack of some sort on that property. From what I understand, he'll be living there," said Harry.

"What about him driving?" asked Bryce. "The judge took his license away but he'll need a license to get around if he lives on that woodlot."

"They may give him a restricted license limited to essential travels," said Harry. "But unless his mother helps him out, he won't be able to afford a car."

Jason asked, "What's he going to live on? Welfare?"

"Probably. That, and what he can make from selling firewood," said Bryce.

"What should we do if he comes around?" asked Stella. "If that man sets one foot on our property, I'll shoot him," she declared.

"Call the police or get to the station to let them know he's there," said Bryce.

"If he really gets out of hand I'll pay him a visit," said Phillip.

In a voice that her children called "The Commander," Rosalie said, "You will do nothing of the sort, Phillip. Stay away from that man. If you go near him you will be the one who winds up in trouble, not him. It always works that way when you try to deal with people of his ilk."

Phillip didn't respond, but his face bore a determination that he couldn't hide.

Candace saw the expression and thought, Ah, Phillip, you wear your emotions on your sleeve. You must learn to be inscrutable like Harry and Bryce.

"I wouldn't know the guy from Adam, and neither would Candace," said Jason. "Is there some way we can get up-to-date photos of the man?"

"I'll ask some people I know," said Harry.

The meal ended with the men retreating to the sitting room with the children while the women talked babies and children as they helped Teensy clean up in the kitchen. Candace spoke of how Bryce was overly protective of her about her pregnancy and Rosalie told her, "He wasn't around Marilyn when she was pregnant, so he has no experience. Give him time, he'll get used to it."

"Just don't let him get out of rubbing your feet," advised Margaret, who by now was in her seventh month with her second child. The women all laughed and offered Candace more advice on the proper way to train a husband.

In the sitting room, the men spoke more seriously. Bryce looked at Phillip and asked, "What kind of shape are you in, Brother?"

"Still good. I can't do as much because of time in school but I can still run 5K without any trouble and I keep my strength up with exercises. How about you?"

"I'm doing a lot in that basement gym I showed you," said Bryce, "and I run three days a week. Swim some too."

Jason sat there and thought, Man, have I got some work to do. I'm not in anywhere near that kind of shape. He vowed to turn over a new leaf.

Harry changed the subject. "Gentlemen," he said, "No matter what you think or feel about Charlie Coe, do not, I repeat, do not, ever say anything about your feelings to anyone, even people who you consider to be your friends. Such words can come back to haunt an innocent man. Are we all clear on that?" And he looked at Phillip until his son nodded agreement. Harry filled them in on a telephone conference he'd had with the DA and Bryce was encouraged by what he heard.

On their way home Bryce and Candace spoke about their reaction to the news.

"After the initial distress, I've settled down," said Bryce. "Coe may not bother us. The DA told Dad that one of the conditions of his probation is that he must stay away from our families. So, if he violates that condition we'll report him and back to prison he goes. He's smart enough to know that."

"Bryce, I know you don't want me to worry, but stop trying to BS me. If Coe is really as nuts as your father and Margaret think, no probation order is going to be enough to control him."

"He's been screwy for a long time. The DA told Dad that Coe must continue with psychotherapy while he's on probation. But, obviously, he can be violent. And he's unpredictable. We'll just hope he keeps away. If he doesn't, we'll take action." Bryce said the last words in a harsh rasping tone that sent shivers down Candace's spine. She glanced at Bryce's profile. Even in the dim light she could see a hardness in his face that frightened her. She stayed silent, calming herself.

When she trusted her own voice she asked, "What does he look like?"

"He has dirty red hair, wears thick glasses. Pale skin. He's about five feet nine and used to be skinny. I think he's gained weight in prison, though. I brought my yearbook with us and I'll show you his picture when we get home. And I'll make sure you see the photo Dad mentioned. And there's something else I want you to do."

"What?"

"Stay in good shape. Keep using our exercise equipment. Call your doctor and ask if it's okay to start jogging again."

"You are worried, aren't you?"

"Yes, and I'm trying to plan for contingencies. If we need to move fast in an emergency, I want you as strong as possible. I don't believe Coe will stay away. The question is what he'll do and when."

Chapter 83

The Sunrise Lumber Company's twin engine prop-jet flew over the paper mill on its descent to the airstrip west of the small Wisconsin town. The sight of the steam emanating from the mill's stack reignited the passenger's worry. He had to find a way to cut costs, or close the place with the resulting blow to the employees and their families and to the economy of the small community. Bryce thought he'd rather go through UDT hell week again. He buckled his seat belt and closed his brief case. Lord, give me strength, he thought.

He and the mill manager arrived at the plant's conference room and shook hands with the union reps and engaged in small talk until everyone had his coffee. Bryce opened the discussions with a review of the financial information he'd previously supplied.

"So you can see we need to cut costs to stay competitive?" he asked.

"How are we going to do that?" asked Yocum, the bargaining committee chairman.

"Eliminate the log stacker, barking drum, washer and chipper."

"So, how are you going to feed chips to the mill if the chipper operation is shut down? You can't just feed whole logs into the digester."

"We're going to use Metro-chippers right at the point of tree harvest," Bryce told him.

The development of the Metro-chipper allowed whole trees to be fed into it at the point of harvest and the resulting chips were blown into large trucks. The trucks then would haul the chips to the mill's stockpile. The system eliminated the need for log-handling equipment at the mill and lowered the cost of producing wood chips for the digester.

Yocum's response was predictable. "But those Metro chippers should be operated by our guys because the equipment is just a substitute for machinery we have jurisdiction over."

"No, it's different. The chippers aren't here in the mill. Your men don't know how to operate the Metro chippers and they've never worked with the lumberjack crews before. I'm not going to start that precedent. The lumberjacks are already trained to operate that equipment and they're the ones who will continue the operation."

"Yer fuckin' us over by contracting out a whole slew of work we've always done."

"Nothing in our collective bargaining contract says we can't do it," replied Bryce. "Besides, John, you know the mill is more costly to run because it's getting older. If we're going to compete we have to save costs."

"Who drives the transport trucks?" demanded Yocum.

"There's a company we've talked with that says it can supply the trucks and drivers."

"More contracting out," complained Yocum. "Why don't you have our company buy the trucks and have our guys drive them?"

"John, that's just trading one costly asset for another. It won't do it for the bottom line."

"That's all you guys think of."

Bryce knew Yocum was grandstanding for the other members of the bargaining committee who sat at the table, so his answer was to all of them.

"We all have to think about profitability. You know damned well there are Canadian mills that are just looking for an opportunity here. You've seen the numbers. Their costs are cheaper and if we don't meet those costs we lose business. Enough of that and we can't operate at a profit. No profit, no mill."

"What do you have to offer in return for the lost jobs?" asked Yocum. "We can't just agree to a loss of jobs," he said. His eyes bore into Bryce's with the challenge.

Bryce returned the stare. So you're threatening to strike. I figured you'd do that. Time to play the ace.

"What if we can figure a way to keep the mill operating for the next couple of years without the prep equipment?" Bryce asked. "That saves most of the other jobs. Then, in two years we take another look at the bottom line. If we're profitable enough, maybe we modernize and keep the place going."

Yocum and the committee knew a strike would kill the bottom line, thus providing a reason to close the mill.

"Can you guarantee this mill will stay operating for the two years?"

"You know that new plywood factory we just built to the north? The sawdust produced there and by others in the area also can be used as feedstock for this mill. That sawdust also will save costs."

Then Bryce played his ace. "The plywood factory has been constructed so that it can be dismantled and moved to another location," he said. "But if we can keep it running at its present location with its present low cost, the plywood mill will stay put, and we can keep this mill supplied with enough feedstock. That keeps this place open for another two years."

Bryce was quiet while the committee considered the offer.

Yocum's face began to turn red. *You son-of-a-bitch,* he thought. "The reason that plywood factory is low cost is because you're paying non-union wages there. And if we try to organize the workforce there, and you know we want to do that, you close it down and move it. Then this mill closes."

"That's a possibility," said Bryce.

"Our committee needs time to talk about this," said Yocum.

"That's fine John. But I'm due to fly out of here by 4:00 this afternoon. My pilot says there's a front coming in and he wants to get airborne before it hits. Can you get back to me before then?"

Yocum looked at his fellow committee members and read worry on all of their faces.

"Yeah, we can do that."

◦≈◦

Bryce flew out that afternoon ahead of the storm front.

"Maybe I'll be able to say hello to the kids before they're asleep," he told himself. On the way back he dictated a report on the day's discussions and decisions. The union had agreed that the changes would be implemented. Bryce settled back to think about how he and the mill management could heal the wounds the employees had taken. It's going to have to be incentives that get the most out of the men and the mill, but we need the union to help formulate them, he thought. Then he settled back for a nap.

Chapter 84

C andace and the children were at the private airport when his plane landed. The look on Candace's face had him concerned before he even kissed her hello.

"It was in the mailbox when I got home late this afternoon," reported Candace. "I've never been so repulsed in all of my life." Her blue eyes were shooting fire and she held the children's hands protectively.

"A dead skunk in our mailbox has kids written all over it," replied Bryce. "They probably found it in one of their traps and stuffed it in the first handy mailbox they saw."

"Bryce, I don't think it was kids," said Candace as they helped their children strap themselves into their car seats. "Darcy, the neighbor across the street, said he saw an old pickup truck stop by our place and then take off. He said an adult was driving. From the brief description Darcy gave, I think it was Coe."

"So that explains why you've met me here," said Bryce.

"Yes. I'm not going to stay around the house without you there."

"I don't have any travel planned for the next ten days. I want to go home first and stay there for a few days. If he comes around again," he rasped, "I'll deal with him."

Candace thought she'd never get used to that voice and the chill it sent down her spine. "Bryce, I don't want you to get in trouble because of him. Please don't do anything foolish."

"That man is not going to terrorize my family in our own home," said Bryce. "I won't allow that. If we have to do it, we can put you and the kids at my parents' house for a couple of days. Coe can't get back to that house without traveling along the lane and we're bound to see him if he does that. But I'm not ready to do that yet."

After the children had been put to bed that evening they talked quietly on the couch in their living room. He had his arm around her and she felt safe as she sat with her shoulder against his chest.

"I'm going to call Detective Miller in the morning," he said. "I want Homer to stop by to meet you and the kids so that if he has to come here later you and the children will know who he is. I'm also going to get a shotgun out of the locked cabinet and put it under this couch. The skirt will hide it. I'll keep the shells on top of the hutch so the kids can't foul up anything. Then his voice took on the rasp she'd heard earlier that evening.

"I'll kill that son-of-a-bitch if he comes around here."

"Bryce?"'

"Yes?"

"Remember when I asked you if you'd teach me how to use your shotgun?"

He saw the expression of determination in her face and said, "Okay, we'll go out tomorrow afternoon. You'll feel like Annie Oakley when we're finished."

"Thank you. Now I have another question for you."

"What, Honey?"

"Do you know," she said, putting her arms around his neck and nuzzling his ear, "that pregnant women who are totally in love with their husbands can really miss them when they're away?"

◦≋◦

"It probably was him," said Homer. "He recently bought an old pickup. He sells firewood and puts the proceeds into the truck. I showed his mug shot in a photo array to your neighbor and he thinks Coe is the guy but he can't be sure. I'm going to have a little talk with Charlie. If he bothers you again, we go for a parole violation. They never should've let him out to begin with."

"Homer, don't let him think we're worried," said Bryce as he walked him to his grey police sedan. "Tell him that he's been seen out here and that we want him to violate his parole."

"My thoughts exactly," said Homer. "I may have to get a little emphatic with him just to be sure he understands, but he'll be the better man for it." He pulled a totally illegal set of brass knuckles out of his pocket so his listener would have no doubt of the emphasis Homer had in mind.

"Homer you be careful around that guy. He's real trouble. Why don't you think about going there with his parole officer? You won't be able to, ah, emphasize your point, but a visit from two people will make him think he could be in real trouble."

"Don't worry about it, Bryce. We'll have our little talk. By the way, your wife is super. Are you really going to teach Candace how to use your shotgun?"

"Yes. She'll never have to use it but it'll make her feel more secure and she won't be afraid around guns if she knows a little bit about them."

Bryce watched Homer drive away. Then he returned to the front porch and Candace

"Why is it you men always have to talk more after you leave the presence of your women? There's nothing you can say that we won't understand."

"I guess we figure that the more you hear the more you may try to keep us out of trouble. And sometimes it's trouble that we really need to find." He put his arm around her waist and said, "Come on, lets get you changed and we'll head out to the gun club. I'm going to give you a thin sponge to place under your bra strap where the butt of the shotgun meets your shoulder. That'll help soften the kick." She nodded and then he asked, "Are Stella and Noah okay with taking the kids for a few hours?"

"Yes. Anne and Stella are going to paint dolls. Noah and Eddie are going to build a model airplane."

While other kids were glued in front of a TV, Eddie and Anne were out riding bikes in the neighborhood and often managed to talk some of the other kids into doing the same. They both were taking piano lessons and Bryce beamed at the progress they made practicing on the used upright that occupied a corner of the living room.

"Otto Schlegel came by today and tuned the piano," Candace told him. "He told me that when you were playing with the Founders that you stopped by Children's Hospital and often read to his son who was badly burned in an accident."

"I remember. He's one of the bravest little kids I ever met," said Bryce.

"Otto said the boy is playing little league baseball now and his uniform number is 51."

☙

Bryce unsheathed a Winchester Model 12 and laid it on a table at the trap range. He showed Candace how to check to determine if the firearm was loaded and how to use the safety. He explained that she never should have her finger on the trigger unless she actually intended to fire the shotgun and then he showed her how to look down the barrel sight to aim.

"Just remember," he told her, "keep the stock tight against your shoulder before firing; otherwise you're going to get bruised up mighty fast. Honey, are you really sure you want to do this?"

"Absolutely. I've wanted to know how to handle a shotgun for quite a while, Coe or no Coe. I might even want to go pheasant hunting with you and Harry."

"We'll have to break that news to Harry very gently," said Bryce.

Candace's eyes danced. "Oh, come on, Harry likes me. And I'd promise not to talk a lot."

"Let's talk about that later. Okay? For now, we'll use some low brass trap loads first and then get into some magnum buckshot shells after you've fired a few rounds. Here, Honey, put these safety glasses on. After you get them comfortable I'll show you how to load and then you can put on the ear protection. The butt of the shotgun is fitted with a compression pad that'll help protect your shoulder from the kick. Did you put the sponge inside your shirt?"

"Yes, Brycc."

"Let's see you hold the butt to your shoulder. We'll get you used to that and then load your weapon." She raised the shotgun to her shoulder and Bryce taught her how to hold the weapon, aim and squeeze the trigger. He had to tell her repeatedly to hold her right elbow out at an angle from the stock. Then he guided her as she loaded the shotgun.

Candace concentrated and squeezed off a shot at a backer fronted with straw bales. A large paper target covered the bales. She was pleased to see the target develop a lot of small holes. She fired several more times, using the pump action to reload. Bryce showed her again how to load the magazine, this time with buckshot shells. Then he unloaded the weapon and watched her load it again.

"Candace, you're not holding your elbow out. Remember what I showed you."

She adjusted her elbow and fired. There was a louder muzzle blast and more of a kick with those shells, but Candace kept the butt of the stock firmly against her shoulder and was none the worse for wear. She watched with satisfaction as the target shredded when the buckshot tore through it.

"Just remember, aim a little low and keep the butt against your shoulder when pumping another round into the chamber," instructed Bryce. "Try to keep the target in sight over the barrel when you're doing that. This shotgun is really too heavy for you, but its right for buckshot and you're doing fine."

"I want to fire it a couple of times without the ear protection," said Candace. "I'm not going to have the ear muffs on in an emergency and I want to know how it really sounds."

Bryce also fired the shotgun a few times, powdering clay pigeons she launched for him. Then they picked up their children and went home.

Coe remained out of sight but Bryce regularly checked with Homer on Coe's whereabouts.

Chapter 85

Phillip had a girlfriend who he wanted to introduce to his family. He and Rita were due at Bryce and Candace's home for dinner that evening. On that early September afternoon when the foliage was just beginning to turn, Candace went grocery shopping for fresh ingredients for the dinner she'd planned. She was wheeling her shopping cart toward her van when a man with terrible body odor appeared beside her. He grabbed hold of the shopping cart handle and said in tones of mock concern, "My dear Mrs. Roberts, let me help you with that. After all, a woman in your condition should not be exerting herself."

Candace turned to face the man and froze. Charles Coe stood smiling beside her, bloodshot eyes looking upward and fixed on her face, his breath foul with cheap whiskey.

In fear, Candace looked around the parking lot and saw several other patrons. She shouted angrily at Coe. "Leave me alone, you drunk!" *Ah, I've got the attention of some people. Shout again and maybe someone will help!*

"Get your hands off my cart and get away from me!" she screamed.

Two of the men in the lot left their wives and began to jog toward her. Coe saw them coming, let go of the cart handle and backed away with his hands raised to his shoulders, palms out.

"Just trying to be friendly, guys. Mrs. Roberts and I are old friends, gentlemen." Then he sauntered toward a battered red pickup. Right before he got in and drove away, he turned and said, "Candace, say hello to Bryce for me."

"Say hello to Bryce for me." *Oh, my God! Bryce told me those were the words he spoke at the scene when he killed Marilyn.*

One of the men said, "Mrs. Roberts, my name is Joe Cleveland. You probably don't remember me but we met at church several months ago. I worked with Bryce years ago at Henry Morton's cabinet shop. Would you like me to call the police?"

"No, no thank you, Mr. Cleveland," replied Candace. "I'll be okay as soon as I stop shaking." She smiled weakly. "What an awful man! He's the one who killed my husband's first wife and he's not supposed to come anywhere near me or our family."

"Where's Bryce now?" asked Cleveland.

"He's at his office at Sunrise Lumber. I'm going to call him the moment I get home."

Cleveland's wife appeared. The matron looked at Candace's belly, and said, "Well at least let us help you get your groceries into your car. Is it that van over there?"

Candace nodded and they walked to her van and together loaded the groceries.

Candace looked at the child seat they still used for Anne and had a terrible premonition that Coe would try to harm her children. Still shaken by the experience with Coe, she thanked the Clevelands for their help, fastened her seat belt firmly below her belly, and sped out of the parking lot toward home and her children.

Cleveland looked at his wife and said, "I'm going inside to call Bryce. If I were him I'd want to know about this right away."

◦≈◦

In her effort to speed home and still keep control, Candace concentrated on the road ahead. As her van topped a rise she did not immediately see the battered red pickup truck sitting back from a stop sign on a street that entered from the right side of the road. Its driver expertly screwed the cap back on to his pint of cheap whiskey, shook his head to clear the burn in his throat and looked casually to his left toward the top of the hill.

"Jesus, she's really pushing that van," he told himself, and he put the clutch to the floor and raced the engine of his old truck.

Blue smoke began to pour from its exhaust pipe and the ancient engine's valve tappets rattled in protest from the abuse.

"I'm going to have to time this jus' right."

As Candace approached the intersection, momentarily her attention was drawn to the cloud of blue smoke and it was only as she began to turn her eyes back to the road in front of her that she realized the source of the smoke was a pickup that was beginning to roll toward the intersection.

It was too late to brake the van. Fear and rage hit Candace at the same time.

"You're not going to get me and my baby, you, bastard!" Her foot jammed the gas pedal.

"I've got to beat him through the intersection!" She steered into the left lane to give herself a little more room to avoid a crash. She felt the bile begin to rise in her throat. The driver of an oncoming car slammed on his brakes and then Candace felt the shock of the collision with the pickup and heard a sickening, banging crunch. She was thrown to her right but managed, with the help of the seat belt, to keep her seat.

The van fishtailed wildly.

"Oh, God, help me keep control! I want to see my family again!" The anger and adrenaline coursing through Candace helped her gain control and she brought the vehicle back toward her lane just before it would have hit the oncoming vehicle which swerved to avoid a collision. As the other driver's horn blared, she looked in her rear-view mirror in time to see the pickup plow into the embankment on the left side of the roadway.

Heartbeat going like a trip-hammer, she tried to accelerate away from the scene. An awful vibrating noise filled the interior of the van and Candace knew it was her rear tire rubbing against the damage caused by the collision. Her heart fell. She slowed down and the rubbing noise changed pitch.

"Dear God," Candace prayed, "just let me make it home." Ahead she saw the familiar curve in the road that she knew was located right before the turn-off that led to her home. Leaning forward in her seat as if she could urge the van onward, she gripped the wheel tightly and steered to keep the damaged vehicle on the highway. The vibrating sound from the rear of the vehicle grew louder and filled her head until she wanted to scream at it to stop.

Behind her, Coe cursed and floored the accelerator to back away from the embankment. The red truck swerved back onto the paved surface and careened down the road in pursuit of the van. Steam rose from under the hood of the pickup as the possessed man pushed his damaged truck to speeds it hadn't reached in years.

Candace drew even with the road into her development and looked into her rearview mirror just before she slowed for the turn.

"Oh, my God, he's following me!" She accelerated again and the rubbing noise grew even louder as she drove toward her home. She felt the rear of the van sink as the tire went flat and began to flop on the macadam. She made the turn from the development's main road into her street. The van careened drunkenly and she fought to keep it headed toward her driveway. Something locked in the rear of the laboring vehicle and it ground to a halt forty yards from her driveway and safety. To the desperate woman the distance seemed as if it was miles. Candace turned off the ignition and bolted toward her home as fast as her swollen belly would allow. *Bryce, now I know why you made me start jogging again. You thought I might have to run from him when you weren't with me.* She looked behind her as she ran into the driveway and saw the smoking pickup turn the distant corner into her street.

Bryce, I need you now!

Chapter 86

This Jeep has a crummy top, thought the woman. It leaks too much air into the front seat and it's too noisy. But I'm not going to say anything to Phillip because he loves this contraption. Rita Sommers raised her voice to the necessary conversation level and asked, "So tell me what Bryce and Candace are like."

"My brother is a very serious guy. He has his heart set on a big family and a career in my father's lumber business. His first wife was murdered and our whole family wondered whether he'd ever recover. I think he has, mostly because he met the gorgeous Lady Candace."

"Is he anywhere near as intelligent as you are?"

Phillip accepted the compliment as due. "More so in some ways. He has the ability to pull back from a situation and see the big picture. And he can plan things to a tee. Once, when we were out riding our old motorcycle I deliberately ran us out of gas just to start an adventure. I thought we were going to have to hike back to a gas station, but he just opened a saddle bag and pulled out a half gallon can of gas. He's uncanny about seeing ahead. I think he gets that from our father."

"And Candace? Besides being gorgeous, what's she like?"

"She's a college physics professor who knows more about lasers than should be allowed, and she's wonderful with children and totally unflappable. And she doesn't take any guff from my brother. But what I admire the most about her is that she can be a tomboy one moment and totally genteel the next."

Phillip maneuvered the Jeep into the road that led into the housing development where their dinner hosts lived and he and

Rita immediately turned up their noses at a cloud of blue exhaust smoke that hung over the street.

"Man, somebody needs to do a ring job on his car. That's just awful!" said Phillip. He looked at the home-drawn map that Bryce had sent to him, passed it back to Rita, and drove further into the development shown on the diagram. They approached an intersection and his girlfriend told him, "It ought to be the next right."

Candace made it to her front door and gripped the doorknob. Locked! She frantically pounded on the door and rang the bell at the same time. "Open! Oh, please open!" The door cracked open and she pushed wildly past the dumfounded Stella and knelt by the couch.

"Call the police, Stella! It's Coe!

Candace pulled the shotgun from underneath the couch and Stella, who was staring in disbelief turned pale. Candace yanked the shotgun from its case, quickly crossed to the hutch and felt the top for the box of shells. Where are they? Where? There!

"Stella! It's Coe! Call the police!" she shouted again, and loaded buckshot shells into the shotgun's magazine. This time the message sank in and Stella darted toward the phone in the kitchen. Noah, who had left the children in the basement when he heard the commotion, saw the determined and angry look on Candace's face but asked anyway.

"Is it Coe?"

She nodded.

"Let me try to talk to that bastard. Maybe I can get him to leave." He made a fist and pounded it into his other palm. "I've wanted to nail him for years."

Candace finished loading the magazine and pumped a shell into the chamber.

"That crazy man tried to kill me, Noah! I don't think he's going to listen to you or anyone else." She dashed toward the front door which had remained open after her entry. She saw Coe get out of his truck and start across the lawn toward the house.

Candace stepped out onto her front porch and Coe saw the shotgun. He paused midstride.

Phillip slowed and stopped at a row of arborvitae that divided the properties. He felt Rita's grip on his arm and looked up to see an ancient red pickup that was the source of the foul haze that hung over the street. Then his gaze shifted when he heard Rita's sharp intake of breath.

"Don't shoot me Candace," implored Coe, "I was just coming by to apologize for my lousy driving, and to tell Bryce I'm sorry that I killed Marilyn," he yelled. His face took on a deranged smile and he raised his hands over his head.

He took another step forward.

Candace brought the shotgun up and fired, aiming low. The pattern didn't have the range to expand completely or Coe would have died right there. A few of the pellets tore through a part of Coe's coat hem that hung loosely away from his body and the rest powered on by him into the lawn.

"Coe! That ought to convince even somebody with your twisted intellect that I'm not going to listen!" screamed Candace.

Coe turned around and, crab-like, trotted back to his pickup as the woman with eyes ablaze pumped another shell into the chamber of the shotgun, descended the steps of the porch, and began a determined walk toward the street.

Phillip glanced at Rita and then focused on the scene developing before him.

"My sister-in-law has to understand that she's never going to hit anything with her right arm tucked under the stock. She has to hold it out almost at a ninety degree angle."

"Phillip! For God's sake, do something!" shouted Rita.

"Why? It looks like Candace has everything under control."

Phillip, fascinated by the unfolding scenario watched as Coe got into his vehicle and the blue cloud emanating from the old truck intensified. Rita had her hand to her throat as Candace began to move into the street, shotgun aimed at the truck. Coe started to pull away in the smoking and still steaming wreck.

Enraged far beyond anything she'd ever felt before, Candace deliberately took aim at the rear of the truck.

"Try to kill me and my baby, will you? Take this!" She pulled the trigger and felt a tremendous satisfaction as the rear windows of the pickup shattered into powder and the right side of the cab developed numerous holes and dents. But the truck kept moving and disappeared around the corner of the block.

"Damn, Candace still has her right arm under the stock," said Phillip. "That causes a push to the right." He turned off the ignition and started to get out of the Jeep.

Rita looked at him with mock puzzlement. "That's the genteel Candace? Phillip, do something to help the poor woman!"

Candace hadn't noticed the Jeep pull up to the edge of her property as she fired at Coe and his retreating truck. She lowered the weapon and, shaking uncontrollably, sat down on the curb. She felt a hand on her shoulder, started, and looked up to see Phillip and a woman she didn't recognize staring down at her. Phillip gently relieved her of the shotgun, clicked the safety on, pulled Candace to her feet and hugged her. Then he turned to the other woman.

"Rita, I'd like you to meet my sister-in-law, Candace. Don't ever get her pissed off at you.

"Candace, this is my friend, Rita Sommers."

Phillip directed his most charming smile at the shaking woman and then asked,

"Candace, Dear, are we still on for dinner?"

Chapter 87

C andace began to laugh hysterically and Phillip signaled Rita to help him walk the wobbly-legged woman back to the house as neighbors who heard the gunfire began to emerge from their houses. Bryce arrived with a police car in pursuit and he ran toward the three people as the policeman stopped at the curb.

Bryce pulled Candace to him, and concern gripping him, cried, "Candace! What happened? Are you alright?"

Then he saw the shotgun in Phillip's hand and he asked him, voice low and rasping, "Was Coe here?"

"Yes, but Candace persuaded him to leave."

Candace's hysteria dissolved into heaving sobs and Bryce picked her up and carried her into the house, followed by Rita. Phillip dropped behind to await the police officer's approach. He put the shotgun just inside the doorway and walked toward the policeman to ease the process. By the time the officer and Phillip entered the living room Candace was sitting on the couch next to Bryce who hugged her between her sips of water from a glass he held for her.

The police officer waited patiently until Candace explained what had happened. Then he went out to his car to radio headquarters to broadcast an all-points bulletin for Coe and his truck. He left a message that Homer was needed at Bryce Roberts' home.

Phillip looked at Candace and said, "Dear, you're obviously in no shape to fix dinner. Why don't Rita and I come back another time?"

"Don't you dare leave here, Phillip!" shouted Candace. "I'm not going to let that son-of-a-bitch ruin our dinner party!"

Stella introduced herself to Rita and said, "Since Candace insists on carrying on, if you wouldn't mind, I'm going to ask your help in preparing some things until it settles down around here." Her eyes shifted to Phillip. "I think there are some groceries in Candace's van. Phillip, be a dear and bring them in."

Rita's expression of incredulity returned as Stella asked Candace about the menu she had planned for the evening. *This is surreal*, thought Rita. *I'm just going to do what I'm told and then Phillip can take me home.*

Candace was grateful for the offer and tried to relax as the other two women worked in the kitchen. Bryce apologized profusely to Rita for the upset she obviously was experiencing and educated Rita about Coe. Bryce opened a bottle of scotch and Rita gratefully had a very brown drink. As she began to understand the background and how Coe had behaved in the past, her feeling that she'd entered another world diminished and her respect and sympathy for Candace grew.

After he again was reassured that Candace was unharmed, Bryce checked on the children who were being kept occupied in the basement by Noah. When he returned Candace was still on the couch. She told them the details that she'd just sketched for the police officer. She ended with tears of frustration and anger.

"I'm just so angry with that bastard! He tried to kill me and our baby! Bryce you have to do something about him!"

"I tried to reach Homer, but he's out of his office for now. I left word for him to call as soon as he checks in. He and the parole agent can pick up Coe and that ought to be it. Back to jail he goes. Candace, Honey, I'm just damned sorry that I wasn't with you today. I feel so guilty about not being there to protect you." *Just like I wasn't there for Marilyn.*

Chapter 88

Rita was a stunning red-head who worked as a nurse in the surgery unit at the Hospital of the University of Pennsylvania. She earned a bachelor's degree in nursing from Hahnemann and then moved on to her present position because she could take courses for her master's degree in the evening while she worked the day shift. Bryce approved of her instantly and jokingly asked her what she did in her spare time.

"I swim," she told them. "That's how Phillip and I met. We both exercise at the University's pool. The man is a natural in the water, and I recognize talent when I see it," she teased. "Then, when I found out he's doing his rotating internship, we really hit it off because we can talk about our professions."

Homer appeared when Candace was on her second helping of salad. The detective made notes as they all again listened and then Homer folded his notepad closed.

"I'm going to contact Coe's parole officer," he told them, "and then we'll pay a visit to Charlie tomorrow morning. He should be behind bars by tomorrow noon. I'll call you when we do that. What's more he should do heavy time for what he did to Candace today. Probably ten years or more on top of his parole violation."

"Can't you go out to his place right now and arrest him?" asked Bryce.

"He's not there. We checked. And his truck's nowhere to be found. We think he's laying low somewhere. He'll sleep it off and we can get him when he comes back in the morning. I don't think he'll come back here and he has no place else to go but to his shack. Don't worry, we'll get him."

He called for a tow truck for Candace's van and they thanked him as he left. Then Stella and Rita put the finishing touches on their main course. Bryce telephoned Harry and briefed him on the situation. The children left with the Colemans who promised to deliver them safely to Midge and Teensy.

After dinner Bryce invited Phillip to see a new piece of equipment he'd added to his basement gym and the two women stayed upstairs and chatted about people they knew at Penn.

Phillip admired the equipment and then said, "Before you say anything I just want you to know that Candace is one hell of a tough lady. I saw her fire your shotgun at Coe and then at his pickup. He's damned lucky to be alive. Bryce, you have to get her to hold her right elbow out rather than under the stock. Now, let's talk about what's really on your mind."

"Phillip, Coe took one wife and untold happiness away from me. I've finally found another woman who I adore and he comes back to torment me and my family again. This time I'm not going to sit idly by and wait for him to do anything more. If the police don't put him back in jail tomorrow morning, I'm going to find him and deal with him in my own way. I don't intend to get caught, but I won't go on like this with Candace living in fear and me worried sick over whether Coe is going to do something else. If I get in trouble over this I want you to promise me that you'll look after Candace and the children."

Phillip nodded, said, "I will," and then was quiet for a while. Finally he said, "If they catch up with him and put him away, he goes back for maybe another seven and one half years. Then what? Another ten if we're lucky? He'll still be young enough to create more trouble when he gets out. How is it that our system allows a shit like him to harass decent people like you and Candace?"

"Phillip, the system isn't to blame for Coe being a psycho, and that's most of the problem. What I resent is the Parole Board letting him out when they know what he's capable of."

Phillip was again quiet and then said, "What are your plans for this Saturday?

"Candace and I are working at a church fall festival for most of the afternoon and then we've been invited to a dance at the country club that evening. Phillip, don't try anything. Coe's my problem, not yours."

"Here's hoping Homer finds Coe tomorrow morning," said Phillip. "But if the police don't get him, we can't let that turd continue to ruin your family's life."

"Lord, we sound awful," said Bryce. "A couple of decent God-fearing men talking like this."

Phillip and Rita left early because she was scheduled to work surgery the next morning. Candace went to bed, exhausted after the emotion-filled day. Bryce stayed up reading until Candace's soft breathing told him she was asleep.

Earlier she had told him, "Bryce, I can't take any more of this. You have to do something about that crazy man. Pay the police to put extra men on shift to find him, whatever's necessary. I could have lost our baby today and I never would have forgiven myself if that had happened. Please, Honey, do something so we have some peace."

As Candace's steady breathing continued, he changed clothes. He dressed quickly in a hooded navy blue sweatshirt, dark jeans and dark sneakers, found his hunting knife, pocketed heavy twine, and left a note on the bathroom vanity telling Candace that he was going to stake out the immediate neighborhood just in case Coe tried to return.

Coe destroyed one family I had, he thought as he quietly closed and locked the door to his home. Now, by God, he won't get the second.

Chapter 89

The next morning Bryce drove Candace to his parents' home before he went to his office. Homer telephoned just before ten a.m.

"Did you get him, Homer?"

"No, we didn't. But Bryce, can I stop by your office? There's something I want to show you."

"What is it?"

"I'd rather you see it personally."

Homer was ushered into Bryce's office an hour later. He set his briefcase down beside the chair he occupied and began.

"Bryce, we were at his shack at dawn and he wasn't there. Apparently, he didn't return last night. His truck's not at his shack. He's probably sleeping one off somewhere in Jersey. Don't worry. We'll catch up with him.

"The parole officer has the right to search his shack without a warrant, so we took a quick look-see. Somebody has been selling him a lot of booze. Nobody from around here, though, because there aren't any state store labels on the bottles. We think he crosses over the river into Jersey to buy it. There are empty bottles all over inside that shack and around the back toward the outhouse. That's enough for a parole violation right there, so a warrant has been issued to include that and the violations regarding Candace."

"Why didn't the parole officer take action beforehand?" demanded Bryce. "Those bottles didn't accumulate overnight."

"After he got his truck Coe was required to go into the Parole Board office to check in and the psychiatrist was sending reports in regularly, so the Parole agent didn't visit for the last couple of months," said Homer. Then he looked at the floor. "The parole office is where I had a heart-to-heart with him after the skunk incident."

"Well, couldn't the psychiatrist tell he'd been drinking?" asked Bryce.

"They have him in group therapy, and I don't think there's much individual attention paid to him. They just don't have the time to do one-on-one for all of the men on parole who need counseling."

Bryce knew that Coe's drinking was not why Homer was there so he'd waited patiently until he could steer the policeman around to the purpose for his visit.

"So, what do you want to show me?"

"This morning when we did a quick look around we found something you should know about and that's why I'm here." He placed the briefcase on his lap, opened it and withdrew a thick folder with a worn and dirty cover. He held it as if it was a treasure and then handed the folder to Bryce.

Bryce put the folder neatly in the middle of his desk blotter and opened it. Dozens of newspaper articles covering his life from high school until the present were inside. There were pictures of the accident scene where Marilyn had been killed and copies of the reports that covered the accident and subsequent court proceedings. The birth announcement for Eddie was in the folder along with squibs covering Bryce's graduation from UDT School and his MBA graduation announcement. The "infamous" picture of him and Candace dancing at a discotheque also was in the folder, along with many sports pages articles covering his time in baseball. The announcement of his marriage to Candace had a hangman's noose drawn in the margin of the accompanying photo of Candace.

Bryce closed the folder and sat back in his chair, appalled at what he'd just seen. Homer retrieved the folder and put it back in his briefcase. Still, neither man spoke. Bryce sat there for what seemed to Homer an eternity, barely nodding his head up and down as he struggled mentally to come up for air.

"Homer, I had no idea the guy is that sick. He's obsessed. I'm going to have to find a bodyguard for Candace when I'm not around. Until you catch up with that creep, I can't allow her to be without protection."

"Agreed," said Homer. "Coe is one sick powder keg waiting to go off. Every law enforcement officer in this area and across the river in New Jersey is now on the lookout for him. We'll find him."

"Good. The sooner the better. Please let me know right away about any developments."

Homer promised to do so and left. Bryce watched out the window as Homer's car exited the parking lot and then he asked his secretary to track down Phillip and get through to him on the telephone. Phillip called back between rounds and Bryce filled him in on the folder and Homer's news that Coe was not found.

When Bryce finished, Phillip said, "Now more than ever, eh, bro?" Then he hung up.

Bryce's next step was to call upon Harry for a favor. Harry agreed to have the company hire a security consultant and provide a housing allowance as well. Armed with that assurance Bryce started his search for a bodyguard.

Bryce explained to his distraught wife all of what he'd seen in the folder and how both he and Homer had concluded that she was going to be protected by a bodyguard. Candace didn't argue. Instead she told him that she wanted to buy a pistol and learn how to use it and then carry it. This time Bryce didn't argue. He drove his family home, keeping an extraordinary lookout in the traffic.

That Saturday they attended the Church festival and later danced with friends at the country club, Bryce being very wary in the parking lot of the club when they left. After church on Sunday Phillip called him and reported, "I know you told me not to do anything without you, but I just want you to know I can't find the guy, Bryce."

"Neither can the police. If I learn anything I'll call you and we can take care of business," said Bryce.

Chapter 90

Three days later the fires began.
The alarms and sirens filed the air early in the evening as fire engines converged on a twenty-acre woodlot that was ablaze.

Bryce knew the man who owned the land because Sunrise Lumber Company managed the woodlot for the farmer. When the fire had been brought under control Bryce approached the owner, Lloyd Boggs, who was sweat-stained and weary from helping to fight the blaze and they spoke about insurance and replanting.

"Thank God your men come in every year or so and thin the brush," the farmer told him. "Otherwise she'd still be burning."

Bryce thanked Boggs for the compliment and then asked if the cause of the fire had been determined.

"No, we don't know yet," the farmer told him, "but the fire chief called the State Police Fire Marshall's office and they're here investigating."

Bryce excused himself and jogged to the area of the woods where the fire was first seen. Two men in police grey coveralls and heavy boots were examining the scene with a German Shepherd. The dog was sniffing at a charred log that had remnants of burnt newspaper under it. Bryce introduced himself and explained his interest in the land.

"Our dog is specially trained to sniff out accelerants and he's indicating a find at that charred log," the corporal told him. "We're going to take samples for testing at the police lab, but I'm pretty sure of what they're going to conclude." He paused for a moment and then said, "Mr. Roberts this fire was set deliberately. Someone used an accelerant, probably gasoline, to get it going."

"Did anyone see anything here about the time it started?" asked Bryce.

"We have some people working on that right now, sir. We don't know anything yet but maybe someone witnessed a vehicle or something else that will help."

Bryce gave the corporal his business card and asked him for a copy of his report so that he could file it with the insurance company. He returned to his parents' home where he had taken Candace and the children and told his father of his conversation with the Fire Marshall. They discussed having their crews check other woodlots under their management and clearing them of brush if needed. Bryce also decided, with his father's blessing, to have the area surrounding the cabin at Sunrise cleared of undergrowth.

A week later a barn located two miles to the north of the burned woodlot was set afire and the building and livestock that couldn't be saved were consumed. Bryce knew the family. When the scene was cleared, he and many of the men in the area appeared to help raise a new barn because the farmer wanted to use wood beams rather than construct a steel I-beam frame.

The old gentleman explained, "Hells bells, I can't nail anything into steel."

The next morning Bryce interviewed another applicant for bodyguard and liked what he exhibited. Phillip's acquaintance, Glenn Foster, had found the man.

Russell Plank was forty seven, in good physical condition and recently retired from the secret service that guards government dignitaries. His references included a recommendation from a former Vice-President. He was divorced and thus had no family to compete for his time and attention. The bodyguard was interested after he learned of the details of the assignment and he and Bryce settled on a fee. Plank would rent a nearby apartment and be ready to accompany Candace or the children early in the morning. When Bryce traveled, Candace and the children would stay with his parents and Plank would occupy a guest room at their home. Bryce telephoned Homer and asked if he'd do a huge favor and fill in Plank on his ongoing investigation of Coe and give him a tour of the area with a detailed map in his lap for guidance.

Homer agreed to do so. Then he asked, "Bryce, do you have a minute for a little news?"

"Sure, what's up?"

"Witnesses have seen an old red pickup in the vicinity of the two arson fires shortly before they started. But no one got a good look at the driver."

"Thanks, Homer. That's just what I needed to hear," said Bryce, and they hung up.

Bryce related the latest news to Plank. Then they left to introduce him to Candace who was at the Coleman's home.

The bodyguard appreciated Candace's unassuming manner and the two seemed compatible enough to suit Bryce as well. Plank's former position made him a shoe-in for the security clearance necessary to guard Candace at her work and he said he was willing to sit through her classes. Homer met Plank at the Coleman's to escort him around the area and Bryce telephoned Mabel to ask her assistance in obtaining an apartment for Plank.

A week later another woodlot went up in flames. This time the arsonist set multiple fires and the crews had difficulty extinguishing the blaze because it developed into a larger conflagration. It was not until the next morning that it was brought under control.

The community held a meeting to discuss steps that could be taken to protect their properties and increase the alert status of all. The fire fighters agreed to use Phineas Williams' pond for a water source because its springs kept its surface from freezing over in winter. Everyone was told to be on the lookout for an old red pickup truck. Then the community went about its business with an eye on the horizons for smoke.

Bryce bought extra fire extinguishers for his home.

Chapter 91

As Candace's delivery time approached, Bryce stopped his travels out of town and they waited as her belly grew the final inches. Two months before, when Bryce said he wanted to be in the delivery room, the obstetrician agreed, provided they participate in a new kind of study for expectant parents: Lamaze classes given in a section of the hospital's cafeteria after the evening dinner hour. They had fun with other couples practicing the breathing exercises and sometimes did them at home in front of their wide-eyed children.

Candace learned the full impact of her practice in view of the children when a neighbor asked her what was wrong with her kids who were puffing and breathing heavily when Plank escorted them around the neighborhood.

۞

Bryce was sound asleep a week before Thanksgiving when Candace nudged him awake. "Bryce, I think you'd better call Plank. I've had a backache for most of the day and I suspected it was labor. I've started to get contractions now so we'd better go."

Bryce made the call and another to the obstetrician.

"How far apart are your contractions now?" Bryce asked as they drove through the darkness lit only by the headlights and the reflection from the centerline in the country road.

"Still seven minutes or so. Slow down honey, we have plenty of time."

As they passed the easterly side of the woodlot where Coe's shack was located, a battered red pickup pulled out of the underbrush onto the roadway in front of them and headed north

in the direction opposite their travel. Bryce slowed momentarily to
try to get a look at the driver, but couldn't see him.

"Bryce! That looks like Coe's truck! It has damage on the
front end!"

"That's odd," he said. "Coe's shack is on the west side of the
lot. There must be an old trail on this side we didn't know about.
Damn!"

Bryce slammed on the brakes. "I should follow him to see if
it's Coe."

"Bryce! My water just broke! Do you want to deliver our baby
in this car?"

Bryce accelerated toward the hospital, hoping to make it in
time. Candace began her breathing as another contraction hit.
Bryce cursed Coe and drove on through the night. He did a
second gear stop at a stop sign and was rewarded moments later
with red flashing lights in his rear view mirror.

"I though all of those guys spent their evenings in a diner," he
told Candace. He pulled over and ran back to the police cruiser,
quickly explained his mission, and the officer agreed to lead the
way with an escort of flashing lights and siren. Bryce felt guilty
about not telling of his sighting of the pickup but he wanted to get
Candace to the hospital first. They arrived at the emergency room
entrance and the officer turned off his lights and siren. Bryce ran to
his car to thank him and tell of the sighting of the red pickup. The
policeman grabbed for his radio microphone as Bryce ran to catch
up with the emergency room crew who had Candace in a
wheelchair on her way into the hospital.

Their son was born an hour later as Candace gave a final
mighty push after struggling to deliver the large baby. She had
cursed Bryce for doing this to her but he knew it was a product of
her pain. Bryce watched as the nurse cleaned the baby's mouth
and his son began to breathe without being spanked. They laid the
crying infant on Candace's chest to clamp the umbilical cord while
the doctor tended to Candace. Bryce felt a tremendous happiness
surge through him at the sound of his son's first cries and Candace
gazed upon her new creation with adoring eyes. The umbilical
cord was cut and bandaged and Daniel James Roberts was given
eye drops and cleaned before he was handed back to his tired but
joyous mother. Candace looked at Bryce and took his hand.

He caressed her face and said, "Thank you." Then he just sat there and, eyes full of adoration, looked at his wife and son.

Candace persuaded him to call their parents and he reluctantly left to find the telephone. Bryce passed on the happy news to the grandparents and then he called Stella and Noah and Jennie and Stan to give them the news as dawn swept over Boston.

By the time he finished the calls Candace had been moved to the maternity ward and he found her nursing their son as he entered the room to tell her of the conversations. He spoke of how happy he had been to be with her when their son was born. "Candace, Honey, the nurses say he is one big baby. Did they weigh him yet?"

"He's eleven pounds three ounces and twenty two inches long," she said proudly. "We have a pitcher in our family." She dozed off when Daniel finished nursing and a nurse burped the baby and then handed him to his father. Bryce opened the wrap and the tiny fingers gripped his index finger with surprising strength. The nurse told him that he should get a close-up photo of that before Daniel began to grow. Several days later he did, and added it to the album he planned to give Candace at Christmas.

He stayed with Candace all day and then remembered he should call Homer for an update on any developments with the red pickup.

Homer reported "No joy," and promised to call with any news.

Chapter 92

Rosalie hired an extra cook to help prepare the family's Thanksgiving meal. Harriet quipped the table of venison, turkey, quail and pheasant reminded her of a medieval banquet. All five of the Roberts children had made it home, including Stephen, who was in his third year at Yale Law School after finishing his tour with the Army Rangers. Candace's parents and her brother, Henry, came, and so did Stella and Noah. Plank also was there at Candace's insistence. Everyone made a fuss over Margaret's and Candace's new babies and the rest of the children. Harry said a particularly poignant grace in which he thanked the Almighty for their many blessings and they prayed for the servicemen and women still overseas in Vietnam.

Bryce looked across the table at his wife. Eight years ago this is where I dreamed I'd be in life. Now I finally have it, he thought. He said a silent prayer of thanksgiving and winked at Candace. Her return look held mischief he hadn't seen for months. Hope again swelled his spirits.

⊙⇒⊙

Early the following morning Harry, his three sons, and son-in-law went pheasant hunting. When they finished plucking and cleaning their birds Harry got them together in the barn where they used the workbenches to clean and oil their shotguns. It was then he put on gloves and showed them what he'd received in the mail on Wednesday afternoon. Using stamp collector's tongs he withdrew it from a large envelope. It was a photograph of the forested hills where Sunrise was located with a cut-out picture of flames at their base. Letters cut out from a magazine and taped across the top read: YOUR NEXT.

"I debated whether to show this to you yesterday but I didn't want to ruin everyone's Thanksgiving. For a day I risked a fire in the Sunrise Hills. Now, we should take this seriously and do something before nightfall. If the arsonist keeps to his habit he'll try something at night." he said. "The weather forecast for tomorrow and the following days is for rain, so, if this isn't a joke, I think he'll try tonight. I want to hear your ideas on what to do without raising a huge alarm all over the area. If this is real, we may have a chance to catch the arsonist."

The men looked again at the letter but didn't touch it. It was Stephen who first remarked on the poor grammar. "That should be YOU ARE not YOUR," he pointed out. "Do we have a half-educated person or just someone who's sloppy or lazy?"

Bryce said, "If it's Coe who did that, he knows better and the letter is deliberately misleading. If it's not Coe we may be looking for a different man. According to what I've read over the years a likely suspect is a volunteer fireman, young, single, with a social handicap. If it's not Coe, I think the guy wants to get even more jollies by putting people in fear. He wouldn't advertise his intentions otherwise."

Then his voice turned harsh. "If it is Coe, the son-of-a-bitch is taunting us. Either way, we have to tell the fire marshal and the local police about this."

Harry and the other men agreed. Phillip suggested that they hire a security firm to patrol the area.

"If we do that," Jason said, "we'll scare away someone who's not Coe. If it is Coe we just make it more of a challenge for a man who's already crazy smart. Besides, the other fires all were started at night. A security guard isn't going to be able to patrol the woods at night and have a chance of catching anyone."

"You're right, Jason," said Phillip, "but I'm thinking of a different kind of security group. I know a man who has former Special Forces people working for him in a security business that is much more than rent-a-cop. If we get them to join Bryce, Stephen and me in setting up a scouting team that stays out of sight we may be able to nab the guy." He told them more about Glenn Foster and they listened with interest.

"Foster told me he has sophisticated night vision equipment that could make a big difference. And we can hook up with radio communication to stay in touch while we're spread out."

Jason said, "I want to help out, too. I've been getting back in shape and I used to be damned good at wrestling in high school." The brothers looked at each other and concurred. "I also think we should alert the fire company and have a pumper standing by," said Jason. They all agreed, but the pumper crew wouldn't be told of the details.

"Phillip," said Harry, "when we get back to the house I'm going to call Homer Miller and then meet with him and the fire chief to show what I have and tell them what we plan to do. Can you try to reach this Foster fellow to find out if he can be of help?"

Phillip said he would and then turned to the married men. "What are you going to tell your wives?"

"Well, gentlemen," said Harry, "I am going to stay here and guard the fort. That leaves Bryce and Jason." He looked at the two men and raised an inquiring eyebrow.

Bryce looked at Jason and said, "I'm going to tell Candace what we're doing. If she knows the truth she'll understand and go along with it, although she won't like it."

"Ditto Margaret," said Jason.

"Bryce, what if this is a diversion by Coe to get at Candace?" asked Stephen.

"She and the kids will be here. Dad and Plank can do guard duty. I don't think Coe will try anything like that, but keep the house buttoned up when sundown arrives. And post Ralph in the barn just in case.

"Just one other thing, gentlemen," said Bryce. "I want first crack at the son-of-a-bitch."

The rasp in his voice made the others exchange glances but nobody said anything in response. They hustled for the rest of the day planning the best places to stake out the arsonist's likely approach routes and the best route they should take to get there. The Roberts men and Jason dug out their cold weather hunting clothes and long underwear. Foster appeared late that afternoon with two other men, one of whom had a German Shepherd with him. They also brought with them an assortment of infra-red gear and night vision scopes that somehow had found their way loose from the military. The personal communication gear was state-of-the-art, individual pieces with single earphones and tiny microphones that were taped to their cheeks or throats. The men used the barn to finish dressing, complete with camouflage paint and head bandanas.

When Margaret and Candace appeared at the barn to drive them to their destinations in the two vans the women used to haul their children about, a bizarre sense of farce overtook the men. With the exception of Jason, they'd often so prepared in previous times, only to climb into helicopters, boats or trucks. Margaret took one look at her husband and started to laugh. "I can't believe we're chauffeuring you men, who all look scary as hell, in vans used to transport children. But Candace and I agree. No one will look twice at a van being driven by a woman. Now you all remember to scrunch down in the seats."

"Scrunch?" replied Candace, "They're going to have trouble just fitting in. Maybe some of you ought to follow in Phillip's Jeep. You can tell anybody who wants to know that you're headed for a dog training session." She covered her mouth to try to keep from laughing.

"It sure as hell wasn't like this in 'Nam," remarked Stephen. The men didn't laugh. They just exchanged looks and set off with Plank driving Phillip and the dog handler in a Jeep at a discrete distance behind the vans. An hour later they did a quiet radio check and then melted into the approaching night at the base of the Sunrise hillside. They found positions with good vantage points and then maintained a stillness that matched that of the trees. Clouds covered the half-moon that otherwise would have helped them to spot movement from below.

An hour before midnight Stephen spoke into his radio, "Someone is coming at the base of the fire trail," and the men on either side of his position moved quietly toward him.

A figure, walking in a halting, surreptitious gait, moved from tree to tree using a flashlight with a red lens to see where he was going. When he got within range, Stephen and a very large security man named Roosevelt, pounced on the shadowy man and had him pinned, patted down and secured within seconds before he started to protest loudly. Stephen covered their prisoner's mouth with his bandana and then shined the red-lens flashlight in his face.

"Homer, what in the hell are you doing here?" hissed
Stephen.

"You know this dude?" asked Roosevelt.

"Yes, he's a local policeman."

"False alarm," radioed Roosevelt. "Maintain positions and
look for other intruders."

"Homer, we're going to let you sit up, but be quiet until you
catch your breath," said Stephen. He felt Homer nod his head.
Roosevelt melted back into the woods to again take up his
position.

Stephen radioed the others that it was Homer and then he
whispered, "Homer, it's me, Steve Roberts. What are you doing
out here?"

"God, you scared the shit out of me," said Homer. "I knew
that you'd be out here keeping watch and I came to join you."

"Keep your voice down, dammit," whispered Stephen.
"Where did you park? If the suspect sees your police car in the
area it'll scare him away."

"I drove my own pickup and I parked it to the west of here in
a farmer's driveway and hiked in. Will you excuse me for a
minute?" replied Homer in a stage whisper. "I need to take care of
business."

"Over there behind those rocks and be quiet when you walk,"
Stephen told him. "Jesus, I feel like I'm in the Boy Scouts. Here,
take your flashlight. Do you want your revolver back?"

"Yes. You won't tell anybody about this, will you?"

"No, Homer, I won't." *But just remember you owe me one.*

"Thanks," he said, relief plain in his tone through the
darkness. He crept off hurriedly toward the rocks that barely were
visible in the beam of the red light.

Stephen took up his watch again, using night vision binoculars
to pick out anything that might have warmth to it on that chilly
night. As Homer was returning, Stephen's radio crackled.

"We have a match being lit at the base of the hill near Bryce's
position. I'm going after him with the dog." Moments later a fire
flared in the night and men began running through the darkness
toward the fire and the sound of the dog snarling.

Stephen called for Homer and said, "Come on, bring that ten
gallon can by my feet. Let's see if we can control the fire. My

father is monitoring our transmissions and he just radioed that he's called the fire company."

Using flashlights, they pounded through the trees and around and over deadfalls toward the fire, awkwardly moving due to the rough terrain and the weight of the jerry cans full of water that they carried. The arsonist had started the fire by gathering a small pile of brush and then soaking it with gasoline that they smelled as they approached. The two men desperately poured and shook their cans of water on the base of the fire and Jason and his security buddy, Foster, did likewise. They stomped vigorously on small twigs that continued to burn. They all gathered unburned loose sticks and leaves from around the edge of the fire and pulled them away. The fire began to dwindle and Jason and Foster ran for more jerry cans they'd stashed near their lookouts. Minutes later the fire was out and Stephen radioed Harry that only one truck was needed to establish a fire guard.

Homer disappeared toward the snarling dog and then he heard a scream of pain as the animal found its prey hiding in a thicket of rhododendron.

"Butch! On guard!" the handler shouted and the screaming stopped to be replaced by a whine of "Get him off me, pleeeaase." Homer got his handcuffs out. When the handler pulled the suspect from the bushes, he 'cuffed their prisoner's hands behind his back.

It was not Coe.

The prisoner felt a powerful hand begin to squeeze his throat and the dim light revealed the camouflaged face and fierce black eyes that belonged to the hand. A deep voice rasped out of the darkness, "Where's Coe?"

Terror gripped the man and he wet himself. "I don't know, honest!"

"Bryce, let me handle this," said Homer.

Bryce shoved the man toward Homer and stomped away.

When the fire truck arrived, the chief identified the man as one of his former volunteers. The other firemen who arrived to stand flare-up watch looked at the man in the beams of the powerful flashlights they carried and grunted in contempt. They didn't have the same low regard for the men in camouflage standing at the fire perimeter waiting for their transportation to arrive.

"Jesus, Bryce," said one of the firemen, "If I'm ever in a fight I want you and your family on my side."

"Wait till you see our transportation before you say anything more," answered Bryce.

◦◉◦

The suspect broke down under interrogation and admitted to setting the other fires. He denied knowing anything about Charles Coe, but told Homer that he'd found the pickup at the back side of Coe's lot when he was contemplating starting a fire there. When he saw the keys were in it, he used it to drive to the fires and then he returned the truck to its hiding place. He abandoned it when it quit running on him and he stole a car to get to the scene that evening. He repeatedly denied knowing anything about Coe.

Homer called Bryce to inform him of the developments and hung up after they agreed that one problem was solved.

But where was Coe?

Chapter 93

As Christmas approached a debate grew in Bryce and Candace's home over whether they should continue with Plank's services. Candace told Bryce that she didn't believe Coe was in the neighborhood anymore because all of the liquor stores for miles around were alerted to him and he hadn't appeared at any of them since the afternoon he'd assaulted her. There were no signs that Coe had returned to his shack and there were no sightings. It was as if the ground had swallowed him. The couple finally reached a compromise. Plank would stay until after the New Year holiday. If there was no sign of Coe by then, Plank would be released from his services. They alerted the bodyguard to their decision so that he could make arrangements with his landlord and give Foster notice that he might be available in January.

At Candace's insistence Bryce began to travel again for a day or two and he stayed at the office later than he had been doing. Plank was with Candace every moment he determined that he should be there and often when she didn't particularly want him to be. He had become quite attached to the children and often took them to and from school while Candace stayed at home behind locked doors with the baby. Her pistol was never very far from her, but out of sight and reach of the children.

Candace began an exercise regimen a week after she delivered Daniel. Her body was becoming adjusted to the routine and she was happy to see her figure begin to resume normal proportions. Bryce worked out with her and gave her encouragement when she despaired of ever having her clothes again fit. In the meantime she put away all her maternity clothes and said she would keep them "just in case" they wanted any more children. With a baby and two children to care for, her days were full and she often retired early.

Bryce caught up with reading in the first weeks after Daniel was born and contented himself with remembrances of past occasions of their lovemaking. This evening the book he was reading on corporate safety methods triggered thoughts of the time he inspected the security measures at her classroom building . . . The invitation in her eyes had been unmistakable, but making love in an office was a new experience for them both.

☙

Neither of them was ready to completely undress.

He pulled her skirt up and realized that she already was moist when his hand slipped under her panties. He kissed her passionately and lightly stroked her until her hips began their rhythm. He opened his trousers and she dropped her panties and stepped out of them, keeping her heels on. He turned her to face the window that was on the other side of a sturdy table.

"Put your hands out on the table," he said, voice husky with desire. She did so and felt her skirt go up and his hands grip her hips. She spread her feet to make herself open to him. Then her fingers helped his huge erection find the opening her wet lips offered. His finger began to titillate her and she moved her buttocks against him, burying his cock deep inside her. His breath was hot against her neck and then shivers of ecstasy shook her as she centered on the sensations now consuming her. He felt her getting close to a climax and slowed his movements to prolong their pleasure.

"Oh, don't stop . . . Not this time, Honey . . . Just keep going." She pushed her hips against him and turned a face filled with wanting toward him. He obliged and thrust deeply into her again and again until he could feel her being transported by wave upon wave of rapture.

The intensity of their passion, brought on by the darkened room looking out over the campus, fueled them both, and his movements turned wild as he lost himself in her. She felt him begin to come and pushed her womanhood close and ground herself against him, thrilled at the intensity of their joining and his reaction to her. A long, low moan escaped from her throat and then she collapsed over the table.

They remained that way until she again turned her face toward him, smiled her teasing way, and told him, "That's the wildest ride this mare's ever had."

"My stud service is free any time."

Their walk to her train was a time when they were aware only of each other.

⊙≫⊙

Bryce came back to the present and took a cold shower before joining his wife in bed. He wrapped his arms around her as she slept. "Tomorrow morning I'll talk her into something," he told himself.

Chapter 94

On the day after Christmas the family was out on new cross country skis in the snowy fields behind the homestead. Their time together made Candace forget all about Coe who had lurked in the backs of their minds in the days leading up to Christmas. Anne was having a ball learning to ski and Eddie enjoyed showing off his skills. Daniel, dressed in a tiny snowsuit, and wrapped in a blanket with only his eyes showing through an opening, was strapped, papoose style, in a carrier on Candace's back.

Harry had a new toy as well. He came buzzing over the fields on a snowmobile with Rosalie hanging on and squealing with laughter as he sped over small bumps in the surface of a pasture. He stopped long enough to tell Bryce and Candace that they had to stay for dinner and then they were off again, headed down a trail the horses used in the warmer weather. Candace turned longingly toward the barn and Bryce read her thoughts.

"After New Year we'll go riding. I promise. Your doctor said not to push it before then."

They returned to the house when they saw his parents speeding back toward the barn. Midge took the two older children to roast marshmallows at the fireplace and put Daniel in a cradle nearby. Rosalie and Harry invited Bryce and Candace to go for a short ride in their four-wheel drive Jeep. They drove east over a small hill along a narrow track through the trees and stopped on the other side in a clearing that once had been open field. Harry asked them to get out and they stood looking at a beautiful view of the sun setting through the trees to the west. They could see the Sunrise Hills to the north. It was quiet, as the breeze had stopped when the sun began to go down. Only the sounds of their breathing broke the winter stillness. Harry and Rosalie turned to them.

"If you want it," Harry said, "this ground is yours on which to build a home. When Rosalie and I get older, if you would like to do so, we can swap houses."

Candace started to cry and Rosalie hugged the taller woman. "You need a place for your growing family and we want to be near our grandchildren," she said. This will work out fine for everyone."

Bryce said, "I gather you've spoken with my brothers and sisters about this and they have no objection?"

Harry looked at him and said, "Correct. They love the homestead as we all do; but they each have plans to live elsewhere."

For the first time in a long while, Bryce hugged his father. Then he hugged Rosalie. Turning to Candace he said, "What say you, Sweetheart?"

"Oh, thank you Harry and Rosalie, of course we'll accept." She stood there looking around at the views and said, "The first time Bryce brought me here I told him I thought it was heaven. I hoped then he and I would share a life together, but I never dreamed we'd live here in this place. She hugged Harry and Rosalie again and then said, "I'm really looking forward to having you as neighbors."

(≈)

New Year's day arrived and Candace and Bryce told Plank he was free to leave when he got things in order. He said he'd been delighted to be of service and told them he didn't think Coe would return to the area.

"Everyone around here knows he has a warrant out for him, and he knows that too, so I think he'll stay away."

Chapter 95

The intercom buzzed and Mabel told Bryce, "Detective Miller is here to see you."

Bryce looked out at the late February afternoon overcast and then turned back to his desk.

"I'll be with him in a couple of minutes. Ask him if he wants some coffee."

Bruce was reviewing operating costs for a furniture factory in northern Pennsylvania. If the price was right and modernization costs made sense, he intended to buy the factory. He finished the section on the business's medical costs, jotted some notes, and then buzzed Mabel to invite Homer to join him.

Bryce rose at his desk as Homer walked across the room toward him. They shook hands and Bryce said, "It's been months since we spoke. How have you been?"

"Oh, you know, police work never ends," replied Miller in a tone that instantly put Bryce on the alert.

"And policemen never lose their walk, either," countered Bryce. "Even though you're not in uniform, when you walked across the room toward my desk, you had that uniformed policeman's half-swagger and you held your right arm out from your waist so it wouldn't swing into your sidearm when you walk."

"You're good, Bryce. Do you want to work part time as a detective?"

"No, thank you. I have enough excitement in my life without dropping in on crime scenes at four a.m."

"We did find a body, or more accurately, what's left of it, this morning," replied Homer. He watched Bryce's face carefully as he spoke the next words. "We think it's Charles Coe."

Bryce was aware of the scrutiny. He leaned forward and his eyes bore into Homer's. "What do you mean, you *think* it's Charlie Coe?"

"The body is badly decomposed. He's been dead for a long time."

"Where did you find him?"

"Some kids putting in a trap line found him on the woodlot where he lived. Bryce, parts of his remains are missing or disturbed. Foxes, crows and buzzards have picked him pretty clean so there's only about ninety percent of the skeleton remaining. The coroner is there with a forensic pathologist but there's not much left upon which to perform an autopsy. His remains were next to a small boulder. There's a dent in his skull that may have come from when he fell and hit the rock. Left untreated, that could lead to his death."

"You think that's what happened?"

"Probably. There was an empty whiskey bottle next to the remains. We think he got even drunker than usual, wandered off toward where he hid his truck, and fell. There are some big tree-roots near the rock that he could have tripped over. He probably got a brain hemorrhage and just never woke up after he hit his head."

"Does the pathologist have any idea of when he died?" asked Bryce.

"He thinks he's been there between five and six months," replied Homer.

Bryce leaned back in his chair and Homer watched him withdraw into his own thoughts.

Finally Bryce spoke. "Homer, I have to tell you, it's a relief to know what's happened to him, and that he's no longer a threat to my family. But it's a shame his mother is going to have to face the way he died. Have you located her?"

Homer was surprised at Bryce's regard for the family of the man who had plagued him, and a new layer of respect was added to his book on Bryce Roberts. Thoughts of homicide retreated farther from the range of possibilities he was considering, but still there was a nagging piece of the puzzle missing.

"The only thing we know is that she's living in Colorado. We can track her down through her social security number that's still on file in the local tax office archives."

Bryce was anxious to have Homer leave so he could use the telephone. He stood and shook the policeman's hand.

"Homer I really appreciate your coming here in person to tell me about this. If the coroner makes any significant findings, please let me know." He walked the detective to the door and then stood back from the window of his office until he saw the grey sedan leave the office lot.

He pushed the intercom and asked Mabel to track down Phillip and Stephen and get them on the line for him. Then he called Candace. He could hear Daniel crying in the background when Candace answered and then his crying was replaced by silence. "I bet I know what you are doing," Bryce told his wife.

"He's hungry and this is the best way I know of to quiet him. Patience, dear. Your turn will come." Bryce could hear the teasing in her voice and imagined the mischief in her eyes.

"Sweetheart, are you sitting down?"

"Yes. Bryce, please don't give me bad news right now. I've had a long day and all I really want is for you to come home."

"Honey, I just learned that Charles Coe is dead. They found his remains this morning. I know a death is never good news, but in this case you can at least know he's no longer out there somewhere stalking you."

There was a long silence as Candace digested the news. Then she said, "Bryce, this may sound awful, but when you come home, we're going to open some champagne; not in celebration of a death, but in happiness over the huge weight that's been lifted from your shoulders and mine. You don't know how many times I feared for myself and the children, and to hear this is just what I need right now."

"I'm with you on that, sweetheart. See you around six." And they hung up.

"She's right," he said to himself. "That man tormented me and my family for a long time. I am going to celebrate."

The intercom buzzed and Mabel told him Phillip was on line two.

"Phillip I have something that will interest you," said Bryce.

"Make it fast, brother, I'm due to report to the pathology lab in about five minutes."

"Charlie Coe is dead."

"What did he do, drink himself to death?"

"In a manner of speaking." Bryce went on to explain the details that Homer had related. "So for all of these months we've been worried about nothing," he concluded.

"Did you ask Homer for a copy of the autopsy report?" asked Phillip. "They're a public record if requested by the coroner, so you shouldn't have any trouble getting it."

"I won't have any problem," Bryce said. "The Coroner is a Republican and he's up for re-election next year."

"One other thing," said Phillip. "If there are any x-rays, I want to have a look at them. Our family is obviously suspect in this until the Coroner makes a ruling, and we want to know as much as we can."

"Phillip, don't be paranoid. The guy tripped and fell and that's it."

"Bryce, do us all a favor. Don't talk to any more people in law enforcement until you've cleared it with your brother-in-law or somebody he recommends. I have to go. We can talk more later. Ciao." And he hung up.

Bryce stared at the phone, stressed over Phillip's remarks. He thought he might call Henry Hawkins just in case.

He pressed the intercom. "Mabel, how's the search for Stephen going?"

"His roommate said he's due back shortly. He'll have him call."

"I'll hang around for a bit to wait for the call," said Bryce. "You can scram if you want to."

"Okay, don't forget your seven o'clock meeting tomorrow morning with your father."

"Thanks, I've got it in my book. Goodnight." Bryce exhaled slowly and began to clear his desk of the day's notes and work. He paused and picked up the slim, beautifully finished three-sided length of dark cherry wood. Attached to one side was an engraved brass plate that held his name. A second brass plate that faced him read: *Omnis Sap re Corum Palpitat.* Savor every heartbeat.

Now, maybe we really can do that. He smiled at the thought. Candace had given him the memento for Christmas. He thought about the gift of a photo album he'd given her. Their favorite picture that had turned out well, but quite by accident, was taken on Joseph's sailboat with Candace showing off her brand new engagement ring and the two of them looking incredibly happy.

That one was featured on the first page. Others showed Whispering Falls as it looked on their first visit and during the other seasons, and them on horseback both with the children and by themselves. The visit to St. Michaels was there, along with a photo of many ducks taking flight on the Wye River. He recently had taken some tasteful portraits of Candace nursing Daniel and he planned to include them in next year's album. He was gazing upward and thanking God for sending Candace to him when the telephone rang.

He answered and filled Stephen in on the details about Coe and then Stephen asked him if he'd spoken to any law enforcement people other than Homer.

"You're the second person who's asked me that. What's going on with you and Phillip?"

"Bryce, the police have a dead person on their hands and they don't know for sure how he died. That gets their suspicions all cranked up until they can rule out homicide. If they start thinking Coe was a homicide victim they'll have only a few suspects, if you get my drift, and we don't want to talk with the police about anything until we hear what the coroner rules on the cause of Coe's demise."

"Lawyers! You're not even out of law school and you're telling me I shouldn't talk to a man I've known since high school?"

"Bryce, I'm telling you," lectured Stephen, "when it comes to an investigation and you are a potential suspect, the police are never your friend. Never. Don't talk to the guy."

"What if he wants to talk to me? What do I tell him?"

"Tell him I told you not to speak with him and then remind him about the night Roosevelt and I took his pistol away from him. Tell him I never told anyone except you about that."

"I can't say that. I'll just tell him I'll talk with him only after the Coroner rules on the manner of death. If he doesn't like that, tough darts."

"Now you're cooking. How are Candace and the kids?"

"Everybody's fine, Stephen."

They chatted about Stephen's plans following graduation and then said goodnight. Bryce was glad to get off the phone and head home to his family.

◦═◦

Candace greeted him dressed in a full length pearl-toned silk robe, high heels and stockings that matched the robe, and a filmy outfit underneath that was not meant for sleeping. The robe was closed at the waist but open enough at the top to tease. Her dark hair shone lustrously, and her blue eyes were emphasized by the shimmer of the robe and silver pearl earrings. He feasted his eyes on her as he took off his coat and tie and she handed him a glass of bubbly from a bottle that she'd opened when his car pulled into the garage.

"Anne and Eddie are with Stella and Noah, who I told about Charlie Coe. Daniel is asleep and there is a bottle for him if he awakens. I'm going to enjoy as much champagne as I want this evening," she said as the mischievous look began at the corners of her eyes.

They toasted "to fate and us" and sat together on the couch in front of the small fireplace that held a fire. He put his glass down and kissed her, gently at first, and then passionately. She returned his kisses and they held each other for a long time, glad of the warmth and closeness.

"I gather you want to dine later?" she teased.

"Ummmm. That is good champagne." He nuzzled her neck and said, "Let's neck in front of the fire for a while. I'm going to change into a robe and I'll be right back."

"I shall miss you." She pouted coquettishly.

"I'll be back before you can count slowly to one hundred." And he was.

Their time since they had witnessed their first sunrise together made them knowing of each other's desires and special places, and tonight they gave of themselves, neither willing to reach the ultimate act until they had fulfilled the other's wants. Later, when they moved to the bedroom, the love they shared was so intense they felt as if they had become of one mind.

At the end Bryce allowed himself to lose control. For the first time in his life he wept with joy.

Chapter 96

C andace awakened, stretched, and blushed as she remembered the events of the night. She lay in bed thinking about those pleasures until Daniel's cries brought her back to the present. She arose, changed his diaper, nursed and burped him, and put him in his playpen. Then she continued her morning over a cup of coffee and the local newspaper that Bryce had put on the kitchen table for her.

Her eyes settled on the right hand column of the front page.

Body Found in Woods read the headline. The article reported that:

> A body suspected by the coroner to be the remains of Charles Coe was found yesterday morning by two boys setting a trap line in the woods near the shack that Coe occupied. The deceased is suspected to be the same Charles Coe who killed Marilyn Roberts, the former wife of Founders left fielder and now Republican business leader, Bryce Roberts. Coe was released from prison last spring and he had been having difficulty complying with the strict terms of his parole. The coroner estimates the badly decomposed body has been at the spot for five to six months. There has been no ruling on the cause of death, but it appears to have been accidental. Sources close to the investigation told this reporter that Coe has been missing since last

September when he was last seen after
he attempted to run down Candace
Roberts, the present wife of Bryce
Roberts . . .

A shiver ran down Candace's body as she thought about how close she'd come to being Coe's second victim.

"Thank God Bryce taught me how to use his shotgun. He knew how dangerous and obsessed that horrible man was. And he stayed up most of the night patrolling the neighborhood to make sure he wouldn't get near me if he came back. But he never came back . . ."

The telephone rang.

"Mrs. Candace Roberts?" asked an unfamiliar voice.

"Yes, this is she. Who's calling, please?"

"Mrs. Roberts, this is Leon Porter. I work for *The National Gazette & Tattler* and I'd like to ask you a few questions if you'd be kind enough to spare the time."

What an obsequious voice, thought Candace. "Mister, er, Porter, is that the tabloid I see at the supermarket check-out?"

"Why, yes it is, Candace. Do you read our paper?"

"No. And it's Mrs. Roberts."

"Oh, I'm sorry. I had imagined I was speaking with a younger woman, Mrs. Roberts."

"What do you want, Mr. Porter?"

"I wanted to ask how you feel, now that Charles Coe is gone. After all, it must be quite a relief to you and your husband to know that the man who tried to kill you is dead."

Anything I say to this creep will be quoted out of context, thought Candace. The silence deepened as Candace fought to control her revulsion. Then she spoke.

"Mr. Porter, our family's thoughts are personal and I don't wish to share them with you."

"Not even if I told you that the Coroner has not yet ruled out homicide?"

"I'm not familiar with the Coroner's investigation, Mr. Porter. Now, good day to you and don't call back." Candace hung up as Porter started his next question.

What an awful man. She thought about phoning Bryce but she knew he had meetings scheduled most of the morning. I'll call him this afternoon, she decided. She sipped her coffee and tried to erase Porter from her thoughts. She looked out the window at the crocuses blooming in the back yard, but Porter's words still came back.

Homicide? How could that be? Bryce said the police think Coe's death was accidental. If it was homicide, he was killed right around the day he tried to get me. And here we were with a bodyguard when Coe was dead the whole time . . . Not quite the whole time. Bryce didn't hire Plank until after Coe's folder of newspaper articles was discovered. And by then Coe had disappeared. I wonder . . .

Chapter 97

M abel handed Bryce a mug of coffee as he entered his father's richly paneled office at 6:55 a.m.

Bryce said good morning to his father and turned when a movement caught his eye. Seated at the small conference table toward the corner was a man dressed in a tweed sport coat and khaki trousers. Alfred Cunningham, the chief forester, had a firm handshake and a genuine smile lit his round face as the two greeted each other. Over coffee the three men discussed the battle with the Gypsy Moth that recently had become a serious plague to the hardwood forests in Pennsylvania and New York. Spraying infested areas of the forests with insecticides had been the only effective means of combating the threat.

Environmental protection groups were up in arms and had tried to obtain an injunction to stop the issuance of spraying permits in Pennsylvania, but the court denied the complaint because the environmentalists could not show 'irreparable harm' to the public from spraying on privately held lands. Sunrise Lumber Company therefore made it to the top ten of the environmentalists' bad guy list. The logic of such attitudes was incomprehensible to men who saw entire forests, and the ecosystems they supported, threatened with devastation if nothing was done to prevent the spread of the moth.

"Of more concern at the moment," Cunningham began, "are Professor Berger and his allies. Last spring we received a letter from the professor requesting permission to do a study in the mature growth forest we own in Tioga County."

"The one we use to supply lumber to the furniture factory?"

"Yes. Anyway, Berger requested an access permit. So we did a background investigation on him just as we check on anyone who asks permission to go on that land. Berger was reported as being a strong environmentalist, so we spoke with him about his intentions. He convinced us he wanted to study the warbler population and we said okay."

Cunningham paused to gather his thoughts and then continued. "When Burger arrived at our mill offices we invited him in for an orientation meeting. While he was inside we had his station wagon searched pursuant to the terms in the application he signed to get his study authorization. Hidden in a small cargo space in his station wagon were two cages with bats in them. Our man removed the cages, and the bats were identified by Jamie Hirsch, one of our forestry group who was there at the time, as *myotis sodalis*, Indiana bats. Turns out the bats are an endangered species. We don't have them in most of our medium and new growth areas. Jamie thinks some may live in our older growth areas, but we're not sure of that. In the summer the bats live under loose bark or in hollows in the older trees. We don't mind them in the hollows of old sycamores or pines, but if they get into cherry trees, or other hardwoods, we have to wait until the breeding season is over to harvest the timber. Lately the environmental extremists have been trying to stop logging altogether in the bat's habitat, similar to what they are trying to do over the Spotted Owl. What they need, however, is proof that the bat actually lives in our tracts of forest. Enter Berger. He releases the bats, and, *viola*, we have somebody claim they are in our woods and then we're in a fight to log our own forests."

"And we're in a fight to keep our furniture factory customers supplied from alternate sources that are more expensive," said Bryce. "We can't afford to let that happen. If we lose those factories as customers we're out very lucrative deals and our crews are out of work. Al, this is confidential, but we're considering buying one of those factories if we can find the right people to run it. If we can't supply the factory with our own lumber, the deal won't work. Now, where were we?"

"Jamie called me out of the meeting. When she told me what they found, I instructed the men to return the cages to the car, just as they'd found them, and then we called the game warden. We confronted Berger over the bats and he was arrested for possession of an endangered species without a permit. Berger tried to tell the warden that we planted them in his car but the warden didn't buy any of it. Berger is going on trial in federal court next month and he's been wailing long and loudly about how he's been framed. He's claiming the bats really were from our woods. Some of the newspapers are beginning to pick up on the story and we could be in for rough public relations. We need to discuss what to do about heading that off or dealing with it if it goes ballistic."

"What happened to the bats?" asked Bryce.

Harry said, "I talked the game warden into releasing them into the custody of a bat expert from Penn State, who confirmed they were Indiana Bats."

"Dad, where are the bats now?"

"I applied for a permit and released them in the Sunrise Hills. That forest is old growth, it will not be cut and we can help preserve an endangered species. Plus there's no evidence they're in our particular trees in Tioga County."

"Have you told anyone what you did?" asked Bryce.

"No, I just filled out a report and sent it to the US Fish and Wildlife Service."

Bryce thought for a moment and then said, "We should call Harriet. Her firm does P.R. work and I think we're going to need some help if Berger builds a press following."

Bryce turned to Cunningham. "Harriet is my sister," he told him. "The other thing we need to do is call that bat expert and find out more about the life and loves of *myotis sodalis*. If they are in our trees, we're going to have to figure out what to do about it."

The meeting broke up and Cunningham left for a small office that visiting employees used when they were in town.

"Dad," said Bryce, "there's some news I want to share with you. I learned late yesterday that Charlie Coe is dead."

"Yes, I saw the newspaper. I'm not surprised," replied Harry. "That man didn't have much going for him. What really happened?"

Bryce told him everything he knew, plus the comments of Phillip and Stephen.

"Keep me informed, please. And give our regards to Candace. I'm sure she's relieved to hear the news. Oh, one other thing. When Detective Miller calls you, try to get the full name and address of Coe's mother from him."

That afternoon Stella telephoned him to advise that Detective Miller had been to see them about Coe's death and that he'd asked a number of questions about Phillip and him.

"I told Miller I couldn't remember much. He particularly asked if I could remember anything about the day and evening when Coe tried to kill Candace. I just told him that we left your home after dinner and came back here after we dropped off the kids."

Bryce thanked her for calling and tried to console her when she began to lament Marilyn's death, a loss from which she and Noah had never recovered. He was able to hang up without a long discussion only by telling her that he had a call waiting on his other line.

Then Bryce asked Mabel to try to reach Phillip. His brother answered the page and Bryce filled him in on Homer's visit to see Stella and Noah.

"Phillip, do you remember what time you and Rita left our place that evening?"

"It wasn't that late. Why?"

"I just was curious as to what you'd tell Homer if he inquires of your whereabouts after you left here."

"I took Rita back to her place and then I went back to my apartment. I was in school the next day. If Homer wants to talk about it with me, just have him call."

"Okay. Let me switch gears for a moment. I'm really impressed with Rita. Are you going to make an honest woman out of her?"

"There's a very good chance that I'm going to be competing for Sunrise time with you," he responded. "Rita loves the out-of-doors."

"Glad to hear it. I'll call if I hear anything more."

Bryce spent time conferring with Harriet over the 'bat case' as he called it, and she asked him to provide her with the name and telephone number of the expert Harry had mentioned.

"I'll run this through a session at my agency after I talk to the professor and maybe we can come up with a press release to counter the tree huggers," she promised.

Bryce had an early dinner with Candace and the children and then left for a Republican Committee meeting. He had to head off a fracas that was developing over who was going to run for the open County Commissioner seats.

Chapter 98

The coroner was at the committee meeting and he filled Bryce in on the autopsy that the pathologist completed that morning.

"It wasn't much of a process. We compared the dental x-rays from prison with x-rays of the skull's teeth. It's definitely Coe. The only other interesting thing we found was that underneath the boot remnants, his left ankle was broken. I think that gives me adequate reason to rule the death as accidental. The guy tripped, broke his ankle, and hit his head when he fell."

"Would that fall be enough to kill him?"

"He probably had a brain hemorrhage as a result of the dent in his skull."

"Did you gents do any x-rays of the skull or any other parts?" asked Bryce.

"None except for the teeth."

"What's next?"

"That's it. His mother is here in town, staying at the Hummingbird Bed and Breakfast. Her funeral director will claim the remains tomorrow."

A few minutes later Bryce excused himself and telephoned his father with the information.

Late the following afternoon an attorney representing a small land development corporation called on Mrs. Coe with a quite reasonable offer to purchase her woodlot. She accepted and signed the deed in the parlor of the Hummingbird, witnessed by a notary the lawyer brought with him.

Coe's remains were laid to rest two days later. His mother and several of her old friends from the area were the only attendees at the cemetery. Mrs. Coe ordered a nice headstone, and paid for it with a miniscule portion of the proceeds from the sale of her woodlot.

As Mrs. Coe's Denver flight left Philadelphia International Airport the next morning, a bulldozer was demolishing the shack in which her son had spent the last months of his feckless life. The remnants of the shack and its contents, except for a carton of personal items Bryce saved for Coe's mother, were hauled to a landfill to begin the process of decay that its former occupant already had completed. The ground where Coe's shack was located and where his remains were found was cleared, plowed, and replanted with Pennsylvania cherry trees.

◦◦◦

The following Sunday evening, there was a burglary at the police station which was not manned after midnight on Sunday. There were no alarms to sound and the burglar moved noiselessly in the penlight's beam to the desk in a cramped but neatly kept office at the end of the hallway. A quick examination of the desk and its drawers by thinly gloved hands didn't reveal the object the intruder sought. The file cabinet's top drawer yielded the folder just where it should have been. The burglar removed it, quietly closed the file cabinet drawer and found the copier where, agonizing over the slowness of the machine, he made a duplicate file. The burglar replaced the original folder, and left through the side door, the lock of which he'd picked to gain entry.

◦◦◦

On Wednesday evening a car slowed as it passed the dirt road into the woodlot where Coe's shack once stood. Its driver looked through the darkness in that direction. I forgot something that night, but it's probably too late to do anything about it now. Damn! I should have thought of it then . . .

Six months ago he'd stolen the motorcycle because its exhaust's sounds were well muffled and its odometer cable was easy to disconnect. Its new rider found his destination and pulled off the quiet country road, made sure the bike was hidden by the brush that grew along the roadside, and then, using a red lens flashlight, he began the approach to the shack through the woods.

His heartbeat increased as the adrenaline began to load his system and his hearing became ultra-sensitive, listening for any sounds not usual for the woodland. The rear of the small building loomed darkly ahead. The figure didn't move to the shack but instead slowly and quietly circled it, staying within the border of the woods and stopping often, remaining motionless as he listened for any sounds and watched the habitat for any signs of life within. He saw no vehicles in the well-worn track that led in from the road and no lights burned inside. Yet, he sensed that the shack was occupied.

Stepping carefully to avoid bare ground and strewn refuse, he closed the distance to the side wall away from the road and listened intently.

Snoring!

He moved quietly and listened at each side of the shack, trying to determine which wall was closest to the sound. Satisfied with his assessment, he moved to the door, and with a gloved hand slowly tested its crude latch. The door moved. *Why would it be bolted? There's probably nothing worth stealing inside.* He gently pressured the door a centimeter at a time, trying to detect whether the hinges would squeal if the door were opened wide enough to admit him. *Come on baby, no squeals, please.* The snoring grew louder as the door opening expanded and the intruder stepped lightly into the fetid space, almost overcome by the stench of body odor, garbage and stale urine that assaulted his nose.

My God! I may vomit over this awful smell!

Get hold of yourself, man! You have work to do!

He risked a quick look at the floor with the red light and then moved swiftly on his toes just as the body on the other side of the divider wall shifted and the snoring changed to gurgling sounds. The intruder froze, heart still pounding, pulse rushing in his ears, waiting to hear the snoring resume its natural rhythm. It did. Furtively, the dark shape moved to the doorway of the room from which the snoring came. Again, he risked the briefest of red flashes from his flashlight. The bunk was against the divider wall. In it Coe lay on his back, partially covered with a blanket, head lolling on a filthy pillow. The shadowy man replaced the knife he had withdrawn from a sheath strapped to his belt at the back of his waist. *I'll use it only if I have to.*

He kept the flashlight turned on and quietly placed it on the crude nightstand. He struck quickly, pulling the pillow from under the sleeping man's head. He covered the snorer's full face with it, while at the same time slamming his knee with tremendous force into the gut, just below the diaphragm of his victim. Keeping enormous pressure on the pillow and most of his weight on his knee, the man held the now struggling body under him. Muffled screams came from under the pillow, and hands frantically grabbed at his sleeves and gloves, until the movements wavered and then stopped. Still, he held the pillow tight against the face, unwilling to chance that the motionless figure was alive. They made a strange scene as the killer held his prey in the red glow of the flashlight, almost as if they were insects whose mating ended in death. Five minutes passed and the terrible pressure continued. It struck the murderer how his breath came loud in the quiet and his victim breathed no more. Seven minutes elapsed; and, finally, the pressure was relieved and the pillow removed. The man pulled off a glove, and with fingertips lightly finding the right place, for over a minute checked the throat for the carotid pulse, just to be sure. Nothing. Coe was dead.

Good, you son-of-a-bitch!

Then the man put his glove on and pocketed a half-empty pint of whiskey from the table next to the bed. He pulled the blanket back. Coe was completely dressed.

Died with his boots on. What a pig.

He hoisted the corpse in a fireman's carry, and stepping carefully in the light of the flashlight he held in one hand, he carried the foul smelling deadweight outside, closed the door, and, deep-breathing with the exertion, hauled his load deep into the woods away from the road. Avoiding overhanging branches, he continued until he found a large rock and dropped the body. He arranged an ankle under a protruding root and maneuvered the body, twisting it over the top of the root until he heard the leg bone snap. He placed the head on the large rock, carefully drew it back and then violently smashed it back onto the rock. He let go. The head fell naturally to the side. The bottle was dropped near the torso and the ground around the place checked for footprints in the white beam of a clear-lens flashlight. Satisfied, the killer returned the red lens cap to the flashlight and carefully made his way back to the stolen motorcycle. The whole stalk and kill had taken less than 35 minutes.

The stolen motorcycle was returned and left a block away from where it had been taken. The odometer had been reconnected. Its owner blamed neighborhood kids for the theft that he'd reported to the police and was just grateful to recover his bike undamaged.

⊙≈⊙

The car continued on its way through the moonless night, its driver feeling not the least remorse over the crime. He slept soundly that evening as he had every evening since the night Coe died.

Chapter 99

In the early 1970s protesters still gathered, but they'd changed from the dedicated to the shrill. They marched without a parade permit; and when their leadership was arrested for blatantly violating the law, they claimed the arrests were a denial of free speech. Four students at Kent State were shot dead by National Guard troops called in to put down rioting that included the burning of a college building in protest of troops entering Cambodia. Busloads of kids from Scarsdale chained themselves to Federal Buildings and then demanded the release of the likes of Daniel Berrigan, a rebel Jesuit priest, who had trespassed on a military reservation in order to sabotage weapons stored there. The remnants of the counter culture still were carrying on their duel with the "establishment."

The demonstrators didn't appeal to the vast majority of America, who by then were tired of their antics, but they received the all-important news coverage from the fourth estate who hated Richard Nixon's administration. Joining the political protesters were people from the environmental movements who now regularly attempted to use the tactics of protest to influence legislatures.

The picketing around the court house began in March, a week before Berger's trial date. The local newspaper printed daily quotes from Berger's allies but repeatedly refused to print the statement issued by Sunrise Lumber Company detailing the care it exercised in its stewardship of its lands. Harriet sent a copy of the statement to all of the elected officials in the area as well as the top people in the state's Department of Environmental Resources and its forestry service. Still the newspaper refused to print their statement, even though Bryce delivered it at a hastily called "press conference." It seemed to Bryce that the environmentalists and the media could have cared less for the truth surrounding the arrest of one of their own. Bryce finally bought advertising space in the local paper which grudgingly printed the statement buried in the small section devoted to business.

For once, Fate, or Divine Providence, or Karma, or God, according to the philosophies of the disparate group of protesters and their foes, took a hand. On the day of the trial it rained and rained in a cold, teeming downpour. The protesters at first attempted to brave the elements, but they weren't dressed for it and their numbers dwindled by mid-morning to a handful of very wet and shivering people. Without a group carrying signs and chanting trite slogans, the fodder the media called news, the TV crews and commentators packed their cameras and rolled away in their trucks, forced to rely on the few reporters who could fit into the small courtroom used for the trial.

It was a four witness prosecution: the game warden who testified that the professor had no permit to possess the bats; a searcher who produced the contract authority for the search and who testified how the bats had been discovered; the Penn State expert in bats to verify the species involved; and, a distinguished older gentleman to testify regarding the disposition of the blind evidence.

When Professor Berger testified that he'd been framed, the prosecutor produced the receipts for the purchase of the bat cages and asked the man how they found their way into his business expense records that had been obtained via a search warrant. The judge had to cover his mouth over the stuttering response that the receipts also had been planted. It took the jury about twenty minutes to convict Berger and the judge deferred sentencing until later in the month to allow a pre-sentence investigation to be completed.

The older gentleman witness was escorted to the court house basement garage where he entered a nondescript van and was transported to the airport to board his private plane. On the way home Harry seriously considered donating funds sufficient to name a chair in the Penn State biology department for his fellow witness, but he concluded that would appear to be a payoff, and so he turned to business matters. His son wanted to buy a furniture factory whose lumber supply was now assured.

Chapter 100

The rains followed Harry and Bryce home and continued the next day. But that didn't deter Bryce from visiting the recently purchased Coe woodlot to check on the progress the work crew was making in clearing the undergrowth, vines and scrub trees from choking the timber.

Bryce picked his way back to the site where Coe's body had been discovered, turned, and carefully assessed the narrow pathway that lead toward the shack's former location. Over the raindrops falling into the trees he could hear the sounds of chain saws off on another section of the plot. He checked a newly planted cherry tree that someday, he hoped, would provide boards for Morton's cabinet shop. As he walked back toward the road he felt the small paper bag deep in his raincoat pocket and carefully considered dropping its contents beside the trail. But the crack of a twig drew his attention to a man standing near the shack site who was watching him approach. Bryce, ever cautious, chose to keep the bag in his pocket.

The stranger wore a transparent plastic raincoat over a powder blue sport coat, bright yellow shirt, and faded pink slacks. His footwear was a pair of low-cut white goatskin boots with large, hairy tassels covering the top laces. The tassels were bedraggled from the rain and the boots mud-spattered. His hat was a totally inadequate light blue pork-pie, better used as a sun shield on a golf course.

As Bryce approached, the man smiled ingratiatingly, revealing heavily stained teeth.

"Mister, you look lost," said Bryce.

"Well, if these are the woods where Charles Coe died, I'm not. I'm Leon Porter and I'm investigating Coe's death." He reached out to shake hands with Bryce.

"Well, Mr. Porter, I'm Bryce Roberts." Bryce shook hands perfunctorily. "You don't appear to be from a law enforcement agency. For whom are you doing your investigation?"

"My newspaper, *The National Gazette and Tattler.*"

"Never heard of it. Where are you based?"

"Florida. But we have a nationwide circulation. I was in Philadelphia when the discovery of Coe's skeleton broke and I smelled a story when I learned he'd killed a woman whose husband is a former Navy SEAL. Now I get lucky and meet the man I want to interview." His smile was half triumphant, half leer.

Bryce had only the briefest of mental debates before he decided to turn the tables and pump the reporter. "First, let me tell you I was not a SEAL. I was a member of a UDT unit that helped to train SEALs. But let me ask you, how does the Navy SEAL connection come into play?"

"Those guys are trained killers. I wanted to interview the man with that background about how they were taught to kill without guns or knives. Might make an interesting story coming from the man whose wife was Coe's target."

Bryce remained stone-faced but underneath he battled to keep himself from demonstrating exactly what Porter wanted to talk about. He eyed Porter's throat and then regained control.

Porter saw the anger in Bryce's eyes and backed away.

"What do you expect to see here, Mr. Porter?"

"The death scene. But the evidence is all gone, Mr. Roberts. Whose idea was that?"

"It's a boring matter of safety and taxes, Mr. Porter. Without any improvements on this property, the insurance premiums are lower and it's assessed and taxed at a lower rate."

"And the investigation into Coe's death is at an end. Right?"

"Presumably, Mr. Porter. Perhaps it would benefit you to return to Florida at this point?"

"I came all the way out here for a story, Bryce. I think I'll hang around for a few days."

"Suit yourself, Mr. Porter. Do you have a business card?"

Porter reached inside his raincoat and produced a vinyl business card holder. He handed Bryce a card.

"This has my office telephone and address on it, Bryce. Call me if you think there's anything more to be said."

"If you print your unfounded speculation, you and your paper may be facing a lawsuit."

Porter laughed uproariously as he headed toward his rented car.

Bryce's face remained inscrutable.

∘≋∘

When he arrived at his office Bryce made two telephone calls. The first was to Foster's office. The second was to an agency in Boston for which Mabel gave him the number. Bryce scheduled urgent appointments with both.

When Harry returned to the office Bryce told him of Porter's interest. Harry gave instructions to forbid Porter's entry at company offices.

That evening Bryce and Candace lingered over their tea after the children asked to be excused from the table. Candace listened to the account of Porter's visit to the woodlot and then she spoke.

"A man by the name of Porter called me last week to ask questions. I was going to call you at the office and then I realized that you'd be in meetings most of the morning. And then I didn't want to mention it before you left for the trial in your bat case."

"What did you tell him?"

"He asked what my feelings were now that Coe is dead, and I told him that was none of his business. Then he asked me what I would say if I knew that the police hadn't ruled out homicide as a cause of Coe's death and I just told him I didn't know anything about the investigation and hung up."

"Way to go. If he ever contacts you again, don't talk with him. Just let me know if he tries to speak with you again. Okay?"

"Okay . . . Bryce, what if Coe was murdered?"

"I don't think he was. The coroner believes his death was accidental and that's good enough for me."

"Well, from what you said, this Porter character may try to cook up some kind of story hinting you killed Coe. What're you going to say if he does publish something?"

Bryce paused, exhaled, and then looked at his wife. In a hard voice he said, "Candace, you've had time to think about things since Porter called you. And now what you really want to know is whether I had anything to do with Coe's death, right?"

"Am I that transparent?"

"Only when you're worried. Honey, I didn't kill the guy. I admit I thought about it if the police didn't do anything. But when they couldn't find him, I just did what I believed was best and hired Plank."

Candace's eyes looked directly into his. "Are you sure, Bryce Roberts? Why were you out half the night when he tried to kill me?"

"I've already told you that I was hanging about outside the house and in the neighborhood in case he came back. I figured that if he did come back, I could intercept him before he got too close to the house, nail him, and hold him for the police."

"Nail him?"

"He wouldn't be on the alert until he got close to our house. I could use that to my advantage to surprise him, overpower him, and tie him up."

The mischief look appeared in Candace's face. "You know, that's something we've never tried . . ." *I'll pry it out of you when I have you tied up and right on the edge. You usually can hide anything from me if you want to. But there are ways . . . I'll call Rosalie tomorrow and arrange an evening when she can take the children.*

Bryce smiled and shook his head back and forth at his wife's humor.

Chapter 101

Later that week a long-time secretary at the executive offices of *The National Gazette & Tattler* elected early retirement. Her decision was unexpected and management hadn't trained anyone to replace her. A help wanted ad for an executive secretary who could work under pressure deadlines was placed in Florida newspapers. Hyman Abrams, the editor, chose the applicant with the largest breasts. He considered her a perfectly reasonable selection when he learned that the attractive woman was a skilled typist.

Chapter 102

Henry Morton, the cabinetmaker, gave Zeke Alexander's name to the Roberts. When Alexander heard who had referred him he accepted Bryce's telephone call and listened to his invitation to meet him in Williamsport for lunch and a tour of the furniture factory. When they finished their tour, Zeke told him he was disappointed over the outdated manufacturing methods and the lack of modern machinery.

"Zeke," said Bryce, "we've agreed to buy the place on condition we can modernize the facilities to run efficiently. We want you to give us all of your recommendations and an estimate for carrying them out. If we think it's doable, we buy the place, modernize it, and you run it. What do you say?"

"I'm interested. But I'll need to stay here for several days to really get the best handle on things. Then we can talk. Okay?"

"Yes. I'll speak with the owner and clear you for re-entry. Call me when you're finished and I'll send a plane for you. We can talk at our headquarters."

"Just one thing, Bryce. Have you thought about the supply line for this business?"

"Zeke, we grow, harvest, dry, and mill our own hardwood, so we can eliminate the lumber brokers and other middle men. We also have our eye on a stain and finish business. If we purchase it, we can sell most of its output but reserve a portion for us at close to cost."

"I have some ideas, Bryce. Give me some time and I'll call you."

Chapter 103

"**N**oah has lung cancer," said Stella. She delivered her message to Candace as if she believed that the world would end.

Candace stood and hugged the older woman whose face had become noticeably haggard over the previous weeks. "How bad is it?"

"He's going to have surgery tomorrow. They'll be able to tell us more after that. He's been acting strangely for the last several months. I just thought he was going into one of his blue funks, but I think he knew something was wrong. He finally told me two weeks ago."

"Noah doesn't smoke. I wonder what caused him to get lung cancer?"

"They aren't sure," said Stella, "but when Noah told the doctors that he worked as a brake mechanic to put himself through college, the doctors said they think it could be caused by asbestos."

"Where's Noah now? I want to tell him that Bryce and I'll be praying for him."

"He's downstairs in the den asleep. I'll tell him what you said. And there's one other thing. We still want Eddie and Anne to visit here."

"Don't worry, Stella, they'll always be around for you. Call me after you have news, Dear."

Candace left in time to meet the school bus that carried her children home.

Anne was crying when she alighted from the bus. Daniel's lower lip was quivering and he sported the beginnings of a black eye. Candace led them away from the curb and then bent down and hugged them both.

"What's up kiddos? Why the tears?"

"The kids on the bus were talking about us," cried Anne.

"Eddie, what were they saying?"

"They said our father's a killer." The warmth of his mother's arms opened the gates for his tears, and he, too, began to cry.

"Your father is not a killer. Do you understand that?"

The children each nodded hesitantly and Candace's face got a knowing look. "Did the kids on the bus say why they were teasing you like that?"

"Randy Mower said his mom read it in the newspaper," wailed Anne.

"Porter, I'll bet. Come on kids, we're going for a ride to the supermarket."

"Do we have to go inside with you?" asked Eddie.

"No, Dear, you don't. Nobody will see you crying if you and Anne stay in the van while I go inside. I'll only be a minute."

Candace went directly to the newsstand when she entered the store. "Sold out" read the backer in the empty space usually occupied by *The National Gazette and Tattler.*

"Oh good lord, everybody in the whole community except me must know what that paper says." She turned to leave and then decided to head toward the manager's space near the entrance.

Tom Blake saw her approaching his counter and reached into one of the spaces next to his desk. He handed Candace a folded tabloid when she got to the counter. She didn't have to ask him what it was.

"I don't believe a damned word of it," he said.

"Thanks, Tom," she said. "What do I owe you for this?"

"On the house, Mrs. Roberts. I've known Bryce since he was a kid when I had just a little country market. He no more did that than spread wings and fly to the moon."

Candace returned to the van and her waiting children. When she arrived home she called Bryce and explained why she'd interrupted him in a meeting.

"Read it to me."

Oh, Bryce, I'm so upset, I don't think I can."

"Read it to me."

Chapter 104

The large-breasted secretary who the editor of *The National Gazette & Tattler* had hired walked into his office and handed him a Special Delivery letter with a certified mail tab on the opened envelope.

Hyman Abrams stared in appreciation, lowered his eyes to the envelope, and said, "I thought I told you never to sign for one of these, Dolores."

"Oh, I'm sorry, Mr. Abrams, I just plain forgot. It's not often one of these comes in when I'm taking a turn at the reception desk. By the way, Porter got one and so did Mr. Cowper."

"Damn it! Cowper chews my butt off every time we get one of these. Who's it from?"

"A lawyer in Pennsylvania named Mattison who demands a retraction and a printed apology for a story about some guy named Bryce Roberts."

"Ah, yes. The 'SEAL and the Skeleton.' Porter found some interesting stuff up there. As a matter of fact, he's leaving this afternoon to fly back to Philly. Seems there may be more than he originally thought."

"Oh, Mr. Abrams," said Dolores as she gripped the edge of the desk and leaned forward, "do you think Porter has found something wicked?"

Abrams tore his eyes away from her cleavage. "I dunno. He got a phone call from someone who said he wants to tell all. So maybe there's a story up there."

Chapter 105

"Bryce," said Saul Mattison into the telephone, "*The Tattler* article comes about as close to libel as possible without actually going over the line. These people are expert at walking the tightrope and they've done it here."

"Have they responded to your letter demanding a retraction?"

"No. I told you that tabloids of this kind rarely retract anything. We haven't heard a peep from anyone."

Mattison could hear his client's fist pound the desk in frustration. "The article ends with a promise of more next week," growled Bryce. "If they print another word, I want you to sue the bastards. Saul, that one article already has cast suspicion on me and put my whole career, my whole future, in jeopardy. I can't allow that."

"The moment they print another word, you come into my office and we'll talk. But I want to repeat what I've already told you, a libel case is very difficult to win."

"As far as I'm concerned, they've already defamed me."

"I know that's how you feel, but we must have a stronger case to prove malice."

"Malice? Christ! They know they're printing a lie. Didn't you tell me that they don't even have to know it's a lie?"

"True. But a case like this is only worth pursuing if we can get punitive damages, and that'll require us to prove malice—that they deliberately and knowingly printed a lie."

"Call me the minute you hear from those turkeys. I have to put up with a couple of kids who are looking at me as if I'm some kind of fiend and a wife who, God help me, still has doubts."

Bryce said good-bye and then asked Mabel to try again to get Homer Miller on the telephone. Homer had not returned his call of several days ago and that was unlike Homer.

"He's ducking me," said Bryce.

Then he left to visit with Noah. Bryce had a small paper bag in his pocket. He and Marilyn's father had a long conversation.

Chapter 106

Zeke Alexander had found a major problem. He wriggled to a more comfortable position in the leather passenger seat of the twin-engine prop jet and reviewed his numbers one more time. Bryce Roberts wasn't going to like what he'd hear in less than two hours. But Zeke wasn't going to try to snow the man with the piercing black eyes. Even if it meant he was out of a job before it began.

Zeke again thought about his conclusion. The most practical machinery to use in upgrading the furniture factory was expensive and could produce furniture in quantities far in excess of the company's annual sales. On top of that, he doubted that the local forests owned by Sunrise Lumber Company could supply the larger quantities of lumber needed to keep the modernized production line going at a profitable pace.

Bryce's plan to eliminate the lumber middle men was impractical because they'd have to buy lumber from outside sources to run at a profitable capacity. And the showroom dealer base had to be built up if the capacity was to be worthwhile. That would take years, and, meanwhile, the updated factory would operate with a huge overhead investment in this cyclical and competitive industry.

The co-pilot opened the curtain and signaled him to fasten his seat belt and the plane began its descent. Zeke tried to keep his spirits from descending with the plane. He wasn't ready to give up yet. And there was one other piece of news Bryce Roberts definitely would want to hear.

Chapter 107

At the Philadelphia International Airport the reporter from Florida moved through the terminal toward the luggage pickup area. He didn't notice the large black man dressed in a Skycap's uniform who walked behind him but kept at least two people between them.

When Porter collected his luggage he was grateful for the help of the Skycap, who almost immediately upon their exit to the terminal sidewalk found a limo looking for a return fare to Doylestown. The limo driver allowed himself to be bargained down on the fare and he held the door for the suntanned passenger with the garish clothing. Porter couldn't believe his good fortune in finding the ride. He tipped the Skycap, but not generously.

◦═◦

Bryce Roberts still seethed as he read *The Tattler's* article once again. "Damned garbage pit that calls itself a newspaper." Then for the tenth time that day he muttered, "I can't understand why anyone reads this crap." The cover page of *The Tattler* featured an obviously doctored photo of a woman who claimed to be the half-human daughter of an alien from outer space.

The story that so angered Bryce appeared on page three where the "National News" section began:

The SEAL and the Skeleton
People in the sleepy community of central Bucks County, Pennsylvania, actually have something to talk about

these days. Do their police think they may have an unsolved murder on their hands? It's a big question, but the alleged victim, Charles Coe, is now just a skeleton, picked clean by the buzzards and whitened by exposure to the winds and sun; and he isn't talking, of course.

Coe's remains were found on land owned by the millionaire family of Bryce Roberts. Roberts' first wife was murdered by Charlie Coe, a small man who sold firewood for a living.

Roberts, who trained Navy SEALs in the art of the stealthy kill, has not spoken on the subject. But suspicions about his possible involvement in Coe's death are circulating among the people of this community because Roberts had a motive to celebrate Coe's death. Informed sources tell the Tattler that Roberts and Coe were enemies from as far back as high school in the late 1950s. Now, only one of the two men is left alive.

Coe was last seen threatening the life of Bryce Robert's present wife. Coe had not been heard from since – until his remains were found. Has passion raged and violence had its way? Police investigating the death still may have questions about the dent in the skull of Coe's skeleton and how it may have gotten there, even though the coroner has ruled the death was accidental. However, nobody will be able to investigate the death scene, because the Roberts family has obliterated all traces of Coe's cabin that once was on the lot where his body was found; and, the spot where the skeleton was discovered has been plowed over and replanted with trees. There's perhaps more to this when the investigation is finished. The Tattler

```
will follow any new leads and advise
its readers.
```

⤬

"Bryce, believe me," said Homer into the telephone, "I never even talked to the asshole who wrote that shit."

"Well, what's this nonsense about 'police investigating the death still may have questions'?"

"I don't know. It's nothing I said. I think that reporter must have read the autopsy report in the Clerk of Court's Office. He could get information on the damaged skull from that report. Honest, Bryce, I never talked to the guy."

"Who in the Police Department did?"

"Nobody I know of. And I think I'd have heard about it if one of the other officers talked with the guy."

"Homer, could you check around the department and find out if anyone did speak with that slime?"

"Sure, Bryce. I'll let you know if I learn anything."

"Thanks, Homer."

Bryce hung up and Mabel entered his office.

"Mr. Alexander is here for his appointment. Do you want a minute to calm down?"

"What makes you think I'm upset?"

"Because that article is on your desktop blotter and you were just on the phone with Detective Miller."

"Good catch. I'll take a moment to wash my face. Where's the file on the furniture factory?"

"Behind you on the credenza. You asked me for that file this morning and I brought it to you."

"Yes, so you did. Mabel, I'll buzz you when I'm ready to see Mr. Alexander." Bryce headed for the private lavatory shared by his office and his father's.

"Damn! I can't let that newspaper interfere with my concentration on this project."

Chapter 108

"Where are the kids?" asked Bryce.

"On an overnight with Rosalie and Harry. Teensy promised to take Eddie and Anne fishing tomorrow. Daniel is taking a nap after a very busy afternoon." Candace handed Bryce a scotch on ice.

"Thanks. How did you know I could use one of these?"

"It's Friday and you've been in a black mood all week. And my spies tell me that you've had a bad day at the office."

"That damned Coe! Even from the grave he's haunting us. Homer finally returned my call today and he denied having spoken with that slime reporter. I don't know whether to believe him or not. Stephen said never trust a policeman who may have you under suspicion. So now I have to be overly cautious about everything I say to Homer, just so he won't misinterpret it."

"Why would Homer suspect you of anything?"

"I don't know. He's a policeman and Stephen thinks he'll always wonder if Coe was murdered."

Bryce downed the last of his scotch and Candace poured him another. He carried his fresh drink into the bedroom and began to change out of his suit. Candace followed him to the bedroom and sat on the edge of the bed as he began his ritual by hanging up his suit just so.

"Honey," said Candace, "this will blow over. Right now there are a few gossips who are entertained, but it won't last." She stood and reached to unbutton the last two buttons of his shirt. "And I have just the way to make you forget all about that dumb old Coe." She put her hands behind his neck and began to kiss his neck with butterfly kisses. Then she pulled his shirt off and dropped it behind him.

Bryce had a large sip of his drink and then held her to him. "And what about you? Are you still suspicious of your husband?"

"All I know is that I'm married to the most wonderful man in the world, and even if you did do it, it wouldn't change anything between us."

"You're wrong, Candace. Things would change. You'd always go to sleep thinking that you were lying next to a murderer." She felt his hands move down to the back of her waist as he leaned back to look her in the eyes.

She leaned back too, but surprised him with mischief in her expression. She began to unbutton her blouse while he watched, fascinated with her long fingers working the buttons and the progressive opening of her blouse. Candace watched his eyes as she began slowly to unfasten her bra that hooked in the front. *Gotcha, mister.*

"What do you say we try out that 'lying next to each other' theory right now?" she asked, voice sultry and eyes inviting. She slipped out of his hands and handed him the rest of his drink.

He took a large swallow and his teasing half-smile appeared. "You're trying to get me drunk and then you're going to take advantage of me."

She returned to the bed and half-reclined on it facing him, blouse open and elbows tucked by her sides and propping her up. She knew her breasts were particularly attractive in that pose. She kicked off her shoes, tilted her head and looked up at him with teasing eyes. He grinned back at her.

She pointed her toes at him, and said. "Help me pull off my slacks."

"What am I going to find underneath them?"

"See for yourself," came the lush reply.

Royal blue bikini panties.

"My favorite color on you."

She stood on the opposite side of the bed and he pulled the bedcovers open with a single sweeping motion.

"Bryce, Honey, lie down here. There's something I want to show you."

"Oh? What do you have in mind?"

She pulled off her blouse and bra and tossed them toward the foot of the bed. His eyes feasted on her body. "Just lie down and I'll show you. It's a surprise."

He dropped his skivvies and joined her on the bed. Kneeling, she reached under the pillows and withdrew long, heavy silk cords with tassels on the ends.

"Where in the world did you get those?"

"I bought them at a drapery shop in town when I was ordering drapes for the house." They'd gotten into the habit of referring to the new home they were building as "the house."

"These are extra-long drapery ties. The saleslady told me she sells quite a few of them. Here, let me put one on your wrist."

"I don't know about this. I'm not sure I want to give you all that control."

She leaned over, brushed his chest with just the tips of her breasts, and kissed him wetly, passionately. "Trust me," she breathed. Then she began to tie his wrists to the headboard posts.

⊚⧭⊙

The limo dropped Porter at the gas station where once before he'd rented a car. He paid the limo driver and carried his bag to the small office that was filled with sales displays of automobile accessories, a cigarette vending machine, and a metal desk with a glass top from under which an area map was visible and family photos kept watch.

"Yes, sir," said the attendant. "I have a late model Chevy that I can rent to you if you plan to return it here."

"Sure thing, Buddy." Porter had already had made up his mind to drive the rental car back to the airport. Damned if he was getting stuck with a junker to drive back to the airport. "Do you have a map of the area?"

"Yes, but it will cost you seventy-five cents. Do you want me to add it to your bill?"

"Mind if I look at it first?"

"Not at all." The attendant opened a drawer, reached in and withdrew a folded map that he handed to Porter. "Here you are. Where 'bouts are you headed?"

"I'm looking for a public park that's supposed to be to the north of town. Some place with an Indian sounding name."

"Nockamixon?"

"Yea. Is it on here?"

"Yep. Here, I'll show you . . ."

When the newly washed Chevy rental car left the gas station, Porter had an escort that went unnoticed. The tail soon realized that Porter either was lost, or that he'd lied to the gas station attendant. The tail radioed for another car to join him and stayed back so that he kept the Chevy just in sight. Soon he'd be able to close the gap because it was getting dark.

⁓

Stella Coleman kissed her husband good-bye and backed her car out of the garage. She felt guilty leaving Noah at home by himself, but she needed to get out of the house for an evening of cards with her bridge club. Noah was so depressing to be around all of the time. Besides, she would be the center of attention with all of the gossip circulating about Bryce and Charles Coe. She couldn't wait to tell "the girls" about the time Candace had shot at Coe. Deep in thought about the coming gossip, she didn't notice the late model Chevy that passed by her on the road that lead to her home.

Chapter 109

Harry entered the sitting room where Zeke Alexander stood looking at original paintings of hunting scenes that Harry had commissioned years before.

Harry had a sip of wine, waited long moments for his guest to finish his perusal, and then asked, "Do you hunt Mr. Alexander?"

"Once in a while I go grouse hunting in the mountains near my home. But it's a lucky day to kick one up and even luckier to actually shoot one."

"Ah, yes. It's a challenge. Now, can you tell me more about this Macgregor fellow that you mentioned to Bryce? Do you know his first name?"

"Yes, it's Ian. And speaking of first names, please call me Zeke."

"I know him, Zeke. Ian Macgregor runs a competing lumber company based in Virginia and West Virginia. Bryce told me that you've discovered some interesting information about some of his, ah . . . connections."

"I discovered that by accident. When I was doing a quick study on the availability of timber for the factory, I checked out the environmental groups that have been leading the opposition to your lumbering operations in the northern tier counties. If the protesters are well-funded they could be a problem. I asked a friend of mine to check Harrisburg's public records of the environmentalist's funding. He reported that a foundation has been donating heavily to the chapter that has been leading the protests for Professor Berger and picketing some of your mill operations. It also seems there have been lobbying efforts by a "separate" organization that happens to have many of the same members on both boards of directors. The foundation is funded by Macgregor and a non-profit corporation he set up for the purpose."

"Do you have any documents or reports that back up that information, Zeke?"

"I gave the few I have to Bryce. But I'm sure there're more. I just didn't have time to get it all because I wanted to work on other information regarding production equipment."

"Do you have any suggestions on steps we might take to minimize the 'environmentalists' opposition?"

"I think that's more in your department, Mr. Roberts."

"Would you care for more wine, Zeke?"

⌒☞⌒

"Candace, baby, you're driving me nuts. You can untie me now."

"Ah, is my big man all excited?" she said in tones of mock pity. "Now what do you think we ought to do about that?"

"Untie me, damn it."

"Not until you tell me more about the night you say you were patrolling outside this house in case Coe came back." She again began to tease him with her mouth and tongue.

". . . I've . . . already . . . told you . . . that's all there . . . was . . . to it."

She stopped and grinned lasciviously up at his eyes that now were even darker than usual. Facing him, she spread her legs over his torso, knees at his armpits, and sat lightly on his chest with her womanhood inches from his face. She began to slowly caress herself.

"You wench, that's just not fair."

"Really? Oh, but, Honey," she said, voice rich and mellow with lust, "we still have so much to talk about . . ." and she lightly ran a moistened finger down his nose and across his lips.

⌒☞⌒

A second car arrived in the quiet neighborhood and parked on a cross street near the target house. Its driver got out of her vehicle and walked unhurriedly down the block past the house that Porter had entered. The streetlights were old and dim and her dark clothing made her difficult to distinguish. The woman reached deep darkness under the shadow of a big maple. She stood next to the maple's trunk and quietly performed a radio check into the tiny microphone taped to her neck.

"Bluejay, this is Robin. Where do you want me?"

"Robin, this is Bluejay. Naked in our bedroom."

The woman smiled at her husband's remark. Foster's couple perpetually teased each other.

"Robin, can you see the house from your vehicle?"

"Affirmative."

"The blue Chevy in the driveway is our car. Return to your vehicle and keep the Chevy in sight. When it moves, we follow."

"Roger, Bluejay. I have a thermos of coffee with me. Do you want me to leave it for you?"

"Thanks. Leave it by the tree where you're standing."

She smiled again and began to walk toward her car, exaggerating her hip swing for the benefit of the man who would be watching through his night vision goggles.

Bluejay heard a telephone ring inside the house. He could just hear a man's voice that was muffled as it came through the window near where he stood concealed by a tall juniper.

The telephone conversation ended and Bluejay moved away toward his thermos of coffee in preparation for what he believed was an imminent departure. He was wrong. He had to wait another half hour.

⊙⋙⊙

"Candace, untie me. This isn't fun anymore." His voice lacked any inflection of passion or humor and Candace realized with dread that she'd gone too far—way too far—with her questioning. She stopped what she was doing and untied his right hand.

"It's obvious this act has been a sham to question me about Coe . . . and I'm just plain pissed. Now, let's call it quits for tonight.

"What really upsets me is that you haven't trusted me enough to take my word that I had nothing to do with that little shit's death." He used his free hand to attack the knot at his left hand while she began to untie his feet. Bryce sat up in their bed, face tight with anger, coal-black eyes boring into her.

"Trust, Candace. Marriage is founded in trust, relies on trust, and lives on trust. It dies without it." His voice had an edge to it that was like a whip cracking across her face.

"Now, what's it going to be?"

She felt terribly exposed in her nakedness before the man who suddenly seemed a harsh-tongued stranger. She resisted the urge to get up and put on a robe. *I can't do that. He'll think I'm walking away from him over something that needs to be said right now. Lord! I must tell him the truth. He's always understood before and I can't wreck our marriage with a lie.*

"Bryce, Honey, I'm so sorry . . . so sorry." Tears began to drop from her cheeks to her breasts. "It's just that I . . . know that you . . . that you have this undying hatred of Coe. You've told me about it and I've heard it in your voice when you've spoken of him. And I believe that you would've killed him to protect me if the police didn't catch him. In a strange way I think I was flattered that you'd do that and I guess I was just fantasizing that you might have . . . Tonight was just another part of that fantasy. I imagined that I could give you a way—an excuse—for admitting it, if you did do it. Darling, I meant no harm or mistrust. Had you admitted it, to me that would have been another way of you saying that you love me. That's really all I wanted to hear out of this. Please . . . try to understand. Bryce, I love you so much. I just wanted to share everything."

The anger left his voice and he spoke in a tone of wonderment. "Even in death that son-of-a-bitch haunts us—right into the bedroom." He paused as he pondered that thought.

"We can't allow that," he said. "Do you remember what you told me about trust the first time we made love?"

"I told you that I chose you for my partner because I trusted you."

"Do you still?"

"Yes, more than ever."

Life appeared at the corners of his eyes and played ever so slightly around his mouth.

Candace's breathing eased as the tightness in her chest dissipated.

He put his hand gently to her cheek and said, "Woman, you have one hell of a good interrogation technique." He gathered up the bonds and his teasing smile began.

"Now let's see how well you hold up under my questioning."

༺═══༻

The telephone rang and Bryce arose to answer it. Candace yawned and rolled over, sated by their recent passions. Bryce listened intently for a long minute and then asked, "Is his wife with him?"

"No, sir," came the reply. "She does not appear to be home. There's only one car in the garage. The subject is with him."

"Let me know if you're able to determine anything else, please." He hung up after the caller promised to do so. The caller disconnected alligator clips from a telephone line that led to a darkened house.

"Who was that?" asked Candace, her voice heavy with approaching sleep.

"I have an eye on a business rival, and I think he's misbehaving. I'll tell you about it later." He gathered her in his arms and said, "Let's get some sleep."

Chapter 110

A fixture was missing from Rosalie Roberts' kitchen. Midge's relatives in Scotland had demanded one last visit from her before age prevented her from traveling to a reunion.

In her absence Rosalie prepared the tea and served Candace. "When will your new home be finished, Candace?" asked Rosalie. She sipped her tea and looked across the table at Candace who had come to collect her children.

"We'll be neighbors in about two weeks if the decorator keeps his word. I can't wait."

"Let us know if we can help with anything. Oh, by the way, will your children still be attending the same school?"

Ah, thought Candace, *now we're getting to the real subject that interests you. Your Quaker pacifism has you worried about more confrontations.*

"We're going to have them finish out the year there."

Candace kept control of the subject. "Bryce and I think that pulling the kids out of public school now would send the wrong message to the community and to our children. So the kids will stay there."

"Isn't that going to inconvenience you? There's no nearby school bus stop, so you'll have to drive them."

"We'll manage."

"Is that the remains of a black eye I saw on Eddie?"

"Yes. But from what the teacher told me, the other boy looked even worse. And, you know what? The other kids don't tease our children anymore now that Eddie has defended his father's honor."

Rosalie saw the affection for Eddie in her daughter-in-law's face and again thanked God for the wonderful stepmother He had given to Eddie. Rosalie would have been aghast had she known the origin of the tiny rope burn that irritated Candace's ankle.

"We all hope this nastiness will go away, Dear."

"It will. Right now I'm more concerned about Noah. Yesterday I saw Stella at the grocery store and she told me Noah has been going downhill faster than they thought he would."

"It's mesothelioma, right?"

"Yes."

"I'm sorry to say this, but Phillip told me it's always fatal. Noah probably will be gone within a few months."

"Then what will Stella do?" asked Candace.

"Stella is a survivor," said Rosalie.

◦✒◦

Porter rushed to his office from the airport and finished typing a draft of the sensational story he'd composed on the flight south. Then he dictated a memo as the sun began to set. He put the memo tape on Dolores' desk and headed home to spend time with his wife and children before he was off on another assignment on Monday. On Monday morning the memo would go to the editor and publisher along with the draft of the story.

"What a coup," thought Porter. "The big issue now is whether we change the thrust of the first article or go with the second account. Well, I'm going to let it up to Hy and Derek."

Chapter 111

Bryce and Harry were deep in conversation with Zeke Alexander.

"We either develop a business plan that will show a profit within three years or we drop the whole idea," said Bryce. "We can't produce enough of our own lumber so we have to find another source. Do we purchase more timberlands or do we go into the wholesale market?"

"Wholesale," said Zeke. "We keep your overhead lower."

"The nice thing about a forest, Zeke," said Harry, "is that even if you don't harvest any trees, it continues to produce value. Trees grow larger and are worth more when they finally are marketed. In the meantime, the only fixed expenses are taxes and insurance. Maintenance usually involves thinning and clean-up where needed. We may want to look at a purchase."

"Any ideas on where we could find that kind of asset, Mr. Roberts?"

Bryce looked at Zeke and then at his father.

"We're going to the Forest Products Association national convention in a couple of weeks. By then we'll have some feelers out and maybe we can pick up options on timberland. If we can get the options for a decent price we can assure ourselves of an additional lumber supply without having to buy land or timber rights up front.

"Now, the other point is whether we can modernize the factory in stages and where we start."

"The facility that needs the most work is the finishing department," said Zeke. "And we may be able to get a break there because there's some good used equipment for sale in New York."

"Zeke, check it out and also please contact used equipment brokers," said Bryce. "Maybe we can pull this off with good used or rebuilt machinery. Let's talk more after you have some quotes.

"Now, I'm going to change the subject. Who is your contact in Harrisburg who can help us with more information about the funding of our environmental nemeses?"

The meeting ended after the information was exchanged and Zeke left with a bouncier step than upon his arrival.

Bryce asked Mabel to make a reservation for himself and Harry at the convention hotel and to schedule the company plane for a quick flight to Harrisburg. He needed to meet the man who could help him investigate Ian Macgregor's treachery.

When Bryce told Harry what he had in mind, Harry beamed over how Bryce was going to turn a problem to an advantage. Such stratagems usually came only with exceptional maturity.

This is going to be fun to watch, thought the older man. Harry retreated to his office where he telephoned his friend, Judge Cohn, and invited him to meet for lunch. Then he booked the company plane for early the following week. By then he would have an appointment scheduled with a title abstractor who had offices in Pennsylvania and West Virginia.

Chapter 112

Eddie and Anne had new ponies. An elderly couple's grandchildren had outgrown the steeds and Candace promised to give them a good home and pay the couples' outstanding veterinary bills if she could have the ponies. In return her children learned early in life to groom their mounts and muck out a stall.

The family was returning to the stables on Saturday afternoon when they saw Teensy waving to them from the terrace of the homestead. She had a newspaper in her other hand. Bryce invited Anne to ride with him toward Teensy and when the little girl began to guide her pony in that direction, Teensy shook her head vigorously in the negative. Too late, Bryce realized that the newspaper was a tabloid. He shouted to Teensy that he understood and would talk to her later.

"Daddy, did that bad man at the scandal sheet write more bad things about you?" asked Anne.

Bryce had to smile at the nomenclature Candace had taught their daughter. "Even if he does, Honey, they aren't true, so don't you believe anything that's printed in that awful paper. Come on let's head back to the stable."

"I know. It's not a real newspaper; it's just a scandal sheet. But it still makes Mommy cry."

"Oh? When did you see Mommy cry?"

"That day we went to the store and Mommy brought that scandal sheet home."

Bryce tried to keep his face from showing his anger over the innocent revelation as he held Anne's pony while she dismounted.

When the family was finished grooming their mounts, Bryce walked to Ghost's stall and gave his wife a long hug.

Candace stayed in his arms, enjoying the embrace. When Bryce released her she looked at his eyes and saw the distress. "More *Tattler*?"

"I think that's what Teensy was waving at us."

"Okay. I'll take the children back to the house. The carpenter is due in an hour to measure for more closet shelves and I want to clean up before he arrives. Oh, Bryce, it's so good to be in our new home! I just hope that awful tabloid doesn't ruin our joy."

"It won't. But if they print more of that garbage, I'm going to sue them for libel. Sweetheart, I'll see you back at the house. I'll collect Daniel and bring him along after I see Teensy."

Candace led the children toward the hill that separated their new home from the stables.

Bryce made a conscious effort to hold his head high as he walked toward the terrace of his childhood home.

◦≋◦

By Monday Saul Mattison was working on the final draft of the defamation complaint he would file in federal court. Exhibit "A" was the original article. Exhibit "B" was the letter requesting a retraction, and Exhibit "C" was the article that appeared in the previous week's edition of *The National Gazette & Tattler*. Exhibit C read:

The SEAL and the Skeleton - Part 2

The Tattler has learned that Charles Coe, who killed Marilyn Roberts, was himself murdered - smothered to death in his own bed. The killer crept silently into Coe's shack, and using brute force, held a pillow over Coe's face and pinned him down with it. The victim struggled but he could not escape the man who was there to avenge the death of Marilyn Roberts, wife of the former Founders star and former Navy SEAL, Bryce Roberts. Driven by love for Marilyn and hatred for her killer, the murderer hauled Coe's body

deep into the woods where he dropped
the lifeless remains onto a rock. That
rock shattered the corpse's skull.
Hatred does strange things to a man.
When there was still doubt over whether
Coe was breathing, the killer trapped
Coe's leg under a tree root to keep him
there. That broke the dead man's ankle.
Coe paid for his own victim's death
when the man who held her dear got a
chance to do the deed. Next week The
Tattler will feature the latest
developments in this ongoing
investigation.

Saul Mattison's legal complaint that would start the lawsuit ended with a demand for punitive damages.

Bryce reviewed the final draft as it slowly rolled off the facsimile. Then he called the attorney and told him to file the complaint. His order was accompanied with a huge sense of guilt. He kept thinking about what he could have done to keep the situation under control, yet he knew it was others who had brought on the trouble. The Roberts family would now be in the public arena, a role they had shunned for more than two centuries. But his good name and the reputation of his family was on the line. He had to protect them both. If they became tarnished, his future and his family would be ruined. He thought about the reaction of his children to him and how they seemed almost fearful of him for the first time in their lives.

"Damn those people at the *Tattler!* Just when our family was beginning to gel, and my work is getting challenging, this garbage comes along." Had Porter been there, he would have been terrified by the facial expression Bryce directed at the folder of legal documents and him.

Bryce correctly anticipated Harry's opposition to the defamation suit, but during a long talk, Harry finally agreed that the family's reputation and Bryce's future had to be defended.

"They've picked the fight," Harry said. "Let's just make sure we win it."

Harry had not given in easily, and so, it was with the idea of mending fences that Bryce looked forward to their trip to the convention.

On Thursday evening of that week he and his father flew to the Forest Products Association convention in Memphis. Bryce had a portfolio of documents that he was eager to share with Ian Macgregor. He and Ian would have lunch to discuss Sunrise Lumber's purchase of options on prime timberland that Ian owned in Western Pennsylvania. Harry promised not to intervene. He eagerly anticipated watching how his successor would handle the situation.

Winging northward on that same evening was a large-breasted secretary who was on a long weekend vacation from her job at the *Tattler*.

⊙✍◎

On Friday afternoon, the telephone in the study of Candace's new home roused her from a daydream she was enjoying as she relaxed in a deep and comfortable sofa. The book in her lap dropped to the hardwood floor and she paused to orient herself to her still new surroundings. The caller kept on ringing and Candace got up and answered.

"Candace, it's Stella. Honey, Noah's dying. The doctor just left and he says that he may have another day or so. Noah wants to talk with Bryce. Mabel told me he's out of town. Do you know when he's due back?"

"Oh, Stella, I'm so sorry to hear that Noah is going so quickly. Just a few weeks ago we thought he still had some time left."

"I know. But it's not to be. Now do you know when Bryce is expected to return?"

"He and Harry are due back on Sunday. But I'll try to reach him to give him the news and your message. In a little while I have to come into town to pick up the children at school. I'll leave early and stop by just for a quick visit on my way."

"Okay. But try to call Bryce first."

Candace dialed the hotel in Memphis. The operator connected her with Harry who had answered the page. He listened grimly to the news, told Candace to cajole Noah's message to

Bryce out of the dying man, and promised to tell Bryce of the situation.

Bryce, he informed her, was in a delicate negotiation.

Chapter 113

"Delicate," thought Harry, as he rejoined the meeting in a quiet corner of the hotel restaurant, really wasn't the right word for the language that Ian Macgregor was using in his discussion with Bryce.

"Ian, cussing will get you nowhere," said Bryce. "You and I both know that if the Association finds out that you're sponsoring environmental protests against one of your fellow members, you'll be black-balled in this business for the rest of your life. Nobody will buy your lumber. You may get lucky enough to sell some of your trees for firewood. But that's not going to pay off your mortgages on the West Virginia properties, now, is it?"

"You prick. How'd you find out about my mortgage?" Macgregor shifted his raw-boned body and Bryce read the worry the movement conveyed.

"Mortgages, Ian. They're a public record recorded in the court house, Ian. It just took a skilled abstracter to find them under a fictitious name you registered. Now, Ian, what do you say we have another look at this long-term option on your Pennsylvania land?"

"That's my best tract of forest and I plan on starting operations there next year. You can't have that one. Give me a break and I'll make it up to you somehow, Bryce."

"Ian, what you did was just plain dirty pool, so you're not getting any breaks. Now here's what we want: a twelve-year option on your Pennsylvania tract and a written acknowledgement that you sponsored the environmental protesters. We keep that acknowledgement in a safe place along with your "foundation" records just in case we need a renewal of the twelve year option."

"Renewal?" Macgregor's flushed face paled and Bryce knew he had the man.

Harry pinched his lower lip. Then once again his face became inscrutable. Nice touch, Bryce, he thought. Lord, even I didn't think of that angle. Ah, you remember well my lessons about life. When someone deliberately tries to harm you, show no quarter in defending yourself. Humph. Ancient phrase, but apt. Show no mercy, no quarter. Go to it lad, you've got him on the run now!

"I'll give you a break on the renewal," said Bryce. "Seven years instead of twelve; and, it'll be for a lease of the timber only. And we do it all for the princely sum you scoffed at earlier in our meeting, plus lease payments at half the rate then generally in effect; but, with a cap in case inflation goes hog-wild. It's all here as drawn up by a very good lawyer."

"Jesus! Do you want my first-born, too?"

"Ian, do you recall the oversized luggage carts the bellhops use here?"

"Yeah, Bryce. What's your point?"

"There's one of those carts in storage at this very hotel. It's full of cartons which each hold hundreds of copies of these documents that show you up for your, uh, environmental concerns."

"Ah, shit. You wouldn't do that . . ." Ian Macgregor looked across the restaurant table at the dark eyes facing him and was the recipient of the "Dombrowski Look."

". . . Jesus . . . I think you would. Gimme the damned papers. I'll sign."

"A notary who works at the hotel office will be here in just a moment," said Bryce. He turned and signaled a bartender who reached for a telephone.

The notary appeared, Macgregor signed, and headed for the bar with the Sunrise Lumber Company check. He looked at it one more time before pocketing it. There just weren't enough numbers to the left of the decimal point.

Harry kept a straight face while they still were at the table, but on the way back to their suite he asked, "A whole cartful of documents?"

"Nah. But I needed just one more item to put the deal over the top."

The message light on the telephone in their suite was blinking when they returned. Bryce rang the desk and returned Mabel's call. He reached her at home. Then he made another telephone call and listened carefully to the information that was relayed by Saul. Bryce chuckled after he hung up. Harry looked a question at Bryce.

"Saul said he has a date tonight. I guess that man does have time for a social life."

It was only then that Harry told Bryce of Candace's call and message regarding Noah's condition.

Chapter 114

N oah looked terrible—even worse than Candace had expected. She sat in the chair by the side of his bed as he drifted in and out of consciousness, his breath coming in gasps and rattles around the oxygen tube fastened to his nose.

"Where's Bryce?" he managed.

"He's in Memphis, Noah, and he won't be back until Sunday, the day after tomorrow. He asked me to take your message to him." *Actually, Harry asked me to do it, but I'm not going to tell you that because it's the right idea, anyway.*

She could tell Noah was weighing whether to speak to her. Then he struggled to try to fill his inflexible lung tissue with air. Candace bent low to hear him.

"Tell Bryce . . . I delivered . . . the glasses . . . and I'm sorry."

"What glasses, Noah?"

But Noah lapsed into unconsciousness from the effort.

"Stella, do you know what he's talking about?"

Stella, who was holding Daniel, shook her head, no.

Candace was anxious to pick up her children in time to keep them from enduring more teasing from their schoolmates while they waited for her. She stayed with Noah, nervously glancing at the clock, but Noah spoke no more. Candace left and sped for the school.

"Maybe that message will make sense to Bryce. But I don't think that's what Noah wanted to tell Bryce in person. Glasses, Huh? I'll call Bryce later tonight and tell him what Noah said."

⚬⚭⚬

"Hi, Honey," said Candace into the long distance line. "I went to see Noah today. He had a message for you. Get a pencil and paper because I wrote down just what he told me . . . You have it? Okay. He said, 'Tell Bryce I delivered the glasses, and I'm sorry.' Honey does that make sense to you?"

"No," said Bryce. "Did he say anything else?"

"I think he wanted to say more, but he drifted into unconsciousness. Bryce, I got the distinct impression that he wanted to say something different to you than what he told me."

"Sweetheart, I have no idea about what he wanted to say. If he's still alive when I get home I'll go straight over to his home from the airport. Now, tell me, how are you and the kids doing?"

"We're all okay. There hasn't been as much teasing at school because the ringleader still remembers his broken nose. We're going to have Rosalie and Teensy over here for dinner tomorrow night. That'll be a switch. What about, you? Did your negotiations work out okay?"

"I'm fine but I miss you and the children. And my negotiations went even better than I expected."

Okay, honey, I'll say goodnight. I love you, Bryce."

"I love you too. See you Sunday."

Chapter 115

Saul Mattison was a bachelor and he intended to remain so. It wasn't that he didn't enjoy the company of women. He did. And his dinner companion that Saturday evening represented the female of the species in her most voluptuous form. Her auburn hair and lovely cheekbones gave her face a raw beauty that its owner had refined with only touches of make-up and a necklace and pendant that called attention to her generous cleavage that was exposed by a low-cut blouse. The lawyer began to make plans for later that evening as he raised his glass to toast his new friend.

"Dolores, for whatever it was that made you decide to come to see me, I'm grateful."

"The cause of honesty and truth, Mr. Mattison."

"Call me Saul. And, yes, those are admirable traits. I may be able to shorten the process of pre-trial discovery as a result of your honesty. Now, have you decided what you'd like to order?"

"Well, my husband usually orders for me when we dine out, so will you do that for me? These long menus take forever to go through and I just want to enjoy something good."

Damn! thought Saul. There goes a glorious evening. The ring on that broad's finger doesn't look like a wedding ring, but I guess it is.

"I think you'll like the seafood, Dolores. They really do it right here."

"Oh, thanks, Saul. I love a good northern lobster. I'll just have that."

Saul's lament deepened. She goes for the most expensive item on the menu and I'm not even going to get laid. Ah, well, the fee

I'm going to earn on this case will pay enough to buy lots of dinners for lots of willing ladies.

"Tell me, Dolores, how is it that you came to work for the *Tattler*?"

"I answered a want ad and they hired me. I'd only been looking for a job for a few weeks after we moved to Florida from New Jersey, so I think I'm really lucky. Now, this week I have an opportunity to visit with my family here and enjoy dinner with you. Nice, huh?"

"You still have family in New Jersey then?"

Yes, my brother, Nicco. But he already had a date tonight, so here I am. Thank you so much for inviting me."

"You're welcome. Perhaps if you return to this area, I could help you find work. In the meantime can you get copies of those documents to me?"

"You're sweet, Saul, but I think we'll be staying in Florida. And yes, I'll mail copies to you."

Chapter 116

Noah breathed his last as the Sunrise Lumber Company's propjet was still an hour away from home. There was a message for Bryce at the airport that Candace was at Stella's house, and that Noah had died.

Bryce headed for Stella's house.

Harry went home to his wife and grandchildren. Rosalie, contrary to her custom with her own family, fed the grandchildren early and waited to eat her dinner until Harry could join her. Over their venison steaks Harry regaled her with the tale of Bryce's dealings with Macgregor and of other anecdotes from the convention.

Rosalie knew her husband well enough to understand when he was avoiding a subject by talking about other matters. Their conversation fell silent because she didn't participate. She waited until Teensy cleared the table and then got up and walked behind her husband's chair. She bent down, put her arms around him and spoke softly in his ear.

"What's really bothering you? Is it that awful newspaper article?"

Harry's hands came up to hold hers.

"Yes. Bryce has approved going forward with a lawsuit for defamation and I'm not sure this family should be exposed to the publicity that's going to generate. Always before we've stood above such things; but, times have changed. America has lost much of the genteel nature we had up until the decade of the '60s. Now, newspapers are becoming much bolder and America is becoming more and more crude. Damn it, Rosalie, this country has lost its dignity!"

Rosalie moved around him and sat in Harry's lap. Her hand gently brushed his cheek.

"It's really Bryce's decision, isn't it?"

"Yes. And I can't blame him. He told me he has to show his kids that he's not a murderer. He wants to be sure his and this family's name is cleared, and he and Saul Mattison believe they can do it in court. Rosalie, we have to protect the good name of this family."

"I know you will. But there's something I want to ask. Harry, do you think Charles Coe was murdered?"

"I believe he was."

Rosalie paled and Harry immediately understood her distress.

"Here's the way I see it . . ." he began, after swearing his wife to secrecy.

Chapter 117

Noah's funeral gave Candace an opportunity to satisfy her curiosity about Marilyn's gravesite. She and Bryce paused there with Eddie after Noah's graveside service ended. Anne walked with Bryce's parents toward their car. Candace stood reading Marilyn's epitaph for a moment and then gave Bryce a kiss on his cheek, gently ran her fingers along Eddie's head, and left them at the stone. She deliberately avoided Stella and was grateful when she saw that the widow was escorted by her brother's family. Candace didn't want to encourage Stella's over-dependence upon her that she suspected Stella would try to establish.

"Dad?"

"Yes, Eddie?"

"Why did Mom walk away?"

"She's a very understanding wife. She knows it's emotionally difficult for me to visit your mother's grave and so she just wants to give me some time by myself with you here."

"Dad, . . . do you still love my mother?"

"When I think about her, I do so with love in my heart."

"Does Mom know that?"

"Yes. But she also understands that I love her, too . . . very, very much."

"I'm glad . . . May we go now?"

"Yes, let's each go give my wife and your mom huge hugs."

Eddie ran ahead of him toward the waiting limo.

Bryce gave a final moment to Marilyn and then looked heavenward. "Noah, I hope you heard that conversation," Bryce said quietly. "But what in hell did you mean about being sorry?"

Chapter 118

Mabel brought them each coffee and then closed Harry's office door. Harry spoke first. "What has Zeke told you about the used equipment? Did he find anything?"

"He can provide a like-new finishing room for about half of what we'd pay new."

"Is it worth doing?"

"Yes. That's the oldest part of the factory and the one that will benefit most from an upgrade. If we can do that, the finish quality of the products will be improved immediately and that's the first thing a customer sees."

"Bryce, I'm still not convinced we should put the company's money into this project. I want to see the revised business plan before we commit."

Harry watched as Bryce held his temper and his disappointment. A dawning respect entered the older man's thoughts and he decided to push harder. "What are you going to do about increasing the number of dealers for the furniture?"

"Go into the South and Midwest. Right now those markets are dominated by factories in North Carolina. But I'm convinced we can compete on quality. If we can get just eleven outlets in the populous areas of the South and Midwest we can make a profit on a reasonable volume."

"And the volume?"

"We promise the new dealers that we'll advertise heavily in their territories. We also subcontract with other furniture manufacturers to produce some of their products."

"What's your advertising budget?"

"It's on an increasing scale as the dealers come into the fold. Here, let me show you. I've worked out some numbers with Harriet's help . . ."

"You've talked with Harriet?" Bryce could hear the pride in his father's voice.

"Yes, last week. As soon as she returns from Florida, we can talk more if you'd like."

"Florida?" asked Harry.

"She said something about doing marketing research on the coverage of some of the newspapers down there."

"Oh? Did she mention which ones?"

"No," said Bryce. "She's going to cover both coasts. She promised to share her results. By the way, I'm going to fly down there the day after tomorrow to try to close a deal for newsprint. Who knows? Maybe I can meet Harriet. Now, where were we?"

⁘

In offices north of Fort Lauderdale, Derek Cowper, publisher of the *Tattler*, finished reading the thick Complaint that had been served by a Federal Marshall. Over half-glasses Cowper looked at his editor, Hyman Abrams, and spoke querulously.

"Hy, I want answers. Why has this attorney sued you and me as well as Leon and the corporation? What makes him think he can prove the articles are false and misleading? I want you to check this lawyer out. Find out what kind of reputation he has and what his skills are. I don't like being sued. Not at all. Particularly in federal court."

"I already checked on the man. Saul Mattison is forty-four years old and is managing partner of a small law firm in Philadelphia. He has a very good reputation and is rated AV. That's the best of the best according to the lawyers' own rating system. According to our lawyers he's the top guy for defamation suits in that part of the country."

"Hy, lets pull the third article that Leon did. No sense in pushing this any harder, even if our circulation in the Philadelphia area is up by forty percent."

"It's too late Derek. Because of the short holiday week the paper went to press yesterday and it's in trucks headed for the north now."

"Can we recall it in time?"

"Not without pissing off a whole bunch of advertisers. That's our second biggest market."

"What do our lawyers say?"

"They're worried, Derek. They want to settle cheap and get out fast."

"We never settle and they know that."

"Derek, this time we have a wealthy and angry adversary. It's not going to be the usual process where we grind the guy down with pretrial maneuvers that cost him a boatload."

"Hy, you tell our lawyers that we don't settle. They know damned well that if we start that policy we'll go down the tubes. Everybody we offend will be encouraged to sue."

☙❧

"Bryce," said Saul Mattison, "I got a call from the Lewis firm today, and they're trying to feel us out about settling."

Bryce switched the telephone receiver to his left hand and found a pen. "Why would a big gun law firm like that offer to settle, Saul? Do you think they're serious?"

"No. They just want to cover their own butts by going back to the client and telling them that they tried to get us to be reasonable and that we aren't."

"Did they make an offer?"

"No. They want us to make a demand. I told them $2.5 million just to see what would happen. They may come back with something, but I doubt it."

"Saul, I want to bleed those bastards. Don't settle for anything less than two million."

"Bryce, even in today's world, that's unheard of. But I'm going to find out if they have insurance for any of this. Maybe we can work a deal. But in the meantime I just served them with discovery requests. They'll have to produce all of their rough notes about the investigation they did and any internal memos they wrote about the story."

"You can get that kind of stuff?"

"Under the new rules of court, yes. But don't hold your breath on whether they produce the documents, even if they have them."

"Okay, Saul. Keep me posted on what's going on, and keep the pressure on."

"Will do Bryce. Take it easy."

Chapter 119

Bryce sat at an outside table in the shade of an umbrella. He was on the second story deck of a restaurant near Fort Lauderdale, Florida. The marina below held, as the discrete business card of the manager stated, "yachts of distinction." Glen Foster, the investigator, joined him at the table and they shook hands. It was 2:30 in the afternoon and most of the lunchtime patrons had left, leaving Bryce and his investigator to themselves in one corner of the deck. They ordered iced tea, glad of the shade offered by the table umbrella. A warm breeze came in off the waterway, heralding the seriously hot weather to come.

"Thanks for meeting me here Mr. Roberts. I thought you'd want to see this first hand. We discovered Cowper owns a yacht when we followed him here. Apparently it's his pride and joy. He brings his mistress here but the yacht doesn't leave the dock when she's aboard."

"Which one is it?"

"The Golden Silence over there." Foster gestured with a slight motion of his head.

Bryce took in the scrupulously maintained mahogany and teak and the magnificent lines of the sixty-footer. "She's beautiful. How's she owned?"

"It's registered in Panama to a corporation chartered in Delaware. Cowper owns all of the stock in the corporation."

"Stupid," said Bryce. "He needs an offshore corporation to really hide things and avoid taxes. Is the yacht financed?"

"Surprisingly, no. Not that we can determine from his tax returns. We managed to obtain copies of his returns for the last three years. He claims the yacht as a second home and office and depreciates it."

Bryce raised an eyebrow at Foster and the investigator answered the query. "An agent of ours, posing as a mortgage broker, offered him a lower interest rate on his home mortgage. Of course, to qualify, Cowper had to produce his tax returns to verify his income."

"And, of course, he didn't qualify."

"Regrettably, the broker's financing at that special rate was consumed by other deals. Part of the application stated that the financial records Cowper provided would be returned, and they were. But, through a careless error, portions of them were copied and misplaced in another file."

Bryce did not smile, at least not outwardly.

"How about Hyman Abrams. What do we know about him?"

"He was divorced two years ago. As part of the settlement he kept the house and paid his wife for her share. The house is in a very exclusive neighborhood bordering on a golf course. Earlier this year Abrams used an inheritance to pay off the mortgage."

"Children?"

"His wife had two by a former marriage. They're both in college. As far as we can determine, their father pays the children's bills."

"And Porter?"

"A wife and two children. A boy, 12, and a girl, 10."

"Debts?"

"A mortgage and car payments. But he owns three antique cars that he keeps in a separate garage. Apparently all of his savings go into his car collection. He has a 1932 Cadillac that's really a gem. The others are good too."

"Glen, you've done well. Thank you. Now all I need is a good verdict."

Chapter 120

To Bryce it seemed as if they would never get to trial. Saul Mattison had persuaded the judge to whom the case had been assigned to put the matter on a scheduling "fast track," but the pretrial wrangling and motions still seemed endless. Bryce's deposition had twice been postponed when opposing counsel had a court date to keep. Bryce learned even more patience with the court system than he had with Harry over the purchase of the furniture company.

Saul finally went to the judge and obtained an order that Bryce must be deposed by a date certain or his deposition would be waived. Opposing counsel waited to schedule the deposition until the last possible day, which happened to be Bryce's wedding anniversary. Bryce doubted that the scheduling was a coincidence because he'd previously responded to written interrogatories in which he had to provide his date of marriage. The only good thing about today was that it was Friday, and thus it wouldn't interfere with the rest of his workweek.

The Lewis firm's lawyer, J. Henderson Abbott, was nicknamed "The Glacier" by the plaintiffs' bar and asked questions at the same pace his icy namesake moved, a talent developed because he was paid by the hour. Bryce followed Saul's instruction and answered only what he was asked. By eleven o'clock that morning, two hours into the deposition, Bryce still was seated calmly looking across the table at Abbott. Thank God for UDT training, thought Bryce. That discipline never has left me and now it's a piece of cake to sit here through this.

"Uh, Mr. Roberts, how long was it that you served in the Navy SEALs?"

"Mr. Abbott, I told you that I did not serve in the SEALs. I was a UDT officer who helped train the SEALs.

"When was that?"

"During most of 1964".

"What were your duties in training the SEALs?"

"I was responsible chiefly for getting the men into excellent physical condition and for instructing in small boat operations."

"Anything else?"

"I, along with others, taught the men how to use scuba gear and underwater propulsion equipment."

"What did you teach in the way of hand-to-hand combat?"

"Nothing. That was done by specialists other than me."

"Mr. Roberts, are you saying that you have no experience in violent hand-to-hand combat?"

"No, that's not what I said. I told you that I didn't teach the subject."

"What is your experience in hand-to-hand combat?"

"I received a standard course in the subject as part of my UDT training."

Bryce watched as Abbott reached inside a large upright briefcase and withdrew a slim folder. *Here it comes*, thought Bryce. *Just stay cool.*

"Mr. Roberts, have you ever been known to have violent propensities?"

No way do I answer that question. It's too wide open, thought Bryce.

"Mr. Abbott, could you define what you mean by 'violent propensities'?"

"Oh, come, come, Mr. Roberts, surely you know what that term means. Now, answer my question."

"I will, if you will define what you mean by the term so that we both are of the same understanding."

"Mr. Roberts, I repeat, have you ever been known to have violent propensities?"

"Objection!" said Saul. "Hendie," he continued, deliberately using a nickname Abbott hated, 'violent propensities' are relative. To a pacifist they are at one level and to a policeman at another level. Please define what you mean by 'violent propensities.' Moreover, you're asking about reputation and character. That's established through other witnesses, even assuming it's admissible in a civil trial. Now, if we can't resolve this we can call the judge. What'll it be?"

Abbott, perfectly aware that the judge might someday read the deposition transcript, chose to curry favor with the court. "Mr. Mattison, you know perfectly well that would unnecessarily inconvenience the judge. Let's move on and I'll rephrase the question. Keep in mind that Mr. Roberts claims the *Tattler* sullied his reputation, so we think that his violent propensities are at issue."

"No, Hendie, there's nothing to establish that."

"Oh, I disagree," said the glacier. "But we'll move on. Now, Mr. Roberts, I show you what has been marked as Defense Exhibit 12 for purposes of identification. Have you seen that document before?

Bryce carefully read the five pages of the exhibit while Abbott fidgeted with his pen.

"Yes."

"Where and when did you previously see it?"

"I read it last week in Mr. Mattison's office."

Bryce watched Abbott try to hide his crestfallen expression. *Thank you, Saul, for your preparation.*

Abbott knew he had been upstaged but chose to make light of that fact.

"What is it, please?"

"It's an incident report prepared by a Transit Authority police officer."

"And do you have a starring role in that report?"

Bryce didn't rise to the bait. He looked across the table at Abbot and responded.

"Mr. Abbott, the report says what it says. How you interpret it is up to you."

Abbot was not used to a witness who remained unintimidated. He paused and then continued. "On the occasion described in that report, did you dislocate the elbow of a gentleman named" . . . he shuffled through the pages . . . "Leroy Carter?"

"That's correct," said Bryce in a matter-of-fact tone.

"'That's correct?' That's all that you have to say about it?"

Bryce interlocked his fingers, placed his hands on the table, looked sincerely across the table at The Glacier, and replied:

"Is that a question, Mr. Abbott?"

Saul looked out the window of the conference room at the city skyline and gave a silent cheer. Abbott was rapidly learning that Bryce would make an excellent witness on his own behalf, a point Saul was sure that Abbott would report to his client and their corporate counsel.

Because Coe was dead, Abbott had to rely on other witnesses to prove the theme of his defense, which was to portray Bryce as a violent man whose open hatred for Coe really did convince the newspaper people to believe Bryce could have murdered Coe. If the Tattler's lawyers could show that belief was legitimate, Bryce's claim for punitive damages could be dismissed and the opportunity for a big, punishing verdict would disappear.

Abbott had to use the man who sat across the table from him to prove that point, so he began a new tactic.

"Mr. Roberts, what did you think of Charles Coe?"

"On the one hand I felt sorry for him. He was pretty much of a poor soul. On the other hand, I hated him for what he did to Marilyn and later to Candace."

"How much did you hate Coe?"

"Fiercely, at first. Over the years after Marilyn's death, it dissipated, particularly after I met my present wife and we became a family."

"But then when Coe assaulted your second wife, that fierce hatred returned, didn't it?"

"Not like it used to be. At that point I considered him more of a problem, a very dangerous loose cannon, who had to be guarded against."

Abbott was thorough, and he followed up into the unknown. He knew that depositions are the time to ask questions to which he did not already know the answer. No jury was watching or listening. So Abbott plunged ahead.

"You guarded against Coe? What did you do?"

"I hired an experienced security man to guard and escort my wife while I was away from home."

Abbott probed the details of Plank's experience and his duties in the Roberts household. Then he returned to his attempt to establish Bryce as a violent man.

"But you didn't need Mr. Plank when you were at home because you could take care of things if Coe appeared?"

"The need was relative. Although Mr. Plank is a very decent and conscientious man, we wanted privacy when I was able to be home."

"But you could have handled Coe if he appeared?"

"I would have called the police first. Then I would have done what was necessary to defend my family."

"How long did you keep Mr. Plank on duty?"

"For several months after Coe tried to harm my wife."

Abbott knew the impact that news would have on a jury. He could hear Saul asking the jury why Porter, the *Tattler* reporter, didn't inquire more about the Roberts family's situation from Homer Miller or others. And Saul would ask why a man who supposedly had killed Coe would hire a bodyguard if he knew Coe was dead? Damn! This was going to be a bitch of a trial!

An hour later Abbott reluctantly ended the deposition after Bryce had described the mental stress he and his family had undergone as a result of the articles, particularly the third article of the series that contained an outrageous suggestion that Bryce had persuaded Noah, Marilyn's father, to take the blame for the murder of Coe because Noah was a dying man.

⊙≋⊙

When Bryce arrived home much earlier than expected, Candace was dressed in her riding outfit of jeans, half boots and an athlete's bra under a heavy shirt.

"Come on, we're going riding," she told him. "It's a beautiful spring afternoon and there's a bottle of chilled Chablis for me and a good red for you. I've packed some goodies and we can have a picnic."

"How did you know I'd be home early?"

"I reminded Saul that today is our anniversary and he had his secretary call me the minute your deposition was over."

"What did you do about our children?"

"My parents volunteered to meet Eddie and Anne at school and keep them overnight. They have a change of clothes at their home. Daniel is with Teensy. Tomorrow morning David and Alice get to revisit the Franklin Institute with another set of children who will be just as well behaved as my brother and I were many years ago."

"How do you do it?" asked Bryce, love and admiration blending into his smile.

"Do what?"

"Effortlessly organize things."

"Honey, I took a page out of your book. I had my parents lined up three weeks ago. They were going to sit with the kids while we went out to dinner, so I just called and they moved things up a bit. Same for Teensy. Now go change and let's get over to the stable."

"Aye, aye, ma'am. Just be sure to pack a corkscrew."

They rode for almost an hour and then put the horses on halters and long leads pegged to the ground. They spread their blanket in a sunny spot by the stream that Candace loved to ride along. Puffy white clouds dotted the sky that showed through the treetops. A light breeze brought the scents of clover fields and wild apple blossoms. Candace sat in the sun's warmth, listening to the stream splashing over rocks as it made its way toward the river. She tasted her wine and then broke their reveries.

"I'm going to stay on the subject only briefly, but I have to know. Must I testify about the stress that awful scandal sheet has caused?"

"Probably. Saul doesn't think that you'll be on the stand very long because the other side won't want to appear to be picking on an adoring and supporting wife."

"I'll do it for us, Bryce. There's just no way that rag is going to create such havoc in our lives without both of us defending you."

"My lady in shining armor. Candace, what would I do without you at my side?"

"Oh, you'd do all right. By now you'd have made the All-Star team a couple of years running and probably would have a woman in every city in the league."

"You're the only one I'd chase after." He raised his sterling silver julep cup that they used for wine on such occasions. "I salute the woman who put me in touch with life again."

Candace batted her eyelashes, put on a mock southern accent, and said, "Why, Bryce Roberts, that's the sweetest thang y'all have said to me in evah so long. Honeychile, are y'all tryin' ta git in mah britches?"

"Well, Candace-Lou, this heah blanket is big enough . . . and there ahren't many buuugs this time of yeahr . . . and ain't nobody 'roun' . . ."

For years afterward they teased and debated about which of them removed his or her clothes the fastest.

Chapter 121

Trial day. As directed by Saul, Bryce dressed carefully in a plain dark suit, white shirt, bright but tasteful necktie and an inexpensive wristwatch. Saul's appearance was in sharp contrast. He wore a rumpled suit, a worn necktie and shoes that looked as if he played sandlot football in them. An uncontrollable lock of hair kept falling in his homely face. Candace said his appearance reminded her of an unmade bed. But the look gave Saul a humility that he believed appealed to the jury. He was addressing them now in his opening statement.

Saul began, businesslike, covering the events and history that intertwined Bryce and Coe. He warned Bryce that he had to do that, so by the time the defense got around to that subject it would be "old news" with much less an impact. Saul now was getting to the meat of his opening.

"So here we have a decent family man and new father, whose first wife was killed by a mentally unbalanced man. Bryce Roberts wept, and he mourned, and, yes, he'll tell you that, at first, he hated Charles Coe for what he'd done. But years went by, and Bryce Roberts found a new and happy life with a new wife and more children . . . only to have his family again tormented by Coe attempting to kill his second wife.

"Bryce Roberts will tell you when he learned that Coe was even more deranged than he thought, he didn't take the law into his own hands. Instead, Bryce hired a body guard to protect Candace when he couldn't be with her. You'll learn that the bodyguard was on duty for months after the time an expert pathologist said Coe died. You'll ask yourselves why Bryce Roberts would hire a bodyguard to protect his wife from a man who he knew was dead. You will answer that question by reasoning that Bryce Roberts hired a bodyguard because he did not know Coe was dead. And therefore, Bryce Roberts did not kill Charles Coe.

"The people at the *Tattler* could have asked the same questions that you will answer, but they didn't. As you'll hear and see, the people at the *Tattler* learned who the real killer was. They even heard him confess, yet their articles continued to infer that Bryce Roberts murdered Coe. We're going to prove to you that none of what the *Tattler* published about Bryce Roberts' so-called involvement with Charles Coe's death is true. We are going to prove to you that everything the *Tattler* published about Bryce' so-called involvement with Coe's murder is a pack of deliberate lies . . . *deliberate* lies, ladies and gentlemen."

Then Mattison laid his trap. "And, we are going to prove that the people at the Tattler knew they were publishing a pack of lies. That's libel, ladies and gentlemen. We are going to prove that deliberate libel was done simply because the people at the *Tattler* did not care a plug nickel for a good man's reputation or for a good man's family. We're going to prove that deliberate falsehood has caused people in the business world to question Bryce Roberts, some people in the community to avoid him, and many to rally to his cause. But you'll also hear how, sadly, his children were picked on and bullied at school because the people at the *Tattler* insinuated their daddy is a murderer when those people at the *Tattler* knew he isn't a murderer. That's why we have sued not only the corporation that publishes the *Tattler*, but also the publisher himself, Mr. Derek Cowper, the editor, Mr. Hyman Abrams and the reporter . . ." he said "reporter" with a terrible sarcasm in his voice . . . "Mr. Leon Porter."

The trap had just been baited. Now, prayed Saul, let's see if the bait is swallowed. Hendie, let's see if you get up and say your guys aren't liars.

Saul concluded, "At the end of this trial ladies and gentlemen, if I have kept my promise to you and proved everything I've said, we're going to ask you to return a verdict in favor of the Roberts family and," Saul pointed an accusing finger at the defense table, where the three men sat, "against the people at the *Tattler*."

The courtroom was silent for a long moment. Then the judge invited J. Henderson Abbott to address the jury.

The Glacier rose to his feet and walked confidently toward the jury box.

"There are two sides to every case, ladies and gentlemen, and we ask that you be fair and listen to both sides as the oath you took requires you to do, and as you want to do.

"The *Tattler* is what you and others call a supermarket tabloid. It sells thousands of copies each week, so a lot of people enjoy reading it. Its purpose, as you will see from copies that will be in evidence, is as much to entertain, as it is to deliver news. Much of what's written in the *Tattler* is gossip, as you also will see. The line between the *Tattler's* gossip and hard news is often blurred. That's what we'll show you about the articles that mention Bryce Roberts. We'll show you that what's really printed about Mr. Roberts is gossip, only gossip, and no more. The articles never actually accuse Mr. Roberts of murder. They're written in a style that the author of those articles and his editor will testify is meant to titillate the reader, not to defame Mr. Roberts."

Abbott paused and had a sip of water from the glass on his counsel table. He mulled Mattison's claim that he has proof that his clients knew they were lying. *Do I deal with that now or wait? I don't know what he means or what he might have. So, don't get into it now. Wait and see what he tries.*

Abbot continued. "Nobody likes to be the center of gossip as Mr. Roberts was. But Roberts is a public figure, a former pro baseball player and prominent in his local political circles. Our law provides that such people are "fair game" for criticism in newspapers. And that is what was done here. The newspaper took a public figure and held him up to criticism and gossip. But, gossip is not libel, as we will prove to you. By the end of this trial you will be convinced that my client did not print a libel against Mr. Roberts and we will ask that you find in favor of my client, *The National Gazette & Tattler.*"

Saul groaned inwardly. *Abbott had not taken the bait and had not defended his individual clients from Saul's accusation that they were liars. Instead Abbott completely ignored the three men and spoke only of the* Tattler. *Looks like we go to Plan B.*

The judge told Saul Mattison to call his first witness.

"Thank you, your Honor, we call Detective Richard Miller."

"Homer" Miller was sworn and identified himself.

"Detective Miller," asked Saul, "were you the police officer who was in charge of the investigation of the death of Charles Coe?"

"Objection, your Honor, leading," said Abbott.

"Oh, I suppose it is," ruled the judge. "Objection sustained. But Mr. Abbott, we're going to be here for a long time if you keep that up. Mr. Mattison, just don't lead your witness when you get to the substance of his testimony."

"Yes, Your Honor. Thank you. Detective Miller, what, if anything, were your duties with respect to the investigation of the death of Charles Coe?"

"I was officer in charge of the investigation of Coe's death."

Jurors number one and two looked at each other and then at Abbott. They were frowning. What the hell was Abbott objecting to?

"Did you examine the scene where Mr. Coe's remains were found?" continued Saul. *Go ahead and object to this one, Hendie.* There was silence from defense counsel.

"Yes sir."

"What did you observe?"

"Skeletal remains were found on the woodlot where Coe lived. The skull was near a large rock. There was an obvious indented fracture in the right forehead region of the skull. The right leg was tangled in a tree root. The rest of the body did not appear to be damaged, but due to the advanced state of decomposition, we couldn't tell if there were other wounds or damage. I attended the autopsy and the remains were identified as Charles Coe. It was determined that one of the bones in the right lower leg, the leg tangled in the tree root, was broken. The Coroner ruled Coe's death was accidental. That he tripped, broke his leg, and hit his head. And that he probably was so drunk, he never regained consciousness."

"Did you make any other investigation of the scene?"

"Yes, sir. Several days later I realized that Coe's glasses were missing. I knew from previous experience with Mr. Coe that he always wore glasses, thick-lens glasses. He was practically blind without them. I went back to where his remains were found, and searched for his glasses, but I couldn't find them. I also checked the shack where he lived but I didn't see them. Later, I also checked with Coe's mother and she didn't have them either."

"Did you ever tell anyone about the missing glasses?"

"No, sir."

"Why not?"

"I figured that if Coe had gone on his own to the spot where his body was found, his glasses would have been found there. If his body had been placed there by someone, he probably had been murdered by a person who didn't have Coe's glasses with him. The missing glasses would be a clue that I would keep to myself. If someone else ever mentioned it, I could focus an investigation on that person."

"Did you ever make a further investigation?"

"Yes, sir. I read an article in that tabloid, the *Tattler*, and I followed up."

"Detective Miller," asked Saul, "what tabloid article was it that made you perform your investigation?"

"In April of this year the *Tattler* published an article about the person who supposedly killed Coe. In that article a stolen motorcycle was mentioned as the means of the killer's approach to the scene. After reading that article I checked our police records regarding thefts of motorcycles during the time frame that the pathologist gave for the death of Coe."

"Describe your investigation for the jury, please."

"I went back through police reports of criminal activities right around the time Coe disappeared. I found a report of an incident that didn't make sense at the time it happened but now is clear. A resident at 1548 North Fernwood Street reported that his motorcycle had been stolen. Hours later it was recovered a block from his house. The odometer hadn't changed by more than a few tenths of a mile, but the fuel in the tank was much lower and there were no signs the tank had leaked. There were graphite smears on the underside of the speedometer. It appeared as if someone had deliberately disconnected the speedometer cable, gone for a ride, returned the bike, and reconnected the cable."

"What effect would that business with the speedometer cable have?"

"Nobody could tell how far the bike had been ridden by the thief, and thus we couldn't determine where he might have been."

"Why would someone want to hide that information?"

The Glacier was on his feet. "Objection, speculation."

"Sustained," ruled the judge.

Saul didn't care. The question had been asked and the jury now had a mystery to think about. He'd hooked them right at the beginning of his case.

"Your witness, Mr. Abbott," said Saul.

The jurors leaned forward in their chairs.

Mattison, you're a prick, thought Abbott. This witness didn't do a thing to prove libel against my guys, so there's no reason to cross examine him. But you leave me with a mystery the jurors want explained. Abbott hesitated, shuffled papers on his counsel table and whispered with Porter and Abrams.

The judge interjected. "Mr. Abbott, do you wish to cross-examine this witness?"

The Glacier rose to his feet. "Yes, Your Honor, just a few questions."

"Detective Miller, can you describe Mr. Coe's height and weight the last time you saw him alive and tell us when that was?"

"I saw him several weeks before his death. He was about five feet nine and weighed approximately one hundred sixty pounds."

"Detective Miller, do you know Bryce Roberts personally, and if so for how long?"

"I've known Mr. Roberts since high school."

"In your opinion is Bryce Roberts strong enough to carry a deadweight of one hundred sixty pounds?"

"Objection!" cried Saul. "That question calls for speculation."

"Overruled," said the judge. "Mr. Mattison, you opened the door to this subject, so I'll allow the question."

"Yes, I think he's probably strong enough to do that," said Homer.

Abbott paused as if thinking of other points. Then he told the court, "No other questions, Your Honor."

"Mr. Mattison, call your next witness," said the judge.

"Your Honor, the Plaintiff calls Leon Porter as on cross examination."

Because Porter was an opposing party, the law allowed him to be called as a witness by the Plaintiff and be subjected to cross-examination, a much more effective, no-holds-barred, form of questioning.

Abbott objected. "Your Honor, Mr. Porter will be testifying on direct examination later in this case. He'll be available for cross-examination then."

"Objection overruled, Mr. Abbott. Mr. Porter, come forward and be sworn."

Porter came forward, took the witness' oath and identified himself. Mattison had him admit that he authored the first two articles and required him to read them aloud to the jury. While Porter was reading, Mattison displayed poster sized copies of the articles on easels for the jury to follow along.

Then Saul asked, "Did you ever speak to anyone in law enforcement regarding the death of Charles Coe?"

"Law enforcement? No. But, I read the Coroner's report and I tried to make an appointment with Detective Miller, but we didn't connect."

"Who did you contact about the appointment with Detective Miller?"

"Someone in the police department, but I don't remember who."

"Did you speak with anyone else about the death of Charles Coe?"

"Yes."

"Who?"

"Noah Coleman."

"Is he any relation to the late Marilyn Roberts?"

"He said he's her father."

"When and where did you speak with Noah Coleman?"

"April of this year at his home."

"What was his state of health at that time?"

"He said he was dying from cancer."

"Following your conversation with Noah Coleman did you write two more articles for the *Tattler* in which Charles Coe's death was the subject?"

"Yes."

"I show you what's been marked as Plaintiff's Exhibit five. Is that the edition of the *Tattler* in which your third article was published?"

"Yes."

"Will you read the article aloud to the jury, please?"

"*The Tattler* has learned more about the murder of Charles—"

"Excuse me, Mr. Porter. Will you start with the headline, please?"

The SEAL and the Skeleton - Part 3

Bucks County, PA - The *Tattler* has learned more about the murder of Charles Coe. A relative of Bryce Roberts has come forward to shoulder the blame for killing Coe. He denies that Roberts had anything to do with Coe's death. But there's a problem. The relative is dying. And with his death will go any means of confirming that he actually did what he takes the blame for. Is he telling the truth, or, is he trying to draw suspicion away from Roberts?

The relative claims that he stole a motorcycle to drive to Coe's house where he stealthily broke in and smothered Coe to death. Then he carried the body deep into the woods, dropped his head on a rock (that explains the fractured skull found on the skeleton) and put his foot under a tree root to make it look like an accident. It was good enough to fool the Coroner into thinking the death was accidental. However The *Tattler* has revealed that Coe was, in fact, murdered.

The article went on to again describe Bryce's relationship to Marilyn and the fact that Coe had killed her. The article ended with a report that, shortly after Coe's body was found, "the Roberts family interests bought Coe's land," and promised, "Next week's issue will feature more on this developing story."

Saul turned toward the jury before he continued his questioning. "Mr. Porter, did Noah Coleman tell you that he killed Charles Coe?

"Yes."

Saul waited for the jury to react and absorb the response.

"Did Coleman tell you anything else that's not printed in your story?"

"Not that I recall."

"What did he tell you about Charles Coe's eyeglasses, Mr. Porter?"

"I don't recall."

"Didn't Noah Coleman tell you that he forgot to take Coe's glasses out of the shack where Coe lived and drop them near the body?"

Bryce Roberts felt his pulse escalate and he forced himself to breathe slowly. He deliberately relaxed his back and neck. Saul had learned of the missing glasses. Now let's see how he uses that point, thought Bryce.

"He might have," said Porter, "but I don't recall that."

Saul looked upward and rolled his eyes in disbelief. "Mr. Porter, are you telling the jury that you can't remember details of an interview with a killer who told you a secret?

"I don't recall that." Porter's tone of voice was flat, unemotional.

Saul faced the jury and his expression returned to incredulity. "Even after Detective Miller's testimony?"

"That's correct."

"Mr. Porter, do you remember being served with written questions asking you about this case and written requests requiring you to produce any notes about your investigation and reporting of Coe's death?"

"Yes."

"And you answered those questions and requests under oath, didn't you?" Saul looked at the jury to let them knew something important was about to be revealed.

"Yes."

"Were all of your answers truthful?" Again Saul looked at the jury when he asked the question and the jury looked at the witness when Saul turned his head toward the witness stand.

Porter began to squirm and looked across the courtroom at The Glacier. His lawyer remained stone-faced.

"I believe so."

"Yes or no, Mr. Porter. Were all of your answers to those questions and requests truthful?"

"Yes."

"And you specifically responded, under oath, that you did not have any notes of your investigation?"

"Yes."

"Mr. Porter, I ask you again, did you make any notes during your investigation, particularly notes of your conversation with Noah Coleman?"

"I might have, but by the time you asked for them, I didn't have any."

Nice dodge, Porter, thought Saul, *but you're not going to get away with that.*

"Mr. Porter you and the *Tattler* were served with the complaint in this case before the third article you wrote was published, weren't you?"

"Yes, I believe so."

"Did you use your notes as a reference for that third article, Mr. Porter?"

"Yes."

"What did you do with your notes, Mr. Porter?"

"I threw them away."

"After you and your colleagues knew you were being sued?"

"I didn't need the notes anymore."

"Mr. Porter, let's go back and have a look at your third article."

Saul got the poster board and held it up so the jury could see it. "Don't you promise your readers that, "Next week's issue will feature more on this developing story."?

"That's what it says."

"Mr. Porter, if you were going to print 'More on this developing story', wouldn't you need your notes?"

"Yes, but we didn't publish any more stories."

Saul walked toward the jury box and stood immediately in front of the jurors. "Mr. Porter, did anyone tell you to get rid of your notes of the Coleman interview after the *Tattler* was served with this lawsuit?"

Porter made a mistake. He looked across at his attorney and editor. Then he answered.

"Not that I recall."

Liar! Liar, pants on fire! thought jurors number 7, 9 and 12.

Saul bored in. "Did you go to the police with what you learned?"

"No."

"Why not?"

"I wanted to protect the privacy of my source, the man who admitted to the murder."

"Did Mr. Noah Coleman ask you to keep his identity a secret?"

"I don't recall."

"Oh, come on, Mr. Porter. You've just testified that a man admitted to you, personally, that he committed murder. Are you telling the jury that you don't remember whether he asked you to keep that admission a secret?"

"I don't recall."

"Mr. Porter how was it that you came to interview Noah Coleman?"

"He telephoned me and told me he had some information on the Coe case."

"And he told you he wanted to clear Bryce Roberts' name didn't he?"

Porter hesitated. He was unsure whether this was an educated guess on Mattison's part, or whether the lawyer who now was tormenting him knew something. He'd known about the glasses.

Saul stalked toward the witness. "Yes or no Mr. Porter?"

"Yes, he said that he wanted to clear Mr. Robert's name."

"So there was no reason to protect the identity of Noah Coleman, was there?"

Porter looked at his feet. "No, I guess not."

"Noah Coleman expected to have his admission printed, didn't he?"

"Yes."

Saul turned to face the jury. He looked them in the eyes as he asked the next question.

"So, there really was another reason why you kept your information from the police, wasn't there?"

This wasn't what Porter had expected. He was being made to look like the obfuscator and liar that he was. He again looked at his attorney's table and Abbott returned his gaze with just a hint of a smile.

"Yes. I thought if I kept the identity of the murderer secret, I could milk the story for a few more weeks."

"That story was selling a lot of papers in this area, wasn't it?"

"Yes, it was. Our circulation was up by forty percent."

"And you didn't tell your readers that you'd learned Noah Coleman was the murderer, not Bryce Roberts?"

"We weren't sure who killed Coe, or even whether he was murdered."

"Isn't the real reason the fact that if you had revealed Noah Coleman's identity, your circulation in this area would have plummeted?"

"Objection! That question is uncalled for!" shouted Abbott, who'd been mentally squirming and dying through the examination.

"Objection overruled," said the judge. "Mr. Porter please answer the question."

"I don't know, maybe it would have," weaseled Porter.

Saul was shaking his head in disbelief but when he looked at the jurors, he saw the same expression on some of their faces. He resumed pummeling Porter.

"Mr. Porter, I'll ask you again. Did Noah Coleman say anything to you about Charles Coe's glasses?"

"I told you, I don't remember."

Saul shook his head in disbelief and sat down. "Your witness Mr. Abbott."

Abbott rose and walked toward the front of the jury box where he stopped and stood on his toes.

"Mr. Porter, was Noah Coleman telling you the truth when he spoke about his killing Charles Coe?" asked The Glacier.

"I don't know."

"Was anyone else there at the time you spoke with Noah Coleman?"

"No, sir."

Abbott assumed a look of innocence. "When you mentioned Bryce Roberts in your articles, did you have any personal anger or animosity toward him?"

"No. I just knew from researching articles about him at the local newspaper that he was an ex-SEAL and ex-major league ball player."

"Did you mean to libel him when you wrote your articles?"

"No. I just was trying to get our readers interested and excited."

Abbot turned toward the bench. "That's all I have, Your Honor."

Mattison saw an opening and jumped into it. He rose from counsel table and walked toward Porter.

"Did you care at all about Mr. Roberts' reputation when you wrote your articles that mentioned him and murder in the same paragraphs?"

"I'm used to people getting mad at me for what I write, Mr. Mattison."

"That wasn't my question. Mr. Porter, let me repeat: when you wrote your articles, did you have any care or concern for Mr. Roberts' reputation?"

"We care about people. It's just that I didn't think Mr. Roberts would get so offended."

"You didn't expect a man to be offended when he's wrongly accused of Murder? Do you really expect the jury to believe that?" Porter's face took on the look of a cornered animal.

"Come on Mr. Porter, answer my question, which I shall repeat once more.

"Mr. Porter, did you have any care or concern for Mr. Roberts' reputation when you wrote those three articles?"

Saul looked at the judge when Porter continued to hesitate.

"Mr. Porter, that is a proper question," ruled the judge. "Answer it."

"I wasn't thinking about that when I wrote the articles."

"So your answer is no, you didn't have a care about Mr. Roberts' reputation when you wrote your articles? Correct?"

"I suppose that's correct."

Saul knew when to sit down. "No further questions," he told the judge.

Abbott could not let that be the last testimony the jury heard from the witness. But, Christ, he thought, how do I rehabilitate this guy? He rose and asked, "You said you didn't think Mr. Roberts would be so offended. Why was that?"

"I thought he'd be a tough guy, what with his SEAL background and all.

"Thank you, Mr. Porter." Abbott got a better answer than he'd hoped and he knew when to quit.

Mattison asked only one follow-up question.

"Before you printed the articles, did you show any of them to Mr. Roberts and ask him what he thought about them?"

"No, sir."

The judge called the morning recess and reminded the jury the case still had more witnesses and directed them not to talk about the case among themselves.

"Who do you call next?" asked Bryce, as he and Mattison headed for the men's room.

"The editor, Hyman Abrams. He's going to have some explaining to do."

Chapter 122

Hyman Abrams was called as on cross examination. He didn't look like a newspaper editor. He looked like a golf pro—deeply tanned face and hands, light green sport coat, pale toned shirt, striped tie and loose, beautifully creased slacks with woven leather shoes. His reading glasses were tucked in his jacket's outside pocket.

Abbott was groaning inwardly over his client's appearance. He'd told Abrams to dress as if he were attending services at his synagogue. Damn! I should have been more specific!

Mattison led him through the preliminaries of his testimony and then got to the heart of his examination of the now worried witness. Saul picked up a blue-backed legal sized bundle of papers and asked the court's permission to approach the witness.

"Mr. Abrams, I show you what's previously been marked as Plaintiff Exhibit 6. For brevity we can agree that this is a copy of our pretrial interrogatories and requests for production of documents addressed to you?"

"Yes."

"And this is Plaintiff's Exhibit 7, a copy of your signed answers that you gave under oath?"

Abrams looked at the last page and saw his own signature. "Yes."

"Mr. Abrams will you please read aloud to the jury question number 8, the one I've marked with the red tab?"

Abrams pulled out his reading glasses and focused on the document. "Do you or the *Tattler* have in your possession or control any notes, memoranda or other written material prepared by you or any other employee of the *Tattler* regarding any statements by any person with knowledge about the matters set forth in the complaint filed against you?"

"And, under oath, you answered "no" to that question, didn't you?"

"That's correct."

"And that would have included any notes made by Mr. Porter regarding his interview with Noah Coleman?"

"Yes, I suppose so."

"Mr. Abrams, did you ever see Leon Porter's notes of the interview he had with Noah Coleman?"

"Yes, I believe I did."

"Do you know what happened to those notes, Mr. Abrams?"

"No, I don't."

Saul moved to his counsel table and opened a thin exhibit folder. He provided a copy of documents to Abbott and the judge. Then he asked the court stenographer to mark the papers as Plaintiff's Exhibit 9.

By the time the stenographer was finished marking the exhibits, Abbott was on his feet.

"Objection, Your Honor, these documents were not provided to me before trial. I have no way of authenticating them and they appear to contradict Mr. Mattison's own witness' testimony."

"Mr. Mattison?" asked the court.

"Your Honor, these documents are not offered for the purpose of contradiction. They're offered for the purpose of showing malice, an essential element of proof of libel; and, also to prove that the editor of the *Tattler* knew that his articles insinuating Bryce Roberts is a murderer are false."

"Why didn't you provide them to defense before now?" demanded the judge.

"May counsel approach sidebar, please?" asked Saul.

"Yes." The judge motioned to the court stenographer to join the attorneys at the bench where they spoke in hushed tones out of the hearing of the jury and others in the courtroom.

"This had better be good, Mr. Mattison," said the judge. "I don't permit trial by ambush in my courtroom."

"Your Honor, I received these documents yesterday morning before we picked the jury. I didn't know whether they're authentic until last night when my associates checked them out with the source. I was concerned for the physical safety of the individual

who provided them to me. And I also was concerned that the
originals would be destroyed if they were revealed before now."

"Why haven't you produced the originals?"

"They are . . . in transit at the moment."

"What are they?"

"Leon Porter's notes."

"Let me see them, please." said the judge. He adjusted his
glasses and reviewed the documents. Then he looked at Abbott.

"Mr. Abbott, I think these documents do more than self-
contradict a witness who is testifying as on cross examination.
Under the new rules of civil procedure that's not a valid objection
anymore. In the interest of truth I'm going to allow the witness to
be questioned on these documents. Mr. Abbott, you may have an
exception to my ruling. Mr. Mattison, when will the original set be
available?"

"By tomorrow, Your Honor."

"You shall allow Mr. Abbott to review them before court
convenes tomorrow morning. All right, counsel, let's continue with
the examination of this witness," said the judge.

Saul returned to the floor in front of the witness, waited
politely for the court stenographer to put her equipment back in
order and then resumed.

"Now, Mr. Abrams, I believe you had just told the jury that
you didn't know what happened to Mr. Porter's notes of his
interview with Noah Coleman?"

"Yes."

"Mr. Abrams, I show you what has been marked as Plaintiff's
Exhibit 9. Can you tell the jury what those documents are?"

Hyman Abrams turned through the pages. As he did a red
line began at his collar and worked its way up his neck and face
until he was crimson to his balding pate.

"This looks like a copy of Leon's notes."

"Notes of what, Mr. Abrams?"

"His interview with Coleman."

"Do you recognize Mr. Porter's handwriting?"

"Yes, this is his handwriting."

"How about the different handwriting in the upper left corner
of the first page? Whose is that?"

Abrams hesitated for a long moment and looked at Abbott
for a hint on how to handle the question. Abbott was of no help.

"It's mine," he said in a low voice.

"What does your handwriting say, Mr. Abrams?"

In barely audible tones he said, "Burn these."

"I'm sorry, Mr. Abrams, I don't think the jury heard you. Please repeat what your handwriting says."

"Burn these."

"To whom did you give those instructions?"

"Mr. Leon Porter," answered Abrams in a tone that said he was glad to have someone else mentioned.

Saul's voice turned accusatory. "You knew that if the notes were found, they could be used to show Bryce Roberts had nothing to do with Charles Coe's death, right?"

"That's one possibility."

"Mr. Abrams, in here there's a note that Porter made about the glasses and how Noah Coleman forgot about them, isn't there?"

"Yes."

"And you and Porter knew that the fact the glasses were missing was never revealed to the public?"

"Yes."

"And thus only the murderer would know about the glasses?"

"There was some thinking like that."

"Coleman knew about the missing glasses and therefore he could be the murderer as he claimed, right?"

"I suppose so."

"And if you and your tabloid kept insinuating that Bryce Roberts murdered Charles Coe you could be sued for libel?"

"Well, we could be sued, but whether we're guilty is another matter," Abrams said in a condescending manner.

"Mr. Abrams, if a newspaper knows that an article about someone is untrue and deliberately publishes it anyway, that's libel, isn't it?

"Sometimes."

"Mr. Abrams, isn't that what you and the people at the *Tattler* did? Knowingly publish a lie when your tabloid insinuated that Bryce Roberts murdered Charles Coe?

"Well it could have been true, too."

"Why, Mr. Abrams?"

"Coleman could have been lying."

"Wouldn't Porter's notes help you prove that one way or the other?"

"They might have."

Saul pointed an accusing finger at the witness. "Mr. Abrams, isn't it true you ordered those notes burned because you thought they would incriminate you and your paper?"

"Not really. I just didn't want them around."

Saul turned toward the jury and rolled his eyes. Then while still facing the jury he asked again.

"Oh, come on, Mr. Abrams. Admit you ordered those notes burned because you thought they could burn you and the *Tattler*. Yes or no, Mr. Abrams, and then you may explain."

"Well, it depends upon how you read them."

Saul knew he'd made Abrams look like the liar he was and he decided to move on to another point.

"Did Mr. Derek Cowper know the stories about Bryce Roberts were untrue?"

"Objection!" cried Abbot. "The witness is being asked to read another man's mind."

"I'll rephrase the question," said Saul.

"Did Mr. Cowper see Porter's notes?"

Abrams cringed. He looked at counsel table and his publisher, and then shrugged his shoulders as he answered.

"Yes."

"So the same information that led you to believe Bryce Roberts was not Coe's killer was available to Mr. Cowper?"

"He knew the same things I did."

"Do you know why he allowed the articles to be published?"

"Those articles were selling a lot of newspapers."

"Did Leon Porter know the articles about Coe and Bryce Roberts were untrue?"

Glad to shift the blame elsewhere, Abrams responded, "After he interviewed Coleman, he may have. Ask him, not me."

Saul turned, moved to the front of the jury box, and paced back and forth as if in deep thought. Then he asked his next question.

"Mr. Abrams, did you once, during the time that your tabloid, the *Tattler*, was publishing the stories about Coe and Roberts ever pause to think about the harm the *Tattler* was doing to the reputation of Bryce Roberts?"

"No, sir."

Saul shook his head in disgust. "Your witness, Mr. Abbott."

"Counsel, and members of the jury," said the Judge, "we're already into the lunch hour. This is a good time to take a recess. The jurors are reminded not to discuss this case among themselves or with others."

The court crier banged his gavel and announced that court would be in recess until 1:30 p.m.

The newspaper reporters in the courtroom made mad dashes for the telephones. Derek Cowper wanted desperately to call his office but there were queues at each of the phones in the court house hallways. Damn the delay!

Chapter 123

Cowper made his call from the payphone in the restaurant where he and The Glacier, as well as Abrams and Porter, had gone for lunch.

"What do you mean she called in sick yesterday?" ranted Cowper into the mouthpiece. Then he listened. "Why didn't someone tell me about this? . . . Where is she, damn it? . . . What do you mean you don't know? . . . Okay . . . Yes, call Mr. Abbott's office the minute you locate her." Cowper hung up and returned to the table.

"Hy, your Ms. Mammaries dimed us. She called in sick yesterday and today. No one answers at her home phone."

Hy Abrams put his chin in his hands. "Derek, we have to settle this before the jury gets this case. If we don't, we're going to get clobbered."

"He's right, Derek," said Abbott. "The question now is how much do we offer?"

"What was their last demand?" asked Cowper.

"2.5 million."

"Jeezuss Ke-riiist! We can't afford that! The *Tattler* will be out of business at that amount."

"What should we offer?" asked Abrams.

"What if one of us wants to settle and the others don't?" asked Porter.

Abbott looked at Porter. "At the beginning of this case you three signed an agreement and waiver that you'd use me as your attorney despite a possible conflict of interest if I represent all defendants. Now that conflict has come into play. I can try to settle you out, Leon, but the other two of you are going to have to agree to my negotiating just on your behalf."

"Is there any way you can get the insurance carrier to change its mind about coverage?" asked Abrams.

"Not without a lawsuit," said Abbott, "and after what I heard today, there won't be coverage because the jury would be entitled to find the libel was deliberate."

Their sandwiches came and the four men gobbled down their lunch and headed back to the courthouse.

"Leon, let's wait until the end of the day to talk settlement for you," said Abbott as they walked up the steps inside the court house. Right now I have some damage control to do."

"How? With what?" asked Cowper.

"The law. What you printed was deliberate but there's still a question over whether it actually defamed Roberts."

⸻

Bryce sat in Saul's office conference room at the end of the first day of trial. He waited until Saul quickly returned telephone calls and that gave Bryce time to ponder his approach to Saul. He had to learn how much more Saul knew.

Saul entered the conference room. He was smiling until he saw the expression on his client's face.

"What's up, Bryce?"

"How did you get Porter's notes?"

Saul looked curiously at Bryce. "A woman who worked for the *Tattler* has a conscience. When she saw what they were doing to you, she kept some documents rather than destroying them as she was instructed. She delivered them to me two days ago."

"Did you do anything to check her out?"

"That's why I couldn't produce the notes right away. My staff worked overtime to investigate her background. She came up clean. She is who she says she is."

"Why didn't you tell me about this?"

"I needed to concentrate on how best to use the notes and I didn't think you could be of any help in that respect."

Bryce was quiet for a long moment, then he asked, "What else did she give you?"

"Another internal memo and the latest financial statements for the corporation that owns the *Tattler.*"

"May I see them, please?"

"They want to settle," said Saul. "But the price isn't right. They offered two hundred thousand dollars. So we continue with the trial tomorrow. When you see the financial statement you'll understand why we're being low-balled in the negotiations." He pulled a folder from among the several thick files on the table and handed it to Bryce.

Bryce's practiced eye quickly reviewed the columns of numbers, some of which astounded him.

"They make that much on advertising?"

"Yes, and they pay out a minimum in costs. They don't own their own printing presses, so they go out to several printers and get competitive bids."

"Saul, it's my family's principle to give no quarter when we're attacked. I really want to put these people out of business. What do you think the jury will do with this bunch? Do we go with the jury or do we settle?"

"Let the jury decide. I think they'll whack 'em pretty hard. But keep this in mind: juries can be fickle. I've had cases where they should have brought back a big award and they came through with a pittance."

"After Abbott's tedious cross exam do you think the jury will favor that bunch of creeps?"

"Abbott may not have made too many points with the jury, but he did okay with the judge. The judge first must rule on whether the articles could be defamatory. If the judge thinks the jury could determine that the articles, under the law, could be defamatory, the jury gets to decide the case. Abbott basically was arguing to the court that each individual sentence in those articles doesn't amount to libel and, therefore, the case should not go to the jury. It's technical, but that's all that he has left to go on, so he's doing the best he can."

"What do you think the judge will do?"

"I don't know because he has to hear the whole case before he rules. Meanwhile, let's concentrate on our case."

"Does Candace testify tomorrow?"

"Yes, after Deforth and Jamison testify about their reactions to the articles and the reaction of the community. Don't worry, Bryce,

I put Candace through a tougher practice cross-examination than Abbott will give her in the courtroom. She'll be fine."

"What about this other document that you mentioned the *Tattler* employee gave you? May I see that please?" asked Bryce.

"I want you to testify before you see it, Bryce. Then you can have a look at it."

Chapter 124

C andace Roberts' hair was done in a conservative curl
that framed her fine-featured face. She wore a beautifully
tailored bankers' grey pinstriped double breasted suit. The narrow-
pleated skirt extended slightly below her knees, leaving just
enough of her model's legs exposed. Her light blue silk blouse was
complimented by a string of small pearls. Her high heels were just
short enough to be appropriate for court, but high enough to give
her walk to the witness stand a beautiful rippling movement in the
pleated skirt.

Every eye in the courtroom followed her to the witness stand.
Even the Glacier felt himself stirring as she walked. Then he
chastised himself. Damn! The woman's gorgeous and there're six
men on the jury. I should have taken her deposition. But the guys
at the *Tattler* were too damned cheap to spend the money. Now, it
comes back to haunt them.

Mattison led Candace through her biography, education, and
employment, and then began the meat of his questioning.

"Mrs. Roberts, are you related to Bryce Roberts?"

"He is my husband."

"How long have you been married?"

Candace turned to the jury and spoke to them while she
responded to the questions that followed.

"We had our second anniversary in May."

"Do you have any children?"

"Yes, Edward, who is eight; Anne, who just turned seven;
and, Daniel, who was born last November 19th."

"Mrs. Roberts have you read the three articles published in
the *Tattler* that mention your husband and Charles Coe?"

"Yes."

"Do you know if your children are aware of the articles?"

"Yes, Edward and Anne are."

"Please explain your answer."

"In March the day the first *Tattler* article was published the children came home from school. When they got off the bus, Anne was crying and Eddie had a black eye. I learned that the kids on the bus had been teasing them. They had called . . ."

"Objection, hearsay," said Abbott. He had to do something to throw this lovely woman off her stride. She was the epitome of femininity and professionalism rolled into one, and, she was talking to the jury about children. The expressions of the men on the jury showed they were just plain enamored of her and the ladies showed none of the catty reactions usually brought on when faced with a more attractive woman. They seemed willing to listen to a woman who had advanced to the rank of professor and they were charmed over her talk of children.

"Your honor," responded Saul, "if Mr. Abbott wants us to drag a couple of children into this courtroom we can produce them. More to the point, the testimony is not offered for the truth of the statement but rather to explain a course of conduct," replied Saul.

Candace turned and looked at the judge with her deep blue eyes.

"Objection overruled," he said.

"Mrs. Roberts, you may continue, please," said Saul.

Candace again turned toward the jury.

"I put my arms around them and asked what was wrong. They told me the kids on the bus had been mocking them. The other children called their father a murderer. Eddie got into a fight over that and I later learned the school bus driver had to stop the bus and separate Eddie and the boy who was talking the loudest about it."

"What did you do next?"

"I asked the children what made the other kids say that their father was a murderer and they replied that the other kids' parents had read it in the newspaper. Then I put it together. Mr. Porter had telephoned me earlier that month and asked me what I thought about Charles Coe's death. I didn't reply and just hung up. I also learned that Porter had spoken with my husband about

Coe's death, so I put two and two together and went to the supermarket. The *Tattler* was sold out, but the manager had saved a copy at his desk. He saw me and gave me that . . . tabloid.

"Sold out did you say?"

"Yes. Most of the time when I go to the supermarket there are always copies of that . . . tabloid on the racks. But this time none were to be seen."

"How did that make you feel?"

"Just plain awful. I knew that the whole community would hear about my husband being labeled as a murderer."

"Objection! Cried Abbott. "It's for the court and this jury to decide whether the article made that accusation."

"Your Honor, the witness can testify about her own feelings."

"Objection overruled."

"Mrs. Roberts, what did you do with the copy of the *Tattler* that was given to you?"

"I took it home, found the article, read it, cried, and then telephoned my husband."

"Afterward, did you notice anything different about the way your two older children behaved around their father?"

"Yes. They actually seemed afraid of him when he first got home. He sat on the couch and took one in each arm and talked with them about the situation. They understood that the article wasn't true and they began to warm up to him. But it took a couple of days for them to really get back to the way they usually are around Bryce."

"How is that?

"He and the children are very close. Family means everything to my husband."

"Mrs. Roberts what did your husband do after he talked with his children?"

"We let the children go out to play in the back yard. Bryce just sat there on the couch and tears came to his eyes. He looked at me and said, "My god! My own children are afraid of me! How heartless of those . . ." and then he used some very . . . descriptive language about the *Tattler*.

Several of the jurors grinned and Candace smiled back at them.

"What effect has the series of articles had on your marriage?"

"Each time another one was published we had a strain on our relationship because the articles would put my husband into a foul mood that made him difficult to talk with and be with for weeks afterward."

"How are things with your husband and children now?"

"The emotional strain is still there, but we're doing our best to deal with it."

"That's all I have from this witness, your Honor," said Saul.

J. Henderson Abbott rose to his feet but stayed at counsel table. He began his attack immediately.

"Mrs. Roberts, do you think that your husband was capable of killing Charles Coe?

"Objection, your honor," cried Saul. "It's irrelevant what Mrs. Roberts thinks in that respect."

"What is the purpose of your question, Mr. Abbott?" queried the judge.

"The jury may have to determine that issue, Your Honor. What better person to ask than the wife of the man who claims he's not a killer?"

"Your honor," replied Saul, "my client is not on trial here, the defendants are."

"Your Honor," countered Abbott, "even if my clients heard Coleman admit he killed Coe, the jury still could believe our doubts about Coleman's confession were enough to turn suspicion toward Roberts and remove the malice claimed by the Plaintiff."

"It's close, but I'll allow the question," ruled the judge.

"Mrs. Roberts, do you remember my question?"

"Yes. You want to know if I think my husband was capable of killing Charles Coe. My answer is: perhaps, in an abstract sense. But in reality, he's too self-disciplined and too decent and kind to do something like that."

"You love your husband very much, don't you?"

"Yes. In every way."

"You would say then, that he is not capable of violence?"

"You said that, I didn't."

"Then, is your husband capable of physical violence, Mrs. Roberts?"

"I've seen it only once when he rescued me from people who had threatened to blow up the college building where I and other faculty members were being held hostage."

"What kind of violence was that, Mrs. Roberts?"

The jurors leaned forward, all attentive, now.

"Bryce overpowered one of my captors. He hit the man in the back, right at the neck and then he punched him in the stomach."

"What else did you see your husband do to that man?"

"He tied him up with duct tape and made him tell where he put the dynamite."

"Made him tell? Mrs. Roberts, how did your husband do that?"

"Grabbed him by the hair and asked him. The man then told him, and Bryce telephoned the police. Then he and his brother got me and all of the hostages out of the building."

"But he left people who were tied up in a building full of dynamite?

"I think Bryce felt nothing could happen if those people were tied up. Also, Bryce didn't know it at the time, but as you can see from that police report in front of you, the captors used fake or dummy dynamite."

Saul's signal and preparation had worked perfectly. He was holding a pen horizontally under his chin to indicate that Abbott was using the police report. But Saul had his eyes on the jury to determine their reaction. Several of the women were smiling.

"So the dynamite was a fake. Then why the violence?"

"Perhaps you misunderstood. We didn't learn the dynamite was fake until afterward. Bryce didn't know that and acted accordingly."

Abbott regrouped. Nobody is going to say I didn't do my best in the defense of this case, he thought. Onward and upward!

"Mrs. Roberts, do you and your husband know a man named Abraham Rabinowicz?"

"Yes. He's a sweet, elderly man who owns a jewelry shop in Doylestown."

"Are you familiar with an incident in which your husband beat up three men who were annoying Mr. Rabinowicz?"

"Mr. Abbott, the three men were trying to rob Mr. Rabinowicz in a train station in Philadelphia. My husband intervened. From what Mr. Rabinowicz later told me . . ."

Let's see if Abbott objects to the hearsay response to his own question, thought Saul.

Abbott didn't object because he knew what the jury's reaction would be.

". . . Bryce tried to talk the robbers out of it and when they didn't go away he used the minimum force necessary."

"Do you consider a dislocated elbow minimum force?"

"I . . . I wasn't there to see what was going on, but I understand that one of the men pulled a knife and tried to stab Bryce. He defended himself. Isn't that what your copy of the police report says?"

"Mrs. Roberts did your husband hate Charles Coe?"

"He had mixed feelings about him. On the one hand he felt sorry for Coe because he was not all there, mentally; but, on the other hand, I think there also was hatred."

"Particularly after Coe attacked you?"

"At that time my impression was that Bryce was more concerned about our family's safety. He hired a bodyguard to protect me and the children. I think he saw Coe more as a menace to us than a target of hatred."

"But you're not denying your husband hated Coe?"

"I think that question is better directed to my husband. After all, he's the one who experienced the emotions first hand."

"Did your husband ever talk to you about his feelings?

Saul Mattison rose to his feet and stood near the jury. "Objection. Marital privilege," he told the court.

The judge paused. He knew it was underhanded for Abbott to ask that question and require Saul to object. It made it appear that the Roberts were hiding something. The judge then instructed the jury.

"Ladies and gentlemen of the jury, in general, it is the law in Pennsylvania that confidential communications between a husband and wife are not to be inquired into in court. The rule preserves the privacy that's needed to foster good communications in a marriage. Therefore I will sustain Mr. Mattison's objection."

Saul was grateful. Under the guise of instructing the jury, the judge told them that Abbott was out-of-bounds.

"Did you hate Charles Coe, Mrs. Roberts?"

"It was more fear than hatred toward him. What I hated was living day-after-day not knowing whether Coe would come back again to try to attack me or the children."

Abbott finally gave up. Candace Roberts was one of the most well-prepared witnesses he'd ever examined. Saul, hat's off to you.

"No further questions, Your Honor."

"Any re-direct, Mr. Mattison?" asked the judge.

"No, Your Honor."

"Mr. Mattison, how many more witnesses do you have?"

"One, possibly, two, Your Honor. It will depend upon whether Mr. Abbott intends to call Mr. Cowper to the witness stand." Saul looked at Abbott. Let's see if I can smoke Hendie out on that.

Abbott wouldn't go for it. "I may call him, your honor, but at this point I want to be flexible on that."

The court then recessed for lunch. Candace, who had remained in the courtroom, held her husband's hand as the jury filed out. Then she joined Saul and Bryce for lunch.

After lunch a very large man, who bore a striking resemblance to a part-time skycap, escorted Candace to her car. Bryce wasn't taking any chances with the guys from Florida in town and he couldn't be with Candace because his testimony was to begin that afternoon.

Chapter 125

B ryce Roberts wished fervently that he could just get off the witness stand and do something physical like joining Phillip in a swimming pool for laps and informal races. He endured Saul's leading him through an extensive biography and the account of Coe's murder of Marilyn while he was home on leave. Then it was on to UDT, baseball, Wharton, and his marriage to Candace and his business experience. Bryce genuinely disliked talking about himself, and it showed through on the witness stand. What he didn't realize was occurring during the time Saul prodded him along was the growing respect the jurors developed for the thirty-two year old man who had accomplished much in his short lifetime and thus had a lot to lose if his reputation was ruined.

Then Saul took him through the anguish the articles had brought: first, to him and his family and then in public life. Bryce related how he was up for election to an assistant chairmanship of one of his Republican Committees, only to have the nomination tabled as a result of the articles. Saul took him through the incidents with Abraham Rabinowicz to get a first-hand account and then more briefly with the rescue of Candace.

Then Saul wrapped up his last questions.

"Mr. Roberts, how well did you know your former father-in-law, Noah Coleman?"

"I knew him from the time I was a teenager when Marilyn and I began to date."

"Was Noah Coleman a strong man?"

"Yes, he lifted weights for all of the time I knew him."

"Did you ever see him ride a motorcycle?"

"Yes, he owned a mid-sized Harley Davison and helped me learn how to drive a bike with a passenger on the back."

"What were his feelings about Charles Coe after Marilyn's death?"

"He took Marilyn's death very hard, as we all did. She was his only child and the apple of his eye. He never was the same after she was killed. Noah hated Charles Coe and used to get angry with me when I would remind him that Coe was not all there, mentally."

"Mr. Roberts, in your mind, is there anything inconsistent with Noah Coleman murdering Charles Coe?"

"Objection, Your Honor," called Abbott. "He's asking the witness to speculate, and that's really a question for the jury to decide."

The judge looked at Saul, and said, "Well, Mr. Mattison?"

"It's a layman's opinion on a subject of common observation, much like a lay witness can testify to his opinion on another's intoxication."

"Your question asks Mr. Roberts to probe the psyche of another man. I'm going to sustain the objection."

"I'll move on, Your Honor." Saul turned and looked at the jury, almost as if he was asking them the next question.

"Mr. Roberts, did you kill Charles Coe?

Saul turned toward Bryce and every eye on the jury followed.

"No, I wanted the law to deal with him. I figured he'd be arrested soon after he attacked Candace. I knew he'd go back to jail because he was in violation of his parole; and, then he'd have to answer for his felony assault on my wife. Coe would be in jail and out of our lives for a long time—probably twenty years or more. There was no need to kill him in order to protect my family."

The recess began and The Glacier stayed at his counsel table and worked desperately to develop a counter punch to the last testimony given by Bryce Roberts. But how do you argue with common sense? You don't. You admit it and propose other alternatives. But which ones? Abbott thought for minutes and then feverishly worked on fleshing out an idea.

Chapter 126

"**M**r. Roberts," began Abbott, "let's talk about the land where Coe lived. Are you familiar with it?"

"It's a forty acre woodlot."

"Who owns that lot now?"

"It's owned by a division of Sunrise Lumber Company."

"And who owns Sunrise Lumber Company?"

"Sunrise's stock is owned by members of my family, including myself."

"When did your company buy that land and from whom?"

"The week after Coe's body was found. I don't remember the exact date. Coe's mother owned the land and Sunrise purchased it from her."

"And then didn't Sunrise immediately bulldoze the house where Coe lived?"

"Yes, but it was a two room wooden and tarpaper shack in very bad condition."

"What was done with the rubble from the house?"

"The wood and tarpaper were hauled to a local landfill."

"Why was that done so soon after Coe's death?"

Do I correct him on the date of death or do I let it go? thought Bryce. Correct him. He saw Mattison rising to his feet to object.

Saul reasoned that no way would he allow the jury to lose sight of the fact that Coe disappeared and Bryce had a bodyguard for months afterward.

"Object to the form of the question, Your Honor," said Saul. "The evidence shows Coe's death was determined to be in the fall of last year. His remains were discovered in February of this year. The property was purchased thereafter."

"I'll rephrase the question, Your Honor," offered Abbott.

"Wasn't the house demolished the same week Coe was buried?"

"Yes. The shack was in horrible condition. It had a very bad sanitation problem and was a fire hazard. Kids play on that land and some run small game trap lines on it. We didn't want children playing in that shack or trying to start a fire in the Franklin Stove. We also promised Coe's mother that we'd tear it down. She didn't want such an awful place as a memorial to her son."

"And the area where Coe's remains were found. What did you do with that?

"Sunrise Lumber Company cleared it and replanted the area with trees. We believed that would keep curiosity seekers away and satisfy Mrs. Coe's concerns."

"Didn't those actions, the rapid demolition of the house and clearing of the land, hinder the investigation into Coe's death?"

"The coroner ruled the death was accidental. So there was no concern about an investigation."

"You moved quickly, right after the discovery of Coe's body, to buy that land, didn't you?"

"Well, correction. I didn't buy the land or make the decision to do so. That was my father's decision. Sunrise is in the lumber business and that land is forested. We believed that the property should be conserved in its natural state rather than become a housing development. So it was good for that purpose, and, eventually, its trees could be selectively harvested."

"So your family will make money off that land?"

"Perhaps, someday. If we take care of it properly, the land will repay us, just as a farmer's fields repay him with a good harvest."

"That's valuable land, then, isn't it?"

"Yes."

"But it didn't come on the market until Mrs. Coe's son died?"

Saul looked at the jury and decided not to object. Hammer him Bryce, just like we practiced.

"Until Charles Coe's remains were found, yes. Mrs. Coe lived in Colorado. She had no practical way of overseeing the land from there and she wanted to sell so she would have a secure retirement. She received a very fair price. There was nothing devious or suspicious about the transaction. Your clients' tabloid is the only thing that's devious and suspicious, Mr. Abbott."

"Your Honor, I move to strike that last response!" screeched Abbott.

"It's stricken. The jury will ignore the last comment regarding the *Tattler*."

But the damage had been done.

Abbott then tried to take Bryce through his use of force but didn't do any better at trial than in Bryce's deposition. It was late in the afternoon when he finished his questioning.

Saul had only a few questions on redirect and then the court recessed for the day.

Bryce made a beeline to counsel table and asked to return to Saul's office before he went home.

"You really want to see that other paper I have, don't you?"

"Yes. What's in it?"

"We're going to use it with Cowper . . ."

⊱≋⊰

When Bryce arrived home that evening Candace was trying on her maternity clothes. His heart melted at the sight. He knew that Candace had waited until he was due to arrive at home before she got the clothes out of mothballs. It was her way of telling him the news and doing something practical at the same time. Wordlessly, they embraced long and lovingly.

"When is he due?"

"Don't you think it's time for a girl?"

"Okay, when is she due?"

"February." Candace watched as Bryce did the mental calculations.

"That picnic by the stream?"

Candace nodded and the mischievous look began in her eyes.

"Woman, you're just plain devious." Then, still hugging her, her husband laughed at how she had maneuvered him into the tryst.

"We're going to have to think of a very special name for this one. Maybe something like, 'Picnic'."

"Perhaps something more subtle, so the kids won't tease her. How about 'Brooke'?"

"Perfect. Why did you wait so long to tell me?"

"This pregnancy has been different. I wanted to be sure. Honey, I think we're going to have twins."

Bryce continued to hold her and his grip gentled. "What does the doctor say?"

"He says it's too early to tell, but I think it's twins. They run in my family."

"What are we going to name the other one?"

"Let's wait to be sure. In the meantime are you okay with twins?"

"I'm okay with that," he said softly, not wanting to let go of the woman who now was giving them another life, and, perhaps, two.

"Bryce, when you arrived home there was something upbeat about you. What happened in court today?"

"Today went okay. It's tomorrow that I'm going to enjoy. Saul wants you there for the last day and the closing even though you wiggled out of court today. If Saul can pull this off, you're going to love it . . ."

Chapter 127

First thing in the morning, Saul called the publisher, Derek Cowper, to the witness stand.

Cowper was fat, but his tailor's skill in crafting the custom-made silk suit hid some of his corpulence. Cowper's custom-made shirt and necktie went perfectly with the suit. He was balding over much of his head and his clipped black moustache was neatly groomed.

As Cowper moved past his table toward the witness stand Bryce could hear his labored breathing, characteristic of obese people when they had to make even small exertions. Cowper took the witness stand and his scalp began to glisten with a thin film of perspiration. He smiled ingratiatingly at the jury but his light brown, squinty eyes couldn't hold on the juror's faces.

After eliciting his identity and responsibilities at the tabloid, Saul showed him a copy of the letter he sent to the Tattler that requested a retraction of and apology for the first article.

Cowper admitted he received the letter.

"But the *Tattler* published no retraction and no apology?"

"That's correct."

"Mr. Cowper, are you the person at the *Tattler* who decides whether the paper makes a retraction or apology?"

"Ultimately, yes."

"Do you confer with others at the paper before deciding?"

"Sometimes."

"Did you speak with anyone about Mr. Robert's request for a retraction and apology?"

"I spoke with Porter and Abrams."

"Did either one of them advise you to apologize or print a retraction?"

"I don't remember what they told me. I just remember deciding not to consider your request."

"Were there any memos or other notes passed among you regarding the requested apology and retraction?"

Shit! He wouldn't be asking me that question unless Ms. Mammaries gave him something . . . Damn, I honestly don't remember . . . Oh, wait a minute there was a memo from Porter, but what the hell did it say?

"I remember Porter gave a memo to Hy Abrams and me, but I honestly don't remember its details."

"Did you produce the memo as part of the request for documents that was served upon you?"

"No, I don't think so."

"Where is Porter's memo, Mr. Cowper?" Saul walked toward his counsel table and the small stack of exhibit folders sitting ready to be used.

Several of the jurors moved to more attentive postures.

"I don't know."

"Did you or anyone else at the *Tattler* give instructions to destroy the memo to which you are referring?"

"No. I think it probably just got thrown away."

"Mr. Cowper, if you could see a copy of the memo, would that refresh your recollection of what it says?"

Aw, shit! "Obviously."

By then Saul was at his counsel table and opened a thin folder. He handed a paper to Abbott, who began reading it. Abbott huffed repeatedly as he read. Bryce thought he appeared ready to go ballistic.

Saul had the court reporter label the exhibit and hand it to the judge. The judge examined it and put it on the bench in front of him. Saul handed Cowper a copy and asked the witness with a now very worried expression,

"Is this a copy of the Porter memo to which you referred?"

"Yes."

Abbott rose and objected. "Your Honor, under the rules of discovery, we should have been furnished with this memo as soon as Mr. Mattison obtained it. I move that it be stricken and that the witness not be questioned regarding it."

"Your Honor," replied Saul, "they're the ones who didn't produce this memo as required by our pretrial document requests. Now we have the pot calling the kettle black."

"Your Honor," countered Abbott, "this witness thought the memo had been thrown away. That's why the *Tattler* didn't produce it."

"Gentlemen, come to sidebar," instructed the judge. The lawyers complied and huddled with the judge and court stenographer.

Bryce and Candace said silent prayers that the judge would rule that Saul could use the memo.

"I've heard enough," chastised the judge quietly. "I think both your clients, Mr. Abbott, and you, Mr. Mattison, have played fast and loose with the rules. That being the case I'm going to rule on the side of rough justice. The memo may be used and the witness questioned on it. I reserve my ruling on whether it may be admitted into evidence and shown to the jury."

Saul returned to a position near the jury box and continued his questioning. He saw that Cowper had turned quite pale under his Florida tan and that he was sweating profusely from the top of his head.

"Mr. Cowper, will you please examine what has been marked as Plaintiff's Exhibit ten? Go ahead, pick it up Mr. Cowper."

Cowper picked it up and the paper shook as a result of his nervousness.

"In that memo does Porter attach a copy of his first article he wrote and my letter requesting a retraction and an apology to the Roberts family?"

"Yes, that's what it says."

"Do you remember whether you saw Porter's article at the time you first read this memo?"

"I must have."

"Whose initials appear in the upper right corner of the memo?"

"Mr. Abrams'."

"So he saw the memo and passed it on to you?"

"Yes."

"What did Porter write in the memo?"

"'These are decent folks. No skin off our noses if we do apologize or retract.'"

"What did you respond, Mr. Cowper?"

Cowper sat there in the witness' chair, silent, but looking in desperation at his attorney. Abbott stared back but said nothing. The collar of Cowper's custom made shirt began to stain from his perspiration.

Saul's voice grated as he repeated his question. "Mr. Cowper, what is the response that you wrote on the request for a retraction and apology?

"PISS ON THEM."

"Your words are all in capital letters?"

"Yes."

"Mr. Cowper," asked Saul in a tone that was pure ice, "at the time when you wrote 'PISS ON THEM' had anyone in the Roberts family, Candace or Bryce or their children, ever done you or anyone else at the *Tattler* any harm?"

"No."

The tone in which Saul asked the question reminded Bryce of the family principle he'd spoken of in Saul's conference room. When someone has deliberately tried to harm you, give no quarter in defending yourself.

Saul was giving no quarter. He walked back to his counsel table and opened another folder. Every one of the jurors leaned forward. Looking from the folder to the witness, Saul asked:

"Mr. Cowper, do you know where Charles Coe's glasses are right now?"

Cowper vomited—all over his custom tailored trousers and Italian shoes.

The judge turned to his court clerk and instructed him to call a recess. The jury returned to their deliberation room and Abbott ushered his wobbly client to the men's room. Custodians appeared and began to clean and disinfect the witness stand. The stench of bile gradually was replaced with the odor of pine.

The Glacier returned to the courtroom and huddled with Saul Mattison in the front corner away from the witness stand. From his seat at counsel table Bryce watched as Saul listened politely. He saw his lawyer nod in understanding and then walk toward him. Saul picked up a legal pad, wrote $500,000 on it and showed it to Bryce.

The Glacier feigned a conversation with Abrams but he really was watching Bryce. Bryce knew that and shook his head firmly and negatively. Saul wrote a question mark below the $500,000 number. Bryce, still aware he was being watched by Abbott, took the pad, wrote $4,000,000 in bold numbers below the question mark and handed it back to Saul.

"Bryce, if I show that number to Abbott, the janitors may have another clean-up job on their hands."

"Show it to him. If he refuses, tell him we'll ask the jury for lots of punitive damages." Give no quarter.

Saul crossed to defense table and laid the tablet in front of Abbott who had returned to his seat. The Glacier listened to Saul, stared at the ceiling as if to seek the Almighty's intervention, shrugged his shoulders, and disappeared to find Cowper.

Bryce left to telephone his office. He wanted to check with Zeke Alexander on the progress regarding a price he'd obtained on some used planers. Things were starting to look doable on that deal. And he needed to check on another matter.

⊙≈⊙

Abbott returned and Bryce reentered the courtroom. It still was in recess.

Abbott told Saul, "Porter wants to settle on his own. He's offering $50,000 spread over four years."

Saul didn't even pause. "We settle all or none, Henderson. By the way, is Cowper cleaning up? I haven't finished cross examining him yet."

Saul scratched his left ear. A small man in the rear of the courtroom got up and left.

"He sent to his hotel for a change of clothes," said Abbott. "I don't know whether or not he'll be able to resume the stand. Look, Saul, we've always been able to deal before . . ."

Abbott saw motion at the rear of the courtroom. A woman with a voluptuous figure entered in the company of a large black man dressed as a chauffeur. The woman wiggled her fingers and smiled at Abrams, who also had turned toward the motion in the hope his boss had come back into the courtroom.

Saul pretended to think about what Abbott had said but his true attention was focused on Abrams. He watched as Abrams paled at the sight of his former secretary.

Abrams rose, pulled on Abbott's coat sleeve, and beckoned him away from his conversation with Saul.

"Don't look now," whispered Abrams to the Glacier, "but Dolores, the woman who dimed us, just came into the courtroom. She's sitting next to a large black man in the rear of the courtroom. What do you suppose she's doing here?"

"She's probably here to listen to our side of the case and then testify in rebuttal," said Abbott. "Can she hurt us any more than she already has?"

"She knows everything that went on. Probably stuff I've even forgotten about," said Abrams.

"How long did she work for you?"

"Since my other secretary retired. Let's see, it was about March of this year when Dolores started. Why do you ask?"

"When did Porter write his first article? March, right? She probably does know everything. I'm going to have to tell Cowper she's here." Abbott left the courtroom to convey the latest news to an already disheartened client. He stared at Dolores on the way out and understood completely what led to her employment.

Saul scratched his right ear and Roosevelt and Dolores rose and left the court room. Twenty minutes later she was on her way to her brother's house in New Jersey. No one at the *Tattler* knew his real name and address.

Dolores was planning a vacation in Italy.

⊙━⊙

Court reconvened and the judge summoned the jury after he was satisfied that Cowper could continue. Despite the threat of Dolores, Cowper had defied all further counsel to settle, he thinking that the jury would not award what Bryce and Saul had demanded. He was dressed in another custom tailored suit and breathed in his labored way as he again took the witness stand. Saul resumed his cross-examination.

"Mr. Cowper, I remind you that you still are under oath. Do you understand that?"

"Yes."

"Will the court reporter please read back my last question to this witness?"

The reporter pulled a section of the recording paper out of her stenographer's machine and read:

"Question: Mr. Cowper, do you know where Charles Coe's glasses are right now?

Then I have a note that the witness vomited."

Saul again consulted the folder in front of him.

"Mr. Cowper, please answer that question. Where are Coe's glasses?"

"I believe the late Mr. Noah Coleman gave them to Porter."

"Do you know why he did that?"

"To prove he knew a key detail about Coe's death that was not public knowledge."

"Why was that important?"

"Coleman's objective was to give his own story credibility and cast doubt that Bryce Roberts murdered Charles Coe."

"Did Porter tell you that?"

"He gave me a memo on it."

"Do you know if Mr. Abrams saw the memo?"

"Yes, just look at the copy in your folder, you'll see his initials on it."

Saul closed his folder, put it on counsel table and paced toward Cowper. He crossed his arms over his chest and in a voice that accused Cowper of being the devil incarnate, asked:

"Mr. Cowper, are you telling this jury that you, Abrams, Porter and the *Tattler* published these two follow-up articles suggesting that Bryce Roberts was a murderer when you believed that was not true?"

"Objection, your Honor," cried Abbott. "It's for the jury to determine whether the articles were defamatory!"

Objection overruled, Mr. Abbott. The question goes to the state of mind of the defendants. Mr. Cowper, answer the question."

"Yes. We knew."

Saul's voice had a whip-like crack. "Knew what?"

"That Bryce Roberts was not the murderer."

"But you and the *Tattler* published those articles anyway?"

Cowper nodded his head.

"You have to answer audibly, Mr. Cowper."

"Yes."

"Your witness, Mr. Abbott."

Abbott saw a hole in Cowper's testimony and went right after
it.

"Mr. Cowper, the evidence from detective Miller shows the
glasses were not with Coe's body. Did Porter's memo show how
and why Noah Coleman possessed the glasses?"

"Coleman said he remembered them when he was leaving
Coe's body in the woods. He went back to Coe's shack, er, house,
and got the glasses so he could put them with the body. But a car
passed by on the road and he became frightened the police would
return to the shack looking for Coe. So he left without taking the
glasses back to the body. After that he never went back and just
kept the glasses at his home."

Too late, Abbott remembered the first rule of a trial lawyer:
never ask a question to which you don't already know the answer.
In his eagerness to punch holes in Saul's case, he'd forgotten the
rule and dug his own hole deeper.

Abbot used the rest of the day to try to convince the jurors
that the actual words and phrases in the three articles didn't
defame Bryce.

The next morning Saul gave a stirring closing that had Bryce
and Candace silently cheering. The verdict came in at 3:00 in the
afternoon: three and one half million dollars, one million in
compensatory damages and two and one half million in punitive
damages, both against the *Tattler* and all three individual
defendants.

The judge dismissed the jury and adjourned court.

One of the reporters in the courtroom broke for the door to
the hallways and the telephones. Others followed as Abbott
worked his way toward Saul's counsel table to shake his hand.

Candace quietly hugged Bryce as the jury filed out. Then she
hugged Saul who looked even more rumpled than usual.

"Thank you for everything, Saul. Now, let me see the memo
in the last folder you used."

Saul pulled a folder out and handed it to her.

Candace opened it and said, "Oh, you didn't!" She dropped
the folder onto counsel table, and hugged Saul again. The folder
fell open on the way to the table. The papers that floated to the
floor were copies of Saul's favorite recipes.

"Dolores told us of the memo," said Saul, "but someone at
the *Tattler* either destroyed it or lost it. We had to use the PISS

ON THEM memo to convince Cowper we had the one that told how Coleman gave the glasses to Porter. I figured Cowper bought it when he got sick right on the stand."

"Now what?" asked Bryce.

"Abbott will call me in a couple of days and try to get us to agree to a reduced verdict in return for them not appealing. As I see it, an appellate court will sustain the verdict of liability and punitive damages, but it could order a reduction in the amount. The verdict gave us a judgment of joint and several liability, which means any one of the defendants can be made to pay the whole amount."

"We'll think about that," said Bryce. "May we call you with our decision?"

"The appeal period expires in thirty days. Just make it before then."

Chapter 128

A week after the trial ended Bryce entered his father's office. He'd waited until late in the afternoon to have this talk with Harry. Bryce sat at the round conference table. He didn't want to have this conversation across a desk.

Harry looked up from his desk, nodded, and resumed his review of a report on the paper mill in Wisconsin. The union members had developed good ideas on efficiency and it looked as if there was a turn-around in progress, sufficient to keep the mill operating.

We have to do more of this with our employees, he thought, particularly those at our new furniture factory. Then he rose and joined Bryce at the table. His expression turned neutral.

"That verdict is an outstanding achievement, Bryce. I'm glad for you and Candace, but just as importantly you've established a reputation as a fighter if someone meddles with you. I'm puzzled, though. How did you persuade Noah to confess?"

"What gave you the idea I did that?"

"He and I talked after he knew he was dying. He told me you two had spoken several times. He hinted that he killed Coe, but I got the distinct impression he was not telling me everything you and he discussed. He said he was afraid that Coe would get to Candace before the police could catch him. He didn't want Eddie, the only grandchild he'd ever have, to lose another mother."

Harry paused and then looked Bryce in the eyes. "Those could have been your motives too."

Bryce's expression hardened. "Dad, I admit I thought about killing the son-of-a-bitch. Maybe the only reason I didn't is because Noah beat me to it. We'll never know."

Harry smiled, looked out the window, and watched two squirrels chasing each other around the trunk of an oak. No, we never will know for sure, he thought. But I suspect you did it and talked Noah into confessing. Even though you hired a body guard for Candace, and acted the part, underneath you were way too relaxed after Coe attacked her and then disappeared. To be that relaxed you either have incredible self-control or you had to know he was dead and no longer a threat. The only way you'd know he was dead . . . Which is it?

"Son, you're right, we'll never know for sure whether you would have done it. Either way, though, this family will continue strong with you leading it."

Harry turned away from the squirrels and changed the subject. "My friend in Boston mentioned you retained his services. He gave no details. He's too discrete for that. But can you tell me why you hired him?"

"There were two reasons. The glasses, and that creep, Porter. The day before Coe's shack was demolished I looked through the box of Coe's personal items that were gathered by the workmen. I didn't want to send Coe's mother anything that would be an embarrassment. The glasses were in the box. I suspected they belonged back in the woods where the body was found, so I removed them from the box before I sent the rest of the stuff to Mrs. Coe."

"Why didn't Homer see the glasses in the shack?"

"I think the glasses wound up on the floor where Homer didn't see them among the junk that was littered all over the place. Or, he went there after the glasses were removed in preparation for the demolition. Homer may not have been completely truthful in his testimony about his search for the glasses. He can tell half-truths, like the time he let me think he'd 'visited' Coe at his shack when it actually was downtown at the parole office.

"But, Homer Miller is no dummy. I had to find out if he realized the glasses were not with Coe's body. If he knew that, he could conclude that Coe had died elsewhere, and that meant a probable homicide. I didn't want him dredging up problems that might threaten our family. So, with Foster's help, I, uh, obtained Homer Miller's investigative report. The report stated that Homer knew of the missing glasses and he also suspected Coe was murdered."

Harry's expression turned to admiration. "I saw the report on your credenza," he said. "You were gone for lunch and I went into your office to get a file on the furniture factory. I read over the report and wondered why you had it. When I read that Homer suspected a homicide I got the chills but I kept quiet. I wanted to see what you'd do."

"Why? Did you suspect me?"

Harry looked into a face full of challenge. What do I say to my son to keep his trust?

"Briefly. But, then when I really thought about it, I realized that you're too decent a man to murder even the likes of Coe. And you're too methodical and detail-oriented to have forgotten Coe's glasses. That made Noah the only other suspect, so I stopped worrying until that damned tabloid published its first piece."

Harry cocked his head and asked, "Bryce, what's the second reason you hired our Boston friends?"

"After Porter came by the woodlot that day, I went down to Tom Blake's store and bought a copy of the *Tattler*. When I read and saw how they write about people I was absolutely convinced a pack of trouble was headed my way. So I asked for help. I needed to know what the enemy was doing. Sun Tzu, the Chinese general said a good spy is worth ten divisions. So our Boston friends found a spy for me."

"Dolores?"

"Yes. She was a legitimate hire after Hy Abrams' secretary was "encouraged" to retire early."

"What's going to keep the original secretary quiet?"

"She's receiving a monthly supplement to her pension. The supplement ends next year when her social security kicks in. Then there's another lump sum down the road. Besides, she hates Derek Cowper.

"But to get back to the story. Dolores, who is the daughter of the Boston agency's founder, was placed at the *Tattler*. I strongly believed that Porter intended to write unflattering articles about me and I wanted to get the jump on him. Dolores was there in time to learn everything from the beginning.

"I just couldn't let Saul know who she really was. I think he suspects that Dolores was bribed. Let him. He'll never know for sure and that's the way it should be. My problem was timing when to have her provide Saul with the documents."

"You set up your own lawyer?"

"It worked, didn't it? I had to get those bastards at the *Tattler*. They meddled and they were going to pay."

Harry whistled in admiration. "So, what did you and Noah discuss?"

Bryce gathered his thoughts and then continued. "After Noah had lung surgery, I paid him several visits. He knew then that he was dying. We got to talking about old times and how we both had hoped for so much for Marilyn and me. When he read the *Tattler* article he invited me to his home and offered to set the tabloid straight. It was then that we discussed his confession and I gave Noah the glasses. I told him to use them to authenticate his story. He loved the idea. Later, after his interview with Porter he told Candace he'd delivered the glasses, but I couldn't verify that. Then Dolores telephoned me about Porter's notes."

Harry looked at Bryce in amazement. "You're a better plotter than I ever was. Talk about taking advantage of what looked like a terrible situation . . . Bryce, why are you looking like that?"

"Damn that Coe! I want to use my imagination for constructive things, not on chicanery. Instead, even after he was dead, Coe forced me into a bad spotlight that put me through the ringer. Damn him!"

"You still hate him, don't you?"

Bryce nodded.

"Look at it from another perspective," said Harry. "Coe brought us closer as a family. Even you and Noah grew closer. And, I'll bet Coe had the same effect on you and Candace."

Bryce's fleeting smile told Harry he was on target.

"I thought so," he said. "You have a good wife, Bryce. I think she'll always stand by you. Never forget, family is everything. Whatever you do, never put anything or anyone ahead of family. It was family that made Noah confess that he was a murderer. It was family loyalty and protection that made you set up the people at the *Tattler* for a fall after they attacked you. That kind of strength always will keep the meddlers at bay."

Harry paused to acknowledge Bryce's nod of thanks. Then he continued.

"I believe that Coe and the people at that tabloid aren't that different. They're what I call 'small people.' They try to make themselves feel big by tearing down others. Abe Lincoln said that 'you cannot strengthen the weak by tearing down the strong.' And you told Coe the same thing at his sentencing. Lincoln was right and so were you. But the weak can't or won't understand that.

"Coe had nothing, so he picked on you, the strongest man he knew. He did a lot of damage, but you're still here, stronger than ever.

"The *Tattler* people tried the same thing. Rather than revealing that a relative nobody killed Coe, those men at the tabloid picked on you and our family. Had they gone after Noah, they wouldn't have achieved the empty power that bringing us down would have made them feel. But you used our strengths and resources to defeat them, and you gave no quarter. It's the only thing to do when people attack you and meddle in your affairs."

Bryce looked out the window and watched the breeze working though the tall pines that bordered the property. He knew his father was right and his anger over Coe's meddling retreated. The hardness in his face was replaced with introspection.

"Thanks, Dad."

"You're welcome. Now, tell me what you and Candace have decided to do about that three and a half million dollar verdict. By the way, did you know that amount set a record here in this area?"

"Saul told me that the other day," said Bryce. "He's on cloud nine because of the notoriety he's received.

"Anyway, Candace and I have decided to put that paper out of business, at least in its present form. Even with a reduced verdict the *Tattler* would take years to recover from paying the judgment. The financial statements that Dolores gave to Saul show it's mostly a paper corporation that generates a lot of cash with advertising. It probably would declare bankruptcy if the judgment is upheld on appeal."

"Bryce, I think I know where you are headed and if I'm right, I think you're crazy. You can't make a silk purse out of a sow's ear. You can't assume control of that awful rag."

Bryce held up a hand.

"Hear me out. We'll record our judgment in Delaware where the *Tattler's* corporation is registered and in Florida where its assets are located. We execute on Cowper's stock which is the controlling interest in the paper and we buy the rest of the stock for a pittance from shareholders who think it's worthless. Then we run the paper, but completely change it to a weekly political news reporter. We simply shift the focus of the dirt that the staff and reporters dig up. It'll take time, so we start out mainly with the Federal government and the more populous states. We report on all of the back-alley politics and the seamy undersides to expose the hypocrisy and corruption that's rampant. Most of all, the articles must be fact-based. We run an editorial page that has a line right down the middle from top to bottom. The left side will be for liberal commentators; and, the right side for conservatives."

"Bryce," said Harry, "I've spent decades building relationships with some of the people that you likely would expose. I know who and what they are, so I don't waste time with ideals and vice-versa. A nationwide paper like that will run into all kinds of opposition. Your advertising revenue will go to hell in a hand basket because the affluent businesses won't want to support a newspaper that pillories their politician friends."

"Dad, as it stands, the *Tattler* would be worthless after we collect its accounts receivable and empty its checking account. Those assets aren't enough to pay the judgment. Besides, there are a lot of *Tattler* advertisers who don't need the protection or largess of politicians. So we may as well try to make something out of it. We start out as a muckraker, but slowly upgrade the articles and news to focus on the civic and political education of our readership. Oh, we'll keep the exposé aspect because that sells papers, but we'll also build a reputation for accuracy. Once that's in place, influence and power follow."

"Who would you get to run the paper? Certainly not the bunch that's there now?"

"My friend, Peter Chase. I've had several long talks with him and he figures there's nothing to lose. Peter's been a journalist on the political beat for several years now, and he despises hypocrisy and corruption in politics. Why not give him a go at it? There really isn't much to lose and there could be a huge amount to gain."

"Now, where do you fit in the newspaper scheme?" asked Harry.

"I don't at first. I just stay out of Peter's way and learn and observe as time permits. But I'll have a say in editorial policy."

"You really have caught the fever, haven't you?"

"Yes, but I also have Sunrise Lumber to think of. There are things I want to do with our company. There's some land in Arkansas that I have an eye on –"

"–Whoa. I've heard enough. It's your verdict, so do what you want to with it. By the way, what are you and Saul going to do about the three men who hurt you so badly?"

"That's where Foster comes in. He found assets they own free and clear. I'm going to clean out Cowper and Abrams. Porter still has young kids, so I won't bankrupt him, but I've found a way to teach him a terrible lesson."

"Good. What have you learned out of all of this?"

"Candace and I talked about that last night. We both decided we're too damned oriented toward perfection. No one's capable of living a perfect life. Someone or something is always going to interfere or intervene to foul things up. But we still can pursue our dreams and adjust along the way. And I've learned how to meddle, even though I never wanted to. If we're going to stay strong, I'll have to get used to the idea of using that tactic. I've even learned to enjoy the challenges it requires of me. But I don't want to spend my life doing it."

Bryce got up to leave. "I've had enough for one day," he said. "I'm going home to my family. I'm going to hug my wife and play with my children. And then I'm going to play my new piano."

"Before you go, I have one more question," said Harry. "What are you going to do about the hatred you still feel toward Charles Coe?"

"I'm not going to dwell on it. I may even forgive him for what he did. But it's going to be on my own terms. Years ago I made Charlie a promise. Someday I'll keep it."

Chapter 129

Saul negotiated a deal with Abbott. In return for a reduction of the punitive damages, the defendants would not appeal. Abbott told him that his three individual clients thought themselves to be "judgment proof" so they weren't concerned about what could be done to them personally. They conceded that the *Tattler* probably would be wiped out. Saul nodded as if in agreement, but inwardly he was rejoicing.

⌒⌐⌐⌐⌐⌐

For the second time in two months Derek Cowper vomited in public. This time it was at the marina where his yacht, *Golden Silence*, was docked. He waddled jauntily along the dock toward his pride and joy with his mistress in tow. As he arrived at the portable steps that led from the dock to the yacht's deck he observed a bright yellow notice taped next to the varnished mahogany door leading to *Golden Silence's* main salon. He moved quickly for a fat man, climbed aboard and read the legal notice. It informed him that his stock in the Delaware corporation that owned *Golden Silence* had been seized in partial satisfaction of the judgment against him. The Federal Marshall had levied upon his yacht. It would be sold at public sale the following week. *Golden Silence* was not to be moved in the meantime. Cowper made it to the railing of the yacht before he threw up. His mistress called a taxi and went home by herself.

Hyman Abrams didn't vomit. He fainted when he read the notice of levy and sale attached to the door of his lovely home by the golf course. He'd put the house in the name of a business corporation in an attempt to work a tax dodge, but the stock of the corporation had been traced through a maze of dummy businesses to his ownership. The stock was seized, and the Marshall now would supervise the auction of the stock and the house. The Maserati in the garage had a similar notice taped to its windshield.

Leon Porter wept as his antique automobiles were loaded onto carriers to be taken to a specialty auction house. The driver who steered the 1932 Cadillac into an enclosed transport truck smiled as he carefully maneuvered the classic up the loading ramp. He would be sure to tell the Roberts about Porter's tears.

In a Fort Lauderdale suburb Peter Chase held several meetings with employees of *The National Gazette & Tattler* to announce the new mission and policies of the paper. He was pleasantly surprised with the enthusiasm shown by the staff and reporters.

By then Bryce, Harry and their families were enjoying an early fall vacation in Maine.

⚭

It was Candace's first trip to the Maine home. Members of the extended family made her feel welcome and as comfortable as her favorite sweatshirt. She sat in a rocking chair on the front porch of the rambling house, content in the afternoon sun as she watched Bryce supervising Daniel's exploration of the grounds. Other children, watched by Teensy and Margaret, played at the water's edge and their shouts drifted on the breeze that came in off the water. The faint gong of a distant buoy added to the scent of salt air and seaweed that pleasured her senses.

She now was the proud and happy mother of three children who delighted her; and, growing in her womb were two more. The thought of three children in diapers was daunting, but she and Bryce wanted to have children early in their marriage due to the late start after Eddie and Anne. She relaxed, and her thoughts drifted into the decade of the Sixties they all had just lived through. She reflected upon how they found strength in each other to meet and overcome its challenges, celebrate its glory, and prosper. Bryce now was established in the forest products business and his interest in the politics of the turbulent times brought him new vistas. For now she was content to be a full-time mother, but looked forward to the day she could return to her work with lasers.

Maybe, she mused, in the meantime I can teach at Bucks a couple of days a week, just to keep my hand in. She smiled at the thought, and Harry, who had awakened from a nap in the Adirondack chair beside her, saw her expression and delighted in it.

"Candace, I can't help but ask. What has you smiling so contentedly?"

"Dad, I'm thinking about teaching at Bucks. And I'm thinking about the last ten years. We've fought a war in Vietnam, invented the laser, enhanced women's status in the workplace, seen civil rights vindicated, mourned Kennedy's passing, have landed men on the moon, and gone crazy over the Beatles. And I was thinking about what happened to me.

"I lost a good husband, and despaired until I met Bryce. Now I have three wonderful children and am expecting twins I feel as if I've made one of the greatest comebacks of all time. That's why I'm smiling."

Harry nodded. "I understand. I think that during the past decade parts of our society have been unraveled and rewoven into new cloth. We've kept many of the good threads, and added some, and we shed some bad ones, too.

"Rosalie and I often talk about the differences between our generation and yours. But what concerns me the most is that nowadays people are unwilling to allow full development of things that take time. They want to change processes again when results aren't immediate.

"But in the ways that count we're the same. Our families have fought and struggled through tough and exciting times; but always, we've stuck together and had hope for our future. Candace, it's good to see that in you too."

Harry paused, deep in reminiscence. Then he came back to the present, cocked his head and looked toward the top of a tall pine tree silhouetted in the sun. "It's pretty late in the season for that cardinal to be calling," he said.

Candace raised her face toward the treetop and said, "Oh, no it's not. You beautiful bird, you just keep on singing."

She stood up, bent down, and playfully kissed Harry on the forehead. Then she walked toward the husband she adored. Bryce saw her approaching and, grin lighting his face, held his arms open, beckoning her.

Candace started to run.

Epilog

January, 2007

Bryce paused in his reading and gazed at the fire in the centuries-old fireplace. The huge bronze-faced andirons stood resolute, glimmering in the heat as they had done since his great grandfather had commissioned a local foundry to forge and cast them.

Behind him quiet footsteps sounded on the polished plank floor.

Which one of my grandchildren is tiptoeing up on me? He smiled and closed the book in his lap in case Timothy, the three-year-old, tried to jump into the big leather chair he occupied.

No Timothy. Instead, a card, tossed from over his shoulder, landed in his lap.

Bryce retrieved it and turned the plastic laminate in his hands.

"So, you have it now, Lucas. When did you pass the driver's test?"

Lucas came around to the side of Bryce's chair. "A week ago. I got it when you and grandmother were in Florida."

"Candace and I wondered why we haven't seen you lately. I'll bet you're finding any excuse to get behind the wheel. Where have you been driving?"

Lucas dropped his lanky frame into a chair on the other side of the hearth and stretched his feet toward the fire. "No wonder you spend time in here. This room just invites you in and then holds you. Do you think our ancestors felt the same way?"

Bryce let his imagination run with thoughts about his colonial ancestors' conversations at the hearth. "No doubt they talked about crops and the cold and snow just as we do. Only there would have been more of them in here to enjoy this warmth.

"But you're ducking my question. Where have you driven since you no longer need another driver with you?"

Lucas looked into the fire for long moments. "Do you think it would upset Grandmother Candace if she knew I visited Marilyn's grave?"

"No, and it wouldn't bother me either. But why did you go there?"

"I can't explain it completely. Perhaps I was hoping to better understand how you felt when you lost her all those years ago."

Bryce inhaled deeply and then slowly breathed out. "Well, did you glean anything from your visit?"

"I think so. Even her epitaph tells the reader that you had a hard time letting go."

"True. But, ultimately I did let go. We all have to learn to do that with parts of our past."

"Then I have a question if you'll talk about it. Why did you wait so long to piss on Charles Coe's grave?"

For long moments Bryce stared at his grandson, pleased by his desire to understand.

"I waited because my hatred of Coe had become a part of me, driven me. I knew it wasn't right, but once something like that gets inside a man it's tough to shed it. When Coe stated in court that he wasn't sorry for what he did, I hated him even more. Because he never asked forgiveness I let my hatred continue to burn, even after he died."

Bryce brought his dark eyes to bear on Lucas' hazel eyes. "Ultimately, I understood that my hatred was the product of my own anger over never having control of the situation, never having closure, never completely understanding why God would allow Coe to kill Marilyn. Most of all, I realized that part of what I've achieved was driven by that hatred . . . and that's no way to live."

Bryce took a sip of wine, and then got up and put another log on the fire. He turned to face his grandson.

"I could have done that for you," said Lucas.

"I know. But I've been sitting for a while and I needed the stretch. But, to get back to your question.

"On the way home on the afternoon when I pissed on Coe's grave I became ashamed of what I did in front of you. It was as if I was trying to pass my hatred on to another generation. But I couldn't see the sense in that, nor could I ask that of you. So I decided to show you and tell you what was behind my actions that day. I figured that if I didn't tell you, someday you'd regard me with contempt for pissing on Coe's grave. So, I had to tell you why I did it. When I began to talk with you I felt that hatred ebbing away."

Bryce smiled at Lucas and there was a hint of mischief in the older man's eyes. "I needed to finish that process. That's why it took you a little longer to get your driver's license."

Your voice no longer holds that awful roughness when you speak of Coe, thought Lucas. "So, now you've forgiven Coe?"

"I couldn't. Coe never showed remorse, although I think he was capable of it. Without that, I believed forgiving him would be accepting the evil he did. You see, in order to forgive someone, the transgressor first must confess that his act is wrong; truly repent; and, then ask forgiveness. Coe, of course, never did that. So, I've asked God to forgive him. Putting that on His shoulders will have to suffice. Now, at least I've been able to finish this life without that burden interfering."

Lucas nodded in understanding, paused for a moment, then stood and retrieved his driver's license from the table where Bryce had put it.

Marilyn's grandson gave Bryce a "high five" on his way out.

The End

About The Author

Wallace Eldridge is a graduate of Dartmouth College, The U.S. Naval Officer's Candidate School and Dickinson School of Law. He has served as an Assistant District Attorney in Pennsylvania and later worked in civil practice as a litigator and business attorney. His interests include handling trials with unusual twists, hiking, sailing, soaring, naval history and college football. He resides in the Lehigh Valley with his partner, Mary Ann Madl, and a Jack Russell named Holly.

...ents

T...					ho had first crack at editing
Medd...					y helpful ideas as well as
gettin...					d.

J...					from her job with a noted
publi...					of	editing,	critique	and
enco...					needed. Jean, your assistance
was ...

...					er, high school friend and pro
base...					ough life in the minor leagues
in t...

...					version and encouraged me to
fini...

Thanks also to .... Ochs who patiently guided me
through the steps required to publish *Meddlers*. Chris, your
assistance was invaluable to this first-time book author who needed
all the help and advice you so generously gave.

And Mary Ann Madl—You have been my best friend and
cheerleader who prodded me when my writing stalled and
encouraged me when I needed it. Thanks for your patience and
understanding while I disappeared to write *Meddlers* and for your
love when it mattered most.

Bibliography

C. David Callahan, et al, *Images of America: Historic Newtown*, Arcadia Publishers, 19??

Stanley P. Cornils, *The Morning After – How To Manage Grief Wisely*, R & Publishers, Saratoga Calif. (1990).

Wm. W.H. Davis, *History of Bucks County*, Lewis Publishing Company, 1905

Kevin Dockery, *Navy SEALs, A History, Part I. The Early Years*, Berkley Books 2002

Kevin Dockery, *Navy SEALs, A History, Part II, The Vietnam Years*, Berkley Books, 2002

John Steele Gordon, *A Thread Across The Ocean*, Walker Publishing Company, Inc. New York, 2002

Mark Lipper, Ph.D, *Paper, People, Progress, The Story of P.H. Glatfelter Company*, Prentice-Hall, Inc, 1980

Thomas J. DiLorenzo, *How Capitalism Saved America*, Crown Forum, New York, 2004

Charles Murray, *Losing Ground, American Social Policy 1950-1980*, Basic Books Inc. New York, 1984

William L. O'Neill, *Coming Apart, An Informal History of America in the 1960's*, Quadrangle Books, 1971

Carolyn E. Poster, et al, *Images of America: Quakertown* Arcadia Publishers, 19??

Rich Westcott, *Philadelphia's Old Ballparks*, Temple University Press, 1966